MW00768116

Sea Change

An Example of the Pleasure Principle

A Novel

By Ken Anderson

Herndon, Virginia

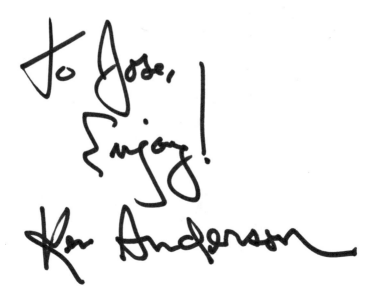

To Jose,
Enjoy!
Ken Anderson

To Dori,

Enjoy!

[signature]

Other books by Ken Anderson

The Intense Lover: A Suite of Poems

*Someone Bought the House on the Island:
A Dream Journal*

Hasty Hearts

The Statue of Pan

Acknowledgement:
"A Sprig of Rosemary" was published in *Velvet Mafia.*

Published in the United States by STARbooks Press, PO Box 711612, Herndon, VA 20171. Printed in the United States.

Many thanks to graphic artist John Nail for the cover design. Mr. Nail may be reached at tojonail@bellsouth.net.

Herndon, VA

to Sonya, the sister I never had

"Which of you shall we say doth love us most?"

– King Lear I, 1, 52.

"I know I made a lot of mistakes, bringing you up,
but they were love mistakes."

– my mother

Contents

Chapter 1: In Medias Res

A young faun named Daniele got up to pee late one night at the edge of an abandoned olive grove high above a cottage near Amalfi. By day, he ran a small tour boat between Amalfi and Grotta Smeralda, but that night he had been alternately making love to and sleeping in the arms of his girlfriend on a tattered dhurrie in a cleft in the roots of a five-hundred-year-old olive tree. The cozy hollow made a rustic bed, the arched branches above them a wonderful ceiling that swayed in the wind. They had such great sex there he figured the tree must be sacred, the haunt of some ancient fertility god.

As he stood, nude, peeing off the cliff, he could see only the front of the terrace below, the latticework of tiles and the railing, not the cottage itself, but as he was shaking the last drops of urine from his cock, he noticed what appeared to be a slim, young woman strolling nude across the terrace, intent on something in her hands. When she turned, Daniele was close enough and the moon was bright enough for him to see that the person was actually a young, well-endowed man. Daniele stooped behind a rock and watched as the young man leaned against the railing, tied the ends of a wreath, and crowned himself with it. Then the young man turned around again and leaned on his elbows on the railing, gazing down into the sea. After a while, he glanced over his shoulder toward the cottage, then out to sea.

Another man strolled across the terrace, and when he reached the younger one, he stood behind him, put his hands on the younger one's hips, and just stood there. When he began bumping him, Daniele smiled mischievously, absently twiddling his goatee. He thought of white horses coupling in the night, felt privy to some crude rite, some coarse suggestion whispered in the leaves of the olive tree. The man seemed bent on satisfying himself, Daniele thought, the boy on calmly letting him, and there was something so simple and natural about it that he clearly understood why the two would do it. Watching them whet his appetite for his lover's lips again, for the damp embrace of her thighs. In fact, at the moment, the whole night seemed under a deep, erotic spell.

Then the man did something strange. He climbed over the railing and held on to it, suspended over the cliff. Daniele thought he was climbing down to something, but when the young man grabbed him as if frightened, realized he wasn't. When they began shouting, he knew they were speaking English, but did not know the language, except for the word *OK*, which they repeated several times. Besides, he could barely hear them over the wind. Then the young man grabbed the man's right wrist. The man let go of the railing with his left hand, swung out over the cliff, and looked down. But what was he looking for? He could hear the two talking. Then the man let go of the railing and leaned back farther, kept from falling solely by the grip of the young man.

The man yelled, "OK," and when he climbed back over, the young man led him toward the cottage and out of sight.

Daniele stood and, scratching his pubic hair, wondered how he could put all these puzzle pieces together. Perhaps only a lover's quarrel. Speaking of lovers, he thought, his cock still pleasantly sore and swollen from their last round. He pivoted toward his love nest, stumbling over some clothes fluttering in the breeze.

"Torna da me, amore mio," the girl moaned sleepily, reaching for him. *Come back to me, my love.*

"Certo," he whispered, lying next to her. *Of course.*

And again they tied the tight knot of joy.

Chapter 2: A Family Outing

Tyler was sitting in the bow of an old, flat-bottom skiff plunging across the smooth, clear-gray water between Bailey Island, Maine, and Ashe Island, about three miles east. He was facing forward, hands on gunwales, catching the occasional spray, and enjoying the wind ruffling his Izod and cooling him off on such an unusually hot day. He had not thought about sunscreen, the trip being short, but his skin felt raw and vulnerable in the sun, as if near radiation, and he wondered if he were going to start things off with a sunburn. He glanced over his shoulder at the others in the boat: Karen, his ex-wife, at the helm, Alice, his younger daughter, next to her, and Linda, his older daughter, on the amidships thwart, all passively rocking with the swells and squinting in the glare. The sun was straight up, an immense spotlight blinding the sky, and if the boat had stopped, there would have been no breeze, as if the strange stillness, like the women's reticence, were somehow connected to the total eclipse that Linda had told him would happen that night.

The main reason for the trip was quality family time before Linda's "test days," a couple of exploratory brain surgeries in preparation for a final surgery which allegedly would stop her sporadic seizures, but Tyler figured that the reunion would be good not only for the physical ordeal to come but also for the emotional one from the past. For Linda's sake, Karen had apparently put aside her bitterness over the divorce, and he gave her credit for that. If the broken family could be set like a bone, perhaps it could heal.

"For Linda, sure," he agreed on the phone. "Should be good for Alice, too, for us all."

"If you say so," Karen replied.

Linda told Tyler that her first seizure had happened in class. Out of the blue, she started trembling, then had auditory and visual hallucinations. The teacher's voice began crackling as if on a staticky radio. The writing in white chalk on the board turned green. Then everything went black. When ten, Linda had been struck by a car while riding a bike. It was assumed that her concussion was the source of her seizures. Later, however, when a doctor suggested tests, it was discovered that the seizures were from oxygen deprivation to the brain during a severe asthma attack, so severe, in fact, she had gone into a coma and had come out of it only when a respirator burned her arm, leaving a milky, heart-shaped scar. He knew she was taking Dilantin daily, an anticonvulsant, and thought he remembered her telling him that she also took folic acid and had altered her diet to include beef liver and more beans, peas, and green, leafy vegetables, though, at the moment, he could not recall why. He also knew that Karen used valerian, small amounts of lobelia, and other herbs in formulas for the disorder.

Prior to Linda's seizures, Tyler was familiar with them only through Samantha, his dog. Sammy's prodrome consisted of walking around the perimeter of a room as if looking for something. During the seizure, she would stiffen and fall onto her side. At times, Sammy staggered from the phenobarbital the vet had prescribed, and Tyler had noticed that Linda seemed drowsy and slurred slightly and figured she was not as sharp as she would be off her meds. He wondered if driving in her condition was legal and, if not, why she did and why Eddie, her husband, let her. He also wondered how difficult it would be, if she had an attack, to grab the wheel and step on the brake.

On prior visits, Tyler and Linda had taken boat excursions around Casco Bay, to Bailey Island, and to Monhegan, and when the idea of a family outing came up, he suggested that, if they were interested, they should look into the possibility of a whale cruise or something similar, something out on the open sea. It was then that he learned that Ashe Island, named after Eddie's family, had belonged to them for generations and that, since they didn't use the house there, Karen had, especially on summer weekends. In fact, according to Linda, the house had become an informal lab for the collection, labeling, and processing of indigenous medicinal herbs. So the decision was to spend a long weekend there. It was an economical alternative, and being thrown together in close quarters, he thought, would force them to communicate.

It was for that reason that, earlier that morning, Tyler found himself at a boat ramp on a beach near the Jetsam Inn, a classic Maine inn where Linda and Eddie had held their wedding reception. When he and Linda arrived, she pulled into a small, sandy lot and parked next to her mother's old, black Escort and boat trailer. Karen and Alice were standing by the skiff below, apparently ready to go. They had run the prow aground and thrown the anchor up shore. Tyler grabbed his bag and jacket from the back seat, Linda a big bouquet of peonies. Then she locked the car, and they strolled down the beach. Meanwhile, Karen picked up the anchor, rolled up the line, and set them in the boat.

Tyler had worn jeans, a salmon Izod, and Nikes and, since he had expected Maine to be cool, had carried a brown leather jacket on the plane, but as soon as he and Linda had stepped out of the airport in Portland, it was obvious that the jacket was not necessary. The scene at the ramp was no different. The humidity was stifling, the cove, littered with lobster buoys, perfectly still, the slate ocean, flat to the horizon, stark silent as if the entire coast were holding its breath. Perched on a cliff, the inn and cottages, mute as a painting, may as well have been abandoned, all the details – rugged boulders, shake siding, Adirondack chairs – blanched by the sun to a meaningful lack of color. An atomic explosion could not have brightened everything more.

"Hey," he began, dropping his bag and jacket in the boat. "How are you?"

"Fine," Karen replied, brushing her hands off.

He was intuitively poised to greet them in whatever way they wanted, warm or cold, but the formal handshake with Karen was almost laughable. A plaintiff and defendant were about as cordial.

"Good, good," he smiled.

Over the years, Karen had grown big as a seal, as he thought of it, while he had slimmed down to a lean, sinewy thirty-inch waist. Her face had hardened, set in a sour expression, and her hair was choppy, as if she had cut it herself (to save money, he wondered), a strange croissant of curls with ends dipping down each side of her forehead. He noticed the dark circles around her eyes, but didn't know what they meant. She was wearing leather sandals, khaki slacks, and a pink, short-sleeved shirt with a yellow floral print, a frank attempt, he thought cynically, to make herself look fresh and happy.

Then he turned to Alice. "Hey, sweetie."

She took a step back, as if from heat, then forward and hugged him mechanically.

"Hi, Dad."

Her clothes seemed wrong for the ride, a white, frilly, sleeveless blouse, short, checked skirt, and black pumps, but then it was hot.

"How you doin'?" he asked.

"Great," she said, pulling her neckline. "I'm head of my department now."

"Wonderful," he said. He knew she meant a credits and collections department at a phone company. "You'll have to tell me all about it when we get there."

Generally, she was reticent apart, but fine around him, his "sometime daughter," as in *Lear*, and, as always, there was an air of nervous vulnerability about her. She had been with a friend when she drowned, swept away by the current as they crossed a flooded bridge, and had never really been the same since: on the surface, smug and indifferent, a Stepford daughter with a pretty, mischievous smile, underneath, hurt and angry, a sullen volcano that could erupt resentfully at any moment. Once Samantha had popped the cruciate tendon in her right rear leg, but had come hopping into the kitchen happily for food as if nothing were wrong. Sometimes he wondered if Alice, in essence, were doing the same, pretending nothing was wrong when, in fact, her heart was broken. That was why he felt he always had to be very careful with her. There was no point in hurting even more someone as injured as she was.

"Well," Tyler said, facing Karen, "thanks for putting the trip together."

"It's nothing."

"No, it's something," he claimed.

5

"Let me assure you," she said, briefly closing her eyes, "it's nothing. We'd be going out there anyway. Just one more set of linens."

"OK," he chuckled.

"Shall we?" Karen asked, meaning to board.

"Sure," he said. "Can't wait to meet Caliban and Ariel."

She paused, looking down to her left. "What?"

"A literary joke," he smiled.

The boat was a tough, wooden, two-oar rowboat with a pointed prow and flat stern. The Ashes had bought it from a lobsterman and bolted a 10-horse-power Honda motor to the transom. At twenty feet, it looked, to Tyler, big enough for the ocean on a good day, not a bad one. The bottom was black, the hull oyster white with dents and scuffs, and where the paint had peeled off looked like holes in cloth. Without the motor, it would have passed for something out of a Homer Winslow painting.

When Tyler held out his hand to help Alice step in, she jerked her hand away as if burnt.

"I can do it," she said, her eyes darting right and left.

She climbed in, rattling an oar, followed by Karen, then Linda with the peonies. Near Linda's feet sat a crate with a black cat he knew was Karen's pet, Peeve, to which she knew he was allergic, as was Linda for that matter. He had brought antihistamine, and the cat would probably run loose on the island. He would figure out what to do about it, if anything, when he got there.

As the women put their orange lifejackets on, Tyler put his shoulder against the prow, then, feet planted firmly in the gravel and sand, pushed the boat off, grabbed an oarlock, and swung aboard. He sat facing them, and as he watched them fastening the jackets, he sensed the exclusive rapport among them the way a mare and fillies naturally move in tandem.

The boat swiveled slowly away from shore, and when Karen turned the key in the ignition, he asked Linda, over the noise of the motor, "Hand me one of those, would you?"

As he slipped the lifejacket on, Karen shifted gears and throttled forward, cautiously guiding the boat through the maze of buoys. They looked like colorful tops, some solid, some striped, all radiating bright, silvery flowers of light. Sometimes two or three were tangled together and, as the boat passed, bumped together, clicking like teeth.

When he and Karen were married, he was used to her not being able to do things. She couldn't drive, swim, drink liquor, or smoke pot. When she drank or smoked, she unraveled mentally and emotionally, but not in the fun way most people did. He lost his inhibitions. She lost control. After the divorce, she had to learn to drive to survive, had taken lessons, and bought a car. Still, though he didn't consider the idea sexist, it just seemed odd that she went out on the ocean in a small boat on a regular basis. It seemed out of character, too adventurous, too risky for her.

When she caught him smirking, she asked, "What?"

"Nothing," he said. "It's just that I know how you are about water, especially deep water."

"Think I can't steer a boat?"

"No, no, no," he blurted.

Karen glared at him, then tilted her head, gazing around him. Linda and Alice glanced at him with a blank expression, then gazed toward the inn, both hugging themselves as if against cold.

"So you've learned to swim?" he asked.

When Karen ignored him, he pivoted, swinging his legs over the seat, and faced forward. She was obviously navigating by sight, he thought, and he wondered how she would get to the island and back under different circumstances, for example, at night or in fog.

Outside the cove, the motor roared, the boat sped up, and the prow lifted, tipping him back so that he had to grab the gunwales. He leaned forward, regaining his balance, in about the same headlong position he would be if speeding down a highway on a motorcycle. When he had settled into the rhythm of the boat, he let go of the gunwales and, elbows on knees, hands clasped, just took it all in: dead ahead bright white, blurred with mist, shading into gray toward the sides.

Now that the awkward meeting was over, he could relax and enjoy the ride, and since he was going to be a prisoner on the island for a few days, he was determined to enjoy that, too. From the start, he had assumed a stoic attitude toward the visit. First of all, he feared being hated by his daughters, but lately his relationship with them had been improving dramatically, and if Karen started in with the recriminations again, she would only reveal what a "herbicidal maniac" she was, as he joked to himself. Second, at this point in life, he was pretty much impervious to her accusations. The reason: he was simply not the monster she made him out to be. Free spirit, yes. Devil incarnate, no. He could take her emotional battering the way he was taking the wind and spray at the moment – with pleasure. Third, the writer in him had always been curious and experimental, searching for experience and understanding, the fodder of fiction. If she weren't careful, she would give him something he could use. And last, he loved his daughters, even Karen, and appreciated the opportunity to be with them. All he wanted was to enjoy himself and enjoy them enjoying themselves and the beautiful seascape that stretched away from them in all directions. He would not let himself be drawn into drama.

And it was with that attitude, that of focusing on the present, that he, in a sense, began anew with Linda the moment he met her at the airport. She had a childlike way of standing with her feet turned in, which endeared her to him, and though she was dressed boyishly in jeans and a white T-shirt, her young, cherubic beauty still shone through, brightening him. He smiled, set his bag down, and, when she hesitated, made an open gesture as if to ask, "Well?" Then they embraced warmly, a gratuitous courtesy which he appreciated more than most in his life, including even winning the Sparky Award, a film-festival prize for one of his screenplays. As they separated, she even let him kiss her fondly on the cheek.

"Good to see you," he smiled.

She squinted into space, then glanced at him. "Thanks for coming."

"You look great."

"How was the trip?"

"Not bad," he said, slipping his bag strap over his shoulder. "Forgot how short the flight is, just a couple of hours."

Again, she squinted into space, her face dimmed with concern. Then they moved on.

"Do you need to go to baggage claim?" she asked.

"No, this is it. So," he hesitated, "how are you?"

"Well," she began, looking at him askance. "For someone about to undergo brain surgery, not bad."

"Good," he urged her. "Keep your eye on the goal, getting rid of the seizures. When they're gone, it'll all be worth it."

"That's what I keep telling myself."

"Have to do anything to prepare for the test?"

"Other than being positive, no."

He knew that Eddie loved her dearly and would be a great emotional support in the days ahead. She taught elementary school, and from what Tyler had heard about her class, he knew that her children loved her. He loved her too, told her so on the phone, and hoped that Karen had not been poisoning her against him again. Accusations, like chlorine, might clear Karen's image in Linda's mind, but they were still poison, and it was important that Linda, for her sake, wasn't conflicted about his feelings toward her and, thus, hers toward him. Such lies were nothing but lies, but everything if Linda believed them, and she needed to believe that everyone loved her now, even him.

When young, Linda had made Tyler a god's eye, an object made of colored yarn woven around two crossed sticks. At first, its only significance was that Linda had made it. He was fond of it for that reason alone: it was an extension of her. Later, he read about it as a two-way magic portal through which he

8

could see into the spiritual realm and through which god could see and protect him, not the Christian god, a nature god with the four points representing water, earth, air, and fire as well as the four directions with the fifth being the eye itself, the spiritual direction, inward. Now what he hoped was that, as ultimate truth, it would shield him against lies.

When they got to Brunswick, he asked her to take him to a wine shop, where he bought several bottles of Sangiovese and packed them in his bag, rolled in his clothes.

"Don't like wine," she said, driving off.

"You don't?" he asked, surprised. "God's blood."

"Referring to communion," she asked, "or some pagan deity?" She knew he was an atheist and, as far as he had influenced her, had raised her as such.

"Dionysus," he laughed. "The joy god."

When they passed a flower shop, he asked her to stop, went in, and, in a few minutes, came out with a big bunch of purple peonies.

"For you," he said, getting in the car.

"For me?" she asked, smelling them.

"Well, for everyone really."

"Thanks. They're beautiful."

The large, showy flowers were filling the car with a pungent rose scent. She lay them on the back seat, and when she turned to start the car, a young man strolled past, carrying an air-conditioner on his shoulder.

"Probably the last one in town," she said, turning the key in the ignition. "Most people up here don't have air-conditioning."

Besides the wine and flowers, Tyler had also brought gifts for everyone: for Karen, a copy of *Herbs of the Ancient Greeks and Romans*, for the girls, a couple of sheer, cotton, floral-print tea dresses from Laura Ashley, mauve for Alice, her favorite color, blue for Linda. He did not have a clue about buying dresses, but they looked feminine and pretty with a flared skirt, V-neck, tie front, and puffy sleeves. He didn't see how he could go wrong. He also bought Linda a few volumes of Ann Sexton since she had taken a few creative-writing courses and had writing aspirations: *Love Poems*, *To Bedlam and Partway Back*, and *All My Pretty Ones*. But he would have to give them to her when Alice wasn't around. Alice was always accusing him of favoritism.

"Last night I had a terrible dream with you and Mom in it," Linda said, backing out.

"A dream?"

"Yeah," she said, pulling away. "In the dream you were a compulsive bike thief who had to try to clean up your act so you could take care of me. Mom was a constant traveler, but she wouldn't tell me where she was going next.

She promised she would send me a postcard when she got there and then I could write her. She gave me a nickel. She said she knew you could turn things around because you were very devoted to me. As I was talking with her, you were stealing a bike in the background. God was it sad."

"Hmmm," he mused, noticing her pink fingernails. "I've never been good with dreams. Of course, *thief* is pretty clear. Question is: What does the bike represent? What do you associate with it?" When she didn't answer, he said, "With divorce comes a sense of loss for everyone. Your mom as a traveler is practically literal. You've lived a lot of places over the years, and I guess that, now that you're married, you feel you're losing her, too. But you have Eddie. As far as I can tell," he smiled, "he makes up for a lot."

"Yes," she agreed. "He does."

"The nickel must mean poverty," he went on, "and we've certainly been that, poor."

"Some more than others."

He knew what she meant, but decided not to engage her on the topic. He didn't know why Karen had never asked for much in the first place. Not that he had it. And technically he had never missed a child-support payment. Then, years later, a three-hundred-pound state trooper knocked on the door and served him with a subpoena. She was suing him for more, which he gladly paid. On that point, his conscience was clear, as clean as Linda's white socks. In some larger sense, he had been cheap, yes, but had to be. He didn't have money. If he had, he would have given it to them.

Of course, now, everyone was better off. Linda taught in an elementary school and was married to a mechanical engineer at Bath Ironworks. Alice had a good job and was living with a young Italian security guard. Karen taught classes at a branch of the state university system. She also wrote newspaper columns and counseled people privately in holistic, alternative healing. He taught and finally was collecting royalties from books and residuals from screenplays, especially from his script for *The Crystal Ball*, a cult hit.

"As for turning things around – " he continued.

"Too late."

"What?"

"It's too late."

"No, it isn't," he insisted.

"It's too late for a normal childhood," she said. "Too late for a normal family."

"You're right," he conceded, "but I'm here now in the car with you, and we still can enjoy ourselves. Why spoil now with the past?"

He had had a couple of other problems with her over the years, philosophical differences, as he called them. First were their attitudes toward his writing about them. He saw it as an expression of love, she as an invasion of privacy. Second were their attitudes toward distance and time. *Wuthering Heights* was the first and, thus, most formative novel he read. It shaped his Romantic view of things. Space and time, he believed, didn't matter to people who loved each other, and so, though he was far away physically and saw her only once a year, he still felt close emotionally and mentally. He gazed at baby pictures of her in big, white, bib-sized collars and felt close. During her adolescence, he pretended to reprimand her on the phone for her mother's sake and felt close. At her wedding reception, he danced with her on the porch at the inn and felt close. It didn't matter whether they were actually together or not. He felt close. She didn't.

Romance with a capital *R*, however, came with a real price. She soon discovered she was sterile due to an undiagnosed gonococcal infection as a teenager. And Tyler had connected the dots this way: his absence and permissive attitude equaled pathos – the rebellious Linda slipping out a window late at night to meet her black or Latino boyfriend. Or as King Lear says, "Nothing will come of nothing." At the time, he had scoffed at the hypocrisy of reprimanding her for doing exactly what he was doing: sleeping around, a dialectical response to the oppressive Southern Baptist milieu in which he had grown up.

But he wasn't being oppressed now, and they were doing something about what they could, in fact, do something about: stopping her seizures. They had ridden down Highway 24 on Orrs Island, one of the most beautiful scenic experiences anyone could have – lush forest, craggy cliffs, rocky tidal inlets draped with seaweed – and now they were having another, only on water. He shaded his eyes and peered toward what looked like a pod of whales. Gradually, the pod flattened to the dim, gray line of an island. One small cotton ball of a cloud had popped up, and at the top of the sky, almost blotted out by glare, a wavering wedge of geese was flying south.

The outing on the ocean and the fatherly issues stirred up again by his visit made him think of one of Ariel's songs from *The Tempest*:

> *Full fathom five thy father lies,*
> *Of his bones are coral made,*
> *Those are pearls that were his eyes.*
> *Nothing of him that doth fade*
> *But doth suffer a sea change*
> *Into something rich and strange.*
> *Sea nymphs hourly ring his knell.*

He wondered if he could transform the sober occasion of the trip into something constructive and fun, as he had wanted to transform the catastrophe

11

of the divorce into the good he thought would come of it eventually, a better life for all of them. When he glanced back, Linda was lying on the thwart, eyes closed, a tennis shoe on the floor to either side, her silver watch band, bracelet, and wedding ring incandescent in the intense light. The peonies were lying on the floor as if tossed in a grave. He glanced at Karen's hand on the tiller. She wasn't wearing her wedding ring, but then, neither was he. When he glanced at her, framed in the wake, she gave him a harsh look. With a look like that, he knew, she couldn't be enjoying herself. Something was on her mind as clearly as if there had been a big, black tick on her forehead.

For some reason, the look made him think of Wyeth's painting *The Intruder*, in which a dog is pointing toward something hidden in the woods. Then he thought of one of the girls' visits, when he had driven them and a friend of theirs to his lake house. He had put a can of gasoline for his boat on the floor of the back seat and, while driving, kept smelling it. Before he realized it, Alice had lit a cigarette and wouldn't put it out. When they got to the house, he noticed that the can had a tiny hole in it and had been leaking. The thought of what could have happened was nothing short of horrifying. Here, too, he felt he was in a volatile situation which could easily blow up. This wasn't just a family outing, he realized. His intuition told him something was up, but whatever it was, he would accept it, go along with it, make the best of it, submissively sacrificing himself to whatever they felt they needed to do or say. Oh, God, he thought, more recriminations. And he despaired that Karen wouldn't forgive him and move on.

To him, the marriage was ancient history, something you read about, not real. He remembered a page in his mother-in-law's Bible, one on which his and Karen's wedding date was recorded with random, what he thought of as Spenserian capitals: "This certifies that Tyler Richard Lynn and Karen Collier Stickler were united in holy matrimony at Two o'clock p.m. on the 7th day of the Seventh month in the year of our Lord Nineteen hundred eighty-nine at St. Mark's Episcopal Church by Rev. George Pardington Palmer. Witness Lloyd H. Stickler. Witness Mrs. G. P. Palmer." The girls' birthdays were also recorded: "Linda Beth Lynn 1-30-1990. Alice Lynn 6-4-92." They had not given Alice a middle name. The idea was to let her, when she grew up, pick one for herself.

The boat sped into the shadow of the cloud, and when the light dimmed, he thought of the eclipse and the strange light in Wyeth's *Big Room*. The ocean changed to a luminous lavender freaked with yellow, a tincture of violets. He figured the lavender glow was some kind of retinal effect after the glare, just as it had taken a while for his eyes, after the glare of marriage, to see exactly what had gone wrong.

One of their problems was mental. After the children, Karen turned conservative while he remained liberal. She wanted to give up their Bohemian life for one more bourgeois, a natural, maternal, protective reaction he understood, but couldn't embrace. He needed to live an unorthodox life, he believed, to be original as a writer, and, of course, to support a bourgeois life, he would have had to take on more teaching responsibilities, which meant he would have had less time to write. Was that the role his life would cast him in, breadwinner?

A second problem was emotional, an indefinable coolness, as he thought of it, on both parts, and, at first, it puzzled him because he thought of himself as basically a warm person, indiscriminately considerate. Then he realized the obvious, that he had married her not so much because he loved her, but because he'd knocked her up.

One night they were making out on the back seat of his car, and when he started to put a condom on, she said, "We don't need it. I've counted the days."

Not that that line of reasoning mattered. He was just as responsible as she was for avoiding an unwanted pregnancy. And the pregnancy, in hindsight, was not, in fact, unwanted. He loved Linda and Alice and wouldn't give them back if he could. What he felt for Karen, though, was compassion, not love, at least not the kind of love for which people usually marry. She was a woman with child, but no means of support. He wanted to love her, but when he realized that he didn't the way he needed to for the marriage to work, it became a kind of remote island from whose shore he was always searching the horizon.

A third problem was sexual. Their sexualities were different, on different levels. Simply put, she was inhibited. He wasn't. In fact, he was open to just about anything. He liked spontaneity and variety. To her, the only thing kosher was the passive role in the missionary position. Everything else was taboo, no 69, not even a hand job. Ironically, the only way he could make her come was to go down on her, but the more she enjoyed it, the more she objected to it and struggled against it.

Question was: Why? One of his theories was that she had, to use psych jargon, internalized the societal notion that sex is bad. The main vehicle of that conditioning, he believed, was her Catholic-school background. Had the repressed nuns and priests figuratively cut out her clitoris the way certain African men literally cut out their wives' so that they wouldn't have fun and leave them? Was there something else in her past that had programmed her to recoil? However she got that way, she had, in short, a problem with pleasure, and as far as he could tell, pleasure was the only reason to live.

He wanted someone he could enjoy sex with, someone who would let herself go. Otherwise, what was the point? It was also an aesthetic problem for him. Complete engagement with someone was obviously more romantic and satisfying than a superficial one. From the beginning, he had hoped that she

13

would change or he would somehow adjust, but there were plenty of others willing to please him. It was perfectly natural that he would start gravitating from dull to exciting, from Puritanical to Dionysian, from frustration to satisfaction.

He wasn't sure what the relationship between good sex and good writing was, but he knew that, for him, there definitely was one. In the past, when certain physical and emotional needs were met, he felt free to engage himself imaginatively. He also believed that, just as sex rites were performed in spring to promote the fertility of the vine, good sex promoted imaginative fertility. He had to experience life intensely, he felt, to write about it intensely, to see it reflected intensely in the mirror of his work.

How he saw his role as writer presented another sexual problem. By nature, he loved to write, and since he was a writer, he felt he needed to be open to new ideas and experiences, to travel, to satisfy his curiosity about things, to feed his imagination, all for the sake of his own personal growth and development of his writing. Thus, he rationalized his penchant for pot smoking and bisexual experimentation, both as rebellious acts in the face of what he thought of as a numb bourgeoisie. At the end of D. H. Lawrence's *Women in Love*, Ursula tells Rupert, "You can't have two kinds of love," but he responds, "I don't believe that." Neither did Tyler.

The beginning and end of his marriage were set off by two choices, like bookends, the two most important options in his life, the choice to get married and the choice to get divorced. The first occurred when he went for a walk in Karen's home town one night. He crossed a bridge, but on the way back, the bridge had been raised for a boat, but, for some reason, not lowered. Thus, he had plenty of time to think. His choice at the time was to stay with her or just walk away, abandoning her with the problem. The right thing to do, of course, was stay, but the right thing to do was a big mistake. The right thing to do was wrong, though the outcome of it was two beautiful daughters that he loved dearly despite the fact that they, because Karen had poisoned them, would never believe that he did.

Five years later, the second choice was clear. He had married for the wrong reason and had been asked to give up, at one end of the spectrum, just plain fun, at the other, his ideas and values, even what he loved most, his passion for writing. Of course, some part of him believed that, if we all are, in fact, free, truly agents of our own being, then he didn't really need a reason, good or otherwise. Boredom was enough or some *je ne sais quoi* between him and her that even he was unaware of, something in their basic natures that didn't fit. It wasn't a false dilemma, he believed firmly. It was them or him.

When they came out of the cloud shadow, the water flashed like a flashbulb, waking him from his thoughts. He shaded his eyes and squinted toward the horizon, where the island's line had swelled to a bump.

When he, pointing, turned to yell, "That it?" he caught them staring at him with a strange look. Three thugs who have cornered a victim in an alley probably had the same glare, he thought, but then the divorce had sullied all their lives and he was, he knew, after all this time, somewhat of a mystery and curiosity to them. A Mona Lisa smile suffused Karen's face, and she nodded.

Then something caught her eye. She flinched and screamed, and as they sped past it, a few yards off port, like a dark phantom in the water's shattered mirror, a huge, bluish-gray shark, the size of the boat, was rolling onto its side, as if basking in the sun, exposing its milky underbelly, and pointing a pectoral fin in the air. Alice grabbed Karen's arm, and Linda sat up, looking aft. Then the fin slipped beneath the surface, leaving a casual trail of sparkling foam on the water.

"My god," he shouted with excitement. "What a monster!"

Chapter 3: A Branch of Wild Cherries

Josh Evans was a kind, affluent, good-looking boy-man who, at twenty-six, had just finished his Ph.D. in architecture and just arrived in Naples at the beginning of a solo tour of Italy. The trip was given to him as a graduation gift by his father, Schuyler (Sky), head of the prosperous architectural firm Evans and Benator based in Atlanta. Sky also thought it would put the finishing touches on his son's education. Josh had been an excellent student. His professors thought he had great potential for success, and, as his father had told him, as soon as he got back, he would make "a great addition to the firm." Because of Pompeii and the temples at Paestum, he had wanted to start the trip in the south and work his way north through Rome and Florence to Venice, Lago di Garda, and Milan.

He had flown into Fiumicino that morning and taken the train to Stazione Termini, then one to Naples. At Stazione Centrale, he took a bus to his hotel, Isola di Capri, where he unpacked, showered, and dressed for the sultry weather: khakis with a blue canvas belt, a short-sleeve, blue and purple, plaid shirt, and blue Superga sneakers. Then he set out on a walking tour of the center of the city: Castel Nuovo, Galleria Umberto, Teatro di San Carlo, and Piazza Trieste e Trento, where he stopped at Café Rosso Pomodoro (Red Tomato) for an espresso.

Before the trip, he had in mind a certain myth of Italy's beauty, which Naples both confirmed with its lovely palazzos, castles, and museums and dispelled with its tropical poverty, grime, and smog. The city also had a certain unreal quality about it, partly because it was simply new to him and partly because it was Sunday and, thus, strangely vacant and quiet. The solitude gave him peace and time to ponder the great exhaustion he felt, sitting, sunk in on himself, in a bistro chair under a big, white umbrella in the piazza.

The first reason for his exhaustion was jet lag. He had taken an Ambien soon after takeoff, but, excited about the trip, had dozed off only a few times. When he just happened to notice the vague, snow-capped mountains slowly emerging from the dark below, he stayed glued to the window to see sunrise over the Alps and as much of Europe as he could: the French Riviera, Corsica, Sardinia, and the misty length of Italy. Now, drowsy, he knew he had to stay awake until bedtime Naples time in order to synchronize himself with his new environment. So he paid, rose, and continued his tour.

The other reason for his exhaustion was the free-floating anxiety he had been struggling with ever since his breakup with whom he now considered a rather sadistic lover, Owen, a charming predator of sorts who had subtly conditioned him to be his own personal masochist. His other secret purpose for the trip was to forget him, but at the moment, his pain over the loss alienated him even more from Naples than he was, a stray colt ambling around the intricate labyrinth of its stone buildings and cobblestone streets. He had been adrift emotionally for months, and now, as the espresso kicked in, he was adrift literally as well, strolling around the littered expanse of Piazza del Plebiscito. The piazza was so littered, in fact, he figured it must have been the site of a rock concert or some similar event the night before.

On one side of the piazza rose the handsome façade of the Palazzo Reale, on the other the long, curved colonnade of San Francesco di Paola, the church where, though an atheist as far as Christianity was concerned, he had hoped to light a votive candle in hopes that some pagan deity like Dionysus would take pity on him and "surcease his sorrow," as he thought of it, misquoting Poe. To his surprise, though, though it was Sunday, the church's huge, steel doors were closed and locked.

He strolled behind the church and, after a few turns, found himself slowly trudging up the long slant of Via Pizzofalcone toward the top of Monte Echia, an old volcano. Colorful laundry, strung on clotheslines, checkered the air above the street.

An old woman in black was perched on a balcony, fanning herself, and when he raised his hand and said, "Buona sera," she smiled and said, "Buona sera."

The street curved to the right at the top, and the view opened into a great panorama of the glimmering bay with Vesuvius hunched in the background. He leaned over a low, stone wall and looked down the sheer cliff into the buildings, bushes, and streets far below, then sat on the wall, his back to the bay, posture drooping, to catch his breath. After the hike up Pizzofalcone, he was winded and, despite the light clothes, sweating. When he looked up, he noticed, in a rock face, the faint imprint of some architectural remains, the arches of a villa which he knew dated back almost three thousand years.

The remains gave him perspective on his depression. He realized that, in the great scheme of things, the heavy lethargy he couldn't set down meant absolutely nothing. Still, it was such a serious burden that he wondered about its nature, whether it was a temporary condition, like a hormonal imbalance, and, thus, curable or a flaw in his temperament that would eventually wear him down. When he was fifteen, his mother, though a good swimmer, drowned one night under mysterious circumstances, but his relationship with his father had always been perfectly natural and proper, as far as he was concerned. His father was busy, but accessible. Josh couldn't see how his parents had contributed to his sexual orientation, let alone to such a grave lack of self-esteem. From the first, he had embraced his gayness like a twin. So why would he efface himself in such a humiliating way with a married man?

18

The downhill zigzag of Rampa di Pizzofalcone crisscrossed below him, but not as steep and tortuous as his downward spiral of self-abasement. Whatever the reason, he was, in fact, sick in some profound sense, but not suicidal. He didn't have the least desire to step up onto the wall. Perhaps an overdose of Ambien, he joked to himself, not jumping off a cliff.

# # # # #

He trekked down Rampa di Pizzofalcone, had Pizza Margherita at Pizzeria Brandi, and, on his way back to his hotel, strolled through Piazza Trieste e Trento again, admiring the lit fountain and the spectacular Galleria down the street. At first glance, what the building had in common with Wright's work, the subject of his doctoral thesis, was the asymmetry of its gracefully curved main entrance and the ornamental detail (in this case, elegant columns, niches, and statues). He was curious about the structural problems of the steel and glass dome and decided he would try to find a shop with copies of its floor plans, perspectives, and elevations.

As he turned onto Via Giuseppe Verdi, he noticed a group of mostly attractive, well-groomed young men loitering among the yellow lights and gray shadows of the Galleria's east entrance. Standing together would have meant one thing, he thought, but they were a few feet apart, set against the bluff of the building's stone façade. Their neat, bourgeois image did not fit his grubby-hustler stereotype, but he was fairly sure he knew what they were up to, and the painterly way in which they had arranged themselves on the sidewalk and steps conjured up a series of intriguing images in his mind: a branch of wild cherries, a stem of wild roses, and, more appropriately, a flock of teenage satyrs mischievously idling in the woods. At first, he did not know where the low music was coming from, strange strains of a lyrical flute and a crisp tambourine, but as he approached, he saw a small, portable CD player sitting on a step.

A hustler with his back to him was singing softly and swaying to the music with his hands in his pockets. He was wearing loose jeans, white Nikes, and a white, sleeveless T-shirt. When he turned and noticed how close Josh was, he froze, mouth open, then lit up as if a bright light had been turned on him. Josh saw how his eyes changed from cool and distant to surprised and fascinated. He didn't know what he represented to the young man, but whatever it was had stopped him in his tracks. Then the young man took his hands out of his pockets and moved toward him head-on with a slow, relaxed swagger.

Josh could tell he was *hot* from his muscular arms, rounded pecs, and the way the tee curved like an hourglass. He tried to hold his gaze, but face to face, blushed and glanced down, first at the small, red bulldog on his tee, then at his hefty package. It pressed against the denim like a long, thick root he had seen trying to press through the vinyl lining of his father's swimming pool. Josh could imagine the branched veins wrapped around it.

Then he sighed and summoned his courage to face him again: the long, wavy brunet hair, the strong features carved into a big block of a face, the sparkling brown eyes gazing at him from long lashes and thick, flat eyebrows, the pink mouth stretched into a wide, lopsided smile, dimpled cheeks, a mole just below his right cheekbone. His jaw was rough with a day's stubble, but even at night, Josh could see the healthy glow of his olive, Southern-Italian skin. In short, the youth was a handsome *paesano*, the kind Josh had hoped to meet in his fantasies about the trip and, in his fantasies, crowned with clusters of vine leaves.

"Buona sera," Josh smiled shyly.

"Buona sera," the young man replied.

"I'm Josh," Josh said, extending his hand.

"Josh?" the man asked, shaking hands. "Valerio." Valerio held his hand in his big, strong hand for a moment longer than necessary.

"Good to meet you."

Valerio's eyes were delighted, but analytical. He was sizing him up, Josh knew, and amused with him, perhaps his naiveté. Josh wondered if he were, in fact, as inexperienced as Valerio apparently thought he was. According to today's standards, Josh, like witch hazel, was a late bloomer.

"What may I do for you?" Valerio asked, his eyes fixed on Josh's.

Josh composed himself, leaned forward, and whispered near Valerio's face, "You wouldn't happen to know where I could get a couple of joints, would you?"

"Joints?" Valerio repeated, his mouth near Josh's.

Valerio's breath smelled of spearmint, his body of aromatic foliage, as if just washed with an herbal soap, and when Josh smelled him, his own body flooded with pleasure. Being grabbed by a gruff carabiniere could not have surprised him more.

"Due spinelli."

"Ah, si," Valerio beamed. "And how do you know I'm not a cop?"

"You're too happy to be a cop."

Valerio laughed, and at that moment, for some reason, the music ended. He gestured for Josh to follow, and they strolled down the sidewalk toward a stout young man leaning against the wall.

"Eh, Rollo," Valerio said privately. "A couple of joints for my friend."

Rollo was standing in an odd way, his head slightly turned to the right, his body to the left, his right hand on his right thigh, his left on his hip, his left foot ahead of his right. Josh wondered if he were deformed or posing in some bizarre feminine way.

"Two?" he asked, droopy eyed.

20

"Please," Josh stared.

As Rollo reached into a pocket, he kept his eyes averted, looking down. Then he slowly pulled out a plastic bag, took out the joints, and put the bag away. He rolled one of the joints back and forth between his thumb and middle finger, showing his wares.

"How much?" Josh asked.

Rollo briefly closed his eyes, then said, "Fifty."

"Thirty," Valerio smirked. When Rollo drowsily lifted his eyes to squint at Valerio, Valerio smiled, "He's a friend." Then Valerio turned to Josh and said, "Thirty."

"I have a lot of coins," Josh said. "Do you mind coins?"

"Coins, bills, watches," Rollo droned. He had a rounded face with some acne, a small mouth, and glossy black hair flipped up at the neck.

Josh reached into his pocket, took out change, and poured it into the palm of his left hand. There, he counted it, pushing it around with his finger, but after he had counted out ten Euros, he decided to give him all of it.

"Here's ten," he said, handing it over. "And I'll give you a twenty," meaning a bill.

Without appearing to do so, he kept his distance from Rollo, not that he was afraid he would pick his pocket. Still, he had an irrational aversion to him, just as he had a natural attraction to Valerio.

When they exchanged the money for the joints, Rollo asked, "Anything else? Coca, hash, cell phone?"

"You're carrying coca?" Josh smiled.

"I can get it," Rollo explained, leaning against the wall. To Josh, Rollo looked as if he could use some coca. "What about videos or DVDs?" Rollo asked.

"Rollo would sell his mother for twenty Euros," Valerio said.

"After all," Rollo agreed, squinting at Valerio, "she is a whore."

"Grazie mille," Josh said.

When he looked at Valerio, Valerio nodded subtly, and they strolled down the sidewalk, stopped, and stared at each other shrewdly, as if sharing a joke.

"He looks young," Josh remarked. "What's the age of consent?"

"Fourteen."

"Looks tired."

"Smokes more than he sells," Valerio explained, stepping close. "He's the least *posato, equilibrato*. What's the word?"

"Together?"

"Yes," Valerio said, "he's the least together of the boys. I think he's positive, but he denies it."

"Positive," Josh repeated. "What about you?"

"No," Valerio stressed. "Not positive. Safe."

"Good," Josh said. "But...." He stared at their shadows on the sidewalk.

"What?"

Josh turned and gestured toward the glossy street. "What about the – the risks?"

"You think I can't take care of myself?"

Josh shook his head. He could imagine what a tiger Valerio would be if a john ever crossed him.

"I've always lived with much greater dangers," Valerio explained, his look suddenly blank. "I enjoy wild things," he said, emphasizing the words with a glance. "When I was a boy, my father took care of orchards where a small red fox would tiptoe up in the evening for a dropped apple or a pear. These days, that little red fox sticks its head around the corner in many other ways: drugs, VD, johns, the Camarro, cops, colleagues. Priests," he added mysteriously. "I forgot priests."

Josh understood.

"I enjoy myself," Valerio claimed. "I enjoy talking with you."

"Me too," Josh confessed.

He knew he was a fool for good-looking men, but there was something more going on here, he felt. Though he also knew it was incredibly stupid to think so, he actually wanted to protect him, a hustler, and a strange one at that.

"Let's say you're out on a walk," Valerio sighed, "and you stop to smell a rose or some rosemary. Well, that's what a trick is to me, a pinch of rosemary rubbed between my fingers."

Josh looked puzzled, skeptical. By definition, Valerio got money and sex, but Josh wondered about the emotional side of tricking. He doubted such a hard life could, in fact, be that easy. A weed poked out of a crack in the sidewalk. He was sure it was bitter, too.

"May I ask you something?"

"Anything," Valerio smiled, in his face again.

"How did you...?"

"What?" Valerio chuckled.

"Get started."

"I clerk at a hotel, La Casa dei Poveri di Cuore," Valerio lilted.

Josh smiled wistfully. He knew enough Italian to know what that meant: The House of the Poor at Heart.

"Franz and Angus, an older couple, noticed my hands and asked if I gave massages. Apparently, I'm a natural, something about my assertive touch."

When he turned away from the light, his eyes went from brown to black, black marbles, peepholes, for Josh, into an florid, exotic, mysterious night.

"Anything else you'd like to do?"

"I'd like to be an Armani model," Valerio laughed. "Really."

Though Josh didn't think he fit the build – he wasn't tall and skinny enough – he thought he'd suggest something.

"There's an Armani shop in Piazza dei Martiri." He had looked up places to shop. "Why don't you drop by there and uh, uh, ask about getting a job? Wouldn't hurt. Later, you can ask about modeling, uh, in Rome or Milan."

When Valerio gazed at him curiously, the attraction was so strong Josh felt that the sidewalk was actually inclined toward him. Good God, Josh thought. He must be more tired than he thought. He was actually thinking of hiring him.

Josh had made reservations for a cottage in Amalfi in a few days and fantasized about taking Valerio there. He had found the place online, a very private *suite nuziale* wedged in a rock face and attached to a small hotel by way of a narrow ledge with a low wall. It was organic in a Frank Lloyd Wright sort of way in that it was beautifully integrated into its surroundings, perched on a shelf with a terrace jutting precipitously over the surf churning below, and one of the pictures of the inside, mainly one large, cave-like room, showed that the wall behind the bed was actually the wall of the cliff. What better place, Josh thought, to let Valerio's hot, olive body writhe on top of him?

The question was: Would such a reckless adventure cure his depression? He definitely needed to be stimulated out of his stupor, but would he just be switching one drug for another, sex for love, methadone, let's say, for Owen? He had read that Pompeians used urine to whiten garments. Perhaps tricking with Valerio would clean out Owen's memory, not that Josh really thought of Valerio that way. Certainly, tricking was safe in the sense that love wasn't involved. The rites and sacrifices, so to speak, were performed outside the heart, not in the main inner body, where only the initiated were admitted. After all, he couldn't possibly fall in love with an Italian hustler, could he? That would be the height of foolishness, even for him.

Sex, however, was a form of escapism, like the joints, not a fix. When it was over, he would still need a fix, the other kind. Early on, his father had talked to him about taking good care of his body, the vessel of his thoughts and feelings, as Sky had put it, telling him how he could spoil his life with diseases like herpes, chronic hepatitis, AIDS. Life was to be savored, he'd said, and sex was one of its great, if ephemeral, pleasures. Why would he want to cut himself off from that? Despite what Valerio claimed, how would Josh know his HIV status? Even playing safe was not fool-proof. And there were other physical dangers implicit in the situation. He was lonely prey, he knew, vulnerable to his own bad judgment. His greatest fear was that, through a series of his own stupid mistakes, he would never find the right person, his "amico del cuore," as they said in Italian, but he had never had enough self-esteem to look for the right person. Perhaps he should now.

"You're not my type," Valerio joked, reading his thoughts.

"Type?" Josh laughed. "Which is?"

"Someone in a uniform, carabinieri, state police."

"You have me there," Josh said, embarrassed. "Architectural students can wear pretty much what they please." A surprisingly cool breeze brushed them as if someone had opened the door of an air-conditioned building. "I think you're kidding me," Josh said, buoyed by Valerio's tact.

Valerio's smile creased his cheeks.

"There's an herb, a weed," he began, slipping his hands into his pockets. "Borsa del pastore."

"Shepherd's purse."

"With small green hearts."

"Like mine," Josh said. "I get it."

Spontaneously, they drifted down the sidewalk into the dark and stopped.

"So, what're you going to see tomorrow?" Valerio asked.

"Caravaggio's *Seven Works of Mercy*. Familiar with it?"

"No."

"I'm taken with this pair of angels, boys."

"Angel boys, huh," Valerio grinned.

"Check it out," Josh suggested. "It's in Pio Monte della Misericorda."

Then Josh realized that while Valerio was gazing at him seductively, he was fondling himself. He figured that he was just having fun with him, still trying to tempt him by displaying his wares, as Rollo had with the joints.

"Tell me," Josh said, changing subjects. "What's the attitude toward gays in Naples?"

"The attitudes of ordinary people are slowly changing for the better," Valerio said. "The whole culture is much more compassionate now. They're not stoning us to death anymore, at least not in the piazza in broad daylight. But the politicians and clergy lag far behind. There's a big generational difference."

"Good to know," Josh said. "I mean about attitudes changing."

A self-conscious silence ensued as Valerio held himself in his jeans.

"I've been having a lot of trouble sleeping lately," Josh said, bringing the conversation to a close. "I'm sure the spinello will help." Actually, he did not intend to use the grass for that. For that, he had Ambien. "I have a sound machine at home."

"Sound machine?"

"It makes sounds like the ocean, a rain forest, thunder."

"Some farmers stuff pillows with hops," Valerio said. "They believe the smell makes you sleepy."

"You should be a gardener."

Valerio pursed his lips and nodded as if actually thinking about it. When Josh extended his hand, Valerio took his hands out of his pockets, took Josh's hand, and looked him straight in the eye. Then he leaned forward to kiss Josh's left cheek, then his right.

"Ciao," he said. "Take care of yourself."

"*You* take care," Josh said.

Josh indulged in one last once-over, then walked away, glad he had met him. The encounter was like "a pinch of rosemary rubbed between my fingers," as Valerio had put it, the memory of whose scent he would take to the hotel and enjoy in his room.

Chapter 4: The Gypsy

As Josh drifted back to his hotel, he was having a *paesano* fantasy about Valerio in a dilapidated barn in the wilds of Campania. He had projected the hustler's relaxed swagger into a relaxed fuck on bales of hay. Then troubled voices ahead brought him back to the moment, and he gazed down the curved chasm of the shadowy street – past dark windows, metal shutters of closed shops, and bags of garbage – until a dramatic study in chiaroscuro swung into view: a noisy confrontation between a well-dressed, middle-aged couple and an old, scruffy Gypsy, all arranged, as it struck Josh, in a artistic composition, like a scene out of Caravaggio, everything scumbled in the dark-orange glow of a small, wrought-iron gas light.

There was a high, burnt-Siena, stucco wall around the hotel courtyard. The wide, wrought-iron gate was solid to neck level, but open with bars at the top. On the sidewalk to the right of the gate was a large, terra-cotta pot with a small, gilded lemon tree, to the left, under the gas light, a white ceramic plaque with the name "Pensione/Isola di Capri" in dark-blue lettering. Below the plaque was a battered intercom. To get into the courtyard and hotel, a guest had to be buzzed in, but the Gypsy was standing in the way, obviously badgering the couple for money in some incomprehensible Neapolitan or Romany dialect.

The woman was standing behind the man, and whenever he would move toward the intercom, the Gypsy would block his way, bark at him bitterly as if they had offended him, and gesticulate with both hands, the right extended more, in a gesture somewhere between begging and making a fist. The man also gestured a lot, as if trying to direct what was happening, but when the Gypsy would lunge toward them irritably, the man's hands went up in a gesture somewhere between *stop* and the way someone would hold his hands up in a hold-up.

"I'm sorry," the man reasoned. "I don't speak Italian."

"We don't have cash," the woman explained, absently touching the silver chains glimmering around her neck, "just plastic. No denaro. Plastico, solo plastico." The Gypsy barked at them again, tapping his left palm vehemently with his right index finger as if they owed him something. "Poor thing," the woman sighed, tugging the man's arm. "Wonder if he really needs to be doing this."

Just as they were stepping back in retreat, Josh casually strolled right up to the Gypsy and body-bumped him so unexpectedly that the couple gasped and the Gypsy stumbled backward a couple of steps, lost his balance, and fell awkwardly to a sitting position, braced against the wall. Josh's sudden appearance apparently surprised everyone to such an extent that they remained speechless, frozen in place.

"Get inside," Josh said. He was facing the Gypsy, but speaking to the couple. When no one moved, he glanced over his shoulder and repeated, "Get inside, please."

He faced the Gypsy again, studying him in the dusk light: the sullen, burnt-brown face, the left eye's nervous twitch, the thick, grizzled thatch and moustache. The Gypsy was breathing harder and sweating, and even in the split second of contact with him, Josh had caught a whiff of a rank, vinegary sex smell, the stink of an unwashed crotch.

When the man pressed the intercom button, a staticky male voice asked, "Sì?"

"Signor Tree, per favore."

When the gate buzzed, the man clicked it open, helped the woman inside quickly, and held it for Josh. "Come on," he said. "Come in."

All at once, the Gypsy snapped to, as if waking from a daze, and struggled to his feet, grunting and pushing against the wall. When he flicked a switchblade open, Josh smiled sadly, even compassionately.

"Oh, my," the man said.

The Gypsy stamped his foot and cursed Josh violently, his face mangled with anger, the face of an angry gargoyle. When he leaned in with the knife, Josh tilted back, but when Josh just stared at him, fixing on the small black cherries of his eyes, the Gypsy stepped back, continued raving, and began rocking heavily from side to side as if he might, in fact, lose his balance again and roll over.

In contrast, Josh just slouched there, shoulders slumped, watching the Gypsy rocking and cursing and twitching. He felt strangely detached from the scene, like someone in the audience of an Italian Neo-Realist movie. If any poor slob had the misfortune of really looking like a criminal, he thought, this one did, *un matto*, a tired, distrustful "crazy man" set loose in Naple's vast, urban jungle. The Gypsy's body was squat, stout, and stooped, the rugged hulk of what must have been, Josh imagined, quite a strong young man. He had a big, creased forehead, a forward, bushy uni-brow, and a wide nose with a scar like lightning on the left. His skin looked tough as leather, spiked with a salt and pepper beard. His clothes showed how incredibly poor he was, the frayed coat and shirt, the worn-out knees of his trousers, the scuffed boots.

When Josh reached out to him, the Gypsy swung the knife, and Josh jumped back and gaped, hands high. Though the blade slit his shirt, the swipe, Josh felt, was more defensive than aggressive, and, strangely enough, he almost laughed. Instead, he contained himself and, with a mischievous look, nodded as if to tell the Gypsy that he understood.

28

"Son, young man," the man said, "what are you doing? Come inside, please."

Despite Josh's reckless, impulsive behavior, Josh knew there was no dispute about the physical hierarchy here. He had no doubts that the Gypsy was a mental case, a felon. He, on the other hand, had never had a fight. If the Gypsy wanted to, he could easily kill him. And yet something else occurred to him. He suddenly realized that some mysterious stranger inside himself was not afraid of the Gypsy, was actually enjoying the unaccustomed danger. But why?

He didn't hate the Gypsy. In fact, he felt a strange sympathy for him, for his wretched humanity. He saw through the negative stereotype of Gypsies, like the stereotype of gays, to the individual in front of him at the moment, unfortunately, in this case, one disturbed and agitated. The Gypsy's obvious misery didn't fit the mold. He thought of him as a mad dog, not a cunning scoundrel. The knife wasn't a knife, but a tooth. However, it wouldn't be so easy to run him off. If the Gypsy were a mad dog, mad dogs could bite.

Josh also wondered if he thought so little of himself that he didn't care if he were stabbed. Was he deliberately trying to punish himself? For what? Nothing. He hadn't done anything wrong. And yet he somehow knew that the nothing he felt here went all the way back to what his affair with Owen had come to, nothing. Talk about structural problems in architecture, he thought. He had a few structural problems of his own, namely desperate tendencies.

At the moment, his depression was taking the form of a passive, inevitable inertia he was bogged down in like quicksand. He knew he had to move, to do something, to say something, but all he managed was to turn sideways and place his hands, as if under arrest, on the wall's rough stucco. Only after he did it, did he realize the submissive message it sent, the obeisant posture that gave the Gypsy his dignity back and symbolic, if not actual, control of the situation. He stared at the stains in the sidewalk, even closed his eyes, making himself completely vulnerable. He was tempted to give the Gypsy money, uncertain what would happen at the sight of a wallet. Such an act of grace would conceivably add to the sum of good in the world. On the other hand, rewarding criminality would only reinforce it, possibly leading to some worse, more violent crime somewhere else. He had no facts, no context, in which to judge the Gypsy, but even if he did urgently need money, Josh decided, threatening the couple was simply wrong. Violence was wrong.

He glanced at the Gypsy, then at the man at the gate.

"You OK?" the man asked, staring at him with concern.

When Josh nodded subtly, the man turned to say something to the woman in the courtyard, and Josh glanced up the street at a tangle of electrical wires, like a modern sculpture, spilling out of a wall.

"Amico," he said, standing up straight and facing the Gypsy. Even if the Gypsy did not understand him, he would catch his calm tenor, he felt, just as a dog would. "Voui un pompano?" Josh's Italian was poor, but he thought he had asked the Gypsy if he wanted a blow job.

The Gypsy's face crimped with confusion.

"Fa il maschio," Josh said. "Faccio la femmina." *You be the man. I'll be the woman.*

He winked at him, and when he reached for his crotch, the Gypsy stepped back, stopped, and stared at him, dumbfounded, working his big, rounded jaws. He spit with disgust, and when he sank into the darkness, the man stepped outside, wrapped his arm like a wing around Josh's shoulders, and led him into the courtyard, a stark, sterile, metropolitan space with large plats of a pale marble tile. A square, contemporary fountain was plashing quietly in the middle of a few scattered, concrete benches, the overall effect the opposite of the warm, romantic image of Naples. The woman shut the gate, then embraced Josh, an arm around his back, a hand on the back of his head the way a mother would cradle the head of a newborn.

"My god, you were brave!" she exclaimed, stepping back, holding his arms.

"It'll hit me later," Josh smiled timidly.

"Not sure I'd call it brave," the man said. "What in hell were you doing?"

"Phil," the woman said. "What did you expect him to do? Jump into a karate stance? I'm Billie," she said, extending her hand.

The courtyard was poorly lit, but even in the weak light, Billie's platinum bob glowed like a big, dim light bulb.

"Billie," Josh said, shaking hands. "I'm Josh."

"Josh?" she asked incredulously.

"Yeah," he said. "Josh."

"Well," Billie said wistfully.

Phil looked from her to Josh. "And I'm her heroic husband, Phil."

"Phil," Josh said, shaking hands. "A pleasure."

Josh noticed Phil's dark hair, but white beard and moustache.

"Interesting evening," Phil commented.

"We were warned about Naples," Billie said. "Should've booked one of those posh hotels near Castel dell' Ovo."

Now that they were safe inside the courtyard, Josh got the sense of things safely locked out and things safely locked in and how alien each world was to the other. Phil and Billie now seemed like humble lambs snug in a pen of comfort, he himself a lonely bird perched in the birdcage of the sheltered life he'd been living. He wasn't here to fight with the disenfranchised, but to enjoy

Italians, an emissary from an air-breathing, affluent upper world of drafting tables, laptop computers, and bookshelves. He was ill-equipped to delve below the surface of things for long and, for some reason, wondered who was closer to nature, human nature, the three of them or the poor wretch who had accosted them.

"Excuse me a second," Josh said, turning to the gate.

Billie gaped, hands open in a surprised gesture. Phil slipped his hands into his slacks and sighed.

At the gate, Josh stood on his toes, peering through the bars. He had decided to ignore logic and give the Gypsy money, but when he opened the gate and looked down the street, all he saw were the cars and scooters parked by the trattoria on the corner. He stepped inside and closed the gate, but as he strolled to Phil and Billie, he felt a slight tingle in his chest and looked down to see a dark stain where the shirt was cut as if the shirt itself were bleeding.

"He nipped me," Josh laughed, actually meaning *nipped*, not *nicked*.

"Oh, my god," Billie blurted, touching the shirt. "You're bleeding."

Phil took out a handkerchief. "Press this against it. Let's go up and have a look at it. We have a first-aid kit in the room."

Chapter 5: A Red Thread

Billie, Phil, and Josh stepped into Billie and Phil's sixth-floor room. When Phil flipped a switch, the ceiling fixture lit up, and the ceiling fan began to slowly swirl into a blur. He strolled to the sliding glass doors, took hold of the curtain wand, and drew the curtain, a wavy expanse of sheer, faded, orange and plaid material. Billie moved to a luggage stand, opened a suitcase, and pulled a yellow first-aid kit from a pocket.

Meanwhile, Josh just stood there, pressing the handkerchief against his chest and looking around the room, practically a duplicate of his, a standard three-star space with a couple of double beds with night stands with a phone, small lamps, and remote controls for the television on the opposite wall and the air-conditioner high on the exterior wall. The plaster walls were tinted lime green below a chest-high rail with a paler shade above. To Josh, the effect was like standing in a big cup of green tea. He noticed the large, framed photo of Pompeii with Vesuvius in the background hanging over the night stand between the beds.

"Have a seat on the sofa," Billie said, facing him.

"Let me step in here a minute," he said, meaning the bathroom.

He flipped the light on, lay the stained handkerchief on the sink, and took off his shirt, dropping it into a trash can lined with a plastic bag. Then he looked at the cut in the mirror: a straight slice about an inch long under the curve of his left pectoral. It looked like a thin, red thread stuck in a smear of lipstick. Then a strange notion came to mind, that the cut had occurred from the inside, as if something inside him, fine as a wine glass, had shattered and a shard of glass pierced the skin. With the pressure off, the cut, like a twig, was budding a bright drop of blood, which he touched with the tip of his index finger, touched to his tongue, and tasted, curious about its rich ferric flavor. Then he cleaned up with a wet washcloth, filled the sink with water, and left the washcloth and handkerchief soaking in it.

When he, shirtless, stepped out of the bathroom, Phil was gazing out the open sliding glass door. A breeze was stirring the bunched curtain and valance ruffles. Billie was sitting on the sofa with the first-aid kit open beside her and a deck chair from the balcony in front of her, facing her.

"I can't get that poor wretch out of my mind," Billie said, tearing open a Band-Aid.

"Don't think about him," Phil said. "I know how you are. You'll just wind up feeling guilty about him instead of seeing him for what he was, a chicken thief."

"Chicken thief?" she asked. "Well, he could have my chicken if that's what he wanted. I can get another chicken."

When Josh snickered, they faced him.

"Well," she sighed, "since we survived it, it will make a wonderful story to tell everyone when we get back."

She patted the seat of the deck chair, meaning for Josh to sit.

"The best revenge is enjoying yourself," Phil said. "Right, Josh?"

"Right."

When Josh hunched on the chair, he was face to face, knee inside knees, with Billie. At first, he bristled at the proximity as if an array of emotional spines had pricked up, defending him against her solicitude. Then he tried to relax, staring at the scatter of granite in the bright terrazzo floor.

"Sit up straight, Josh," she said, pushing his shoulders back. "You look like a hemlock flocked with snow."

"I know," he admitted. "I have terrible posture. Comes from sitting on a drafting stool for six years."

"Drafting stool?" Phil asked.

"I was an architecture student," Josh explained. "I mean, I'm an architect. Just passed the exams."

"Congratulations," Phil said.

"Just a scratch," Josh said, facing Billie.

Billie tore open an alcohol swab and a small packet with a square of gauze. Then she focused on the cut. "May this little bee make up for its sting," she said, "with a hive of delicious honey." She swabbed the cut, dried it with the gauze, and, before it could bleed again, covered it with the Band-Aid. "There," she smiled, showing a perfect set of teeth. "All better."

He thought of the small Band-Aid as a kind of flimsy, flesh-pink medal awarded in the gallant, if thoughtless, defense of fellow tourists.

"Tetanus shot?" she asked.

"Think so," Josh said.

She looked like Vivien Leigh about the time of *Streetcar*, he thought, beautiful and elegant. She was much paler than Phil, and because of her fair complexion, platinum hair, and light brows, her black eyeliner and long, black lashes made her sparkling blue eyes stand out. Since the liner extended a little beyond the corner of her eyes, they had a slightly Egyptian look. Her pink lips and rosy cheeks also glowed against her paleness. Up close, though, he could see the first signs of age etched in her face (in her neck, in the corners of her eyes, in her smile), but subtly, the way a calm sea wrinkles at the first hint of a breeze.

"How long does it take a cut to heal?" he asked, more to himself.

"Depends on the cut," she said. "This one's slight. There'll be a little scab, which will probably fall off in a couple of weeks. It won't leave a scar." She stared at him sadly. "How old are you?"

"Twenty-six," he said. "Why?"

She glanced toward Phil, and when Josh turned, he caught Phil, hand raised, giving her a look as if to say, "Don't."

"Nothing," she smiled. "Just curious." After a moment, she asked, "What's your birth date?"

Phil sighed and flumped on a bed.

"September 18," Josh said.

"September 18," she repeated.

"Billie," Phil said, apparently trying to dissuade her from something.

Josh had no idea what was going on between them and, again, felt disconnected from the scene, a specimen in a bell jar. His detachment, in general, was not unusual, but tonight he had a number of reasons for it. He was exhausted with jet lag with strangers in a foreign country just after an altercation with a crazy Gypsy.

"Where are you staying?" Phil asked.

"Next door," Josh said.

"Here?" Billie asked.

"Yeah, right next door, the next room."

"Another coincidence," Billie said, glancing at Phil.

"Coincidence?" Josh asked. "What was the first?"

"Your name," Phil said. "Same as our son's, except that he always liked to be called Joshua."

Josh caught the *liked*, then changed the subject. "We certainly have great views, the port, the bay, Vesuvius."

"We're about as high as our house in California, " Billie said, eyes blank, as if she were lost in thought.

"What do you mean?" Josh asked.

When Billie failed to answer, Phil said, "We have this great place perched on a cliff off Highway 1. The Tree house."

"Tree house?" Josh smiled.

"Old joke," Billie explained, back in the moment. "Our last name's Tree. You may as well tell him the other one," she said to Phil.

"Two Trees, one trunk."

Josh laughed a little puff of a laugh.

"What's your last name, Josh?" Billie asked.

"Evans."

"Well, Josh Evans," she said, "would you like a glass of wine? Wine is a great antidote for an evening like this."

"Actually, alcohol interferes with my ability to sleep, and if there's anything I need right now, it's a good night's sleep."

He was fairly sure he would feel more grounded in the morning.

"You sure?" she asked. "Sitting on the balcony awhile may help us all wind down."

"Nah, thanks," he said, getting up. "Bed sounds pretty good right now. I was too excited to sleep much on the plane."

"Let 'im go, dear," Phil said, standing. "The boy needs rest."

"Well," she said, rising, "we'll see each other at breakfast."

Josh had picked up on her melancholy and, on some level, realized that, as tired as they were, or because of it, she was having trouble letting him go.

"What time do you think you'll put in an appearance?" he asked.

"Around eight," she said, brightening. "We want to get an early start on the day."

"See you at eight."

"Good."

"Pleasure to meet you, Josh," Phil said, shaking hands. "Despite the assault and battery. Just knock on the door. We'll go down together."

"Sleep well," Billie said, hugging him.

He felt her soft, warm body, breathed the subtle pineapple scent of her perfume. The embrace revived him enough emotionally to respond to her and the great comfort of the couple's natural bonhomie.

"Oh, let me give you something," she said, stepping back. She picked up some swabs and Band-Aids and gave them to him. "You can nurse yourself."

"Thanks," he said. "I will."

He moved to the door, but as he was closing it, he smiled and said, "Phil, Billie."

Chapter 6: A Tall, Strong, Ornamental Sapling

Josh went to his room and stripped. When he glanced at the photo of Capri on the wall, the island seemed so romantic – all the bright, blue and white buildings and boats – that he longed for someone with whom he could share it. To him, going to Italy alone was an oxymoron. It made as much sense as going on a honeymoon alone, yet he was calm, not sad. The trip would be a great distraction, allowing him time to heal. And speaking of healing, his calves ached and his inner thighs had chafed a little from his walk around town. He would smooth skin lotion on and get some rest. He was so tired he was sure he could fall asleep quite easily without the Ambien.

He slid under the covers, turned off the table lamp, and dozed off in a few minutes, slipping under the surface of a shallow sleep in which he could still barely hear the late traffic along the port and, at one point, the distant, pulsing siren of an ambulance. In about thirty minutes, though, he drifted over some rocky ledge in his mind, gliding down into the pitch-black waters of a deep sleep, in which he began dreaming that he could feel his legs and arms growing light and tingling with a strange transformation taking place in him. He turned tan, then brown with a thin, lithe bark, and countless small, yellowish-white scales began growing from his skin, overlapping each other. The scales began fledging leaves, like flames lighting, heart-shaped, aromatic leaves the vibrant green of parrot feathers. He could feel the leaves in his hair, like a crown, all of his hair blending into leaves, leaves sprouting from his brows, sideburns, the light coat of hair on his legs, the crease in his pecs, the hollow behind his knees. Branches forked from his shoulders like wings, and his hands, like branches, burst into shiny foliage.

When he noticed his shadow, it was not the shadow of a man, but a fluid, dancing cloud flecked with flashes of gold. Only then did he fully realize what he had become: a tall, strong, ornamental sapling flowing with the long, luxuriant hair of leaves. He gave his branches a shake and spread them like sails to catch a sudden gust, bent back with the ecstatic gasp of the wind through his leaves.

When he woke, he realized that he had, in fact, gasped bent backward, sexually aroused almost to the point of climax.

"Jeez!" he smiled, taking hold of himself. "What was that about?"

As close as he was, he was sure he would come. He jerked himself and rubbed his abs and pecs, touching the Band-Aid, which he had forgotten. He twisted his right nipple into a little pucker, but the longer he jerked himself, the softer he got. He squeezed a glob of Astroglide on himself and, slicked up, tried again, playing with his balls, but again, got only softer. After a few minutes, he gave up, swung his legs over the side of the bed, and went to the bathroom to clean up. Then he opened the curtain and sliding glass door, stepped to the railing, and – the late air slightly cool against his body – looked straight down at the sidewalk far below. He had heard that a person had to jump from at least seven floors to be sure of killing himself, but couldn't imagine anyone surviving a fall from such a brutal height as the sixth. Then he remembered that in Italy the sixth floor was the seventh. The first floor in the United States was called the *pianterreno* (the ground floor) here.

He stepped back from the railing, sat on a chaise longue, and took in the night, absently fondling himself: Vesuvius outlined against a soft, luminous sky, suburbs glittering at its base like a shoal of diamonds, the moon, above to the right, wrapped in a gigantic cocoon of bright, silvery clouds. Occasionally, a car would rasp quietly along the port, and when he felt relaxed, drowsy, and empty-headed enough, he got up and went back to bed.

Chapter 7: Ashe Island

The bump on the horizon swelled to an island, but between here and there, to port, a coal pile of dull, black rocks rose from the water, like a shipwreck waiting to happen, Tyler thought. As they passed, he noticed the small, shiny seal heads bobbing among the bursts of light – beyond, a sea of dazzling diamonds.

As they approached the island, Karen steered to starboard, following the shore, and as they rounded a craggy point, a stone house, high on a cliff, swung into view, crouching like a fox among the firs. Vintage Maine, Tyler thought. He wasn't surprised to see something like it here, a Realist painting come to life.

As they passed the yellow buoy at the mouth of the cove, he saw the island as laid down in layers, each determined by its proximity to the water. First were the dark, wet rocks, green with seaweed, which would flood with the tide. Next were the dark, wet rocks just above the high-water mark, but not out of reach of the sea; above them, the dry, brown rocks, great granite shoulders bearing the weight of the waves, as Tyler thought of them. For some reason, Charles Atlas, the muscle builder, came to mind. The cliff was crowned with a dense tangle of brown to green bushes and weeds splotched with the yellow of goldenrod, and from this marginal vegetation rose the countless spires of what Tyler thought of as Christmas Tree Land, a thick virgin forest of balsam firs. Live trees embraced the dead and half dead with bare trunks lit with sunlight, set off by the deep, dark-green shadows tucked among the boughs, all the trees etched against a vague sky washed out with haze. He could imagine the forest glistening with picturesque ice, the bitter wind blowing off the ocean, the black surf raking the shore with a deafening roar, slamming against the boulders, and bursting into spray. Then it struck him that something was missing. There were no cormorants, gulls, or terns circling overhead.

The pier was a series of big granite blocks laid end to end like dominoes and framed in thick, blanched pilings with a weathered bench, dirty-gray fenders, and a wooden ladder disappearing into the water. Karen killed the motor, and as they floated in smoothly next to the ladder, everything went warm and quiet. Tyler stuck his hand in the water, which felt unusually warm for Maine, in the upper sixties, lower seventies, he figured, and when the bow thumped a fender, he took hold of the pier, swung his legs over his seat, and reached a rope to wrap around a bollard. Alice moored the boat at the stern, but when Karen stood and shook her hand as if sore from the helm, she wobbled, losing her balance, but grabbed the ladder and righted herself.

Then everyone started placing things on the pier, paper grocery bags, plastic water jugs, tote bags, a cooler, everyone squinting in the glare. Tyler settled his bag carefully on the pier, tossed his jacket up, and lay the limp peonies on top of it. Then he picked up the cat crate, perched it on the edge, and, without disturbing the boat, lifted himself to a sitting position.

"Let Peeve out," Karen said, and when Tyler opened the crate, Peeve yowled, braced against the back of it, then shot out of it, bounding briskly down the pier and up the path through the firs.

Linda was not paying attention, and as the boat shifted, she missed the ladder, stepped into the water, and hit her left arm on a rung.

"You OK?" Tyler asked, leaning toward her.

"I've got it," she said, climbing up.

The women picked up everything but the totes.

"I'll bring the rest," he said, setting his stuff on the bench.

He watched the women trudge up the path, then glanced at the submerged rocks, like big black hearts, off the other side of the pier. The shore was a landslide sinking into dirt-brown sand studded with big, bean-like pebbles. The cove was a mirror image of the sky, and beyond it, past the flat, blank sea, he could just make out, as if making out the future, the thin gray line of Bailey Island, but not the inn.

He slung his bag strap over his shoulder, wedging his jacket and the peonies under his arm, then picked up the totes and started up the hill. The faint path twisted through the trees, and when his arm would brush a branch, swarms of shiny needles would bite his skin pleasantly like black flies, only spellbound flies whose bite didn't sting. At times, the path disappeared over stone, where roots, like veins, ran across the surface as if he were walking not on an island, but something living. Here, he would have to guess where the path took up again, and about halfway up the bluff, he stopped to catch his breath in the relatively cool, aromatic shade of a particularly tall, dense stand. He wanted to brace on a tree, but was afraid to stick his hand into the thick, blue-black needles, someplace he couldn't see. Looking up, he couldn't see the crowns for the boughs, either, and the silence was as marked as a whisper. He looked around to see what he sensed – isolation, unfamiliar terrain – but, feeling foolish, moved on.

He came out of the woods, passed through an opening in a stunted hedge of wild roses, and stepped into a yard of sorts, a rough stone shelf with patches of dirt and weeds. To his right sat four weathered Adirondack chairs. Like ghosts facing the cove, he thought. To his left stood the tall skeleton of a fir with a hatchet wedged in it. The bottom limbs were missing, apparently hacked off up to about six feet. Above that, the thick trunk thinned to a point with limbs shortening from sharp spikes to a splay of sticks and twigs at the top, all the white gray of storm clouds. It looked like the frame for an artificial Christmas tree, reminded him of a Medieval spiked mace.

Straight ahead, the weather-beaten house, nestled in firs, was one step up from a ruin: abandoned, humble, desolate, especially as he imagined it in winter, the house of an outcast deity like Loki in Norse mythology or Eris in the Greek. The wooden roof shingles were bleached and cracked, the brick chimney out of plumb, the walls splotched with crooked patches where plaster was missing and with nebulous stains ranging from the dark gray of mussel shells to the woolly black of mold. The walls had broken up from freezing and thawing over the years, cracking into big puzzle pieces along the lines where the mortar had crumbled between the underlying stones. And he didn't see how the simple windows could possibly keep the cold out any more than the damaged roof could keep out rain and snow.

There were ominous, if incongruous, bull horns over the open door, and when he stepped inside, he had to duck to clear the lintel. He put the totes down, then just stood there, waiting for his eyes to adjust and smelling not exactly a stink, but the strangely aromatic blend of various herbs and weeds. Karen was moving from window to window, pushing aside scraps of curtain to let light in, and when his eyes finally focused, he found himself standing in a dim, cave-like interior gleaming with hundreds of ceramic, clear-glass, and amber-colored bottles, canning jars, and vials and draped with dozens of batches of flowers, herbs, and weeds hanging upside down from the beams in the ceiling. The downstairs was practically one big room with a wide archway into the kitchen to his left, and his first impression of the place was that it was a cross between an incredibly cluttered stockroom and a shadowy witch's den. Because of the plants, he guessed, it had the wild quality of a lair, the kind in which either a wolf or a wizard could live. Spells could be cast here, he thought, alchemy performed. And since, before Karen, no one had lived there for years, it also had, despite the clutter, an empty, colorless feel about it. He could imagine how bleak it was in winter.

To his left was a door with bookcases of jars to either side, and when he heard one of the girls moving behind it, he assumed it was a bathroom. Then he noticed the old, yellow front door to his immediate left. "Come in" was scrawled in faint, blue script across the top, the panels decorated with various vague animals: wolves, mountain lions, dolphins, pigs.

In front of him stretched a rustic table with crossed, x-shaped legs and six old schoolhouse chairs recently painted battleship gray, two to either side and one on each end. On the table were dozens of pewter candle holders of various sizes, some with diseased-looking bayberry candles, a rubble of candle ends, coils of rope, a pair of shears, garden snips, scissors, piles of rubber bands, stacks of labels and tags with date and location lines. Over the table hung a rusty, four-pronged, wrought-iron chandelier dripping with the little, red stalactites of bayberry candles. The fixture looked Gothic to Tyler because the hub was basically two black cones end to end. The cones reminded him of church steeples and pointed hats.

Two extra chairs from the table, both loaded with jars, were backed against either side of the arch into the kitchen, and above them hung sooty kerosene lanterns, which, he figured, would provide some lurid light at night. Through the arch he could see a big, black woodstove angled in a corner and crowded with big, black, cast-iron pots and pans.

To his right, as he looked around the room, he saw a pair of frail-looking rocking chairs to either side of a tea table with a pile of dirty roots. He pictured a pair of old women sitting there, gazing out the window. On the floor nearby were stacks of book-like plant presses bound with leather straps and, near them, three drying racks hung with bundles of herbs and flowers. Across from all this was a couple of long benches laden with jars with a basket of dried herbs between the benches and one on each end like bookends. The walls were a couple of feet thick, the windows inset with deep sills, the ones over the benches thick with colorful bottles of what he figured were intense tinctures or dyes: gory, translucent reds, lurid purples and lavenders, transparent flowers floating in pale green. The multicolored bottles looked as if Karen had bottled a rainbow. There was a corner cupboard, and bookcases lined the walls, all with shelves labeled *Syrups*, *Salves*, *Liniments*, as well as *Infusions*, *Decoctions*, and *Tinctures* subdivided into plants, roots, and barks, shelves jam-packed with labeled glass containers between the door and windows, between windows, every space available, just as there were baskets, kettles, and buckets of dried herbs and weeds in almost every space available on the floor.

When Karen had finished opening the curtains in the great room, she moved to the kitchen, and he strolled to the left of the table and stood there, watching her. She opened the little curtain over the sink and started taking groceries out of bags. There was a big double sink in an old, stainless-steel counter that looked like something out of an operating room.

The cooler was sitting in one side of the sink, the plastic jugs in the other, and when he noticed the arched faucet, he asked, "Where do you get water?"

"A cistern in the boulders above the house."

"You drink it?"

"No," she said, putting bottles and cans in an open pantry to the left: cider vinegar, olive oil, honey, cayenne pepper. "The tank's corroded, but it's good for dishes and cleaning."

A small stick wreath with paper goldfinches hung from the window latch, and the sill was choked with canning jars of nuts, seeds, and bones. Beyond the window: a jade gloom of balsam limbs. He tuned out mentally for a moment, lost in the jumble on the counter: a big knife stuck upright in a cutting board, a mortar and pestle, a glass measuring cup, a postal scale, a vegetable brush, a tea ball. Then he came to, feeling the strain of his shoulder strap.

"Where do you want the totes?" he asked, taking the peonies from under his arm.

"I'll take care of them," she said, folding a paper bag.

"Something I can put these in?" he asked. The flowers were floppy as rags, gorgeous purple rags that smelled like a funeral.

She took a ceramic rooster pitcher from the pantry and ran a little water in it. When she started to hand it to him, he asked, "Where should I put this?" meaning his bag.

"You'll be sleeping there," she said, nodding toward the daybed in a niche near the table.

A frame with cheesecloth stretched over it was leaning against the bed, so he picked it up and was going to stow it in one of what he thought were closets to either side of the niche. He opened the door to the left, halfway expecting, in a place this morbid, to find a skeleton on its knees. What he found was, in fact, a closet, but an herb closet, yet another pantry crammed full of jars. So he leaned the frame against the chair by the arch, stowed his bag and jacket on the bed, and took the pitcher from her, slipping the flowers into it. The awkward rooster was painted red with a green comb and wattle and dotted all over with bumblebees as if, at least from his point of view, the bees were stinging it. It looked like a therapy project from a mental institution, but he didn't say anything because he was fairly sure that one of them had made it.

He made a space for it under the chandelier, then turned toward the niche, apparently a large converted fireplace in the wall across from the front door. The mantel, eye-level, had a stopped antique clock in the middle, an ominous stuffed crow on one end, and a big, washed-out duck decoy on the other. The rest of the shelf was lined with jars labeled with names like amanita, belladonna, catnip, deadly nightshade, green hellebore, hemlock, hops, Saint-John's-wort, tansy oil, verbena, wild lettuce. The bed was backed by a bank of firm, oversized pillows, but covered by a tattered patchwork quilt in faded purples, violets, and blues similar to the color of the peonies, a trellis of clematis, as he thought of it.

"The linens are fresh," she said. "Eddie's grandmother made the quilt."

"The quilt looks a little musty."

Above the pillows, the plaster was discolored with brown and orange stains in which he could almost make out, as in a Rorschach test, the faint design of what he thought must have been a mural. At first, all he saw was clouds. Then he "made out" a winter branch in a russet streak across the wall. He stared at it, decided his eyes were playing tricks on him, and flumped on the bed, knees spread.

43

"Firm bed," he said, bouncing on it.

"If there's one thing we have here," she said, "it's firm beds."

"Great! I'll sleep well."

"Linda's mother-in-law, Helen, bought them."

When he looked down the cluttered table, his line of sight went straight out the front door, and since he knew the door faced west, he wondered, if he followed the line, if he would wind up at the inn. He was sure he'd be able to see its lights at night. Then he noticed what he figured was a walking stick, like a shepherd's staff, standing to the left of the door. When he heard someone moving around upstairs, he glanced at the plants, like Spanish moss, dangling from the ceiling.

"What's upstairs?" he asked.

"Two bedrooms," she said, opening the cooler.

She set some condiments aside, took out a bag of ice, and removed a wire twist from its neck. There was an old wooden icebox the size of a safe under the counter, and she opened it and stood the bag in a top compartment.

"Never seen one of those," he said.

"Neither had I."

As if on cue, the girls appeared. Alice stepped from the bathroom, wearing pink flip-flops and a one-piece light-blue bathing suit speckled with what looked like black and lavender pansies. She was carrying a large, yellow beach towel with a white picture frame printed around the edge, but he couldn't see if there were a picture on it. At the same time, he could hear Linda flouncing down the rickety staircase that dropped to a landing in a corner and hooked into the room. She was wearing blue flip-flops and a skimpy, orange two-piece and carrying a matching beach bag and a frayed brown beach towel with a big, orange seahorse in the middle. When she stepped off the stairs, she just stood there, feet touching, in an S Curve. Alice was slim, but he was impressed with how buxom and nubile Linda was. His "little girl" had bloomed into a married woman.

When he blurted, "Wow!" Karen shot him a sharp glance. "That what I should be doing? Changing into trunks?"

"Why don't you gather driftwood for the stove?" Karen asked, sliding the cooler under the counter with her foot. "I have wood at the side of the house, but can always use more."

Alice was holding her neckline the way she often did. "You have sunscreen?" she asked Linda. When Linda nodded, Alice said, "Come on."

As the girls left, Karen picked up an army-green, canvas log carrier beside the stove.

"What if I cut down that dead tree in the yard?" he asked, getting up.

"I don't think we should be cutting down trees on someone else's property."

"It's dead," he said, taking the carrier. "It could fall on the house. You'd be doing them a favor." When she did not respond, he said, "Well, if you're not going to cut it down, string a hammock from it. It's a great place for a hammock."

As he plodded down the path, he saw some pale brushwood and balsam cones which he thought would make good tinder, but Karen had distinctly said driftwood, so he would save those as backup in case he did not find much along the shore. When he came out of the trees, he expected to find the girls sunbathing on the pier, but they were nowhere to be seen, and he wondered where they had disappeared to. The boulders to the north looked impassable, so he set out over the shingle to the south, climbed the promontory that formed an arm of the cove, and, standing on a boulder, took in the view, the aesthetic solace of nature, as he thought of it: rocks draped with slimy seaweed, trails of suds meandering into the ocean, clouds like wisps of smoke. When he had caught his breath, he climbed down the other side of the promontory, where a stretch of brown sand rose to a grassy dune, behind which lay a large, primal bog. The bog drained to a small, black pool backed with horsetails and, behind them, a wall of shady boughs. In the perfectly still scene, something twitched, catching his eye, and he carefully crept into the bog and squatted to examine a small fly stuck on a pink dewdrop on the tip of a tiny red hair of a strange, prehistoric-looking plant. The plant's stems burst into hairs like fireworks, and the fly had caught on one, from time to time fluttering to free himself. Tyler glanced across the bog into the dark woods and felt the hush. Except for a few gnats, the doomed fly, ironically, was the only sign of life he had seen: no animals, no gulls. Then he remembered the seals.

When Tyler entered the yard, humming "Con te partiro," he saw the almost invisible scarf of smoke suspended over the chimney. The carrier was full of driftwood and brushwood, and he dumped it onto the pile of firewood by the house. When he entered the great room, Karen, despite the heat, was standing by a kettle steaming on the stove. He could barely hear the water bubbling.

"No music?" he asked, tired, but exhilarated from the hike. When she ignored him, he dropped the carrier beside the stove, went over to his bag, and began taking out the bottles of wine and standing them on the table. "Where are the girls?" he asked, sitting at the head of the table.

"Upstairs," she said, lowering a tea ball into a crackled ceramic mug, then draping the chain over the rim. "Resting."

45

"Have a corkscrew?" he asked, gazing out the door.

"We don't drink wine," she said, using a dishcloth to pick up the kettle.

"Linda said she didn't like it," he mused. "Surely you have a corkscrew around here. Been a long day, the plane, the drive, the boat, this bitch of a sun." When he thought of what he'd said, he chuckled. "I'd like to relax. "

"We don't have one," she said, pouring boiling water into the mug, "nor anything else to do with wine."

"Well, you *do* have a carafe," he said, reaching a big one from the mess on the table. He stood it to his left and studied the dozens of dried, dark-red clover heads inside, what he thought of as red cotton balls in a medical jar.

"Here before us," Karen explained, putting the kettle on the stove. "Look. I was making this for me, a sedative. Instead of the wine, why don't you have it? OK?"

"Sedative?" he asked. "Like valerian?"

"Right."

"Sure," he said, leaning back in the chair, knees spread, hands behind his head. "I'd like to find out more about your herbs." He smiled at her affectionately. "A sedative should be interesting."

"Good," she said, resting the mug on the table. "I'll make myself another."

"Thanks."

The tea looked as if a deep-red dye had been diluted in water. She placed a jar of honey and a spoon near him and removed the tea ball, and when he sipped the tea, it tasted like hot beer with licorice in it. When he asked for an ice cube, she reached one from the bag of ice, and he stirred it till it dissolved. She produced a plate of cheddar cheese, Ritz crackers, and a bunch of green grapes from the icebox, then prepared herself a cup of tea and sat down with him. At first, there was an awkward silence.

"Good to see you and the girls doing so well," he said, pulling a grape off a stem.

"Yes," she began, "despite everything, we *are* doing well. I've been pretty successful in a number of ways."

"Good, good." He wondered what she meant by "despite everything."

"I've raised two wonderful girls alone."

"You have," he conceded, popping the grape into his mouth.

On Linda's official wedding tape, there was, to him, a hilarious moment when an older woman he didn't know told him, "You sure did raise a couple of beautiful girls," and Karen chimed in, "Let's get one thing straight. *I* raised them. He called occasionally."

Then Linda said, "Now, Mother."

As far as Tyler was concerned, the moment, comical as it was, should have been edited out.

"The girls are smart," he said, "and, more important, kind, easy to love."

The grape tasted funny, a little sour, and he wondered if its slight "turned" quality were because of the tea. He wanted to spit it out, but swallowed it.

"Yes, I raised them alone," she said, "with no help from you."

"Well," he smiled, "you know that's not true."

Actually, he had sort of laughed, exhaling a sudden puff of breath.

"Is it?" she asked.

He had never missed a child-support check, even long after he was legally required to do so, and he had all the canceled checks to prove it. When the girls had moved out on their own, he sent the checks directly to them. Surely, she knew that.

"You must mean emotional help," he said, unscrewing the cap on the jar of honey.

"And I've come a long way toward healing myself," she said, arms folded across her chest.

If she meant from the divorce, he thought, then good. It was time.

"And I've helped others heal," she added, "friends, colleagues, clients."

He spooned a teaspoon of honey into his tea, and when he stirred it, the spoon rasped against the bottom of the cup audibly in the quiet.

"As an herbalist," he said, more of a question. When the honey was dissolved, he laid the spoon on the table, screwed the cap on the jar, and sat back, hands on the edge of the table, palms up as if at a séance. "There's nothing like succeeding professionally," he sighed. "God knows it took me long enough." He had tried to write artistically and was finally reaping financial benefits from it. "Brew anything for Linda's asthma?"

"Comfrey, mullein, coltsfoot, a drop of lobelia," she said trance-like, staring at his hand like a fortuneteller. "Chewing a little lobelia helps an attack, and I use it in a seizure formula."

"Has she had one lately?"

"What?"

"Seizure."

"Strangely enough," she said, rubbing her upper arms, "she had one during her last consultation."

"With the doctor?"

"Yes."

"Stress about the surgeries."

47

"Living without the threat of seizures – " she said with a shudder, "she'll be a different person."

"You cold?" he asked, puzzled. He couldn't tell if the shudder were real or a gesture for emphasis.

"I'm OK."

She got up with her cup, went into the kitchen, and set it on the counter. Then she cleared a space and started cutting up vegetables on a cutting board with a big cook knife.

"Where's Peeve?" he asked, idly scratching the hair on his sternum.

"She'll come in when she's hungry." She paused, knife poised, then said, "I've often thought of writing you, thought it would help your relationship with the girls."

"You should've," he said, running his hand over the bristly hair on his head. "I've pretty much botched things up." When he felt something in it, he picked it out, a fir needle, and lay it on the table.

"I knew how important a daughter's relationship with her father is."

"Of course," he agreed, his finger through the handle on the mug. "I've heard that men marry women who remind them of their mothers, but not too much, and women marry men who remind them of their fathers, but not too much, and if girls can't work out problems with their fathers, they'll act them out with other men. The father's just the prototype for all the other men in their life."

"Not that you were a real father," Karen said almost under her breath.

Eddie, he knew, was the perfect husband for Linda, but all he knew of Gino, Alice's security guard, was that he was sexy: dusky, well-built, but too pensive for his young years as if worried about something, perhaps losing someone as beautiful and capricious as Alice. He had wanted to be a cop like his father, but couldn't because of a high-school football knee injury.

"I wanted to catch you up on what they had been through," she said, "who they were now, and, since Alice was younger, how she had suffered in particular. As I said, to help your relationship. Not sure relationship is the word," she said, the blade hovering over a carrot. "More like indifference. Really. Wouldn't you agree? Seeing them as little as you have?"

"I'm here, right?" he asked, his face smooth with patience. "You asked me to come, and I did."

If he had been indifferent, he would not have seen them at all, but he had scores of correspondence with Linda about planning visits or commenting on them afterward (hers to Atlanta, his to wherever they were living, Indiana, D.C., New York). On the earliest visit he could remember, he took the girls to a service at Ebenezer Baptist Church. On the next, he drove them to Jekyll Island, where they saw the Atlantic Ocean for the first time. It was a cold day, and the girls had colds, but they ran into the cold water and played, jumping, splashing, and laughing. The moment was one of the few he could remember when Alice was happy. After the visit, he had written them, "We must all go someplace big and open again."

But as they grew older, conflicts during visits became more heated, ending in an embarrassing catastrophe at an opera one night. Louise, a friend of Alice, had flown down with them, and during the performance, Alice and Louise had talked incessantly (mainly about how much they were suffering from it) and managed to ruin the evening not only for him and Linda, but also for everyone sitting around them. Linda left during the first intermission, and after that, she and Alice decided they would make separate visits from then on.

Tyler and Linda had a good time at the zoo on her next trip, and they had even planned on her moving to Atlanta. As she wrote in a letter, "Next year, I'd like to move down, get a job, and go to graduate school there. It would be great to live in the same city with you for a change, to get together whenever we felt like it, to just drive across town. We've always been so far apart." And he believed that too. If they had only lived in the same town or somewhere much closer, he reasoned, he would've seen them on a regular basis. Had he let geography and a couple of plane fares defeat him? "And you didn't seem violently opposed to my living with you, either," she went on. "You actually looked thrilled."

But she met Eddie, her husband-to-be, and stayed in Maine, and after that, there did not seem to be anything Tyler could do to get the two, inseparable as they were, to visit Villa Toscana, as he liked to call his house in Atlanta, even though he offered to pay their airfare and even though they actually took a train to visit friends in North Carolina one summer and were fairly close by.

There were the excursions around Casco Bay with Linda, but he figured his trip up for her wedding would be the final time that he, Karen, and the girls would be together. He was part of the reception line and had prepared a few notes for a toast, but had never been asked to give one, let alone give away the bride. As Linda had put it, she wasn't a cow to be given away. All in all, though, he still considered her wedding day the best day of his life.

Before Linda and Eddie had moved into the house they built, he had stayed at the Jetsam Inn and offered to arrange dinner there for all of them, but Karen and Alice declined. On his next trip, he stayed with Linda and Eddie in the new house, where they showed him the nursery and a crib for the child they were planning to adopt. When Linda wrote him about Eddie's kidney problems, he offered to fly up, but when Eddie's prognosis improved, he didn't. Then out of the blue came the news about her surgery, and here they all were.

His attempts to see Alice had not fared as well. To begin with, she had always been mad at him for the divorce, which she never accepted. She still wanted them to be The Ideal Family. She wanted things to go back to the way they were, which, of course, they couldn't, and to send the girls financial support, he had to go where the jobs were. Karen, understandably, was never inclined to pull up roots and follow him anywhere.

When he was around the girls, a fierce protective instinct kicked in, but Alice thought of it as trying to control her. In other words, she wouldn't let him be a parent whenever he did get a chance to be one. So, after a while, he quit trying. Ironically, she had finally achieved what she had always complained about: not having a father. She had very effectively driven him away, a fact which she herself was well aware of.

In a letter, she wrote, "I've always had this wonderful fantasy of having this big, sweet, protecting dad who really loved me and wanted to take care of me, but you weren't there enough to be that, and when you were, I didn't let you, and you were afraid to try, so it's no one's fault."

Finally, visits (in either direction) had come to an end. In another letter, she wrote, "In regard to your coming up, I won't have any vacation days, so I wouldn't be able to spend much time with you. Maybe next summer." The letter was his last written communication from her, and he could certainly read between the lines: there would be no next time. He offered to pay her airfare to visit him a few more times, but she never took him up on it, and after a while, he gave up.

"I was always very careful," Karen said, "not to say anything negative about you."

Well, he knew that wasn't true. For example, a certain mythic inheritance from his mother, their grandmother, that he had allegedly stolen from them.

"I didn't say anything because I wanted them to get to know you, but then," she said, holding the knife straight out from her thigh, "it finally occurred to me: they don't need to know you. They don't need to know you any more than you apparently needed to know them, your own flesh and blood, for all these years."

"We can make up for lost time," he claimed, lifting the tea. "We're not dead. Thought *that* was what this trip's about, connecting."

"They can get along fine without you, always have, even when we were poverty-stricken."

Ah, he groaned. The financial issue.

For most of his life, he had lived from month to month with no savings and an accumulating charge-card debt. Once in a note with a birthday check for Alice, he wrote, "Perhaps the check will subsidize a nice dinner out for the two of you," meaning her and her boyfriend. "But," he added, "don't cash it till June 1, please." There wasn't enough money in his checking account to cover it until then.

Linda's correspondence with him over the years was riddled with references to and thank-you notes for the monthly child-support checks, as well as for birthday and holiday checks, Crate and Barrel certificates, and gifts such as wine glasses, an Ikea light, items from a bath store, Valentine's cards and chocolates, real and virtual flowers, and packages of books and manuscripts in which he thought she might be interested. He had paid for her, as far as he could tell, to do absolutely nothing but enjoy herself in Santa Fe for a year, quite a vacation. He also had helped her buy cars and car insurance, furniture and a stereo system for her first apartment, eye glasses and contact lenses, and textbooks for college. He had put her on his health insurance when he had it, given her spending money for a trip to England with Eddie (her fiancé at the time), and paid for a substantial part of the catering at their wedding. But one year, he noticed that she hadn't cashed a check he sent her for her birthday. When he reminded her to deposit it, she wrote that she had decided not to cash it. When he asked, "Why not?" she did not respond.

After a trip to visit her, when she had mentioned the alleged inheritance from her grandmother, he said, as he put it, "The only thing she could have left you was nothing because that was all she had a lot of." He sent her a Xerox of the $7,000 inheritance check, a check he had used to buy his first piece of property, a 600-square-foot, one-bedroom condo. He also explained that, under the Napoleonic Code, by which Louisiana was still largely governed at the time, there was no way his mother could have willed the girls anything. Half of his mother's "estate" went to his brother, half to him. If his mother had wanted to give the girls anything, she would have had to do it before she died. Besides, after his father died when Tyler was fifteen, his mother raised him on social security. Where did Karen get the notion that Jewel, his mother, had money?

In regard to Alice, he remembered helping her out with car insurance, car repairs, summer dresses, and a silk outfit to wear at a store opening. He had even paid for one of her two abortions. He had given her $500 as incentive to get her GED. He had also given her a coffee machine, a potted gardenia, and checks and gift certificates at Christmas or on her birthday. He knew the gifts weren't much, but had hoped she'd appreciate, as they say, the thought behind them. He had kept all of her correspondence, among which, he knew, were several thank-you notes referring to "the check," "the dough," or "the gift."

There were times, though, when he, in fact, did not have the money they asked for, but he hoped they would understand that if he didn't have it, he didn't have it. As he wrote Alice, "Don't take the fact that I don't have the money to mean anything other than the fact that I just don't have the money. When I have it, I'm really a very generous person."

One of the reasons Alice was financially destitute for a long time was that she had dropped out of high school. Only after a series of short-lived, dead-end jobs did she come to realize, as she put it, "the literal value of an education." After that, she got her GED, tried cosmetology and paralegal school, and began taking a few college courses. Eventually, she got a good job with a reputable phone company. In other words, her financial struggles had a happy ending, but the fact that the girls had to ask, even plead with him, for money at times had shamed him profoundly, especially when he didn't have it.

"Do we need to do this?" he asked, elbows on the table, the warm mug clasped in his hands. His enthusiasm for everything was going out like a fire from lack of air.

"Do what?" Karen asked, slicing a head of broccoli.

"Dredging up all these toxic issues," he said, savoring the tea's soothing licorice smell. "What will it accomplish? If it's your idea of therapy, I guess I understand, but I don't need therapy. I just want to enjoy my time with you and the girls." The tea was warm now, not hot, so he took a big gulp. The sooner its sedative effect kicked in, he thought, the better. "I can't really see how it's even good for you. Such obstinate anger can't be good. Does it make you feel better? Or worse? This isn't therapy," he concluded, trying to be logical and tolerant. "This is what you need therapy for."

She closed her eyes.

Then he added, "It won't change the past."

"I can tell you what has been good therapy for me," she said, scraping the carrots and broccoli into a bowl with the knife, "the girls. The girls are a gift. Their love is a gift. Because of them, I had to heal myself and heal myself reflected in them."

He thought of a Mencken quote, "Soothe us in our agonies with emollient words," and wished he could help her, but was at a loss.

"And since I did," she said, stabbing the cutting board. When she let go of the knife, it was standing upright again. "And since I did," she repeated, "I realized I needed to write you or, better, see you for another reason. Ouch!" she grimaced. "Bit my tongue. Mmm."

He took another gulp of tea, then asked, "Which is?" He had to see where this was going.

"We need to admit the fact that you've hurt us horribly, me and the girls, those you said you dearly loved."

When she said the word *horribly*, the lightning flash of emotion literally shocked him. She was much worse off than he ever dreamed. He had experienced a similar shock when he had called Brent, a college lover, to ask if he could use a photo Brent had taken of him on a book jacket. Brent's intense anger sounded as if they had broken up a few days ago, not years. Tyler thanked him and hung up.

"We'll never heal if we don't," Karen claimed. "Not talking about it is a denial that it ever happened. You need to face it, too, for your own sake. You'll never wash the dirt off your hands if you don't."

"You know – " he began. His mind had slowed to a snail's pace, and he realized he was losing his ability to focus mentally, to deal with her, to want to deal with her. "You know," he coughed, plunking down the mug, "you're not the only one wounded by a divorce. Nobody comes out of a divorce unscathed. How are you hurt in some way different from how everyone else is hurt?" Her anger was infectious, but he had become immune to it through exposure. If he wasn't capable of loving them, he reasoned, he wouldn't know it. He wouldn't know what he was missing. But he did, in fact, love them. He could remember the tenderness he had felt for them and others and how sweet it was. He felt the same way now. And who was she to tell him otherwise? "As I said," he repeated somberly, "I don't need therapy. My hands are clean."

"Dirty," she insisted, arms folded across her chest. She looked as if she were trying to contain herself, but couldn't. "Dirty as those dirty things you did to me, a young, innocent girl. And they've affected my self-worth and every failure of a relationship I've had with men since, men I could never trust for fear of violence."

"What?"

"I didn't know anything about sex, didn't know what it was, what part I should play, how I should be treated."

"What are you talking about?"

"Abuse!"

"Abuse?" he laughed. "If fucking's abuse, yeah. I abused you four times on the honeymoon."

What in the world was she talking about? he asked himself. Had she transposed some sexual violence from some other man onto him?

"How did I abuse you?"

"Oh, you know how," she claimed, briefly closing her eyes.

"No, I don't. Tell me."

"I don't have to tell you. You know what I'm talking about."

"Are you saying I physically injured you?"

"Of course, you did."

"You know," he sighed, "I wish my whole life were on videotape so I could rewind it and show people exactly what they did and said as opposed to what they think they did or lie about. I wish I could force you to show me exactly what you're talking about."

"No matter how you may remember it or rationalize it, Tyler, the way you treated me was nothing short of rank abuse on every level, physical, emotional, and mental. You even tried to break my soul."

He caught himself starting to fold his arms across his chest as she had.

"Let me get this straight," he said, placing his hands on the table. "The rules are: What I remember is wrong. What you remember is right. That it?"

Preposterous. He was so sensitive about the issue of physical abuse that he even worried about the line between it and discipline when Sydney, an Australian Terrier he loved, kept tearing the insulation from under his sun porch.

"She's so small," he wrote Linda, "and I'm so big."

And if Karen wanted to know about real sexual abuse, she needed to read his friend Sue Silverman's book *Because I Remember Terror, Father, I Remember You.*

The first option, as he saw it, was that Karen was deliberately lying to sway the girls against him. Another theory was that she was in love with the idea of being victimized, playing the role for all it was worth, wallowing in it, like a sow, so much, in fact, she had actually come to believe it, and if she did believe it, then she had lost her mind.

"I don't think you realize it," he said, "but you're equating sex with abuse. That what it was for you? A violation? Rape? No wonder I couldn't get you off." Karen was seeing a shrink when he met her. In fact, the shrink, according to Karen, had advised her to have a fling for whatever reason, probably, he guessed, to overcome her Catholic upbringing. "We had perfectly normal vanilla sex, at first fun, later routine, finally frustrating. The only thing abusive about it was how frustrating it was toward the end." If she weren't frigid, he said to himself, he wouldn't be sitting there. "How many nights did I go in the bathroom and jerk myself off because you weren't in the mood?"

Suddenly, he realized the girls were standing on the staircase landing.

"Oh, my god," he whispered to himself. Then he said aloud, "Sorry, girls. More tired than I thought. Your mom and I were just having a...."

He trailed off, staring, hypnotized, at the panels of light stretching slowly from the door and windows across the floor. Then he shook his head to clear it and smiled at them. They were wearing the same clothes they had worn on the boat, Linda's hair wet and curly, Alice's pinned in a twist on her head.

"You look beautiful," he said drowsily.

And they did, lit up in their skin's pink glow. Alice was just standing there, surprisingly apathetic, especially if she had overheard much of the conversation. There was definitely something missing from her nonchalant expression. He wondered what could be going on in her mind. Linda, however, was smiling smugly as if some awful opinion of him had been confirmed.

When she absently rubbed her arm, Karen said, "Come here. Let me see."

The girls stepped into the room, and Karen took a bottle from a shelf marked *Liniment*, grabbed a dishcloth from the counter, and opened the bottle to wet a corner of the cloth. Alice sat to Tyler's left at the table. Linda went around it to sit to Tyler's right. Karen stood the bottle on the table, lifted Linda's arm, and massaged her arm gently.

After a moment, she smiled and asked, "Feel better?"

Linda nodded, and Tyler noticed that the place where she had hurt her arm was squarely on top of her burn scar.

"Sore?" he asked.

"Yes," she replied, glancing at him. "Read mom's book?" she asked. She was referring to *World Wisdom*, a cross between a meditative diary and a primer on Maine herbs.

"Yes, I have," he said, blinking, "and each time she mentioned you, it was like seeing you walk into the room unexpectedly. You were young and happy, a bright sun breaking through clouds."

"How poetic," Karen said. "You still don't get that words are worthless, no matter how pretty."

"Karen, please."

At this point, he was bovine dull, slipping slowly into a lethargic slump, but he forced himself to sit up.

"Seen *Crystal Ball*?" he asked, glancing at Linda, then Alice.

Alice looked preoccupied, but the way her eyes kept darting back and forth indicated she was aware he was staring at her.

"Seen *Crystal Ball*?" he asked Linda again.

"No, we haven't," she squinted. When the script had been optioned, he sent her a copy out of pride and because of her interest in writing, but she never commented on it. "We don't like horror movies." Then she faced him and smiled sadly, "Dad."

"Yeah?"

"Please don't send me anything as disgusting as that ever again, OK?"

That stung, he thought. He had been stung before, pulled the stinger out, and kept going. This time, though, it was like hearing the first gunshot in hunting season: he was just beginning to pick up on the fact that Linda's venom was affecting him emotionally. All of his gut defenses were failing him. Suddenly, he felt vulnerable.

"I want to go back," he said, struggling to keep his eyes open.

"I'd like to go back, too," Karen remarked. "There're a few things I'd change."

"No," Tyler said, rubbing his eyes with his fingertips. "I want to go back to the mainland."

"In the morning," she said.

"Should have brought Stolis," he laughed to himself, "not wine." He meant Stolichnaya vodka.

Chapter 8: La Prima Colazione

The breakfast room at the Isola di Capri was Spartan with white ceramic floors, contemporary tables and chairs, and a narrow sideboard stretching along a big, blank wall. The room's one redeeming grace was the bright sunlight pouring through the huge plate-glass windows, polishing everything – the silverware, china, and glasses – to a happy, promising gloss. The tables were spread with two cloths, the changeable white one on top and a longer one underneath a shade of rose, the chief splash of color in the room. The only other colors were from the gleaming array of food on the buffet – golden bread, orange juice, marmalade – and the pink paper hydrangea in the little, cut-glass vases on the tables.

For some reason, Billie had chosen the breakfast table to put on her earrings, silver, heart-shaped leaves, appropriately enough, and as she looped them through her pierced ears, she again reminded Josh of Vivien Leigh in *Streetcar*, not the poignantly neurotic Blanche, no, the one with great sensual appeal – for example, that of her full, lovely, maternal breasts, as Josh thought of them, which she apparently liked to display in low-cut clothes, in this case, a bra-less, white blouse. She was wearing the same silver chains as the night before, which he now saw were a pendant necklace with a mahogany tear-drop that looked like a large guitar pick. Occasionally, she would fondle the chains absently, and he wondered if the careless mannerism were her unconscious way of drawing attention to her cleavage.

"Mmm," she hummed over her espresso. "My way of getting in touch with myself in the morning." She savored another sip. "I think this is the best coffee I have ever had in my entire life. Thick as pudding."

"My cappuccino's good," Phil remarked.

Phil's mature, well-groomed good looks were a great complement to Billie's, despite the fact that his teeth were slightly yellow and his brown hair obviously dyed, obvious in contrast with his light facial hair. His white eyebrows, for instance, were almost invisible. At first, Josh wondered why he combed his pompadour straight back. If he combed his hair forward, Josh thought, he could hide his receding hairline. Then Josh realized that he was probably hiding a bald spot.

"Well," Phil began, fixing Josh with his sky-blue eyes, "how are you doing this morning?"

"Reborn," Josh smiled.

"I'm jet lagged," Phil said, "and my back's out of whack from the plane."

Josh started to suggest Valerio as a masseur, but thought twice about it. Though his intuition told him otherwise, Valerio, for all he knew, was a crook.

"Feel pretty good," Billie stated, glancing at Josh. "Take it you slept well."

"Yes. Well," he hedged. When he told them, "I had a little trouble falling asleep," Billie placed her hand on his forearm as if to console him, though he didn't know why.

Phil, in turn, knuckled her arm affectionately, and Josh noticed that they were all touching each other.

"I sat on the balcony awhile," Josh said, "but once I hit the bed, I slept like a baby. Guess I miss my sound machine."

"Sound machine?" Phil asked.

"I fall asleep to the sound of surf every night."

"How primal," Phil commented.

There were other guests in the room, and since the only soft surfaces were the tablecloths, the birdlike chatter and the clatter of china and silver were noisy and resonant.

"Well, you look fine," Billie remarked, removing her hand. "Your cheeks are rosy, rosy angel cheeks."

"Thanks."

"At your age, I'm sure a naughty angel."

"I wish." When he noticed Billie staring at him, he asked, "What?"

"Tell me about your haircut," she said, lightly touching his hair.

"Bill-eee," Phil warned.

Josh's hair was frosted, cut short on the back and sides with a wedge on top parted down the middle.

"It's the way I've cut my hair since a kid," Josh explained. "Why?"

"You're about to enter the professional world, right?" she asked. "Maybe you should consider something more – "

"Mature?"

"Forgive her," Phil said, putting his hands together as if in prayer. "Stay young looking as long as you can. You'll look mature, as they say, soon enough."

"Well, while in Italy, keep an eye out for what the young professionals are wearing."

Phil laughed a little sigh of a laugh, then stared at Billie with amusement. "Young professionals, huh?"

Suddenly, Josh's loneliness looked more like solitude, one which he prized, and he wondered if Billie, unchecked, would try to smother him with attention.

"May I get anyone anything from the buffet?" she asked, rising.

"I'm fine," Josh said.

Everyone was having some form of bread – Josh rolls stuffed with Nutella, Phil plain rolls with butter and marmalade, Billie a large croissant with honey. Instead of espresso, Josh and Phil were drinking cappuccinos and orange juice. Phil was also having a small bowl of corn flakes and milk. In a minute, Billie returned with a small glass of grape juice.

"There was a tea bag over there that said *Bacca di Sambuco*," Billie said, sitting. "Anyone know what that means?"

"*Bacca* means berry," Josh said, sipping orange juice, "but I don't know what *sambuco* means. Raspberry maybe. No, raspberry is *lampone*."

"This grape juice is so good," Billie stressed.

"So is this orange juice," Josh agreed.

Josh thought food tasted this good only when he was stoned.

"And this marmalade," Phil chimed in. "A little bitter in a good way. Hmm, so good."

"Is it the food, us, or the fact we're in Italy?" Billie asked.

Josh just happened to notice that everyone was biting into bread at the same time, devouring the warm, fluffy dough with clear pleasure. Then he glanced out the window at the weathered terrace across the street – the bulky balustrade adorned at intervals with big, chunky urns blowzy with ferns and the red, painterly dabs of geraniums, everything set off against the façade's taupe plaster and teal shutters. Good food, good scenery, good company, he thought, and again he felt comfortable with Billie's zealous interest. So what if she wanted to take care of him? He could use some mothering.

As if reading his thoughts, she asked, "How's your wound?"

"A little sore and itchy."

"Every once in a while, use one of those alcohol swabs on it and replace the Band-Aid." She sipped juice, apparently puzzling over something, then looked at Phil. "I'm still not sure what all that was about."

"It wasn't about anything," Phil said, hands open. "The man's crazy."

"He was angry about something," she countered.

"Life," Phil stated. "He was angry about life. He was trying to tell us that a life of crime doesn't pay as well as it used to. What I can't figure out is Josh here."

Elbows on the table, Josh held his cappuccino in front of his face and, in effect, hid behind it.

"What do you mean?" Billie asked.

"You moved toward him twice," Phil observed, his ruddy face rounding into a sincere parental smile, parental, Josh thought, in the sense of a tough, old oak you could lean on and relax in the shade of. "What were you trying to do, commit hara-kiri?"

"He was protecting us," Billie stated. "That's what he – "

"Let him speak for himself," Phil said, threatening her with his spoon.

"I don't know," Josh sighed, setting the cup down. "I've been strangely detached from everything lately. I mean, way before the trip. You know, on the outside, looking in, a passive observer. And since I was, in a sense, watching some other Josh dealing with him, I wasn't afraid of him."

Josh decided that breakfast on the first day he knew them wasn't the right time to tell them he was depressed as hell nor the reason why.

"He was a sad case," Billie remarked.

"Sad case," Josh repeated ironically. "Guess my life is so boring I actually enjoyed the danger. Don't think I've ever been physically threatened before."

Billie was studying Josh with obvious concern.

"Blood come out of the handkerchief?" Josh asked.

"No," Phil said, smearing butter on a roll. "I sent it on its way with your shirt."

Billie wet the tip of her index finger on her tongue, pressed it against a croissant flake on her plate, and touched the flake to her tongue. Then she swallowed it pensively and fixed Josh with a stare. He could hardly wait to see what she would say.

"So," she began. "You're alone."

Josh nodded

"Why?"

"Gee," he smiled, a finger on his mouth. "You mean why am I not married or why am I in Italy alone?"

"Start with Italy."

Phil rolled his eyes, sipped cappuccino, and licked foam from his lip.

"The trip is a gift from my father," Josh explained. "A graduation present."

"A European tour used to be considered the final touch on a person's education," Phil remarked.

"That's what Dad thinks."

"You say your father gave you the trip," Billie said. "What about your mother?"

"Mom died when I was fifteen."

"Fifteen," Billie mused. "What a tender age to lose your mom." Billie bit her lip pensively, then asked, "Mind if I ask how?"

Phil looked at Josh and shook his head. "Apparently, she can't help herself."

"Actually," Josh said, "it's sort of an interesting story. We have a cabin cruiser and used to moor in a cove on Lake Lanier, this big lake northeast of Atlanta. Dad and Mom drank too much one night, and when we woke the next morning, Mom wasn't onboard. At first, we thought she'd swum ashore and gone somewhere for something, but when we noticed she hadn't used her swimsuit, Dad called the cops. Three days later, a diver found her in deep water about a hundred yards out. The autopsy showed she had lorazepam and, of course, alcohol in her system, so the theory is that she passed out and fell overboard or went swimming in her clothes and passed out, something like that."

"Like Natalie Wood," Phil remarked.

Billie dipped the tip of her croissant in a packet of honey. "And lorazepam is?" she asked, watching the honey slowly form a small, gold bead and drop into the packet.

"I think she was using it as a sleeping pill," Josh said. "I could certainly tell she was relaxed when she took it. It slowed her down."

"Dangerous combination," Phil remarked, "liquor and sleeping pills."

"I'm sure it was addictive," Josh said, picking up a pastry.

When he bit one end of the roll, a glob of Nutella squirmed out of the other, and he licked the chocolate off his fingers.

"Not exactly a healthy breakfast you're eating there, young man," Billie said.

"You think croissants are healthy?" Phil said.

"Know what they call this in Italian?" Josh asked, meaning the pastry.

"What?" Billie asked.

"A *fagottino*," Josh said. "A little faggot. Comes from the same root our word *faggot* comes from, a bundle."

"A bundle," Billie repeated.

"Faggot originally meant a bundle of sticks. Here it means a stuffed pastry that looks like a bundle." He set the pastry down and wiped his fingers on his napkin.

"Interesting," Billie said ironically. "Whenever I eat one, I'll just pretend I'm eating a gay."

"My lord," Phil remarked.

"What would I like to be stuffed with?" Josh wondered, draping his napkin across his thigh.

There was a pregnant pause. Then everyone burst out laughing.

"Wait a minute," Phil said, holding up his fork. "How did *faggot* meaning gay come from *faggot* meaning bundle?"

"When witches were burned at the stake, gays were bundled up and burned with her."

"Women, hedonists, geniuses," Billie lilted, "all good kindling for a nice, warm xenophobic fire."

"On a Medieval winter's night," Phil added.

"What is the word for faggot in Italian?" Billie asked.

"Well, there're several: *checca, ricchione, frocio*, but I don't know the various shades of meaning among them." There was an awkward pause. Then Josh said, "Tell me about yourselves. So far, I've been answering all the questions. How do you two occupy yourselves?"

"We're artists," Phil stated, hand up, thumb and index finger pinched as if holding a brush.

"Painters?" Josh asked.

"Right," Phil said. "I also occasionally sculpt in driftwood."

"And occasionally I like to take a break from painting and do pottery or jewelry," Billie added. "We're what's known as 'prominent local artists.'"

"Great," Josh said.

"We're actually lucky enough," Phil said, "to sell enough to build on a rather comfortable life style. What with the occasional commission or grant."

"Of course, lately," Billie added, "we really started selling. Sold just about everything we have."

"Oh, why?"

Phil shook some milk off a spoonful of cereal and seemed to be pondering the question. Then he said, "Not sure why," and put the spoonful in his mouth. After he swallowed, he said, "Especially off our web site."

"Of course," Billie said, "after a certain number of shows, your name is known, and some people are more interested in having a name than a painting. Imagine someone saying, 'I must have a Tree.'"

"What sort of subject matter do you paint?" Josh asked.

"I like the wine country," Phil said, a hand up in a nondescript gesture. "Landscapes, still lifes, *natura morta* as they say in Italy."

"I like the coast," Billie stated.

"Well," Josh said, "we have something else in common, drawing. Of course, mine are technical, not artistic."

"Some of our work is more commercial than artistic," Billie confessed, "but deliberately. We know the difference."

"I can draw on my computer," Josh said. "Ever try that?"

"Haven't thought of it," Phil said.

"Where on the coast are you from?" Josh asked.

"Full Moon Bay," Phil said. "Between San Francisco and Monterey."

"You said you have a cliff house."

"We were just driving around one day," Billie said, "looking for something to paint, and we took this dirt road off the highway to see where it led, and it led to an abandoned house."

"An abandoned house with an ocean view," Phil stressed. "A Craftsman-style redwood bungalow nestled among some Douglas firs tall as skyscrapers."

"Naturally, we looked into it," Billie added. "Buying it, that is. A foreclosure, a former vacation house fallen into disrepair. We just thought of rundown as Bohemian. It was fine for us."

"Wasn't designed by Wright, was it?"

"We should be so lucky," Phil lamented.

"Well, we are that lucky," Billie commented cryptically.

"We call it Seaweed," Phil said, riffling his fingers, "a pun on Seaward, a house in Carmel."

"You should come and visit us," Billie blurted, her face lighting up.

"Can't beat the view," Phil remarked. "The sunsets."

"Sea lions and seals and gulls."

"Oh, my," Josh joked.

"You won't need your sound machine," Phil said, hand up in a stop gesture.

"Just raise your window," Billie remarked, fondling her necklace.

"I take it there's no beach."

"There is," Phil said, pointing at him, "a little private beach in a cove near the house. Only problem is – the undertow's too strong for swimming. You surf?"

"I'm not the athletic type," Josh admitted, noticing a faraway look in Billie's eyes. Then he noticed that Phil noticed it.

"Well," Phil began again, "you can always sunbathe."

"You can do that on the terrace," Billie said, coming back to them. "That is, if it's warm. And he hasn't mentioned the other problem."

"What, sharks?" Josh smiled.

"No, uh – " Phil hesitated. "Well, there's that, too."

"It's a sixty-foot drop to the beach," Billie stated. "There're stairs, but try getting up them at our age."

"We do have to stop and rest a couple of times," Phil smiled wistfully.

"Great exercise," Josh suggested, elbows on the table.

"I'd rather hike along the trail," Billie remarked, strangely triste.

"A great trail along the cliff," Phil explained.

When Billie said, "Josh, sit up," he straightened up and pulled his shoulders back.

"Yes, ma'm."

"You look like a shirt tossed on a chair, a nice shirt, but rumpled."

"Next, you'll be trying to nurse him," Phil joked sardonically, pointing at her.

When he winked at Josh as if sharing a secret, Josh realized that he would, in fact, enjoy visiting them. Without knowing it, he had become entangled with them emotionally the way lobster buoys become entangled, simply by proximity and chance. He felt that, in a sense, he must have left a latchstring of sorts hanging outside himself, and Billie had come along, lifted it, and walked in, taking over as housekeeper, at least for a few days.

"How long you been in Italy?" he asked.

"Since yesterday," Phil said. "We flew into Rome and took the train down."

"Why the Gypsy made such an impression," Billie commented. "Benvenuti a Napoli!"

"Bet we were on the same train," Josh speculated.

"11:14?" Phil asked.

"Yeah."

"Only we forgot to say first class," Billie explained, "and wound up in a car that wasn't air-conditioned."

"A big birdcage of a car," Phil added, "with a bevy of Italian women all chirping at once."

"Why Italy?" Josh asked.

"Picture-esque," Billie replied, breaking the word in two.

"Plenty to paint," Phil translated. "To be quite frank, lucrative clichés."

"Where next?"

"After Naples?" Phil asked.

Josh nodded.

"We don't have an itinerary," Phil said, waving a no. "Probably Amalfi."

"Me, too," Josh said. "Found this beautiful little hotel just west of Amalfi. Maybe you could stay there."

"By all means," Billie smiled. "We'll look into it."

"Great," Josh said. "What're your plans for today?"

"I thought we'd arm ourselves and hold up Gypsies," Phil joked.

"And why would we want to do that?" Billie asked.

"Irony," Phil said, hand up, fingers spread. "Ethnic humor."

"I can think of better ways to spend the day," Billie claimed.

"Oh, how?" Phil asked.

"Enjoying ourselves."

Josh volunteered, "I'm going to the Museo Archeologico."

"What a coincidence," Billie quipped. "So are we. Want to go together?"

"Sure," Josh said. "There's this fabulous exhibit of silver from Pompeii."

"I have to pee first," Phil said, downing the orange juice.

"Phil," Billie groaned.

"Me, too," Josh said, wiping his mouth on his napkin.

"Shall I call a cab?" Billie asked.

"Let's take the bus," Josh suggested. "Mingle with the natives." When Phil nodded, Josh said, "I have the bus number in my backpack."

Chapter 9: Il Museo Archeologico

In a few minutes, the three were strolling uphill toward the Piazza del Municipio, Josh with his backpack, like a wilted blueberry, crumpled on his back and Billie with a large canvas bag riding on her side. Josh had made her put the bag's strap over her head instead of just on her shoulder as a safety measure. At the piazza, they caught a bus to the handsome, shell-pink Museo Archeologico, and after the chaos of the crowded, bustling streets, the entrance hall immediately cast a peaceful spell on them. They agreed to split up and meet at the snack bar in the courtyard at noon, and as they parted, the Trees set off with sketch pads in hand toward the steps to the mezzanine and Josh with his camera in his pocket for the Farnese sculptures. He looked forward to a long stroll through the shady forest of beautiful objects.

He had the intelligence and sensibility to enjoy the collection, especially the superb statues of nude males, but even though he had heard about it, the machismo of the Farnese *Hercules* was quite a surprise. The stunning virile impression was due in part, he figured, to the ample display of masculine sex traits: the plump genitals, the thick, curly mane of hair and beard, the large size of the figure's shoulders, chest, and hands, the superhuman size of the statue in general. As he slowly circled it, even the two apples held behind Hercules' hip, the way a pitcher would, seemed scrotal. But the trait that said *man* the most was the heavy, massive muscles. The figure was literally swollen with strength. His face was that of a mature man who has endured many trials. He was looking down thoughtfully, and the sinuous posture implied, ironically, how weary he was, slumped against his huge, knobby club, a weapon which seemed to disappear, Josh noticed, into the mouth of the lion draped over it. The phallic club and lion's skin, he thought, were also symbols of power, enhanced by the strength and endurance implied by the tawny marble.

Josh knew that, in the hands of such a powerful man, he would be sexual putty, shaped into any pliable position the man wanted, but the exaggerated musculature held little appeal. Hercules would not be his first choice. He was attracted to the more down-to-earth, though perfect physiques of other nearby statues, sculpture whose sensuality aroused him to the point that he was experiencing a pleasant confusion of impulses, a level of aesthetic pleasure, let's say, higher than that of a straight man. Marble the color of mussel shells, orange discolorations, even the wound-like nicks and chips in the stone were having about the same effect on him as skin tones. In short, he was cruising the statues like men. He even fantasized about one of them, blue with moonlight, coming alive like Galatea, stepping from its pedestal, and wrestling him to the floor, where, bent to the hero's will, he surrendered himself to intense, receptive sex. The notion that an ancient sculptor must have had sex with his creation did not seem all that farfetched.

As he lingered in front of *Achilles and Troilus*, the hero's masculinity, Josh thought, lay more in his outrageous violence than in his rippling physique. The great warrior was caught mid-stride, the ball of his right foot just touching the ground as the toes of his left were lifting off it, the static statue stepping forward in a graceful S Curve as Achilles held Troilus by the ankle, the boy's limp body slung over his shoulder like a fawn. Josh had first come across the story in an undergraduate mythology class. Troilus was the youngest Trojan prince, a boy warrior, and in one version, Achilles captured him in the Temple of Apollo and, taken with his beauty, raped him, then killed him on the altar. Josh had also seen a picture of an ancient vase painting in which the warrior, in full armor, was chasing the naked youth in an exciting, if desperate, scene which could just as well have been erotic as hostile. Par for the course, Josh, no hero, put himself in the place of Troilus and imagined what the cool breastplate must have felt like pressed against his back. He knew that testosterone was the hormone for both sex and aggression and was well acquainted with the idea of love and sex as destructive.

A bizarre form of violence was also the subject of the Farnese *Bull*, the largest sculpture from the Classical Era and one carved from a single block of marble. In the scene depicted, the twins Amphion and Zethos were tying Dirke to an agitated bull as punishment for offenses against their mother, Antiope. The frightened bull had reared in resistance, cloven hooves pawing the air, the bull's head tilted because, on one side, Amphion, nude, was holding a horn and pushing the snout and, on the other side, Zethos, nude, was pulling a rope tied to its horns. Again, as he drifted around the group, Josh was distracted from the composition by the men's firm buttocks and their suggestion of vigorous, satisfying sex.

Besides the scope of its artistic achievement, the elaborate sculpture held a personal fascination for him, and he wondered why. The brawny bull was a traditional masculine symbol, and according to the myth, it was being used to destroy someone. Then it became clear: the sculpture was a simple symbol of Owen's destructive power. The idea that the bull perhaps looked frightened, to Josh, paralleled Owen's apparent dismay at the tragic grief he had caused everyone: Josh, himself, maybe even his wife. Could someone as intimate with Owen as his wife be unaware of his sexual ambivalence?

Just as he had the thought, he noticed a tall, good-looking man step from behind a figure as if he had stepped from the group itself into life. Which character was he? Josh wondered, face brightening. The real-life embodiment of Amphion or Zethos? He touched his shirt over the cut on his chest. Which tragic end would he meet?

One of Josh's first insights into his sexual orientation was his warm response to pictures of Greek statues he had chanced upon in the *Encyclopedia Britannica*. He had gone from flat, black-and-white images, he realized, to bigger-than-life, three-dimensional, golden-hued stone and now to an actual handsome man facing the group and like a moon slowly orbiting it counterclockwise.

Josh had seen waves crash against rocks, then retreat from them in circles of receding counter waves. He felt his pleasant, diffused state of horniness clearly focus on the man, the only attractive male he had seen in the museum, and wondered if the vibes he was feeling were actual vibes or simply his own feelings projected onto and deflected off the man. Was his gaydar really picking up on some subliminal signal, some subtle hormonal secretion, like a flower's, scenting the air?

He remembered his camera, slipped it from his pocket, and casually snapped a few pictures of the group and, when the man was not looking, one of him. He slipped the camera into his pocket, but continued watching him.

The man projected a seriously lean, athletic, masculine image due in part to his long, narrow, angular face. He had a flat, broad forehead, slant, intensely blue eyes that seemed to be caressing everything appreciatively, and light brows that spread gracefully like wings. His flat ears, straight nose, and wide, impassive mouth added to the butch look. His grooming also stressed it. His thick, shiny, light-brown hair was cut fairly short with the hint of a part on the right – Josh thought his hair looked like soft fur, wanted to touch it – and his sideburns trailed down his face, fanning out to a subtle mix of tough stubble and boyish peach fuzz on his jaw, chin, and lips. The fact that his frame tapered to a tight waist made Josh want to wrap his legs around it.

All at once, Josh wondered about his own appearance should the man glance his way: khaki shorts, canvas belt, lime-green Izod, but before he could give it another thought, he almost intuitively became aware of Billie spying on him from the big archway separating the rooms. If she had seen him watching the man or snapping his picture, would it confirm the fact he was gay, if she hadn't deduced it already from his *fagottino* remark? And why did she look so concerned? At that point, she smiled, fluttered her fingers at him, and disappeared behind the wall.

When he turned toward the man, he was strolling toward a bench across from the *Artemis of Ephesus*. Josh's impulse was to follow him. Cruising was fun, whether or not he meant to follow through with it, definitely a harmless distraction from his obsession with Owen. His body seemed at odds with his heart. How could he possibly claim to be depressed over Owen when he was hot to trot after a sexy stranger in a museum?

The man sat on the bench and leaned against the wall, knees spread, hands clasped behind his head, not really seeming to focus on anything. Certainly open body language, Josh thought.

He remembered his own poor posture, straightened up, and strolled over to Artemis, struck with how different the statue looked from most in the museum: stiff, not relaxed; detailed, not simple, the bronze face and hands dark, not marble white. Her rows of breasts, he'd read, were not breasts at all, but bull testicles sacrificed to her in the name of fertility, and, in fact, the breasts, when he looked closely, did not have nipples. Testicles where breasts were supposed to be, he mused. The two equated logically in the sense that both were life-giving: one for the creation of life, the other its sustenance.

The statue was cordoned off with rope, and he moved to the side and pretended to be examining it from that angle, but was really waiting for the man to glance away. When he did, Josh took in as much of him as he could as fast as he could: the square jaw, the blunt chin, the long, taut vines of muscles winding around his arms, the plump biceps set off by the big jonquil of his yellow short-sleeved shirt.

The man leaned forward, elbows on knees, and seemed to be just resting, enjoying the moment. He looked at Josh, and when Josh stared, the man shot him a blank stare in return, a direct, yet aloof look that indicated he was aware of Josh's interest only, not that he was receptive to it or repulsed by it. After a while, he seemed amused by the length of eye contact, perhaps the compliment of a stranger's attention. The hint of a sly smile crept into his eyes, not his face, but when Josh winked, as if they shared a secret, the man's tenuous eye-smile became an earnest, admissive face-smile, a friendly one, but Platonic. Josh knew a serious cruise when he saw one, and this brief exchange wasn't one. Perhaps the man was straight, after all, but liberal, maybe even naïve. Why should he feel criminal about cruising him?

The stone in his chest, like one in a cherry, was weighing him down, Josh knew, but he also knew that, given time, it could sprout into something nourishing and striking. The fact was that he was still in love with Owen, though he shouldn't have been, still foolishly holding out hope that, through some romantic miracle, the young man would come to his senses, abandon his family, and reunite with him. Italy was the land of saints and miracles. Why not here? But if he really wanted it to happen, Josh thought, he would have to work for it, pay for it, give up something, perhaps even something as trifling as flirting with a stranger. He would have to pass, even if the man had, in fact, been interested. On that note, Josh gestured with two fingers toward him, half salute, half wave goodbye, and strolled off.

# # # # #

At noon, when Josh entered the loggia of the quiet courtyard, Phil and Billie were sitting at a bistro table in the shadow of one of the tall palms, their sketch pads leaning against the spindly legs of their chairs. A snack stand was parked nearby in a corner of the yard, and he went there first, ordered a lime granita (flavored crushed ice), and joined them. The greenish granita glistened in a paper cup with a red plastic spoon stuck in it. He set it on the table and took a seat, relieved not to be standing or walking on marble. He was glad to give his sore feet a rest.

"Can you believe they leave the windows open?" Billie asked, her necklace glimmering even in the shade.

"All that car exhaust," Phil remarked.

"I was a little surprised." When Josh noticed the straws and lemon wedges in their drinks, he asked, "What are you drinking?"

"Diet Cokes with lemon," Billie said. "We were tempted by the panini, but wanted to wait on a real meal at a decent restaurant."

Josh spooned up a big chunk of the granita and tasted how tart and sweet it was. Then his sinuses ached with cold.

"Ow!" he exclaimed, shoving the spoon into the ice. "Brain freeze."

"Go slow," Billie smiled.

"So," Phil began, hands up in an open gesture, "what did you like most?"

"You mean archeological objects," Josh smirked, glancing at Billie.

"What works of art?" she parried.

"Well," he said, leaning down to pick up her sketch book, "I guess the greatest work in there, as far as I've seen, is the Farnese *Bull*."

"Why?" Phil asked. "What does it say to you?"

"What does it say to me?" Josh repeated, flipping open the sketch pad. "I guess," he hesitated, "something about the destructive power of sex and obsession."

"What does sex have to do with it?" Phil asked, a hand extended as if to shake hands.

Josh thought. "You're right. It doesn't have anything to do with sex."

When Billie gave him a pleased, sideways glance, as if she understood his train of thought, he felt caught out again.

The bull was being used to destroy someone, a woman, in the name of the sons' cruel sense of justice, but before Josh could organize his thoughts any further, Billie turned to Phil and said, "What about something about the balance of power between men and women at the time?"

"I think you're projecting a modern mentality onto something that happened a long time ago."

"Perhaps."

Phil and Billie sipped their drinks, and when Josh looked at a sketch of a young, powerfully built satyr pouring wine from a goatskin, he realized how talented Billie was. The sketch was amazing, well worth framing. If Phil was in the same ball park, they were both great artists.

"I love this," Josh exclaimed, turning the pad so they could see what he was talking about. "The open stance. Wow!"

The satyr was tilted back dramatically, braced on his left leg, one flexed leg in front of the other. Of course, with the satyr's hips thrust forward, Josh saw the sexual connotation of the pose. The satyr could have assumed the same stance for an even more pleasant reason, his hand holding, not a missing cup, but something else.

"I'll give it to you," Billie offered.

"Would you?" Josh asked. "Thank you so much. Can't tell you how much I like it."

"Imagine him as a fountain decoration," Phil suggested. "Water pouring out of the goatskin."

The next sketch was of Pan teaching a young man to play the panpipes.

"Pan looks as if it's not just the pipes he wants him to play," Josh commented, turning the pad again, "at least not the wooden kind."

"Wooden?" Phil quipped.

"You boys," Billie sighed. "Put that away." She sipped Coke. "You can look at it later."

"Back to my question," Phil said, tapping the table.

"Favorite works," Josh stated, closing the pad.

"The *Bull* and what else?"

"We have to include Hercules," Josh said, setting the pad down.

"What a man!" Billie said, fondling her necklace. "See the butt cheeks on him?"

"Yes, I did," Josh stressed.

"What a great fuck he must have been," Phil stated, surprising Josh.

"The cock seemed a little out of proportion," Josh ventured.

"You never know," Billie remarked. "Small ones can surprise you."

"Really?" Phil joked.

"Notice how one cheek rode higher than the other?" Billie asked. "Part of the S Curve."

"Implying how tired he is," Josh said. "He's slumped on his club for support."

"Exactly," Billie agreed.

"Irony," Phil said. "Even the strongest man in the world gets tired."

"I also liked the statue of Achilles at the other end of the room."

"What about it?" Phil asked, elbow on table, cheek on fist.

"Well, not so much the statue itself," Josh explained. "The story behind it."

"Which is?" Phil asked.

"The boy slung over Achilles' shoulder is Troilus," Josh explained, "the youngest son of Priam and Hecuba. Achilles raped him and killed him."

"Our noble hero?" Phil said sardonically.

"'Fraid so."

"Wait a minute," Billie said, touching Josh's hand. "You like rape and murder?"

"The fate of Troy was linked to the fate of the boy by prophecy. So it may just symbolize the sack of Troy, but it also says something about the violence of sex and the sexuality of violence."

"Sex violent for you?" Billie frowned.

"Hot sex," he admitted. "Maybe *violent* isn't the right word."

"Hope not," Billie said.

"Don't be such a prude," Phil scolded her. "You know you like it rough."

They both laughed.

"What about you?" Josh asked, picking up his cup.

"Do I like rough sex?" Phil asked.

"No," Josh smiled. "What was your favorite?"

"We both liked the *Dancing Faun*," Billie said.

"Speaking of butt cheeks," Phil joked, sitting back.

"Haven't seen that one," Josh said.

"Yes," Billie smiled. "His butt looks like a couple of eggplants. I sketched him from the back."

"I did the front," Phil said. He thought, then chuckled. "Sounds perverse."

"But we decided the reason we liked him so much," Billie explained, "is that he makes a great symbol of joy, sheer joy." She picked the lemon wedge from her drink, squeezed it into it, and dropped it back in. "First of all, he's uninhibited."

"After all," Phil said, eyebrow raised, "he is a faun, an animal."

"He's brazenly naked," Billie said. "And he's dancing," she added, resting her case, "his toes just touching the ground, his hair tossed up, long, flowing hair, I might add."

"He's uncut in a couple of ways," Phil joked, making a scissors gesture.

"He's looking up, smiling," Billie continued, "obviously in the throes of some Bacchic ecstasy."

"In other words, drunk," Phil quipped.

"He really captures a certain *joie de vivre*," she concluded.

"I'll be sure to find him," Josh said. He took a small bite of ice and enjoyed the way the lime flavor melted in his mouth. "Based on the bronzes I've seen, I prefer marble. The stone mimics skin better."

"I like the fact that the physiques on the statues of older men," Phil said, "were just as cut as those on the younger. Gives me hope."

"What a collection of hot men," Billie said, eyeing Josh. "You'd better get back on your exercise routine when we get home," she added, turning to Phil, "if you want to talk about cut physiques."

"You said you use vineyards as subject matter," Josh said, glancing at Phil. "I saw a fresco with Bacchus pictured as a bunch of grapes with his head, hands, and feet sticking out. He looked like one of the Fruit of the Loom guys."

"We saw a bust called *Dioniso*," Phil said, wiping perspiration from his forehead with the back of his hand.

"And a statue with Dionysus as a babe sitting on a satyr's shoulder."

"Been to the Gabinetto Segreto?" Phil asked.

"No, not yet."

"An absolute must."

"I know."

"Those Pygmies really pygmies or children having sex?" Billie asked Phil.

"Not sure the museum can lie to us."

# # # # #

They chatted a few minutes, agreed to meet at the gift shop when through, and split up again, going off in different directions, Josh toward the Gabinetto Segreto, the Secret Cabinet, where he was quite taken with the frank audacity of *Pan and a Goat*. Since he had looked up a dirty-Italian site on line, he even knew the word for goat bugger, *capraro*. His interpretation of the pseudo-bestiality depicted was the wonderful animal nature of sex, a physical act in which we lose our humanness for a moment and become again just the pleasure-driven animal we were to begin with. What a relief sex was in how it made us forget the cares of our complicated, mind-controlled lives. He wondered which statue impressed him more, the Farnese *Hercules* or the one of Pan fucking a goat. The great cultural taboo of the latter intrigued him. Anything different was just more interesting to him than things the same, not that, in reality, much beyond vanilla sex actually appealed to him.

After the Gabinetto Segreto, he wandered down to the glass-enclosed loggia of another courtyard, where he admired another gallery of statues and torsos of broken statues, which he thought of as beautiful carcasses. He figured he could thank some Christian for Diomedes' missing crotch just as he could thank the Fascist-Vatican collaboration for shattering thousands of Von Gloeden glass negatives in Sicily. As he liked to joke, the only Christian he trusted was Christian Dior, and he wondered about the missing top of Psyche's head as well. He was particularly taken with the perfect symmetry of Policleto's *Spearman*, bright white in the sunlight, possibly an image of Achilles, certainly a classical ideal. Its compelling beauty brought up the issue of just what made him want to submit to another man? Attraction to the figure's inherent strength, he reasoned, suggested a lack of it in himself. According to that logic, if he were to survive, he had to seek out someone strong who could help him.

As he was about to round a corner into another loggia, he pulled a "Billie," as he thought of it. That is, he stopped and spied on her and Phil as she, hand on hip, was reading the plaque in front of the *Tyrant Killers* and Phil, a few steps back, was sketching them. Again Josh was struck with Billie's sensual appeal. For a middle-aged woman, she had stylish bangs, a good figure, and strong, shapely legs. And she was dressed smart: flimsy blouse, dusky blue skirt, black flats. Phil's outfit was nondescript: white shirt, khakis, loafers. Josh thought of him as the strong, steady danseur who provided the lift, so to speak, for her dance. They were obviously enjoying each other's company as well as the treasure trove of classical art around them, a happy, harmonious couple freethinking or kind enough to be open to the superfluous company of a young, gay architecture student. Billie stood up straight as if she intuitively sensed something, and as she started to turn in his direction, he stepped back out of sight.

When they strolled into a room of the silver exhibit, he checked out the *Tyrant Killers*, then went out among the palms and stones in the courtyard. As he strolled around, he stopped to admire the *Colossal Head of Vespasian* with its missing nose and chin, then the giant torso and head of Jove, the *Busto di Giove*, Josh's head at the statue's armpit. He thought of its size as the immense power of men in his life. And with that thought, he looked around for the man he had cruised.

Chapter 10: Da Vincenzo

After the museum, they strolled down Via Santa Maria di Constantinopoli to Piazza Bellini, veered toward Da Vincenzo, and took a table on the patio behind latticework with scraggly oleander. The contrast between the afternoon glare on the street and grotto-like shade under the canopy blinded Josh for a moment, but by the time he had clipped his backpack to his chair, his eyes focused, and a waiter in a mauve vest appeared, greeted everyone, and handed out menus in English.

Josh asked for a bottle of mineral water *non gassata*, and when the waiter departed, he asked Billie, "Where's your bag?"

"Right here," she said, indicating the space between her chair and the latticework.

"Do me a favor," he said. "Tie it to your chair." She laughed, said OK, and tied the strap to her chair. "You may want to rethink wearing all that glittery jewelry, too," he added.

When it came time to order, Josh ordered antipasto and a Capri bianco *in ghiaccio* (on ice) for starters and would see after that, Billie spaghetti alle vongole (clams) and a Capri bianco also since Josh had, Phil gnocchi alla Sorrentina and a Peroni.

When the waiter left, Billie asked Josh, "Take pictures?"

Josh did not know if she had seen him snap one of the stranger.

"No."

"Why not?"

"Seemed touristy," he admitted.

The waiter set out the glasses of wine and poured Phil's Peroni.

"See the silver exhibit?" Phil asked Josh, touching a water glass.

"Oh, yes," Josh stressed. "Totally changed the way I thought of Pompeii. Much more sophisticated than I thought. My god, the detail on those cups."

He pictured silver tendrils emerging from the black and brown of aging on a cup.

"I loved the one with the grapes and grape leaves," Billie said, referring to a single-handled cup with grapes and leaves in relief on one side and ivy and berries on the other.

"I liked the skeletons," Phil added, referring to one with eight skeletons under a garland of roses.

"Me, too," Josh said. "Read the notes on 'em?"

Phil shook his head.

"One scene is a little allegory," Josh explained. "One skeleton weighs a bag in one hand and holds a butterfly in the other. A second skeleton is putting on a crown. A third is staring at a mask. The inscription reads, 'Enjoy while you're alive. Tomorrow is uncertain.'"

"So the bag and butterfly would symbolize the material and spiritual choices in life," Billie said, interpreting the scene. "The crown, of course, is power. The mask, I guess, has something to do with pretense or appearance versus reality."

"Very good," Josh smiled. "In another scene, the skeletons of Epicurus and Zeno are standing on either side of a table with dessert. The inscription reads, 'Enjoyment is the supreme good.'"

"I second the motion," Phil agreed.

So many to pick from, Josh thought, ivy and berries, olives and olive leaves, centaurs and cupids, clever, elaborate silverwork adorning cups that had sat on tables in Pompeii two thousand years ago.

"I bought a couple of catalogues for the show," Josh said, "one for you, one for me."

"Didn't have to do that," Billie said, absently pulling a strand of her straight hair.

"Least I could do if you're giving me a sketch. Speaking of which," he added, wiping his fingers on his napkin, "before I get my hands oily, may I take a look at Phil's sketches? You mind?"

"Not at all," Phil said, holding his Peroni.

Billie reached into the bag, pulled out Phil's sketch pad, and handed it across the table. Josh opened it and leisurely flipped through a few pages, drawings of works he recognized, *Hermes at Rest*, *Antinous*, *Sleeping Satyr*, the *Runners*, even the big eyes and long sideburns of Alexander in the big mosaic of him defeating Darius, the Persian king. Phil could draw as well as Billie, Josh thought. In fact, their styles were so similar that, if the drawings were shuffled, it would be hard for him to sort them. His favorite, though, was still the satyr with the goatskin.

"Wonderful," he said, closing the pad and handing it back to Billie. "I really do admire your skills."

"Thanks," Phil smiled, pressing his hands together as in prayer.

The waiter set out the food, asked if they needed anything, and left.

"Sooo," Billie said, drawing out the word, "let's devote ourselves to enjoying some good food."

Josh admired the fragrant dishes, then focused on his own, popping a shiny black olive into his mouth.

"Mmm," Billie hummed with delight. "The pasta's garlicky. Delicious."

"Get around to the bronzes?" Phil asked, picking up a salt shaker.

Josh nodded, chewing a slice of prosciutto. He thought of the elegant pair of bronze-blue deer with their little penises and, as usual, could not help projecting a romantic scenario even on them.

"Can't believe I've dropped into the middle of so much art," he remarked.

"The museum alone makes the trip worth it, whatever comes next," Billie said, fork mid-air.

"And what luck to meet you two," Josh said, "real artists."

"I'd hardly put us in the same breath with the works in the museum," Phil chuckled, halving a dumpling with his fork.

"Let's see," Billie said, balancing her hands like scales. "Harmodius and Aristogeiton on one hand, Phil and Billie on the other." When she dropped the Phil-and-Billie hand on the table, her wedding ring tapped it. "Think we lose." Josh knew she was referring to the *Tyrant Killers*, the statues side by side in the glassed-in loggia, where he had spied on her.

When he recalled the image of the big, powerful men, again his train of thought was nude men, sex, destruction, and he realized, with a sigh, that he needed some serious self-analysis and soon. His train of thought should be, he told himself, nude men, sex, fulfillment, happiness, the difference, as he saw it, between the destructive theme in *Achilles and Troilus*, for example, and the rude mischief of a vase painting he had seen in the Boston Museum, one in which the god Pan, erect, was pursuing a young shepherd. Achilles chased Troilus, raped him, and killed him. Pan, on the other hand, was chasing the shepherd to have fun. The bawdy nature of the scene was perhaps best reflected in the shepherd's wide eye fixed on the god's sizable erection, his expression not of fear, but of pleasant surprise with the hint of a smile. It was the size of the cock that created apprehension, not sex itself. Chancing upon the vase had had a beneficial, validating effect on Josh since its obvious gayness, in this case roguish, connected him with other gays at other times, in short, with the historic gay community. Prior to that moment, he had lived in a gay vacuum of sorts, an immense societal conspiracy, as he thought of it, to deny that gays even existed.

At that point, just as Josh had forked some marinated mushrooms, he noticed a tall, good-looking young man strolling toward the restaurant, a fashion model if he ever saw one. He was wearing shades with big, aggressive lenses, a leather belt and wide leather wristbands as well as a watch, and low-slung, ragged jeans peppered with shiny silver studs. His gauzy, see-through shirt was open to his navel, showing off his slim, curved-in torso. Silver chains, like Billie's, with silver dog tags and a silver crucifix sparkled among his chest hair, and Josh could see, as if through haze, his groin hair and the top of his pubes. As he was about to pass by the latticework, he grabbed his belt the way a man might casually cup his crotch, but since Josh could not see his eyes, he could not tell if the gesture were suggestive, a subtle signal. Josh's eyes turned to follow him as he went by, no more than a couple of feet away, and when Billie noticed Josh's line of sight, she turned to see what he was looking at, then smiled slyly. To Josh the clunk of the young man's cowboy boots on the cobblestones could not have been more evocative.

"So," Billie said, sipping wine, "what's the gay scene like in Naples?"

"Gay scene," Josh repeated, giving himself time to think now that the cards were on the table.

"With churches on every corner," she said, "I'd think they'd be pretty intolerant."

"Surprisingly," he began, "I've read that their attitude's what's called 'Arabian.' They don't really care so much whether you're gay or not as whether you're top or bottom."

"Hmm," Phil mused. "As long as you're top, you're straight?"

"In some sense," Josh said. "Of course, gays who think that are just rationalizing. If you're into men, but say you're straight or even bi – "

"You're deluding yourself," Billie said.

"But," Josh added, "if thinking that way lets Neapolitans accept someone as gay, so be it."

"Any other differences?" Phil asked, raising a fork with tomato and basil.

"Between?"

"Attitudes here and home."

"A lot's the same," Josh said. "In fact, you can spend your whole trip here in a gay environment if you want: gay hotels, gay restaurants, gay clubs, gay shops. But I didn't book that trip."

"Figuratively speaking," Billie said.

Josh leaned on the table, lay an anchovy on a small piece of toast, and slipped it into his mouth. When he had swallowed it, he said, "The gay scene here seems to float more."

"Float?" Billie asked.

"Back home," Josh explained, "there are places you can go every night, here too: bars, baths, cinemas, but here often you learn where things are happening by word of mouth or by calling an info line. The party might be at one place one night, another another, leather night on Thursday, naked night on Sunday."

"Naked night?" Billie laughed.

"Foot-fetish night, uniform night, fist night."

"Fist night?" Phil asked, forehead creased.

"Don't ask," Josh blushed. "Everything goes on later, too, too late for me if I want to see Italy. I've seen a gay bar. I haven't seen Italy."

There, he thought, that was the first time he had explicitly said he'd done something gay, gone to a gay bar.

"Where would you go?" Billie asked hypothetically.

"Well," he said, "there's actually a bookshop and bar somewhere around here, Caffé Intra Moenia."

"Why there?" Phil asked.

"Why there?" Josh thought. "Supposed to be a good place to meet people at night. In fact, the whole piazza's supposed to be a good place to meet people at night. Not why we came here."

"Well, it would've been all right if it were," Billie assured him.

Josh would not have minded meeting someone casually in a "clean, well-lighted place," as Hemingway put it, but he was definitely not into cruising in the sense of going into a sling room or dark room. He wasn't judging anyone. He just wasn't attracted to it. Sex rooms, cubicles, a dark lane in a park – these were places he only fantasized about.

"For someone not interested," Phil smiled, "you certainly seem well informed about the gay scene."

"Well, I am interested in the local gay culture, let's say, but I'm not interested in actually meeting someone. I'm still savoring the last meal, so to speak."

From his ironic tone, it was obvious that the last meal had *un sapore cattivo*, a bad taste. He was now revealing his second secret, he realized, that the man he loved had robbed him emotionally.

He was enjoying the Trees, of course, though he couldn't shake the weight of the guilt he felt over the failed affair. What did he do or not do that drove Owen away? Whatever it was, he knew he would have to forgive himself to live with himself. But he couldn't think of anything he had, in fact, done except perhaps let the injured relationship suffer longer than it had to. Once a deer had sprung from the woods by the road and, trying to leap his car, struck it, eye to eye with him through the windshield for a second before he saw it, out of his side window, cartwheeling into the median. There, busted open, it writhed and jerked till he gave a couple of rednecks permission to shoot it, "his" deer because he had hit it. He should have finished off the affair, like the poor deer, quickly, too, put it out of its misery.

Another way of looking at it, though, was that he simply enjoyed sex with the young man as long as he could. The great pleasure, of course, had a great price, but one he'd been willing to pay. No, he told himself. He hadn't done anything wrong. He didn't need to forgive himself. He needed to move on, though he wasn't sure how. His fun with the stranger in the museum was a good clue that he could move on, though forging himself into someone a man like that would want, he figured, would be about as difficult as pounding cold metal into shape on an anvil. To be malleable, he realized, he would have to be hot, thrust into the intense fire of another torrid romance. His budding friendship with the Trees, coming out to them, leaning against them like a linden for a moment – it was all giving him a chance to catch his breath, to organize his thoughts. In short, the trip was working. Because of its great distraction, he was becoming more and more viable emotionally.

At that moment, he saw the dusky hand stuck in front of him and turned to see the teenage Gypsy murmuring to him through the diamonds in the latticework. He did not understand her soft, mournful voice, but then he did not need to. The hand, palm up, said it all. He thought of her face, what he could see of it, as a Modigliani, a hatchet face with thick brows, prominent nose, and a piteous expression somewhere between strangely calm and glum, all framed in long, dull-black hair swept over her head and hanging down the right as if wind had blown it that way. She was holding a cigar box in her other hand, and when he noticed her old, home-made, black dress, he thought of how hot it must be. Its severity also made him think of funerals, and it gave her a morbid spiritual aura as if she were, in fact, a corpse reanimated by some deep Romany spell.

"Well," Billie said, glancing at Phil, "here's your chance to hold up a Gypsy."

"What?"

"At breakfast, you said you wanted to arm yourself and hold up Gypsies."

He sat back, responding with a goofy look, lips pressed together, cheeks puffed.

"I don't want to give her money," Josh said, "but I'm not sure I can tell you why."

Phil and Billie glanced at each other apparently to see what the other thought.

"You didn't have to scrimp and save to come on this trip, did you?" Josh asked.

Billie hesitated: "Actually no."

"Neither did I."

Josh had absolutely no animosity toward the girl. Treating her badly would have only made *him* feel bad, and he was sure that tourists in general had made her feel bad enough about begging. But he was also sure that, if he gave her money, she would have to give it to someone else, and, if he did not give her money, someone would probably abuse her. Whether he did or didn't, he knew, certainly would not affect the practice one way or the other. He had wrestled this particular ethical bear last night and wound up foolishly chasing after the man, but this present bout was pretty much a draw.

"Vai via, per favore," he said gently. *Go away, please.* He held her gaze to let her know he meant it, and when he whispered, "Vai via," again, she withdrew her hand and shuffled off.

"I wonder if there's anything in our hedonism to guide us in a moment like this," Billie said.

"Well, in hedonism," Phil began, "the chief goal is pleasure or happiness. So the question is: Is giving her money good or bad in light of that goal? Would giving her money make her happy?"

"It would keep her from being beaten today," Josh said.

"But it would perpetuate a system in which she would continue to be exploited," Billie countered.

"Which would make her unhappy in the long run," Phil added. "Inversely, if everyone refused to give her money – "

"She would have to work for a living," Josh cut in.

"Like the rest of us," Billie said. However, Josh sensed her unease with the statement, something about her downcast eyes.

"Of course, the assumption here," he smiled, "is that work would make her happy."

"Better than starving," Phil concluded. "Speaking of starving, what about *your* happiness?"

"What do you mean?" Josh asked, staring at his hands folded on the table.

"You said you weren't interested in meeting anyone, you were still savoring your last meal relationship-wise. Well, a meal only lasts so long, even this one," he said, indicating the table. "Soon you'll be hungry again. And from your expression," he added, "it must've left a bad taste in your mouth."

Billie chuckled and slapped Phil's arm playfully.

"Ashes," Josh said metaphorically, "a mouthful of ashes with some embers among them."

"You should take the necessary steps toward making yourself happy," Phil said. "So the next question is: What *would* make you happy?"

"Unfortunately," Josh confessed, "a good relationship. I'm dependent on someone."

"You couldn't be happy on your own?" Billie asked.

"Well, yes," he admitted. "I could. I am. And that's enough. But I know I'd be even happier with someone else."

"A partner," Phil said. "Me too. Found mine."

Billie made a strange chicken-wing gesture which, Josh knew, meant to hold his shoulders back. So he sat up straight, sticking a green olive into his mouth.

"Nothing will come of nothing," Phil said, forking a dollop of mozzarella. He slipped it into his mouth, chewed it, and swallowed. "If you don't do something to find a partner, you won't. You're smart. You know how to solve problems. You made it through graduate school, for god's sake. Just think of this partner business as a problem to be solved."

"A bed without love is like a lake without water," Billie aphorized, winding spaghetti on her fork. "You need to start filling it up."

Josh puzzled over the metaphor, then let it go.

"Look," Phil laughed, gazing toward the street. When Josh leaned to his right, he saw three scraggly black cats slinking across the piazza. Like evil, he thought, looking for a victim.

While Phil and Billie watched the waiter shoo the cats away, Josh leaned back, rolled a slice of salami into a tube, and poked it into his mouth, reviewing his values in terms of what Phil had just said about hedonism. Tricking with Valerio, for example, he knew, would certainly feel good physically, even emotionally, and he was fairly sure it would go a long way to drive out the chill of Owen's indifference. Good is what feels good, he told himself. Bad, bad. Thus, tricking with Valerio would be good, a pleasure born from the thigh the way Dionysus was from Zeus's, the profane god in all of us that ironically saves us from the profane, the mundane, even despair. And there was certainly nothing wrong with sex for sex's sake, pleasure for the sake of pleasure. It didn't have to be justified or purified with love. The very word *trick*, though, connoted deception, and he thought that perhaps the deception lay in the idea that a trick was *all* when, in fact, it was just *part*. Sex was just one of the ropes that tied people together. The others were emotional and mental. With a partner, sex would be enhanced by love and rapport. A trick was good, he decided, but a partner was better.

After the waiter chased the cats away, he returned to the patio, asked if anyone wanted anything, and slipped the check onto the table near Phil.

When Phil reached for his wallet, Josh did as well, and when Phil said, "I'll get it," Josh smiled, "No, no, no. I can pay my share. I'm not some poor student mooching his way across Italy."

"Didn't think you were," Phil said.

Josh had heard there were three currencies in Europe: money, sex, and charm, charm meaning being engaging enough for someone to want to put you up for a couple of days. He hoped he had all three. He knew he was frugal.

When Phil took out a credit card, Josh said, "We'd better use cash. I read on line that someone on the staff copied a couple of credit-card numbers and cleaned the accounts out before the poor *turista* knew what hit 'im. Have cash?"

"Yes, thanks," Phil said, putting the card up and taking out some Euros.

"That what your last friend did?" Billie asked.

Phil looked perplexed.

"Yeah," Josh grinned. "He cleaned out my account."

"You know," Billie said, "you can't let that turn you into a cold, cynical person."

# # # # #

After lunch, because both taxis and some police cars were white, Josh hailed a police car and asked the cop to drive them to the hotel. When the waiter intervened, Josh apologized, and everyone had a good laugh. The waiter pointed down an alley and told them to stroll over to Piazza Dante, where they caught a taxi to the hotel. Phil and Billie went up to take a nap, but Josh took the taxi on to the Armani store in Piazza dei Martiri, where he bought a black silk shirt for Valerio. On the walk home, he also stopped in an *enoteca* and bought a couple of bottles of local wine.

Chapter 11: La Bersagliera

Around eight o'clock, Billie, Phil, and Josh were strolling along the waterfront on the way to La Bersagliera for dinner, Billie and Phil in front, Josh following, his backpack strapped to his shoulders. He was wearing cargo shorts and a yellow Izod, Phil slacks and a white, short-sleeved shirt, Billie a delicate, light-brown, shoulder-less dress with a silver sash tied in a flower-like bow on the left. Though beautiful, Josh thought, she seemed melancholy, Phil sympathetic, and Josh decided to respect their somber mood by not trying to engage them in conversation. Instead, he simply enjoyed the thrill of being so far from home in what was to him such an exotic place, taking in all the otherworldly details of the languid evening, a summer night in October, as he thought of it. There was no breeze, but the perfect stillness was tranquil, not stifling. He glanced at the blur of a moon projected onto vaporous black the way the sound machine by his bed threw the time, in soothing blue, on the ceiling. Then he stubbed his boot on a cobblestone, realized he was going to fall, and put his hand out, bracing himself as he dropped to a knee.

"Oh, my god, sweetie," Billie blurted, turning. "You all right?"

"Fine," Josh said, standing. He brushed his hands off. "Guess I need to watch where I'm going."

# # # # #

In a few minutes, they were going down steps and through a passage flanked with big terra-cotta pots spiked with palmettos. They came out at the marina and turned right toward a terrace under a canopy. There, the maitre d' greeted them, and as he started to lead them to a table, Josh asked for the bathroom and, on the way there, glanced at the walls of mirrors, photo displays, and plaques. He washed his hands, then joined Phil and Billie at a table in the far corner of the terrace. The table sat four or five with an end against a railing, beyond which stood a hedge of holly. On the other side were the waterfront and marina packed with yachts, a small forest of masts, again all perfectly still and stark silent in a strange, spellbound sort of way. Looming over everything was the immense outcrop of the castle, bulky and heavy as a mountain, practically all sloped walls with a few small windows near the top, everything lit up in the ghostly glow of yellow spotlights.

Billie was sitting in the corner chair, Phil the outer, facing the restaurant. Josh slipped off his backpack, clipped it to the inner chair on his side, and sat, facing the castle. Then he noticed that Billie had put her purse on the hedge.

"Give me that," he said with mock irritation.

"What?" Billie asked innocently.

"You may as well throw it in the bay." She handed him the purse, which he put in his bag, and when they turned to look at the castle, he said, "Castel dell'Ovo."

"Ovo?" she asked. "Why egg?"

"At first, I thought it was because of its shape," Josh said. "Then I read some silly myth about Virgil and an egg."

"I recognize the Italian flag," Phil said, making a vague gesture with his finger. "What are the others?"

Over the bastion nine flags hung stiff as wax in the calm.

"The purple one with gold stars is the European Union," Josh said. "I'm not familiar with the red and yellow one."

An older waiter in livery came and handed out menus and a wine list.

"A bottle of mineral water," Phil began. "What's the word? Still water."

"Non gassata," Josh said.

"Non gassata."

"And I'd like a Campari on the rocks," Josh added.

"A cocktail for the lady and gentleman?" the waiter asked. He had a hard face, grizzled moustache, and slicked-back hair, but when he smiled, a certain warmth softened him.

"Noooo," Phil drawled. "We'll have some wine in a moment."

"I give you a moment," the waiter said and turned away.

Josh unrolled his napkin, letting his silverware clink onto the white tablecloth.

"Isn't that your friend from the museum?" Billie asked.

The maitre d' was seating someone at a nearby table, and when Josh glanced at him, he recognized the sexy man at whom he had winked. Then, despite himself, he blushed all over with a kind of warm, late-adolescent polymorphous perversity, a vague, fuzzy, sexual glow. The man had apparently dressed casually for dining alfresco on a warm evening. He was wearing beige linen trousers, a short-sleeved shirt of a rich, dark-green hue, and a pair of soft, comfortable-looking moccasins. When their eyes connected, the man nodded, smiling a subdued smile, and Josh sat up straight, smiled a clearly embarrassed one, and saluted him with two fingers again, but when the connection failed to break, Josh realized, too late, that the man's eyes had already gotten inside him, looked around, and seen him for what he was, a lonely gay guy cruising him. No stare was more direct, and faced with such fierce confidence, Josh suddenly felt inept as a puppy. He relented, looking down, but when he glanced up at the man's light moustache, some prone emotion, like a compass needle, swung in the man's direction, and he thought how coarse, yet sweet it would be to kiss him.

"Josh," Billie whispered, egging him on.

Josh took a deep breath. "You American?"

The man nodded. "From Atlanta."

"Atlanta," Josh said, eyebrows flared. "So am I. What a coincidence." A yellow Gerber daisy and little fern fronds fanned from a white budvase in the middle of the table. Josh fondled the vase, then looked up. "Where in Atlanta?"

"Candler Park. And you?

"Buckhead."

"Buckhead," the man repeated as if impressed. "I've spent some time in L.A., but Atlanta's home."

"I'm Josh."

"Tyler," the man said, sitting back, half slumped, hands on the edge of the table.

Josh interpreted the man's relaxed posture as sociable, but when Josh hesitated, staring at the salt shaker, Billie leaned forward and said, "I'm Billie. This is my husband, Phil."

"Pleased to meet you," Tyler said.

"Likewise," Phil replied.

"Enjoy the museum?" Billie asked.

"Incredible. Worth the trip alone."

"Here on business or pleasure?" Phil asked.

"Pure pleasure," the man nodded. "You?"

"Same," Phil said, hands open in an *obvious* gesture. "To enjoy each other and Italy."

"How long you been here?" Josh asked, summoning his courage to glance at him again.

"Got here yesterday."

"We did too," Josh smiled, holding his gaze. "How's the jet lag?"

"Not bad. But my shoulder hurts from sleeping in some odd position on the plane. You?"

"Tired, out of sync. Hard time falling asleep last night."

Josh started to mention Phil's back problem, but when the waiter appeared at Tyler's table, Josh pulled himself together and asked, "You alone?"

"Yep," Tyler said, taking a menu.

"Like to join us?" Josh asked.

"If you don't mind."

"We certainly don't," Billie said, motioning toward the empty chair. "Make yourself at home."

Phil stood, Josh slid over and swapped silverware, and Tyler strolled over and sat next to him.

# # # # #

When they had seen each other, the young man took a shine, as Tyler thought of it, like the polished shine on a tuxedo shoe, and he himself, as if recognizing a friend, had also felt something good and pleased about him, if only an aesthetic response to his boyish looks. He was tall and slim with thick, floppy, dirty-blond hair in a sort of Dorothy Hamill wedge, only longer on top. His face was peachy smooth, as if he didn't have to shave, his cheeks rosy, his moist mouth pink as a child's. But if his face said boy, even sly, slutty boy, Tyler thought, his legs said man: legs with big calves in a sheath of fine, golden hair, all tapering to the big, yellow socks rolled around his ankles and a pair of leather hiking boots. And now he was sitting next to him, across from a man who gestured a lot and a woman whose mind always seemed in overdrive.

When Josh's Campari came with a slice of orange, Tyler was so taken with its jewel-like red he ordered one.

"Let's try this Conegliano prosecco," Phil said.

"Very good," the waiter said, setting the bottle of water on the table.

"We'll see how that goes." As the waiter turned away, Phil added, "Some bread, please."

"Ha Lei aceto basalmico?" Josh asked. *Balsamic vinegar?*

"Si, naturalmente," the waiter replied.

"E pepe, per favore." *And pepper.*

Phil assumed the duty of pouring everyone water.

"I'm not that hungry," Tyler said, "but I know I need to eat something."

"What about you?" Billie asked Josh with a glint in her eye. "Been a long time since *lunch*," she stressed. "Ready for *dinner*?"

Josh chuckled, "Think so."

Tyler knew they were speaking in code and had a good idea how to break it.

"What about splitting an insalata caprese?" Josh asked Tyler. "I'm afraid if I eat a whole one, I'll be too full."

Tyler faced Josh. "OK." Up close, Tyler could see that his eyes were pale green and, at the moment, washed out as if he were, in fact, jet lagged.

"Let's split one, too," Billie suggested to Phil.

The waiter returned with a basket of bread, bottles of oil and vinegar, and a pepper mill. He poured some oil on a plate, then took orders. Besides the salads, Phil ordered grilled sea bass, Billie risotto alla pescatore, and Josh spaghetti amatriciana. Tyler ordered penne arrabiata simply because he liked the name. He said he had a thing for words. When the waiter left, Phil took on hosting duties again, spotting the oil with vinegar and dusting it with pepper. To Tyler, the sienna globs of vinegar looked like giant amoeba slowly undergoing mitosis. Then everyone started sopping them up with bread and eating them.

"So?" Tyler began, wiping his mouth on the back of his hand. "What brings you guys to Naples?"

"Culture, food, fun," Billie lilted.

A dusky wine steward with tousled hair appeared with Tyler's Campari and a wine bucket with a bottle of prosecco. He set the Campari on the table, then showed Phil the bottle, but when he turned to uncork it, Tyler could not help noticing his firm, round buttocks. He sensed something, and when he glanced at Josh, Josh had struck a pensive pose, a finger to his lip, as if thinking. He stared at Tyler, glanced at the steward's butt, and stared at Tyler again, perhaps to let him know, Tyler thought, he knew what he was thinking. The cork popped, and the steward turned to pour some prosecco, but when he offered it to Phil, Phil made a brushing-aside gesture.

"It's fine," he shrugged.

The steward filled the glass about half full, and the wine fizzed up nearly to the brim, then fizzled down. Then the steward poured some more and handed it to Billie.

After a sip, she said, "My way of getting in touch with myself at night."

When Phil took his glass, he said, "*My* way of getting in touch with yourself at night."

Tyler and Josh laughed.

"Well, you're right about that," Billie said. "A glass of wine can pique my interest in letting you get in touch with myself at night."

When the steward gestured as if to pour Tyler, then Josh a glass, they shook their heads, and he wedged the bottle in the bucket. When he leaned over the table to collect the extra glasses, Tyler noticed his smooth, dark hands, traded secret glances with Josh, and smirked.

"What about you, Josh?" Billie asked. "Gotten in touch with yourself lately?"

"Well, I tried last night," he admitted, "but then I wasn't drinking."

"Oh, ho," Tyler laughed.

"And you, Tyler?" Phil asked, joining the game. "Gotten in touch with yourself lately?"

"Assuming I wasn't in touch."

"Touché."

"You guys been smoking?" Tyler asked.

"Like to?" Josh asked, blinking.

"Uh," Tyler hesitated, nonplussed. "I'm a little leery of smoking pot in a foreign country."

"You smoke pot?" Billie asked, critical.

"I'm not a pothead," Josh said, hands up in a stop gesture. "Some people have a drink to relax. I have a puff."

"Pressures of graduate school," Phil said seriously.

"I'm not a drug-crazed fiend," Josh swore. "Besides, so far no one's actually put me in charge of building anything. You don't have to worry about a house falling on you anytime soon."

"What are you talking about?" Tyler asked.

"Josh just got his Ph.D. in architecture."

"Great," Tyler said, patting Josh's thigh. "Congratulations."

"Thanks," Josh said, biting his lip. He squinted at him as if his eyes were out of focus, then opened them wide and smiled.

"You know," Tyler said, facing Phil and Billie, "I've always heard that wine is a way of getting in touch with nature. You know, the mystical-unity thing. But, as you said, the only nature I've gotten in touch with is my own."

"Well," Billie conceded, "getting in touch with one's own nature is a form of getting in touch with nature in general. We're certainly still part of it, refined out of it as much as we are."

They heard someone playing the Italian cliché "O sole mio" on an accordion and turned to see a pretty young boy strolling along the waterfront, squeezing and stretching the instrument. As he approached, a man in a suit at another table leaned over the railing, tucked a bill into the boy's pants pocket, and whispered something into his ear. When the man sat, the boy serenaded his table with "Core 'ngrato."

"I notice you're not wearing a wedding band," Billie said to Tyler.

Phil laughed a jerky hiccup of a laugh, then glanced at Billie curiously.

"No," Tyler mused.

"Why's a smart, personable man like you letting all those good looks go to waste?"

"Well, Billie," he grinned, "your question's based on a couple of false assumptions. One, that I am, in fact – How shall I put it?"

"Letting your good looks go to waste," Phil smiled, elbow on table, palm up.

"Right," Tyler said, sipping Campari.

"And, two," Josh said, glancing at Tyler for confirmation, "that you have to be married to enjoy yourself."

"Bitter," Tyler said to Josh, meaning the drink, "but good. I like it."

"You seem like the marrying kind," Billie insisted.

"Oh?"

"Settled, rational, nice."

"Thank you," Tyler said genuinely. "I *was* married."

"Divorced," Billie said.

"About your age," Tyler said, glancing at Josh.

"Must've married young," Phil remarked.

"Knew I was right about you," Billie claimed.

"Well, I did start out pretty romantic."

"And now you're cynical," she said.

"Wouldn't say cynical," he said. "More like realistic."

"What happened?" she asked.

"Billie!" Phil scolded her.

"I don't mind," Tyler said. He thought for a while. "The whole thing turned into a kind of brutal boxing match. It wasn't as if we wanted just to beat each other. It was as if we wanted to beat each other to death. Sorry. Now you're going to think I'm Stanley Kawolski."

"Not at all," Billie said. "We appreciate your honesty."

"And I appreciate your appreciating it," he quipped. "In fact," he added, almost to himself, "I appreciate everything."

"Children?" Phil asked.

"'Fraid so," Tyler confessed. "Two daughters." Parricides, he thought, flashing back to *Lear*.

Josh's response was to lean back, thumbs in pocket, elbows at his sides, and take a good look at him.

"Surprised?" Tyler asked.

"Not at all," Josh said, shaking his head, "but – what did you mean by ''Fraid so'?"

"Familiar with King Lear's daughters Goneril and Regan?"

"'Tigers, not daughters,'" Phil quoted the play. "So, she poisoned them against you."

"I expect it's left you with a pretty dim view of women," Billie concluded.

"Funny you should say that," Tyler smiled, thinking of another line from *Lear*: "The dark and vicious place where thee he got / Cost him his eyes," referring to Edgar's father, Gloucester, and his evil brother, Edmund.

"Why?" Billie asked.

"Well, actually I don't know you well enough to tell you," Tyler chuckled. "I was thinking of a line from *Lear*, and Shakespeare can be pretty raunchy."

"Pish," Billie said with a dismissive wave. "You can say anything you want around us, especially Shakespeare."

"Suffice it to say," he said, "every woman I've slept with has tried to kill me."

"Literally?" Phil asked.

"In fact, I've had such bad luck with women," he joked, "maybe I should try men."

"If you're going to try men," Josh said, leaning forward, forearms on the table, "try me."

Tyler laughed a small cough of a laugh, then glanced at everyone. Phil looked unfazed, Billie as if she were processing the remark as quickly as she could, Josh as if he'd thrown out the line just to see if he would bite.

"Try you?" Tyler scoffed.

"Yeah," Josh said. "I could show you a good time."

"Sorry," Tyler said, composing himself. "That wasn't a hint."

"What better place to try something new?" Billie joked. "New town, new language, new sexual orientation. "

"Let's say you're in prison," Josh said, "and you've lucked out with a cute cellmate."

Josh tilted toward him slowly as if being pulled by gravity so that their shoulders were almost touching.

"Straight men practice homosexuality in prison," Billie claimed, blasé.

"A compatible couple could be happy for years," Phil stated, hands open.

"Well," Tyler confessed, "I *am* a writer."

"Really?" Billie said. "A writer always needs to broaden his – " she paused, "his experience and understanding, right?"

"Josh," Tyler said politely, "I would like to know you better. You might make a good character in a novel sometime. All of you. But, at this point in life, I'm just looking for someone I can trust."

"You can trust me," Josh claimed, sitting back.

"For all I know," Tyler laughed, "you three could be perfidious grifters."

"For all we know, you could be the god of wine," Billie said.

"Exactly."

Tyler thought of the first time a male had touched him sexually, a boy in a swimming pool in Arkansas. Tyler, ten, was hugging the side of the pool with an arm on the coping, and the boy had swum up to him underwater, stuck his hand up a leg of Tyler's swimming trunks, and groped him. The innocent fumbling around was the first chink in the eventual crack and break with bourgeois morality, his first inkling that middle-class values were a lie. What he had been told was bad felt good.

In his hippie, free-love days, he had been bi "in practice," engaging in a few purely sexual adventures for the rebellious, anti-Puritanical hell of it, awkward, confused three-ways and four-ways, even sophomoric orgies of various exotic combinations. In college, he had a friend, Brent, with whom he indulged in a little emotional experimentation, a fun, yet tender learning experience, as Tyler thought of it, which Brent himself ended when he wound up obsessed with him and miserable.

Till then, Tyler considered himself only an amateur libertine at best. A line from Pasolini's *Salò*, however, helped clarify the mysterious blur of his waxing sexuality. Four sadists in the film forced their male and female captives to bend over. Then they examined their anuses, which one sadist said were "physically interchangeable." When it came to intercourse, Tyler realized, the mechanism was pretty much the same, a piston in a cylinder, no matter whose. Either way, it worked. It was not so much that he was bi by nature, he thought, but that through Brent and others he had simply learned the "the ins and outs," so to speak, of that kind of fun and thus felt comfortable in bed with just about anyone he was attracted to, anyone, that is, who passed a certain litmus test of body, heart, and mind. In other words, Tyler, by chance, had somehow become as blind to the sex of his partners as his penis was. The spiritual benefit, as he thought of it, was that he was attracted to the person, not the body. Did it really matter what body the person just happened to come dressed in? With women, he knew to bump the clitoris, with men the prostate to get them off, the goal being to please his partner as well as himself. But then, in his own particular experience, men had been much more enthusiastic and energetic about it, assuming whatever contortionist position he wanted, begging him to fuck them as vigorously as he could, in short, going to a lot more trouble to make sure they enjoyed themselves.

Of course, close on the heels of free love came free thinking. He already valued reason over authority, especially religious authority, and over the years his naïve boyhood insight into bourgeois hypocrisy grew into his own measured, if simple, adult form of Epicureanism based on the pursuit of pleasure and the avoidance of pain. To him, right and wrong were as obvious as pleasure and pain, and that sentence – that "right and wrong were as obvious as pleasure and pain" – was all the philosophy he needed. As far as he was concerned, it was a principle clear enough to guide him through any situation, including the present one. In that light, he asked himself, what were the pros and cons?

On the plus side, he was already fond of Josh because of his good looks, charm, and intelligence. Tyler liked having good-looking people around him because, in general, it was just more pleasant. Not that he couldn't like someone not blessed with a perfectly symmetrical face. Second, it was also just more pleasant to be surrounded by kind and considerate people, people who valued the moment, the fun in life. And it took smart people to realize the hard truth that life was short and shouldn't be wasted on hate and revenge, just plain unpleasantness in general.

The down side was the great unknown. Besides, how could he possibly open up to anyone after the calculated deceptions he'd trumped and absolute horror he'd faced? What did he have to offer anyone except poisonous thorns, permanent scars? His dumb heart had certainly snarled up, a tight knot no one could pick, at least not any time soon. The best tack, he decided, was simply to get to know Josh better.

"I'm not much on wandering troubadours," Billie said, twirling her wine glass, "but the kid with the accordion's good. What a lovely melody."

The boy was playing "Carmela" as if he were older and wiser for failed love. Then out of the dark, an old man with a checked head wrap and gray stubble appeared over the hedge to Billie's right, peddling roses.

He handed one to Phil, but when he started to hand Phil another, Phil said, "No, no, no, grazie. One's enough to remind Billie I love her, not that she needs reminding. Quanto?"

When the man shrugged, Phil fished out a five and gave it to him. Then the man started to hand Josh a rose, indicating that it was for Tyler.

"Grazie," Josh said, making a stop gesture, "ma l'uomo bello non é mia ancora." *The handsome man isn't mine yet.*

"Prego," the man said, backing off and nodding obsequiously.

Tyler caught the words *bello* and *mio*, but asked, "Which translates as?"

"I told him we weren't a couple," Josh smiled coyly.

Tyler looked at him curiously, then faced Phil and Billie. Billie smelled the rose, brushing it gently back and forth across her nose, then lay it on the table.

"Speaking of couples," Tyler began, "where did you two meet?"

"At Cranbrook," Phil said.

"Cranbrook?"

"The art school," Phil explained. "Billie actually won the Outstanding Student Award."

"Gee, golly, guys," she joked.

Then the salads arrived, two oval platters with tomatoes, mozzarella, and basil glistening in golden oil and sprinkled with pepper. The waiter set four saucers on the table, but everyone decided just to slide the platters between them and eat from each end toward the middle.

"Like in *101 Dalmatians*," Josh joked.

"You mean *Lady and the Tramp*," Phil corrected him.

"Oh, yeah," Josh chuckled

"Win any student awards?" Tyler asked him, cutting up some salad.

"No," Josh confessed, shaking his head. "What about you?"

"Me?"

"You said you were a writer."

"Writing awards or student awards?"

"Either."

Tyler stabbed some basil, tomato, and cheese on his fork. "Actually, I have. I won the Caffee Medal at LSU, and recently, thank god, the Sparky Award, sort of a breakthrough."

"Sparky?" Josh asked.

"Doesn't sound like much," Tyler said, lifting the fork. "Heard of Slamdance?"

"Slamdance? No."

"The Sparky is the Grand Prize Winner for Best Horror Screenplay at the Slamdance Film Festival."

He stuffed the food into his mouth.

"Wow," Billie said.

"We're impressed," Phil added.

"Horror, huh," Josh said, absently touching the cut on his chest. "You should sign the guestbook."

"Guestbook?" Tyler asked, chewing. The cheese was creamy, the tomato sweet, the basil crisp.

"Yeah, they have a guestbook here. All sorts of famous people have signed it."

"But I'm not famous."

"Yes, you are," Josh insisted.

"Tyler I nothing am," he said, paraphrasing Edgar in *Lear*. "What about you?" he asked Billie and Phil, changing the subject. "When did you know you were going to make a go of it as artists?"

"Well, we'd been teaching and selling a painting or two out of a gallery where we live, L'Arte per L'Arte."

"Which is where?" Tyler asked.

"Full Moon Bay," Phil said, pointing up for emphasis, "south of San Francisco."

"Then we both got selected for some regional museums," Billie added. "Sort of an art act, a husband-and-wife duo."

"We both have commissions we need to finish when we get back," Phil reminded her.

"It's nice that we all have something in common," Tyler commented.

"L'arte dell'artista," Josh said, "e l'arte dello scrittore. The art of the artist and the art of the writer."

"Actually," Tyler said, "they're similar in that I have to paint pictures that readers can see in their minds."

"And architecture is a blend of art and science," Josh added.

"Well, it's obvious that we're kindred spirits," Phil remarked. "Just look at our shirts. Mine's burnt umber, let's say. Tyler's, I believe, Verde Veronese. Billie's dress ochre. Josh's yellow's as bright – "

"As a sunny meadow," Josh joked, touching Tyler's knee with his.

Tyler gave him a flirty smile, but crossed his ankles, breaking contact.

"Who wears colors like these?" Phil asked.

"If I may ask," Tyler said amiably, "when did you know your son was going to turn out so well?"

"Our son?" Billie asked, forehead crimped. Suddenly, she was somewhere else.

"Yeah," Tyler said, confused. "I have nothing but the greatest respect for people who can do well academically *and* socially. Most graduate types are nerds."

Phil studied Billie with a look of concern.

"Josh isn't our son," he said, smiling at Josh affectionately.

"Not technically," Billie added, coming back.

"Adopted," Josh joked. "No. We just happened to be staying at the same hotel."

"Oh," Tyler said. "You seem so – comfortable with each other."

All at once, Tyler saw them as three stones: two piers and a lintel. They were holding Josh up somehow.

"Well," Billie began, "even though we haven't known him very long, he already feels like family to us, a new-found son. If he moved in tomorrow, I'm sure we'd all feel perfectly at home."

"An adoptive family is your real family if there's that emotional connection, right," Tyler reasoned. He reached into his shirt, cricked his neck, and massaged his left shoulder absently. "More than a biological family who doesn't have the connection. Blood ties don't seem to count for much, if anything. I mean, I was adopted, never knew my real father, and when I grew up and looked up my real mother, it was a terrible mistake. I didn't want anything to do with her. And my own family," he went on, "well, I was never much good to them or them to me for that matter. If family is ever going to mean anything to me, I'm going to have to redefine it."

"Redefine it as love or common convictions," Billie agreed, "something along those lines. Family is those people with whom we have a good time, and I'm having a pretty good time right now."

"We have a lot to be grateful for," Phil agreed, "and we'll have even more when the entrée arrives."

"I'm just grateful to be alive," Tyler said. "Anywhere."

"That include Pompeii?" Billie asked.

Chapter 12: A Bottle of Coda di Volpe

After dinner, everyone shuffled up the steps to Via Partenope, where a handful of macho taxi drivers were idling by cabs across the street.

"Everyone like to hang out on my balcony for a while?" Josh asked. "I have some wine on ice, a bottle of Coda di Volpe."

"Whatever that means," Billie said.

"Whatever it means," Phil joked, "I'm sure you'll drink it."

"I really should be getting back," Tyler objected. "My hotel's in the Vomero, and I think the funicular quits running at ten."

Actually, he was not worried about the funicular. He had let concern about logistics spoil trips. This time he was going to relax. There were always cabs.

"Oh, come on," Billie insisted. "The night is young, and so are you. We'll chaperone you if you think you need it."

"Thank you," he said. "I can handle him."

"And he can handle you," Billie replied.

Phil looked puzzled.

# # # # #

So around eleven, they found themselves on Josh's balcony, sipping wine, chatting drowsily, and occasionally taking in the glittering panorama. Billie and Phil were sitting, Tyler standing near Phil at one end of the balcony, Josh near Billie at the other. The balcony was enclosed by a concrete wall about a yard high with a contemporary, wrought-iron railing running along the top, and Josh was leaning over it, gazing across the glimmering bay. On the far shore, small bubbles of headlights appeared and popped as they rounded a curve. High above, the two black cones of the crater were barely visible against a charcoal sky.

"This may as well be a city on another planet," Josh said. "Still can't believe I'm here."

"Careful there, sweetie," Billie said. "We're about as high as our house in California."

Josh thought it curious that she mentioned that fact again. "Six floors?" he asked.

"About."

"A cliff house," Phil explained, glancing at Tyler.

They discussed whether the hotel were earthquake-proof and how they would try to escape, if they could. When Tyler asked Josh his opinion, Josh said the building looked pretty sturdy. Then they talked about the wine. Josh had iced it in the basin in the bathroom but served it in plastic cups. All he could tell was that it was light and dry, but according to the Trees, it had a mellow, floral taste with a hint of lemongrass. Phil asked Tyler the name of his screenplay, *The Crystal Ball*, and when he asked about it, Tyler said that it was about how a woman lost power over her life, then regained it and that it was more than just cheap thrills, the reason, he claimed, why it had become a cult hit. He also explained that, though he had written Kim, the protagonist, as a heroine, a lot of women saw her only as a victim and accused him of misogyny. When Billie and Phil got up to go, she asked Tyler if he would accompany them to Pompeii tomorrow, and he agreed. He said he was planning on going and would meet them at the bus station on the waterfront at nine in the morning.

Josh set his glass on a nightstand and saw them out, and when he turned toward the room, Tyler was standing, glass in hand, his back against the balcony doorjamb. The room had a king-sized bed, and when Josh returned, he picked up his glass, sat on the bed, and glanced at Tyler.

"They're fun," Tyler smiled subtly. "I like them."

"Me too," Josh said. "Though I can't quite figure out exactly why Billie's taken such an interest in me."

Tyler set his glass down, unbuttoned the top button on his shirt, and reached inside to rub his left shoulder.

"Sore?" Josh asked.

"Yeah."

"Just the thing."

Josh set his glass down and opened the nightstand drawer, revealing an ashtray with a joint and yellow Bic lighter.

"Oh, my god," Tyler laughed. "You do have pot."

"Muscle relaxant," Josh said, picking up the joint and lighter. "Good for your shoulder."

"You didn't smuggle that in, did you?"

"No."

"Where'd you get it?"

"A hustler at the Galleria," Josh said, lighting up.

"You little devil."

When Josh puffed on it, Tyler glanced at the ceiling, apparently checking for a smoke alarm, and when Joshed offered it to him, he pinched it between his fingers and toked. They held the smoke for a moment, then, at the same time, blew it out the door.

"Shit," Tyler laughed, passing the joint. "I'm going to wind up in an Italian jail for the next twenty years."

"No, you're not," Josh said, putting away the lighter. "If you do, at least you'll have plenty to write about."

"I'll never get back to the hotel," Tyler said more to himself.

"Look at the size of this bed," Josh nodded. "Big as a soccer field."

"I don't know," Tyler scoffed.

"Comfortable around gays?"

"I have some very good gay friends."

"Ever slept with them? I mean, platonically."

"Actually, I have."

"It's settled," Josh said, suppressing a smile.

They had two hits. Then Josh tamped out the joint in the ashtray and shut the drawer. He did not want to risk smoking more until he knew how strong it was.

"To be perfectly honest," Tyler admitted, "I had my share of strange bedfellows, as Shakespeare says, in my wild, free-love days."

"Any port in a storm," Josh said.

"Definitely not," Tyler stressed. "I'm very careful where I dock my boat."

"How long did you dock with your wife?"

"Five years."

"What happened?"

"Thought I loved her," Tyler confessed, picking up his glass. "I married her because she was pregnant, but thought I loved her. I was always fond of her, even after the divorce. We were young and foolish, yes, but...." He trailed off. "If you knock someone up, guess you should support the kid, not marry the mother. Nothing good came from marrying under duress."

"Duress?"

"She was Catholic. I was Baptist. So we compromised with an Episcopal wedding, and the priest who counseled us actually asked me if I were marrying under duress. If I had said yes, of course, he wouldn't have married us."

"And she, as Phil said, poisoned your children against you?"

Tyler licked his lip, apparently thinking, then looked at him. "Giving them anything, a textbook, eyeglasses, or just basic affection, was like giving gifts to the bones in the death cults around here. I marvel what kin me and my daughters were, to paraphrase the Fool in *Lear*. If kinship were based on emotions, I had no daughters."

"You're using the past tense," Josh pointed out.

"Yes," Tyler said, sipping wine. "My ex and younger daughter died in a – in a boating accident."

"Boating accident?" Josh asked. "Really?" Then he put his hand up in a stop gesture. "Sorry. This is obviously not where I wanted the conversation to go."

Tyler shook his head apparently at the futility of it all. "And you?" he asked. "Why's a smart lad like you so available and glum?"

"My ex went back to his wife and child," Josh explained. "Need I say more?"

"You can if you want to."

A quiet euphoria was spreading through Josh's body, making him all loose and limber.

"Well, you can argue that he didn't intend to use me, but that's what he did."

"Angry?"

"Maybe I should've been," Josh mused. "Could've gotten even by telling his wife."

"Why didn't you?"

"I wanted him too much to be angry with him, was even willing to work out some arrangement. Never got the chance."

"What?" Tyler laughed. "Be his mistress? That how you see yourself, second best?"

"Guess I was just that lonely."

"And when you feel lonely," Tyler asked, staring into the night, "what does that feel like? Let's say you're the writer, not me, and you have to come up with an image for it."

"Well, love and affection are warm," Josh said, picking up his glass, "so I guess the opposite is cold. Loneliness is winter. I'm a guy in heavy black clothes in the middle of a snowfield."

"Excellent," Tyler said, facing him. "You got it. You know how to write."

"What about you?" Josh asked, sipping wine.

"What?"

"What's your image for it?"

"Me. Let's see. I'm a guy in slacks and a short-sleeved shirt on a hotel balcony on a hot night."

"Yesterday, I felt even more isolated than I usually do. You know, stranger in a strange land. Then I took up with Phil and Billie, and now I've met you. You're a bit of a surprise."

"You never know what's coming, do you?"

"You're right," Josh agreed. "Life's one big blind corner."

"Let's hope there's no unavoidable collision around it."

Josh thought for a second, then toasted, "Here's to avoidable collisions."

They tapped glasses and stared at each other, Tyler's eyes red, yet piercing, his lids droopy. Then Tyler's stare softened to a sleepy smile.

"What an angelic face," he remarked.

"An angel up to no good."

"I'm sure."

Tyler set his glass down, reached inside his shirt, and groaned. When he rubbed his shoulder again, Josh set his glass down and slid back on the bed.

"Come here," he said, patting the bed between his legs.

"What?"

"How 'bout a massage?"

"Massage, huh," Tyler smirked.

"Your shoulder, not your cock. Face the door."

"I know what you're up to," Tyler claimed.

"What?"

"Something about a fly caught in a web," Tyler joked, "in this case a linen fly."

"You're too smart a soldier to be captured against your will."

"Really?"

"Really."

Tyler slouched against the jamb and seemed to be considering the proposition.

"You'd just hate me in the morning," he said, triste. "Or yourself."

"Don't think so." Josh yawned. "Sorry," he said, rubbing his eyes. "Look," he joked. "I'm not strong enough to rape you. If I try anything, just stand up." If Tyler were going to surrender to anyone, Josh thought, why not him, someone with, if not good intentions, at least benign ones, an opponent with a stronger complaisant power? "Let me untie that knot in your neck. OK?"

"Si, Capitano."

Tyler sat on the bed with his back to Josh, and Josh gingerly placed his hands on Tyler's shirt and began massaging his shoulders slowly, yet firmly. Through the supple cotton, Tyler's trapezius muscles felt strong, yet light as nylon ropes.

"Hurts so good," Tyler said, arching his back.

Josh gazed at Tyler's soft, bristly hair, secretly nosing its clean, shampoo scent laced with the pleasant musk of a masculine body slightly moist and redolent of sex from the sultry night. Tyler's own particular civet was nothing short of a pleasant balm to Josh, a healthy, rousing, balsam smell that set off some wonderfully carnal chemical reaction deep in his groin.

105

"There," Tyler whispered, meaning a spot in his neck. "Yeah, that's it."

Josh thumbed the spot, then reached around and began unbuttoning Tyler's shirt.

"Better without it," Josh stated, matter of fact.

"Uh, huh," Tyler said, glancing over his shoulder.

"As I said – " Josh began.

"Just stand up."

Josh gently pulled the front of Tyler's shirt from his pants, unbuttoned the last couple of buttons, and carefully drew the shirt down Tyler's shoulders and below his elbows. When Tyler freed his arms, Josh pulled the shirt out of the back of Tyler's pants and laid it aside.

Then he went back to the massage, focusing on his shoulders again, kneading the tendons in his neck like dough. Then he branched out to his deltoids, triceps, the latissimus dorsi, running his thumbs up and down Tyler's spine, digging them deep into his lower back, treating him to the kind of hard, effective rubdown he himself would have enjoyed, a restrained frottage of sorts. And all the time he was massaging him, he could not believe his good luck, the fact that he had the sensuous feast of this good-looking man all to himself and was enjoying it. Tyler's muscles were well defined not so much because he was muscular, Josh thought, but lean and muscular. He didn't know if he worked out, but there was no fat on him. He could see the details of his musculature flexing every time he moved, his back all flushed and radiant from the workout.

If Josh's fingers could taste, Tyler's taut skin was honey to them, lighting Josh up, through touch, with a good, rosy feeling. All he knew was that to touch the man made him feel privileged and good. So the massage was good for him as well, a great satisfaction. His body went all compliant and willowy, opening up to him in some deep, warm, sentient way. He got an erection, and a slow-burning, sensual fire began playing lightly over his skin. And then he could not help himself: he was so drawn to him he slipped his hands under Tyler's arms and began firmly massaging his pecs.

"Important to you?" Tyler asked.

"What?"

"You know what."

"Your pecs like attention too, right?" Josh said, resting his forehead on Tyler's back.

Tyler laughed a light laugh: "If it makes you happy."

Then they just sat there, coupled, relaxed, Josh's hands squeezing and pressing Tyler's pecs, Tyler's chest rising and falling in audible rounds of calm, yet deeper breaths. But what had started out as a firm massage was now gradually evolving into a delicate, tentative touching. He cupped Tyler's pec with his right hand, his left lying casually on his groin. He barely touched the nipple, teased it with the tip of his index finger until it stood up stiff. When Tyler sighed and tilted his head back, Josh hugged him, held his throat, felt Tyler's light, closely cropped beard, the rasp on his palm filling him with a subtle, yet exquisite forepleasure.

Tyler slipped out of one of his moccasins, toe to heel. "Scoot back," he said, indicating the headboard.

Josh did, placing a boot on the bed, but when Tyler started to lean back against him, Josh said, "Wait a second," and flipped his Izod behind his head. "Now."

Josh pulled him toward him so that they wound up propped against the wall with Tyler's head reclining on Josh's shoulder, Tyler clasped in his arms like a Venus Flytrap. Tyler draped his legs over Josh's comfortably as if offering himself, and Josh nuzzled Tyler's neck and began running his fingers lightly over Tyler's pecs, abs, and groin.

"What's that I feel?" Tyler asked.

"What?" Josh smiled. "My cock?"

"No," Tyler laughed. "On your chest."

Josh was in such an intense state of arousal that even Tyler's voice was now seductive and mellifluous.

"Band-Aid," he said, playing with the fuzz below Tyler's navel. "Slight cut. Tell you about it later." He slipped his fingers under the waistband of Tyler's slacks, grazing his pubic hair. "Vorrei far piacere a te," he whispered amorously, one meaning of which was *I would like to please you.*

"I have a pretty good idea what that means," Tyler said, especially the 'piacere' part."

When Josh saw that he was, in fact, pleasing him, he unbuckled Tyler's belt, unbuttoned his pants, and carefully unzipped them, and as he slowly pulled the fly apart, Tyler's erection popped up, wrapped in the soft cotton of his loose, thigh-length underwear. Josh unbuttoned the underwear, and when he took out Tyler's cock, the shaft was flushed with pinks and lavenders with veins like vines twined around it, the swollen head plum-colored and bell-shaped. A gooey tear was oozing from the slit.

"Same as if you were doing it," Josh said, manipulating it, "only feels better. More fun."

As they lay there, Tyler's back to Josh's chest, hot, moist skin to skin, Josh was so hypersensitive that the almost imperceptible motion just from jerking him was creating almost enough friction to bring Josh off.

"Feels good," Tyler said.

"Is good."

"What's the word for this?"

"In Italian?" Josh asked. "*Sega*. Hand job. There's also the expression *manare l'uccello*, to yank the bird."

"Manare l'uccello," Tyler murmured.

Josh took Tyler's earlobe between his lips and, as he stroked him with his right hand, caressed his chest with his left. He fondled his scrotum through the shorts, and when he nudged the right side of it, he could feel the testicle drawn tight against his crotch and knew he was close. The more excited Tyler became, the more he straightened out, and when Josh felt he was about to come, he took more of his ear into his mouth and tongued the notch behind it. Then Tyler, hips thrust up, straightened out completely, shooting a big, baroque pearl of semen onto his chest, followed by several long, thick strings of it. Then he collapsed against Josh, gasping as if fighting for air.

"You sly fox," Tyler panted, wiping the sweat off his lip.

"Me?" Josh joked, milking him.

He ran the index finger of his left hand up Tyler's urethra till it met the place where his right index finger took over, running up the rest of it till the last gob of semen gushed out, dripping onto his groin.

"Thanks," Tyler said. "I needed that."

"I could tell."

"Could you?"

"Hang around," Josh said. "More to come."

"I'm exhausted. Besides, I'm old enough to be your father."

"No, you're not," Josh replied. "Older brother maybe."

"Much older, ten years."

"So what?"

Tyler tried to glance at him and snorted a laugh. Then they just lay there, head to head, slumped against the wall, Tyler's genitals cradled in Josh's hands, a cozy, modern pieta of sorts, their left legs over the side of the bed, their right stretched out on the covers. Tyler's hands lay by Josh's thighs in an open, receptive, almost sacred gesture, and from the peaceful rise and fall of Tyler's chest, Josh could tell that he had dozed off. He stared at the photo of a snow-capped Vesuvius on the far wall, closed his eyes, and rested for a moment, a patch of Tyler's hair between his lips, his musk in his nose. The occasional traffic on Via Colombo ebbed and flowed with a soothing, lethargic, ocean-like sibilance, but when an ambulance came screaming wildly down the street, he realized he needed to get up and prepare them for sleep.

When he made Tyler sit up, Tyler slurred, "I should go."

"No way," Josh said, getting up. "I'll take care of things, then turn off the lights."

He took Tyler's hands, pulled him to a standing position, and undressed him. Then he turned down the covers.

"Lie down," he said, trying to make him sit.

Tyler resisted, grabbing Josh's arms, but when Josh persisted, staring him down, he sat.

"Go to sleep," Josh said, pushing gently against his shoulders.

Tyler reclined, dragging an arm across his eyes, and Josh gazed at him, taking in all the tight, tan, animal details of him head to foot. When he was satisfied that he was thoroughly familiar with him, or as familiar as he could be at the moment, he covered him to his waist, folded his clothes neatly, and set them on a chair, placing the moccasins underneath. Then he closed and locked the sliding glass door, lowered the metal shutters, and drew the curtain, all as quietly as possible. Next, he turned off all the lights except the small lamp on the nightstand on his side of the bed. He went into the bathroom, turned on the light, and changed his Band-Aid. On the way out, he picked up a hand towel and turned off the light.

The milky juice on Tyler's chest had turned to shiny smears, and when Josh dabbed them softly, Tyler unconsciously lay his hand on Josh's. Josh took it, placed it carefully on Tyler's chest, and went around to his side of the bed. There, he lay the towel on the nightstand, undressed, and quietly got into bed, slipping a foot under the covers. He lay on his side with his leg cocked and began jerking off, focusing on Tyler's arms, facial hair, his sublime smile in repose. When he thought of kissing him, he came, shooting onto the sheet, in the silence, with an audible plop. After he squeezed out the last drop, he wiped the sheet with the towel, lay it on the nightstand, and turned off the lamp. He knew he wouldn't need Ambien nor his sound machine. The room was as black and quiet as a tomb.

Chapter 13: The Silver Tree

About thirty minutes after Josh fell asleep, he dropped into a dream about a bright day in post-war Naples. At first, the sun, in eclipse, was a big engagement ring, but when it peaked around the moon, the diamond lit up, blanching the sky to a blank page. Then the haze ignited, and the gulls, like glass figures, faded into glare.

Along Via Partenope, a short, concrete wall separated the promenade from the harbor, but at one point, in a dry, grassy area, stood a silver olive tree with graceful branches and thousands of tinfoil leaves. In the bright light, the glittering leaves were a galaxy of tiny atomic explosions. Occasionally, pieces of foil would materialize from the air, flutter to the tree as if drawn to it, and attach themselves to the twigs like filings.

The wall along the promenade was topped with a scrolled, wrought-iron railing like the one on the balcony at the hotel, and Josh was a hungry *snaguzzo*, a discarded boy, leaning on it, taking in the scene. He was wearing old leather sandals and a ragged pair of green boxer shorts with a leaf pattern, and the warm, capricious wind lapping his body reassured him somehow, made him feel alive and erogenous, at home in himself.

He heard a vehicle pulling up and turned to see Tyler parking a jeep near the tree. He was a soldier in olive drab with a helmet, and when he turned off the jeep, he took off the helmet, set it on the passenger seat, and stretched, arching his back as if he had been driving for a long time. Then he just sat there, a hand on the wheel, staring at Josh. In the dream, Tyler, like Sky, Josh's father, was distinguished looking with a creased forehead and receding hairline made up for in a way by shoulder-length hair in back.

When Josh approached, Tyler stepped from the jeep, stuck out his hand, and said, "Hi. How are you?"

When they shook hands, Josh massaged Tyler's palm with his middle finger in a secret sexual message.

"Fine," Josh said. "And you?"

"Great," Tyler said, staring curiously. "I do that?" he asked, meaning the cut on Josh's chest.

Sometimes Sky would point at Josh when referring to him or just emphasizing a point as if cuing an instrument in an orchestra, and there was something about the way Tyler pointed toward the cut that reminded him of the mannerism.

"Not yet," Josh said.

When Tyler ran his finger across Josh's chest beneath the cut, his touch felt like the hot, rough lick of cat's tongue.

"Not yet, huh?" Tyler said sardonically.

When the bright tree stirred in a breeze, wavering, stroboscopic spangles of light played over the two like the slow, revolving stars of a disco ball. Tyler shaded his eyes and tried to look at the tree, but blinded by it, squinched his face and glanced at Josh.

"Would you like me more if I gave you a Butterfinger?" he asked.

"I already like you."

Josh shoved his shorts down, turned around, and braced on the jeep's fender. When he felt Tyler's palm on his hip, his pelvis relaxed with a warm, voluptuous sensation, and the tree began hissing in the wind.

"Turn around," Tyler said, removing his hand.

Josh stood and turned, showing his erection.

"I don't want to want you," Tyler said sadly, thumbs in his canvas belt.

"I don't want to want you, either," Josh said, going soft.

They stared at each other with disappointment. Then Josh pulled his shorts up.

"I'm grateful," Tyler said. "Believe me. But I really can't accept it."

When a gust hit the tree, it began dancing and sizzling, and the leaves began sparkling like thousands of sparklers, but when Tyler sat against it, it turned into a normal olive tree, all crooked limbs and little, green leaves, a living chandelier of small, black olives. Tyler clasped his hands behind his head and gazed down the promenade, legs open, knees bent, boots flat on the ground, and while he slumped there, chest moving, eyes heavy, the tree's drooping leaders would sway and dip in the breeze and try to touch him, but couldn't.

"God," Tyler sighed. "I feel like an old dog."

"How's that?"

"Tired."

Josh sat crossed-legged, facing him, an elbow on Tyler's knee.

"Would you come with me to this dream?" he asked.

"We're in the dream," Tyler explained.

"Another one," Josh said. "It's small, no bigger than a hut, and it's old, real old, but I'm pretty sure you'll like it."

"Where is it?" Tyler asked, a hand on the ground, the other on Josh's knee.

Tyler's palm on his knee sent a thrill up his leg, turning him all sun and soft, warm wax.

"On a cliff like Phil and Billie's house, sort of a cross between Kalypso's cave and an eagle's nest, only with a drafting board for me, a desk for you, and a view of the Gulf of Salerno. You can sleep there," Josh added.

"I could use some rest," Tyler said.

"It also has a sound machine which shows the time on the ceiling."

"Good," Tyler said. "I could use some time on the ceiling."

# # # # #

When Josh woke, he did not have the slightest idea where he was. He felt the nightstand, found the lamp, and turned it on. Then the bed moved, and he heard the rustle of linens. When he twisted around, he saw Tyler rolling over, facing away. Then everything came back to him, and he smiled, turned off the lamp, and went back to sleep.

Chapter 14: Dead End

Late that night, Rollo thought he would try Corso Meridionale instead of the Galleria and stopped near Hotel Continental to light a cigarette. He was wearing a tight, blue-and-green striped tank top, grayish-brown khaki shorts, a cracked leather belt, and a pair of old, supple leather sandals. His acne had cleared up some, pink, not red, and he thought the shorts showed off his smooth, olive legs, so he was optimistic about his prospects for the evening. He took a drag on the cigarette, leaned against the building, and stood in the odd way he did to make his back feel better. He was tired, high on pot, and droopy eyed, and when he closed his eyes, his head against the wall, he dozed off. Then it was as if he felt, not heard, a soft swoosh, as if an owl had landed, and when he opened his eyes, an old, four-door Alfa Romeo Giulia with its windows down was parked at the curb.

He squinted at the man leaning across the passenger seat, but could not see much, but when the man said, "Get in the car, son," Rollo dropped the cigarette, strolled over, hiding his limp the best he could, and leaned into the window, face to face with a small, no-neck, middle-aged man with a buzz cut, a day's beard, and skin the texture of distressed leather.

"How much?" the man asked, staring at him with large, black, world-weary eyes.

The interior was cluttered and dirty, and the man was wearing a cheap, gray suit. So Rollo figured he was dealing with an easy trick, not a big shot.

"Twenty-five," Rollo said.

When the man made a strange wide-eyed expression as if surprised, Rollo wondered if he had asked too much or sold himself short.

"Worth it to satisfy a need, right?" Rollo asked. "To have a little fun. To forget the pain."

"The pain," the man repeated, smiling sadly. He seemed amused at Rollo's histrionics. "Yes," he chuckled. "My pain hurts. Let's take a ride."

The man opened the door, and when Rollo got in, the man looked behind them, executed a U-turn, and headed toward Piazza Garibaldi. He took Corso Garibaldi to the port and turned right on Via Nuova Marina. As they drove, Rollo noticed the man's long, feminine fingernails, but when the man glanced at him, Rollo looked at his own rough hands timidly clasped in his lap. When he sneaked another peak, the man was nodding to himself subtly as if deciding something, then steered the car into a large, reflective parking lot crowded with trucks and vans. Incandescent gulls swooped in and out of the intense aura of street lights. Across the lot was docked a lit-up, blue and white car ferry the size of a building with two big ramps down like draw bridges as if waiting to be fed by the stevedores standing around. The man drove into a maze of huge, dark warehouses, zigzagged around corners, and finally turned into an bleak, dead-end alley, rolling to a stop at a bright brick wall.

When the man pulled up the emergency brake and turned off the headlights, Rollo felt a silent, claustrophobic heaviness settle on everything as if they had driven into an ancient underground burial chamber, and it took a while for his eyes to adjust to the misty, moonlit scene. The walls surrounding them gave the effect that they were trapped in a tall, precipitous ravine. In the wall to his right, big, concrete, foundation stones formed a small ledge under a row of big, arched windows clad with metal bars. In the wall to his left loomed huge metal doors. Rollo leaned out the window and looked behind them toward a row of low concrete barricades lined up along the waterfront. Behind the barricades stretched an uneven chain-link fence, and, across a span of water, like a wharf in Styx, a blur of tractor trailers packed another parking lot.

"How did you get your limp?" the man began.

"Fell off a balcony," Rollo said, sitting back in the seat. "At least, that's what my mother says." When the man lightly stroked Rollo's thigh, Rollo felt as if a feather had brushed him. Rollo looked at the man's hand, then at him. The man had a long, pointed nose with small nostrils, and when Rollo said, "The money," the man wiped the end of it with the back of a finger, leaned forward, and reached into his back pocket for his wallet.

When he gave Rollo the money, Rollo put it away, unfastened his shorts, and shoved them to his ankles. Then he sat back, knees spread, and began pulling himself.

"Can a man find happiness with another man?" the man asked, tossing the wallet onto the dash.

"What?" Rollo asked, snorting to clear his nose.

The man lay his arm on Rollo's seat back. "Can a man find happiness with another man?"

"I don't know," Rollo said, puzzled.

"Nice thigh," the man said. "You're a little chunky, but nice thigh. Play football?"

"No," Rollo said, piqued. To calm himself, he leaned back, closed his eyes, and gently stroked his erection.

"I play on a squad," the man said, watching him. "Where I work."

Rollo opened his eyes, tilted his head forward, and pressed his thumb against the stout base of his cock to make it stand up tall.

"I also coach boys for a big-brother group," the man said. "At-risk boys. You at risk?"

"For what?" Rollo asked. He flicked his cock, which sprang up hard, and then he just sat there, hands at his sides, offering himself.

"For drugs, violence, VD, all sorts of things." The man bit his lip and looked as if he could hardly hold himself back. So Rollo was surprised when he said, "That all you got, a little mouse and a pair of dice."

"What?" Rollo balked. "I have a big cock, enough to choke you, cocksucker. Mouse, my ass."

"Have a joint?" the man asked. "I'll think it's larger if I'm stoned."

"Fuck you."

"No, serious," the man said. "Have one? Puts me in the mood."

Rollo stared at the gargoyle of the man's creased face. "Ten Euros."

"Ten," the man said. "Great."

When he reached for the wallet, Rollo relaxed. "And I can get you hash and coca."

"Hash and coca," the man mused, laying the ten on Rollo's side of the dash.

Rollo took it, stuck it in his shorts, and sat back, holding up the joint with his thumb and index finger. The man opened the ashtray and lay it in it. Then he put his arm on Rollo's seat back again.

"Cut your hair yourself, didn't you?" he said, fondling it. "Looks like it."

"Look," Rollo said, "you want to blow me or what?"

A combination of exhaustion, pot, ignorance, superstition, and the man's mixed signals was making Rollo paranoid. His body went numb with a weird fear, his nape hair bristled, and his erection began to wilt. Suddenly, the man's big eyes and aquiline nose looked sinister, predatory.

"You blow me," the man said, his soft hand on Rollo's neck.

"The man," Rollo stammered. "I was supposed to play the man, just me."

"I'll give you fifty."

"No."

"Come on," the man said, trying to push Rollo's head down. "Think about it, fifty. We'll take turns."

"No," Rollo pouted, jerking his head away.

"OK," the man said. "Seventy-five."

"Seventy-five?"

Rollo had never gotten so much for a blow job, something, for him, as easy as shooing a pigeon, and he had certainly performed more contorted acts with less maneuvering room.

"Seventy-five," the man swore.

The man undid his pants and shoved them down, revealing a solid erection. Then he took out more money and, holding it up with his left hand, drew Rollo's head down with his right. When Rollo, staring up at him, was just about to go down on him, the man smiled wistfully and dropped the cash on Rollo's feet. Then Rollo looked down and breathed the man's moist, scrotal smell. When he slid the rubbery foreskin back, he noticed not only the strange shape of the man's elliptical glans, but also how fluffy his pubic hair was, as if the man had used conditioner on it. Once Rollo started giving him head, he lapsed into it mindlessly, and soon the man was lifting off the seat – straightening out, in effect – in an apparent access of release, shaking and panting, holding Rollo's head down with his left hand, gripping the emergency brake with his right. Then he collapsed on the seat with a groan.

When Rollo, drooling, turned to spit the goop out the window, another man in a suit was leaning in it, watching. Rollo screamed and flinched, his arms snapping to his chest.

The man stood, opened the door, and said calmly, "Police. Out of the car."

When Rollo failed to move, the man grabbed him and dragged him out of the car onto the pavement with his shorts around his ankles. Unlike the trick's hands, this man's were strong as talons, iron clamps. The man shut the door, and Rollo rolled onto his hands and knees and looked up at him, a stocky, athletic-looking silhouette with a big head and curly hair. Rollo got up, but as he was pulling up his shorts, the man shoved him against the car.

"Hands behind your back."

Rollo knew he could not outrun him, so he stepped on the ledge in the wall and grasped the metal grate over a window, but the man clutched his shorts and tried to pull him down, pulling the shorts off instead. He dropped them, grabbed Rollo's foot, and pulled his sandal off, then grabbed Rollo's ankle and began a tug of war with him, trying to break Rollo's grip on the bars. When he did, Rollo fell, hands slapping the ledge, and landed on his elbows, smashing his nose on the ground. Near the car stood a metal pole which, at some point, apparently held a sign, and when Rollo struggled up again, the man took hold of his right wrist and swung him around backward, slamming him against it.

Rollo staggered a few steps, stunned, a hand to the back of his head, vaguely aware, out of the corner of his eye, that his trick was bent over, picking the cash off the floor of the car, but before Rollo could come to his senses, the man pushed him against the car again.

"I said, 'Hands behind you back.'"

The man twisted his arms behind him, cuffed him, and snatched his hair, forcing his head through the passenger window. When the trick grabbed his hair and held him in place, Rollo looked up into his faint smile, then looked down. When he realized that the trick really was not a trick as such, but partners with the man, a pair of tectonic plates shifted. He felt something coming, then literally shook with the revelation, his body wracked with wave after wave of chill-like shocks. They had lured him out here, he believed, to do something terrible to him, and there was nothing he could do to save himself.

"What do we have here?" the second man said. "Some joints, some cash, Marlboros. Looks like, uh, seven, eight, nine joints."

"Four for you," the trick said, "four for me, and one for evidence. We'll split the cash."

Rollo felt the second man's hand on his back.

"Would you like to avoid going to jail?" the man asked.

"A favor for him," the trick said, "a favor for you."

The hand slid down Rollo's back to his right cheek. Then he felt the man's left hand on his left. The man squeezed Rollo's cheeks, then let go, and Rollo could hear him unbuckling his belt and unzipping his fly. A moment passed. Then the man spread Rollo's cheeks, prodded him, and, holding Rollo's hips, began dry-humping him. Rollo clinched, then relaxed, opening up to him, and after a while, he was taking what felt like a live coal deep inside him.

"Say, 'This is where my life has led,'" the man said, methodically fucking him. "Say it."

When Rollo glanced at the trick, the trick whispered, "Say it."

"This is where my life has led."

"Louder," the man said.

"This is where my life has led!"

"Say, 'I'm nothing,'" the man said.

"I'm nothing," Rollo cried.

Then he realized that he was, in fact, nothing and always would be. In his own primitive way, he knew that, like a black hole in space, he would always keep pulling his life into the vacuum of himself until he would reach critical mass and die.

"Say, 'I have nothing to lose.'"

"I have nothing to lose," he sobbed. "Nothing."

When the man's thrusts became slower and deeper, Rollo's sobs became a choking, off-key lament of all the disappointment and frustration he had known.

"Say, 'I'm nobody,'" the man said, wedged in him

"I'm nobody."

"Say you don't exist," the trick whispered.

"I don't exist!" Rollo blurted, his face wet with tears.

The man stepped back, slipping out of him, and when the trick let go of Rollo's hair, Rollo backed out of the window and stood up straight, gasping and sniffing. As the man fastened his clothes, Rollo could see him better, the strong jaw, the hooked nose, the sideburns pointing into his cheeks. The man reached Rollo's shorts and sandal and threw them through the back window. Then he gripped Rollo's arm and opened the back door.

"Where are we going?" Rollo asked, alarmed.

"Where do you think?" the man replied.

Rollo had been raped repeatedly and contracted HIV in jail.

"No!" he cried, straining to pull away. "No, please, I beg you."

When the man punched him in the face, Rollo crumpled to his knees, out cold.

Chapter 15: The King of the Party People

Tyler figured he must have dozed off, for when his head bobbed and he opened his eyes, Peeve, the black cat, was hunched, paws together, directly in front of him on the table, staring at him haughtily with amber eyes and swishing its tail languidly as if it were a descendant of some royal Egyptian cat. Its fixed pupils looked like black fangs with a white dot of light, and when it blinked, it had no eyes.

"You know I'm allergic to her," he slurred.

When he reached to brush her off the table, she arched and hissed, showing a little shark's mouth of sharp, shiny teeth. He drew back, and Linda put down the small willow wreath she was weaving, picked her up, and poured her onto the floor in a fluid, serpentine motion. Then Linda sat bolt upright and began braiding her wreath again. Alice was sitting upright across from her, braiding one. He could hear the low gurgle of water boiling, as well as Karen shuffling on the kitchen floor, but he could not see what she was doing. However, he could not believe she was boiling anything in such stifling heat. The bleak room was just as hot at sunset as at noon, if not hotter, and here she was, he thought, slowly filling it with steam. The vapor, he figured, couldn't be good for her herbs.

Then the sun sagged below the door lintel, splaying through the chandelier's bayberry drippings, and through the cleft in the trees where the path lay, he could see it settling on Bailey Island in a sort of Casco Bay version of an alignment of the planets. When it reached a point below the drippings, but above the candles on the table, it was shining directly through the door and into his face, blinding him, and he turned to see the niche, except for his shadow, kindled to an orange glow. As the glow dimmed, he faced forward again, and when the sun sank from view, the sky became a giant jewelweed, all yellow, orange, and red spotted with small, brown clouds. With nightfall, a subtle, balsam-scented breeze washed into the room, and he felt a slight sunburn on his face, arms, and hands. He also became aware of the vast silence in the bay, as if everything in the world, as he thought of it, were waiting for the big black bloom of the lunar eclipse at midnight.

"No music, right?" he asked, pensively touching the light stubble on his upper lip.

"You've already asked me that," Karen groused from the kitchen.

He shoved his chair back and relaxed into an open posture.

"No music, no dancing," he concluded, bracing a foot on a knee. "I could sing something if you wanted to dance," he yawned, unlacing a Nike, glancing at Linda, then Alice. They glanced back askance. "No?" he asked. When they went back to braiding, he took off his Nikes and socks and stood just long enough to set them by the bed in the niche. Then he slumped in the chair again.

"Oh, to dance barefoot," he began slowly, "on an old, wooden floor, face to face, hand in hand, with the one I adore." He smiled to himself, nodded, and continued. "My heart would be bright as the light from the door that blows on the pebbles aglow on the shore." He tilted his head back, gazed into space, and recited, "Yes, my heart would be bright as the light from the door that kindles the buoy that's anchored offshore."

Linda and Alice traded looks.

"No one wants to dance?" he asked, throwing his voice toward the kitchen.

"No, Dad," Linda said finally. "No one wants to dance with you."

"Just like you to quote some romantic poem instead of facing reality," Karen called. She emphasized the word *romantic* with bitterness.

"I didn't quote it," he explained. "I just composed it."

"Whatever," she said, appearing in the archway. She glared at him, wiping her hands harshly on a dish towel, her eyes little jars of hate. "You think we want to dance with you after you've neglected us all these years. As I said, telling the truth is the only way to heal ourselves, you included. Keeping quiet is a way of agreeing to a lie."

"What lie?"

"That you didn't neglect us and abuse us."

"Abuse is a form of attention," he quibbled. "Pick one. Did I neglect you, or did I abuse you?"

"You abused us, then neglected us."

"I see," he laughed feebly.

"You manipulated us like puppets to meet your needs."

"You know, at the moment," he admitted, "I'm just too foggy-brained to know what that means." And, in truth, he felt as if he had had a slight stroke. He knew he knew words, if anything, eye, tooth, hand, foot, but was having trouble recalling them, trying to express himself simply and clearly. "But," he went on, "what I do know is that I was beginning to develop a good relationship with Linda again, and you won't have it. That's all that's going on here."

Karen bristled like a scorpion, tailed arched. The girls froze, stored mannequins. He had criticized St. Karen, the North Star in their night.

"I'm not sure if I'll ever be able to forgive you," she stated.

You smug, self-righteous bitch, he thought more in humor than in anger. Absently, he crossed his arms across his chest, but heavy, they fell open, dangling at his sides.

"I thought maybe I could if you admitted your guilt and said you were sorry," she went on, "said it and meant it."

I wouldn't now if my life depended on it, he balked.

"If the great wound you inflicted had closed," she said, shivering and rubbing her upper arms.

Again, he couldn't tell if she were, in fact, cold or shivering for emphasis. He glanced at the girls for their reaction, but there was none: mindless braiding.

"But, of course, it hasn't," Karen sighed.

Obviously.

He quoted Prospero from *The Tempest*: "The rarer action is / In virtue than in vengeance." He left out the next line, "They being penitent," for he wasn't. That is, he wasn't willing to let her sit in judgment of him. Who knew his faults better and could judge them better than him? If anyone tried him, he'd try himself.

"Maybe I should forgive you," she said, beginning to pace, "whether you deserve it or not."

Why don't you? he thought.

"It would be Good working through you to someone else," he reasoned, "the old-fashioned concept of grace, and good working through you, of course, would be good for you."

"A pardon?" she asked rhetorically. When she stepped on a squeaky board, she stopped, as if awakened, and turned, pacing in the other direction.

"Forget me," he suggested. "Focus on yourself. You talk about healing. Spend your time wisely healing yourself. You're a healer, right? By profession?"

Time, he thought. How long does it take to survive divorce, a life? Surely, there was something better she could do with hers.

But if his mood had been, let's say, cardinal red, it was now mysteriously deepening to imperial purple. It was as if the anxiety of the situation were vanishing like incense, had been turned off like some adrenaline spigot in his chest. He didn't care if she hated him.

"Look at everything in the light of happiness," he said earnestly. "Good is what feels good. Bad is what feels bad. You can't feel good right now. This can't be good for you."

Karen crossed paths with a high-nosed Peeve slinking toward the kitchen. There, the cat jumped onto the counter, sat primly, and preened its sleek coat.

"Let go of the past," he asked. "It's pulling you under like some – " He thought for a moment. "Like some jewelry box you're trying to save."

With the jewelry-box analogy, both girls glanced at Karen as if to check her response, but she only kept pacing dreamily like a tiger.

"We're supposed to be enjoying ourselves out here," he said, "not raking over the coals of every damned thing that went wrong."

The remark's brusque tone was apparently a trip wire. Karen stopped and glared at him again, rage smoldering, lava under snow. The girls looked from her to him.

"How much valerian did you put in here?" he smiled, lightly touching his cup. "I can hardly hold my eyes open." He felt hypnotized, as if he had fallen into a fast trance only she could call him out of.

"Of course, when I think of how you abused the girls," Karen said, "how could I possibly even consider forgiving you? What you did to them is, in fact, unforgivable."

"And what beastly thing did I do to them?" he asked wearily, resigned to fate.

"You never supported them," she stated as fact.

"Financially?" he scoffed. "I never missed a child-support check, not one."

"What checks?" Alice asked, slipping the willow bracelet on and off her wrist lackadaisically.

"The checks you endorsed, Missy," he said point-blank. "Those checks."

She looked down moodily, avoiding his eyes. He supposed she was just trying to please her mom, playing Pinocchio to Karen's Geppetto.

"They never had dental care," Karen said.

Neither did I, he thought. In graduate school, he made $3,000 a year; the first year he taught, $9,000.

"Let alone music or tennis lessons like other kids," Karen ran on.

He remembered Alice's violin, but realized what a primal bog of pettiness they were gradually sinking into.

"They were so poor then," she said, "that now Linda is a tightwad, doing without clothes, and Alice is a spendthrift, making up for all she missed with things."

"They're in the room, you know."

Linda was fanning herself with the fluttery wreath, Alice eyeing him with a finger in her teeth.

"Can't tell you how humiliating it was," Karen said, "to ask my parents for an allowance."

"You didn't tell me they were helping you," he said, downing the last of the lukewarm tea.

"I finally had to get a lawyer to sue you for more."

"More," he smiled. "More implies what I'd been sending. Then the entire state of Indiana sued me for a year's support you said I hadn't paid. Silly me. I had the canceled checks. Hope you got something out of it."

The girls looked up at him, then her. He was not sure, but they seemed surprised by the information.

"You were too cheap even to send them a birthday card," she said, squinting at him, suddenly old with anger. "Or worse," she added, "a get-well card."

He always remembered their birthdays, but often mail and gifts to Alice came back or were lost because she had moved without telling him, and he was usually unaware of when they were sick until long after.

"Not true," he said simply.

"Even when Linda was in a coma from asthma."

"Wait a minute," he puzzled. "You keep cats, to which you know she's allergic, and you wonder why she has asthma attacks, one of which put her in a coma."

There was a world he could have said about that. When he glanced out the door, the bay was black as an oven, and the few sleepy lights on Bailey were brighter than the faint stars pricking the night, a night, at the moment, muted by both the sensual afterglow of sunset and the romantic glow of the rising moon.

"I don't know what's worse," she said, skimming over the accusation, "the way you ignored them before or after you left."

"Meaning?"

"When I was at work," she claimed, pacing again, "you actually locked them in the bathroom so you could study."

"Never happened." He looked from Linda to Alice. "You girls know that isn't true." They stared at him as if he were speaking Italian. "You're not going to correct her?" he asked affectionately. "On which side of the door is the lock in a bathroom, Linda? Alice, which side?"

"Well, there was the time you locked me in the bedroom," she claimed, "a hostage in my own house. You can't deny that."

"Yes, I can."

"I had just written a note to drop out the window when you finally let me out. I was so afraid you'd find it I ate it."

"Karen," he sighed, "we lived in an apartment complex. You could've raised the window and called to dozens, if not hundreds, of people. Notes," he balked, shaking his head.

The girls just sat there, but he could tell they were thinking, conflicted to a point, he hoped to the point of doubt.

"When she was born," Karen said, "you wouldn't even see Alice because she wasn't a boy."

"I think you've been drinking one too many herbs."

"You were kind to me then, pregnant with her, when you thought I might bear you a boy, but that's all I was, just a means to an end." All at once, she looked trapped in the reverie and looked for a way out. Then she found it. "I think you saw her first when she was nine months old."

"You went home to have Alice," he explained, "because we couldn't afford to have her. Your parents could. And if I didn't see her, it was because of what was going on between you and me, not her. I can't believe you're blaming her."

"I'm not blaming her, you bastard."

"I can't believe you'd even mention this sort of thing in front of her."

When he glanced at Alice, she seemed to realize she was biting her finger and took it out of her mouth.

"You wanted a son, an extension of you," Karen said, "to prove something about your masculinity, I think. I could sense you were wrestling with your gender identification."

"Gender identification?" he asked. "You must mean sexual orientation. I'm no more uncertain of my gender than you are."

Alice looked sheepish, Linda amused.

"Whatever," Karen groused. "But you're lying if you say you didn't want a son."

"Yes," he nodded, "I did want one, one of each, a daughter and a son, but I was perfectly happy with what we got, two beautiful daughters. You're taking a balloon and blowing it up to a blimp. Quite a stretch."

He noticed Peeve slip off the kitchen counter, slink across the room, and disappear out the door.

"You loved her most," Alice said quietly.

"What?" he smiled, taken aback.

"You always loved her most. Linda."

"Well, Sweetie," he replied gently, "there's a problem in logic. She's a girl, too."

"Speaking of seeing her," Karen said, eyes far away, "there was that incredible visit when they slept in the same bed with you and your lover. Both

126

naked," she added, focusing on him again. "And you actually had them touch your penis to 'educate' them, as you put it, about boys and sex. "

"Touch my penis?" he smiled to himself. "Karen, Karen, Karen. You should be ashamed." He turned to the girls. "Girls." When they only stared, he chuckled, "Oh – my – God." He thought of Sue Silverman's book, then glanced at them again. "Tell her that didn't happen. That's not me. I know me, and that's not me. You know it's not me. I'd never do anything to hurt you. Linda. Alice."

He vaguely remembered the visit. He was living in a studio apartment with a king-sized mattress on the floor under a big industrial window. Strangely enough, the most vivid detail he could conjure up was the soft, dark-blue bedspread about the size of a fish pond. There was a long, black-leather sofa on which someone could have slept, but he was fairly sure that everyone had, in fact, slept together and had fun, the kind of innocent fun that kids would have building a fort in a living room or pretending to camp out. Try as he may, though, he could not remember sleeping nude with them – it was just too long ago – though he admitted to himself that he could have in some access of naive, if misguided, Bohemian foolishness. He doubted it.

As for the penis story, again he thought she had lost her mind or was deliberately lying about it the way irate litigants do in custody hearings. Because he and Karen had been ignorant about sex growing up, they had agreed from the start to be open and honest about it with the girls. Each bathed with them until it was inappropriate, and Karen, he felt, if she sincerely believed what she said, must have transferred the memory onto the account of the visit. If sex, for her, had always been abuse, as seen through a Catholic lens, then he, to her, was some sort of sex deviant perfectly capable of molesting his children. If the girls believed it, then it was a false memory planted by Karen and given credence through repetition. It had, in fact, not happened. In the context of how Karen was using facts, though, they didn't count for much, hers versus his.

"Well, well, well," he murmured, head down, massaging his neck. "I seem to be in the same box with wife beaters and child molesters. Great. While you're at it, go ahead and throw in murder and bestiality."

"I was surprised they were willing to see you," Karen said, the dishcloth at her lips.

"Who would," he replied, "after the job you've done on them? No," he stressed, head up, looking around at them. "I'm not an evil monster, and there's nothing you can ever say or do to make me think otherwise. If that's what we're here for, forget it. You failed. It won't work."

The only way he could figure out to deal with the situation was to remain calm and try to answer her accusations (to the best of his memory) point by point with the facts in a matter-of-fact tone of voice, and remaining calm, despite everything, was turning out to be amazingly easy. He didn't know where it had come from, but he was wrapped, he felt, in a purple robe of godlike invulnerability.

At that point, Linda and Alice got up, took his hands, Linda his right, Alice his left, and slipped the willow bracelets onto his wrists.

"What?" he joked. "No ivy?"

"Here," Karen said, turning toward the kitchen. She dropped the dishcloth on the counter, reached the stick wreath with finches from the window, and handed it to Linda. "Put this on him," she said. "It'll ward off spirits and spells."

"What about aches and pains?" he asked. "More practical."

"Sorry we don't have the appropriate flowers," Karen remarked.

Linda and Alice crowned him, adjusted the wreath, and twisted the finches so that they were sitting up as in a nest. The finches were what kept it from looking like a crown of thorns. He wondered at all the rite-like mumbo-jumbo, but enjoyed the sudden attention, especially when the girls sat on the daybed behind him and began firmly massaging his hands. While they did, rubbing his fingers and thumbing his palms, he stared out the door, and since he had Wyeth on his mind lately, being in Maine, the obscure yard and trees beyond reminded him of the black backgrounds in paintings such as *Black Water* and *The Intruder*. Lulled by the tea, his languid tiredness, and the warm, implied intimacy of their fingers, he was aware they had slipped something else around his wrists, but not until his wrists bumped together did he realize he was bound with something stronger than willow, something unbreakable he was actually familiar with from binding others in kinky sex: plasticuffs.

"What?" he asked, incredulous, starting to stand up, but Alice sat him down again with a hand on his shoulder, and from the extra tension on his restraints, he realized that Linda had bound his hands to a slat on the chair. There was no point in trying to free himself, he knew. He was as trapped in the chair as he was in his body. Alice bound his left ankle to the chair leg, and when Linda started to bind his right, he lifted his foot, then, curiosity piqued, lowered it, letting her bind it. Besides, he was far too lethargic to resist.

"What a sap," he said, shaking his head, "a bona fide, natural-born sap." Trapped like the fly in the bog, he thought. "I'm the little fly now, stuck to this fuckin' chair!"

"What?" Linda asked, tightening the tie.

"Linda," he said, gazing at her drowsily, "you're my Cordelia. What the hell are you doing?"

"Who's Cordelia?" Alice asked.

"Why?" he asked Linda. "What's going on here?"

Again, his first thought was that Karen had poisoned them. He didn't know what they were up to, and he didn't care, but whatever it was, to get to them to do what they'd just done, bind him to a chair, she had had to poison them as surely as if she had mixed anti-freeze in their Jello. Linda had told him a story about a terrible mistake she had made in the elementary school where she taught. The class project was to go into nature and gather pretty things for a room display. What she gathered, in fact, were the bright red leaves of a clump of poison ivy. The next day, her hands and face were swollen and pink as certain amanita mushrooms, a terrible, maddening condition that would torment her relentlessly for months. Karen's hatred of him was like the poison ivy, he thought. The girls, seduced by its hot passion, had gathered it to their harm. Whatever she had said, they had believed her without question since they owed her allegiance. They owed it to the one person who had stayed with them and taken care of them. Who wouldn't? He thought of lines from a poem he'd written about his mother, a poem set in a cemetery.

> *Then all at once I saw the spiteful dead,*
> *who poisoned at its source the crimson river*
> *flowing through our veins, and knew that we*
> *had poured into our children, poisoning them.*

"The reason for the trip," he began, "quality time, means nothing, right?"

"It's nothing," Karen said, "if it got you here to face the truth."

"It's nothing but a lie," he claimed. "This trip meant everything to me. *Are you having surgery?*" he asked Linda.

"Yes," she said, taking a seat.

He stared at Karen, went into her all the way with his eyes, and, once inside, looked around, sizing up exactly what she was up to. Pierced by his gaze, she put a hand over her crotch and her heart and stepped back, as if instinctively aware of the violation, then, composed again, glared at him, mad as a maenad.

"Facing the truth," he repeated. "That's why I'm here. To hold me accountable in some vengeful court in your brain. Boy," he sighed, breaking his stare, "you really haven't thought this one through." When Alice sat at the table, he added, "None of you have."

"Someone has to hold you accountable," Karen said, strolling toward him.

"You want to rail at me," he said. "Then what? We all have a good night's sleep and boat back to Bailey in the morning?"

"And never have anything to do with you ever again," Alice said, absently pulling her neckline. Despite her smugness, he thought, she was still just as emotionally nude as she was when a little girl.

"Sweetie," he said, "you don't mean that."

"Yes, I do."

"You love your mom," he crooned. "I understand. It's no big, intricate knot."

"I hate you," she snapped, fingers casually resting on her clavicle.

"What a long nose," he remarked.

"You're crazy," she said. "Cordelia, intricate knot, long nose. Why don't you talk like normal people?"

Her "cruelty" triggered a series of negative images in his mind. He thought of Kim, his heroine, chained like a dog and raped repeatedly in his horror script *The Crystal Ball*. He thought of what it must be like to be bound in a chair in a gas chamber, waiting for the pellet to drop. He pictured himself hanging upside down from a beam in the ceiling like a batch of dry, crumbly herbs for a tea, a particularly macabre, but tasty witch's tea. And yet, as these images focused and faded in his mind, again he felt no anger or anxiety, serenely out of touch with the scene, as in an out-of-body experience, separated as an alien from the actual Tyler Lynn in the room.

"Why don't you step back from the edge of the cliff?" he asked Alice. "How's that for clear and simple? Step back from the cliff. And you," he smiled drunkenly, turning to Karen. "I see a short unhappy life for you, Macomber." He was referring to *The Short Happy Life of Francis Macomber* by Hemingway, a story in which a wife perhaps murders her husband when he finally asserts himself as a man.

"Macomber?"

"A Hemingway character."

"Your literary allusions are getting tiresome," Karen remarked, planting her hands on the table to emphasize the word *tiresome*.

"Sorry," he said. "What I do." Then his thoughts went back to the strange notion of his body as tea. "What *did* you put in my tea?" Everyone froze, then looked from one to the other. "So you did put something in it. Valium? Can't believe valerian feels this good. How many?"

"Three," she said matter of fact.

He couldn't tell if she were joking. At this point, he figured he should consider himself lucky she hadn't put rat poison in it.

"Well, whatever your plan was," he confided, "it backfired. I haven't felt this calm in years. In fact, I haven't ever felt this calm. If you killed me now, I'd just come back from the dead."

"Like Jesus, right," Alice scoffed.

"No," he said, smiling a droopy smile. "Dionysus."

"Dionysus, huh?" Karen said.

She walked to the door, picked up the walking stick, and took it to the kitchen, where he could hear her scuffling and rustling.

"Didn't you know what divorce meant?" he murmured to himself.

She stepped into view, took a Tupperware container out of the ice box, and disappeared behind the arch again. A long silence ensued, and he checked the girls' expressions, then bowed his head, staring at his crotch. Then he realized that he must have blacked out and shook his head to clear it, to wake himself up. When he noticed something in his peripheral vision, he looked up to see Karen, feet spread, framed in the archway with the walking stick standing by her side, balsam cones and a sprig of red raspberries attached to the top with florist's wire. For some reason, the stick looked perversely virile to him, the knob phallic, the cones scrotal, even the berries and leaves somehow pubic. He had no idea what she was thinking, but the strange *objet* looked like some sort of primitive staff, and holding it, Karen, in her slacks and floral shirt, some tacky Queen of the Spinsters.

"What's that?" he smiled, dull.

"A scepter for the king," she snapped sardonically, "King of the Party People."

She strolled over, wedged the stick between him and the chair back, and stepped back apparently to admire her handiwork. When the girls sniggered, he imagined what he must look like, some absurd tribal king from *The Golden Bough.*

"And now what are trying to do," he asked, "make me look as foolish as possible?"

"Not that you haven't humiliated me over the years."

"Meaning?"

"Maligning me with the girls."

"Example?"

"Calling me a liar!"

"If that's what you call refuting your lies," he said, "so be it."

She leaned forward and slapped him.

"Mom?" Linda objected.

"Jeez," he groaned, smarting and squinching his nose. "A meat cleaver to the head would've had time to heal by now. You act as if I invented divorce. Divorce is divorce, for Pete's sake. Get over it."

He had thought divorce meant he would go his way, they theirs. He had tried marriage, but failed. It was over. They were all part of a botched life he wanted to put behind him. But even he was wrong.

What was the answer? he asked himself now. Leave Karen, but stay near the girls? He had to divorce her. There was no other choice. But he didn't have to divorce the girls. In fact, he couldn't. Never. No matter what they thought or felt or did or said, they were still his physically, emotionally, and mentally. He should've seen them more.

Linda said that they had moved so many times that once when she and Alice stepped off a school bus, they had no idea where they lived. When he heard that, he felt as if he himself had dropped them off there, like dogs he wanted to get rid of. In short, he had abandoned them.

To his surprise, though, they had apparently divorced him, and this breaking of bonds at the natural center of things did not bode well for anything else holding together. If they would drug him, tie him up, and slap him, anything could happen.

"Girls," he said, "I am so sorry. I can't believe we've come to this. What a waste. You're young. You should be sitting outside and enjoying the night, not –"

Alice jumped up and smacked him so hard his chair rocked, he blinked, and his cheek stung.

"Shut up!" she yelled. "Who are you to be telling us what we should be doing?"

She sat, arms crossed, sulking. He worked his jaw as if she had knocked it out of line. Linda took off her glasses and laid them on the table, but held them, staring at them with a sad, distant smile.

"Guess we've officially gone from daddy baiting to daddy bashing," he said.

"Yes, I was always being told what I should be doing by you and everyone else," Karen claimed.

"And that was?" he asked.

"Playing second fiddle to you," she said. "Another, more subtle way you abused me, by devaluing me."

"How so?"

"It was all about you, your degree. I was just a means to that end, too, the financial means."

"Your job at the phone company?"

"Yes."

"I understand," he said. "But I don't see how you saw your financial contributions as less important than mine. I was getting a measly stipend as a Teaching Associate. You were making a regular salary. It was a question of your support then for my support later, after I got the master's and a job."

"Exactly," she agreed, "when you were supposed to be the breadwinner, and I was supposed to be the housewife and mom. Only that didn't happen, did it? I had to work *and* care for the kids, two roles for which I was hardly prepared after the mind job you and your spiteful mother did on me."

"Mind job?" he asked. "Spiteful mother?"

She was reciting a play she had written and rehearsed thoroughly, he thought, and she was going to stick to the script, irrational and erratic as it was. In other words, she would just ignore his questions and ad-libs. It was almost as if he weren't there. This tragic catharsis, as he thought of it, was something she was going to perform with or without an audience, even with or without the other characters in the play.

"First," she alleged, "you threatened to have me committed to a mental institution so the two of you could bring up Linda on your own."

He laughed an abrupt, drugged cough of disbelief, then, gaping, gazed at the girls, who looked disturbed.

"If you only knew how much I wanted to untie Jewel's apron strings," he laughed again, "you'd realize how truly – " He started to say *crazy*. "How truly sad that sounds. And Tyler, Jewel, and Linda lived happily ever after. Right. Incredible."

Oh, my God! he thought, numb. You *have* lost your mind.

"With just the two of us," she said, "there were always two versions of things. I'd remember what you'd said and you'd deny you'd said it."

"Take, for example, having you committed."

When Linda exhaled a long, deep sigh, he turned and watched her tapping her glasses impatiently on the table with her right hand and twisting a strand of her fine, curly hair nervously with her left. When she glanced at him with a faint smile of what appeared to be apathy, he realized, again, that she was not going to do or say anything.

"You've really set me up," he said, turning to Karen. "If I say it isn't true, then I'm mentally abusing you."

"You *are* abusive," she snarled, lunging at him.

"I'm tied up," he explained. "You slap me and lecture me on abuse. I hope you see the…."

Then Peeve caught his eye. Quietly, the cat leapt onto the far end of the table, almost invisible, black against the night. Spotting Tyler, it froze, then deftly picked its way through the warren of pewter, bayberry candles, and clutter until it halted in front of him, swishing its tail curiously and purring ominously at the sight of such a large, juicy mouse.

Tyler could not help himself. He yowled like a cat, startling everyone, including Peeve, who cringed and hissed. When Tyler saw how irritated everyone was, he burst out laughing, tried to compose himself in snorts and sniffs, then burst out laughing again.

Chapter 16: Pompeii

The morning after the seduction in Josh's room, Tyler, Josh, Billie, and Phil walked to the bus station on the waterfront and bought tickets to Pompeii. Eventually, the bus rolled up and took them on the leisurely trip past Mount Vesuvius. Josh was the tour guide by default since he was the only one who had done any research.

"It became a Roman colony around 80 BC," he began, "but there was something there for hundreds of years before that. The most important dates to know are AD 62, the year of the earthquake, and AD 79, the year of the eruption. The eruption killed about 20,000 people."

"When was the last eruption?" Phil asked.

"In '44."

"How many died then?" Billie asked, absently combing her hair with her fingers.

"Only 26. Based on what I've seen of the shoddy construction in Naples, though," Josh added, "the city is a major catastrophe waiting to happen."

"So many people," Tyler commented, "so little time to get out."

As soon as they stepped inside Pompeii, Josh got confused since he thought they were at Porta Marina, the main entrance, when, in fact, they had entered through a gap in the wall near Porta di Stabia, an entrance on the south side of the site.

"The map doesn't match what I'm seeing," he puzzled.

Everyone had dressed for the warm weather: Phil slacks and a white dress shirt with the sleeves rolled up, Billie a sheer white dress with a white belt and slippers, Josh khaki shorts, a yellow polo shirt, and his backpack with picnic items, Tyler jeans and a white linen shirt unbuttoned over the chest. The shirt looked Hawaiian, only more classy with a dark-blue floral print spilling down the left. The flowers actually looked like cross-sections of pomegranates.

Josh kept glancing at his notes and the structures around them, and as they followed him slowly across the grounds of the gladiators' barracks, Tyler was grateful for the balmy sunshine, pleasant company, and easy ability to blot out his mind with what he was seeing: at the moment, dark cubicles in a long colonnade with a tiled roof. He also realized that he had intuitively paired up with Josh as Phil and Billie trailed behind, and the fact that Josh was literally lost and adrift struck a sympathetic chord. It seemed symbolic of his passive loneliness. Tyler wanted to help, but had no idea how.

When they stepped into the Little Theater, Josh figured out where they were and gave them his notes on the place, and when they had climbed to the top row of seats, they could see the Big Theater next door and up Via Stabia toward Vesuvius, in the heat just a faint silhouette against the chalk-dust blue of the sky. The idle mountain had such an innocent face for a killer, Tyler thought, always in the background of the lives of the Pompeians like the sensual hum between him and Josh as they stood, almost touching, gazing over the ruins. What subterranean pressure was gradually building between them, he wondered. Erupting into what? Friendship, more self-destructive violence, a placid kiss goodbye in a hotel room? He imagined what the immense *crack* must have sounded like when the peak blew, freezing everyone with fear. He remembered Josh's warm breath on his neck and his own exquisite, if reluctant, eruption, but was, of course, more relieved than alarmed by it. He could not deny the young man's sweet effect on his skin. Nor could he see any serious harm in it. A release in tension between emotional tectonic plates, as he thought of it, and the messy afterglow had been restful and comforting.

They glanced at each other with sly smiles, as if they knew what the other was thinking, then, as if on cue, headed down the steep steps gingerly. At the bottom, Tyler jumped down the drop by a thick, muscular atlas and, turning, automatically took Josh's hand to help him, but when Josh hopped down, absorbing the shock with his knees, he did not let go of Tyler's hand. The gesture seemed instinctive, and, on impulse, Tyler decided to conduct a little experiment. He would simply let Josh hold his hand to see what would come of it, which, in fact, was just to stand there, hand in hand, looking up into the weary, eroded face of the kneeling telamon, a big, white chunk of chiseled stone stained black and greenish blue in the creases.

"What a bear," Josh remarked, eyes half closed in the glare.

"Like bears?" Tyler asked.

He understood Josh to be using the word in the gay sense of a big, hairy man.

"Uh, no," Josh said, shaking his head sheepishly. "You're more my type, slim and smooth." Josh looked at Phil and Billie with their backs turned, taking in the view from the top of the theater. Then he let go of Tyler's hand, reached inside Tyler's shirt, and caressed a pec. "Besides," he said, a cherubic twinkle in his eye, "I'd be crushed to a pulp by a brute like him. I need someone who knows how to play a...."

"Fine guitar like you?"

"That's it," he agreed with a coy smile, "a fine guitar like me."

"Bet you can take it," Tyler flirted.

He breathed Josh's male smell (the moist armpits, the glistening flush on the sternum), and Josh's hand on his chest made his pulse flutter, set in motion some slow, tentative momentum in his groin. Toward the bed in the hotel room, he figured. He felt good even walking at his side and casually touching him, even just standing close to him. If his credo were, in fact, that good was what felt good, then Josh was good. It was hard to be cool to him in such heat, he thought metaphorically.

"You never did explain why you have a cut on your chest," Tyler said, glancing toward Phil and Billie.

He pressed the crown logo on Josh's polo and felt the Band-Aid under it. He pulled the shirt out of Josh's pants, slipped his hand under it, and fingered the smooth strip.

"This derelict was bothering Phil and Billie," Josh said, squeezing Tyler's pec, "and when I stepped between them, he took a swipe at me with a knife."

"You're kidding," Tyler chuckled, fascinated. The heroic deed raised Tyler's opinion of him.

"It was nothing, I can assure you," Josh claimed. "He seemed so miserable I felt sorry for him."

"Still."

He was attracted to Josh the way he was attracted to any attractive person. He was shallow that way, he knew. It was just more pleasant. And the modest intimacy in Josh's room last night had led to the subtle rapport between them now. He was connected to someone someway, and connection vs. alienation was also good. Humans, he thought, were social beings, another way of saying a pack. All Josh had to do was lean forward to kiss him, but when they glanced toward Phil and Billie, they were turning around. When Tyler and Josh broke apart, Tyler leaned against the atlas, and Josh tucked his shirt in, laughing a funny little breath of a laugh.

As everyone started up Via Stabia, Tyler realized they would have to set a slow, relaxed pace for the Trees. Getting around the ruins would be rough going. The street was paved with great puzzle pieces of stone fit together with deep cracks between them. They would have to watch their step, or they could turn an ankle. At one point, there were stepping stones across the street, which Tyler figured were there for when water filled it. On either side were the stacked stones of rectangular columns, gated, roped-off entrances, ruins bright in the meridional sun or dark-blue in shadow. As they strolled quietly, the free spirit in him joined the familial pack of the foursome, and even though he and Josh were in the lead, he felt like a stray that had taken up with strangers. Perhaps he was hoping they would feed him in some emotional way eventually with Phil and Billie as parent substitutes and Josh as a brother in some Platonic sense. In any case, his trip so far had been a cool passage leading to the sunlit atrium of meeting them, and explorer that he was, he was eager to see where else the newly formed tour would lead, besides a right onto Via Abbondanza.

"There's graffiti along here," Josh said. "'Albanus is a bugger.' 'Restitutus has deceived many girls many times.' Slurs like that. My favorite, though, is 'Lovers, like bees, lead a honey-sweet life.' On the wall of a house over there a couple of blocks," he added, pointing right. "The House of the Lovers."

Tyler traced a deep track in the street. When he glanced up, he saw a bas-relief of a winged phallus and balls in a small temple with phallus finials.

"I think this is the workshop of Verecundus," Josh said, indicating the wall.

"Oh, my," Billie smiled, shading her eyes.

"Phalluses were not only fertility symbols," Josh explained, "but also protection against evil."

"Art as magic," Phil remarked.

"Mine's always got me in trouble," Tyler commented.

"How much trouble?" Billie asked.

"More than you can imagine."

"How many times did you say you were divorced?" she asked.

"Legally, once."

"Didn't you say you beat your wife?" she joked.

Tyler and Josh laughed.

"It was a metaphor, Billie," Phil said, making fists. "Marriage as a boxing match."

"Boxing match," she repeated. Eyebrows raised, she gave Josh a comic look of alarm.

"I've read that we set our wills aside when we fall in love," Josh said, "then pick them up again when we marry."

"The will asserts itself," Tyler agreed.

Reciprocal relationships, Tyler guessed, were not totally out of the question, but he figured that, to be compatible, two men would have to get the battle of the wills over with first, like two gorillas fighting it out to see who's head ape. Then they could settle down into their harmonious dominant and submissive roles. He remembered the passage in Carson McCullers' *Ballad of the Sad Café*, the one about the lover and the loved.

"I think it depends on context," Josh said. "I'd defer to someone's judgment in areas like painting or writing, but I'd probably stick to my guns when it came to architecture. In other areas," he winked, "I'm versatile."

Everyone snickered.

"Well," Billie said, "we defer to your judgment as to where to go next. Lead on, Virgil."

Tyler smiled at her reference to the guide in *Inferno* and *Purgatorio*. Then they strolled down Abbondanza in silence, taking in the sights: fluted columns, arches, the countless stones in a wall, more bas-relief, broken frescoes with lions, horses, bulls, boars, deer. Tyler studied a fresco up close. On a black background, a gold eagle, wings arched, held a green snake in its beak and talons. Josh pointed out a bar with women's names on the façade. Next came the House of Paquius Proculus with a mosaic of a chained dog. Josh stopped at the House of Caius Julius Polibius and recited a poem that he said was scratched in Latin on a side wall.

Nothing lasts forever. Now the sun shines clearly.
Now it sinks in the sea. The moon is half gone which was just full.
Thus, every feather obeys the wind, the most cruel denial of love.

"Carpe diem, everyone," Billie sighed.

"We're trying, dear," Phil said with mock melodrama.

At the House of Loreius Tiburtinus, Phil and Billie wandered off, leaving Tyler and Josh near a large fountain with wall paintings on either side: one of Pyramus and Thisbe, the other of Narcissus and his reflection. Pyramus was drawn well enough, Tyler thought, but Thisbe's face was oddly flat, her buttocks bulbous.

"Not the best painting I ever saw," Josh remarked.

"Whoever drew the lion," Tyler said, "had obviously never seen one. Gorgeous color on the wall," he added, referring to the maroon stucco. Below the fresco was painted powder-blue foliage.

"What's that on the tree?" Josh asked.

"Uh, her cloak. Familiar with the story?"

"No," Josh said. "What's it about?"

"Forbidden love. They live in houses that share a wall, but there's a chink in it, through which they whisper. They agree to meet one night, but when she sees a lion, she flees, dropping the cloak. The lion, fresh from a kill, gets blood on it. When Pyramus sees it, he thinks she's dead and kills himself. When she finds him, she kills herself."

"Romeo and Juliet."

"Right," Tyler agreed. "Reminds me of Jane Fredericks."

"Jane Fredericks?" Josh laughed.

"This girl who lived next door where I grew up," Tyler mused. "Her father poisoned my father's beagles, so war broke out between the adults, and she was forbidden to cross our property line. If she crossed the line, her father beat her, but we could sit right on the line and talk to each other."

"How sad," Josh remarked.

"Sometimes I think it's colored all my relationships with women."

Josh scraped an arc in the dust with the toe of his shoe. When he glanced up, Tyler stared back. Again, Tyler felt the irresistible impulse between them. Anything could happen.

"Familiar with the Narcissus story?" he asked, breaking the mood. He stepped to the other mural.

"It's a satire on gay culture," Josh joked, trailing him.

Tyler smiled.

"What's odd about this one," he said, "is that he's looking up instead of gazing at himself in the pool."

"It's the moment just before he falls in love with himself," Josh smiled.

"There you go." Tyler sat on the edge of the base of a column. "This is your first trip to Italy, right? Didn't your program have some study-abroad opportunities?"

"The college offered it," Josh replied, "but, at the time, I considered it a distraction. I wanted just to keep plowing ahead toward the degree."

# # # # #

In the peristyle of the House of Venus, the four strolled to a halt in front of a big mural of Venus on a giant clam shell with a pensive Cupid to one side and a rapt Nereid the other.

"These frescoes are badly drawn," Tyler said. "The faces are exquisite, but look how awkward her legs are."

"The perspective's off," Billie remarked. "Her right leg looks broken."

"The clam shell was a yonic symbol," Josh explained.

"Yonic?" Phil asked.

"Vagina," Billie enunciated.

"Probably that cowry shell on her neck, too," Josh added.

"So what's this thing here?" Phil asked, pointing to what the Nereid was holding, a pole with what looked like a small puffed sail.

Everyone stared at it.

"No idea," Josh said.

"Guess this must be where Botticelli got his inspiration," Tyler said, referring to *The Birth of Venus.*

"He never saw this," Josh said. "He was just drawing on tradition."

"So to speak," Tyler quipped.

"Lot of erotic stuff in Pompeii," Billie said.

"After all," Josh smiled, "Venus was its patron deity."

"Art as religion," Phil remarked.

"I'm surprised you didn't bring sketch pads and pencils," Tyler replied.

"Well, I do have the camera."

"And I am taking note of all these earthy colors," Billie added.

At the House of Julia Felice, Phil and Billie strolled down the beautiful portico along the garden, but Tyler and Josh strayed into a strange room where tiers faced a central well and the floor sloped down to the walls. Josh explained that it was a triclinium or dining room built to accommodate reclining guests. To demonstrate, Josh lay with his elbows on the edge of the well and his feet toward the wall. Tyler stretched out beside him. The topic of Roman architecture led to Josh's degree and his thesis: *Learning from the Flaws in the Work of Frank Lloyd Wright*, and soon Josh had drifted off into a free-associative monologue about Wright's idiosyncrasies.

"He was a great architect," Josh said, "but also a power-mad control freak. It was typically his way or the highway. As a result, he wasn't always the best person to hire or work with. He created details to suit his needs, whether or not they had any precedent of success, and so at times, his building would fail: for example, leaks or insufficient protection from the outside temperature. Of course, very frequently his details would succeed greatly, and he'd be lauded as a great thinker."

Tyler turned onto his side, propped his head on his hand, and cocked a knee, watching Josh, lost in thought, staring at the stone wall across from them.

"On a weirder note," Josh went on, "he was a tiny guy, so his rooms were typically very small, his ceilings low, his corridors narrow. In other words, he'd design for himself as much as he was designing for his client. On an even weirder note, he'd design clothes for the owners to wear in his homes."

"He *was* a control freak," Tyler laughed.

He rolled onto his back, clasped his hands under his head, and crossed his ankles, gazing sideways at Josh and occasionally through the high window above him.

"He designed a lot of furniture to outfit the rooms," Josh said, "furniture that's now world famous on its own design merit. While that isn't all that strange, the fact he forbid owners to move it around the house was. He was notorious for visiting his former clients and moving the furniture back to where he had originally intended."

Josh rolled onto his side, head on hand, facing him.

"He was routinely broke," he said. "While world famous, he was also outspending his fees. He didn't exactly die a pauper, but wasn't exactly lighting up cigars with $50 bills."

Josh stared at Tyler and bit his lip pensively, but they could hear Phil and Billie strolling along the portico, and as they passed the door, Phil and Billie noticed them.

"What have we here?" she chuckled.

#

Behind Julia Felice's house was the large, elliptical Amphitheater with seats overgrown with big patches of grass.

"Oldest amphitheater in the world," Josh said. "It held 12,000 and had a velarium or canvas cover which retracted like the roof of a football stadium." He talked about gladiatorial games, sea battles, and the riot between the Pompeiians and Nucerians which resulted in the stadium being closed for ten years. Everyone speculated on what qualities human beings would have to have to watch murder for entertainment.

"Indifference to suffering," Tyler said.

"But what would cause such indifference?" Josh asked, studying him.

"Selfishness in the sense of the inability to see oneself in others," Phil said.

"In short," Billie agreed, "a great lack of imagination."

"Selfishness in the sense of self-preservation," Tyler suggested. "You have to be selfish to survive. The Hollywood hero is a scapegoat. He sacrifices himself for the sake of others, which is noble, of course, but not much comfort in the casket."

Everyone else seemed concerned.

"Well," Billie said, "I started to say that the world was much more violent then. Then I realized that isn't true. We have much better ways of killing ourselves."

They wandered next door to the Palaestra or Gymnasium with its border of giant umbrella pines. The great green clouds of the canopies cast cool, blue shadows on the ground, a welcome relief from the heat, but the lower branches, cut off, reminded Tyler of a mace and the fierce gladiatorial games again. He thought of how the violence in the arena had spread like fire to the fans in the seats, whipping them up to massacre the Nucerians, their guests, an atrocious act which, he knew from literature, violated one of the most sacred codes of the ancients. He glanced down the endless perspective of a colonnade, then, through the columns, across the athletic field and managed to balance the savage gladiatorial vision with a civilized one of the vigorous workouts and athletic competitions centered around the swimming pool, now just a blank depression in the middle of the lawn. Two men wrestling for sport, he knew, were certainly a much better image than two running each other through with swords.

They visited the Orchard of the Fugitives with its thirteen body casts contorted on the ground near a wall. Then they swung by Menander's House in a big loop back up to Via Abbondanza, where they turned west, making their way to the Stabian Baths, the Forum, and the crowds of tourists.

"This is where we should have come in," Josh announced.

"Doesn't matter where we began," Billie said, "or even where we end up."

As she was about to speak, Phil interrupted her: "You're not going to tell us it's the journey, not the destination, are you?"

She gave him a droll, annoyed look, and as Tyler glanced down the Forum toward Vesuvius, he could not figure out exactly what he was seeing: two mountainous cones like shoulders or a cone within a cone or caldera. The lower slopes were dark with vegetation, the upper bare with white streaks like ski slopes. Again, he imagined the heart-stopping *crack* and the pyroclastic flow rolling down the mountain relentlessly. What must the pain have felt like, he wondered. Incinerated in an instant, a long, excruciating instant.

To the right, Josh pointed out the Temple of Apollo with the statue of the god and the column with the sun dial.

"What about a spot over there for lunch?" he asked, looking to the left, toward the Basilica.

They settled on steps in the shade of a wall. Billie sat on the top step near a truncated column with an Ionic capital. The men bumped awkwardly before Phil sat on the step below her. When Josh gestured toward the top step, Tyler sat there, knees spread, and Josh slipped off the backpack and sat below him.

"Let's see what we have in that humble wineskin of yours," Phil said, meaning the backpack.

Josh began unwrapping and setting out the picnic: a Napoli salami, a chunk of Caciocavallo, rosemary focaccia, and a bottle of Aglianico. He cut up the food with a Swiss Army knife, doled out portions on paper plates with napkins, and poured the wine into red plastic cups.

"Sorry about the plastic cups," he said.

"So why is this called a basilica?" Billie asked, tearing off a piece of the oily bread. "Thought a basilica was a church."

"Originally, a law court," Josh explained. "Guess the Christians appropriated them."

Everyone ate, chewing the sweet salami and slightly salty cheese.

"This salami is so good," Phil moaned.

"I know," Josh agreed, glancing at Tyler's crotch. "I actually felt a twinge of remorse, cutting into such a beautiful piece of meat."

"Oh, my," Billie blurted.

Tyler leaned back and looked at him askance. It was good to be sitting in the shade after walking in the sun, he thought, and again, he felt at home with them, a comfortable place where he could be himself. In fact, just being there with them, he was resting in some subtle sense as well, though he could not tell himself from what. The tasty picnic was the least of it.

"Fresh grapes would be nice," Billie said.

"Let's enjoy what we have, my dear," Phil admonished her. "Don't complain about what we don't have."

She said "what we don't have" in unison.

Tyler felt they were talking about something greater than grapes and that they'd had the conversation before.

"You're getting the grapes in the wine," Josh remarked.

"Here's to getting in touch with yourself," Tyler said, parroting the risqué joke from dinner last night.

When he raised his cup, the others touched cups and sipped the warm, garnet wine.

"In touch with yourself," Billie repeated.

Josh set his cup down and cut more pieces of the salami, cheese, and bread.

"More sausage?" he asked Tyler, offering the plate.

"Maybe a little more bread and cheese," Tyler said.

Josh served him, then offered the plates to the Trees.

"Think I will," Phil said, taking a slice of cheese.

There was something solicitous about Josh's manner with Tyler that Tyler noticed that the others noticed. Josh's role as waiter, Tyler inferred, cast him (Tyler) as patron in some psychological sense, and when Tyler's gaze lingered on him thoughtfully, Josh's intent pout changed into such a timid smile that Tyler had to resist the tender impulse to touch the young man's shoulder or, like a schoolboy, poke his neck just to get a rise out of him. Despite himself, Tyler realized that he was responding more and more affectionately to him, that his nerves like wires were becoming less resistant to his suitor's sweet attentions. Wandering around the ruins of his life, Tyler's sense of failure, like a seed, had grown into resigned despair, a difficult, yet familiar fate he could live with, but now, in the shade of a wall, it had bloomed into a sanguine flower of relief. He understood perfectly well what Josh wanted, a friend, but could he be his ultimate friend? And why was he even asking himself such a question. He'd met him last night.

"Soooo," Tyler droned, breaking eye contact with him. "If you're an art act," he said, turning to Phil and Billie, "what sort of act do you do?" Again, he was referring to last night's dinner conversation.

"Seascapes, landscapes," Phil explained, "modern, great color."

144

"Vineyards, orchards," Billie added.

"Lots of those in California," Josh remarked, hunched over his plate.

"Exactly," Phil agreed, wiping sweat from his brow with the back of his hand. "Familiar with Richard Diebenkorn, his *Ocean Park* series?"

"'Fraid not," Tyler said, biting into the soft, yellow cheese.

"Abstract *and* figurative," Billie said. "What about Hockney?"

"I like Hockney," Tyler muttered.

"Hockney-esque," Phil said. "Billie has a show at the Oakland Museum when we get back, and I have a few pieces at the Laguna Beach Museum."

When Billie, thumbs to shoulders, motioned for Josh to sit up, he went from rag doll to puppet on a string.

"Have any art?" Phil asked Tyler.

"A couple of Ansel Adams photos: Yosemite Falls, the Sierras."

"Very good," Phil smiled. "California."

"Italy's such a contradiction," Billie said, staring into her cup. "All this pagan art and its open attitude and the unforgivably priggish Vatican set down in its midst."

"The Vatican has such a privileged status," Phil complained. "It's a huge corporation with hotels, restaurants, shops, and schools."

"Schools for brainwashing children," Josh interjected.

"But it doesn't pay taxes," Phil continued. "In fact," he added, pointing for emphasis, "it's subsidized by the Italian taxpayers to the tune of four billion Euros a year."

"And, unlike other religions," Tyler mentioned, "it's a sovereign state, a tiny state with undue influence!"

"Right," Phil agreed. "It has diplomatic relations with every nation. A lot of EU countries are bound to it by treaty, even though it violates the EU Convention in regard to separation of church and state."

"It's even part of the UN," Tyler said, "where it interferes with birth control, abortion, sex education in general."

"It opposes the UN resolution decriminalizing homosexuality," Josh added. "In fact, when it comes to gays, it opposes human rights. I've read that, when it comes to gays, it believes that civil liberties can be quote unquote 'legitimately limited' and that discrimination against gays is quote unquote 'not unjust,' but 'obligatory.'"

"It's toxic attitudes like that that led to Buchenwald," Tyler mused.

"Toxic as the old lead pipes in Pompeii," Josh agreed.

"That's taught in the schools here, right?" Billie asked.

"Where it ignores bullying and violence, even suicide," Josh said.

"Well, as faith in reason rises," Billie concluded, wiping her hands on her napkin, "the church, I'm sure, will decline."

"The number of first communions, confirmations, even Catholic marriages," Tyler assured her, "is, in fact, falling off."

"Woo," she blurted, wadding up the napkin, "the wine is making me drowsy."

"Anyone want anything?" Josh asked, glancing around. "Everyone done?"

He handed out hygienic wipes and, when everyone had cleaned their hands, held out a small paper bag in which to drop the wipes. Then he packed up, stood, and slung the backpack onto his shoulders. They strolled to the Porta Marina, where Josh asked the guards in Italian if he could go to the granita stand across the street.

When a guard asked, "Per quanto tempo?" Josh said, "Due minuti."

He bought everyone a lemon granita in a paper cone and, as they ate the brisk ice, assumed his duties as tour guide, leading the others up the west side of the Forum to what had been a big granary, now a ramshackle warehouse open on one side but fenced off from tourists. As they idled there, Tyler's gaze strayed over the rows of amphoras, stacks of capitals, finials, friezes, basins, and urns, various architectural fragments. Sitting on a box was the body cast of a man huddled against the heat, knees in the fetal position, hands clasped and pressed to his face as if praying. Though Tyler knew it was only a plaster mold, he felt as if he were, in fact, in the presence of the dead and felt not only a quiet respect for him and the awful fear he had suffered, but also a sense of embarrassment at the indignity of such an intimate moment set on display.

"Think he's called the Mule Driver," Josh said, clutching the fence.

"Reminds us of the transience of things," Tyler mused. "Still, it's odd to think of him sitting here forever."

When they had finished the granitas, Josh handed out another round of wipes. Then they went around the Temple of Jove and headed east to the brothel or Lupanare, the Den of Wolves. There Josh explained that, though most foreigners didn't speak the language, they could point to the picture menu over the cubicles.

"Practical art," Phil remarked.

Over the centuries, the painted vignettes had faded to faint, reddish-brown depictions of couples doing it cowgirl style, doggy style, in the missionary position.

At the House of the Vettii, in a fresco to the right of the door, Priapus was weighing his penis on a set of scales.

"A huge cock must be a curse," Tyler whispered to Josh.

"Yours is just right," Josh whispered.

"Thanks."

"Looks like a bag of coins on the other scale," Josh observed. "Guess it objectifies sex, sex as a commodity."

"You object to that?" Tyler asked. "Sex for sex's sake."

"Uh, no," Josh decided. "And Priapus was a fertility god, fertility in the sense of prosperity. Thus, the basket of fruit in the background."

"Ah," Tyler exclaimed. "The fruits of one's labor."

"This is the house of a couple of very successful brothers."

"Another way of interpreting it," Tyler pointed, "is that it places value on sex and pleasure, as it should. In America, pleasure is de-valued."

Billie had strolled up and been eavesdropping. "Puritanism," she grumped.

"Exactly," Tyler agreed.

At the House of the Faun, they saw a bronze copy of the delightful *Dancing Faun* in the pool in the atrium, and Josh reminded them that the *Battle of Issus* mosaic in the museum had come from there.

"Art as history," Phil remarked.

In the House of the Tragic Poet, they saw another mosaic of a watchdog, this one with the caption *Cave canem*: "Beware of the dog." In the House of the Little Fountain: a mosaic fountain with a bronze fisherman on the lip. In the House of Pansa: a phallus and inscription, "Here lives happiness." They took Via Consolare north to Porta Ercolaneo, through which they exited the town proper, taking Via dei Sepolchri down to the Villa dei Misteri.

"The Villa of the Mysteries," Josh stated, "the best-preserved Pompeian villa and frescoes." They wandered to what Josh called the Initiation Chamber, where he leaned on the gate at the room's main door. "A mystery is a secret ceremony," he explained, "in which the initiate is admitted to a cult, and this is a fresco of the initiation of a young bride into the Dionysian Mysteries. Banned by the Senate, by the way, as a danger to the state."

"Danger to the state?" Billie asked

"Music, sex, wine," Tyler smiled. "Didn't you know that fun's subversive?"

"The scenes go clockwise around the room," Josh said. "The Greek word for rite has something to do with growing up, so the wall paintings are a visual representation of the psychological transition from virginal girl to married woman."

"What a gorgeous red," Billie blurted, referring to the vermillion background.

"In the first mural," Josh began, "what we may have is the mother of the initiate, a priestess, and the initiate herself. As you can see, a nude boy in boots is reading from a scroll. The boots, I've read, are actor's boots and may suggest the theatrical aspect of the ritual." He gave Tyler an odd smile. "The initiate, guided by a priestess, plays a role in the ceremony's drama."

The priestess held a stylus in one hand and a scroll in the other, and Tyler inferred that she was about to add the initiate's name to a list of devotees.

"In the second scene," Josh said, "another priestess is sitting at a table with attendants to either side, one holding a basket from which the priestess is removing a cover, the other pouring water into a basin into which the priestess is about to dip a sprig of laurel. Water's usually associated with ritual purification."

"I could use a drop or two myself," Tyler quipped.

To the right, Silenus, Dionysus' companion, was playing a lyre with ten strings, and in the third scene, a satyr was playing panpipes and a nymph was suckling a goat. Tyler knew that Pan was a half-goat nature god, and a nymph suckling a goat certainly blurred the line between our human and animal natures. Initiation into the mindless ecstasy of sex (marriage) was, without doubt, one way of looking at what the ritual was about. He was well aware that his mind died at climax, but eventually came back. On the right, the initiate, hand up, seemed startled by what lay ahead. Tyler, in turn, interpreted the protective gesture as the superego's fear of a powerful, if not overwhelming libido.

In scene four, Silenus was scowling at the frightened initiate in the prior panel. Appropriately so, Tyler thought, since Silenus, part animal, would represent the direct opposite of her prudishness. He was holding a silver bowl in which a young satyr seemed to be staring at his reflection, but, behind Silenus, another satyr was holding up a theatrical mask which looked like Silenus. From the viewer's perspective, it wasn't clear whether the first satyr was gazing at his own reflection or that of the mask, in which case he would be prophetically seeing himself in old age.

Again, Tyler tried to reconcile all the images by thinking in terms of opposites. What better way to respond to the prospect of old age and death, he thought, than by taking pleasure in the moment, as Dionysus obviously was, slumped drunkenly in his wife's lap and missing a sandal? Tyler also wondered in what other way the initiate would have to die before she could take part in the revelation of the god. She, of course, would have to lose her virginity. The girl would molt, leaving the woman.

In the central scene, Dionysus was wearing a wreath of ivy, and the thyrsus, tied with a yellow ribbon, rested against his thigh. Tyler could not help noticing that the staff crossed the god's lap at exactly the same place and slant his erect phallus would and that, though the staff, of course, was too long, the cluster of ivy at the top made a sort of "head."

"Odd that when the initiate finally has her mystic, life-altering vision of him," Phil commented, "he's soused."

"In the next scene," Josh pointed, "the initiate emerges from the vision, born again, as the Baptists say, that is, transformed into a woman. As you can see, she is about to lift a cover off something, and from the size and shape of it — "

"Like a woman unzipping the pants of a well-endowed man," Billie cut in.

To the right, a winged figure held her hand up as if to say, "Wait." She was also wielding a whip and glancing toward the crouched woman crying in the next frame. Everyone focused on the lash mark on the initiate's hip. She was kneeling with her head in the lap of a woman consoling her.

"Actually," Josh said, "I never found a good explanation of why flagellation is part of the ceremony, though the rites were, in fact, famous for their terrifying ordeals."

To the right, in contrast with the initiate's grief, was the joy of a nude dancing and striking cymbals. Behind the dancer, a woman was bringing a thyrsus, signifying, Tyler thought, the successful completion of the ritual and the initiate's acceptance into the cult.

In the eighth scene, the bride was preparing for marriage, aided by an attendant. A boyish Eros held up a mirror with the bride's reflection, and, symbolically, Tyler thought, both the bride and her new, altered image of herself were staring at the viewer. In the ninth scene, the mature bride was wearing a ring, and in the last, Eros, bow in hand, was leaning on a pedestal, staring at her.

"And they all lived happily ever after," Josh said, smiling at Tyler.

Chapter 17: The Lemon Grove

Everyone returned to the pensione and rested, then around eight o'clock set out for a trattoria Josh had seen behind San Francesco di Paola, the big church with the curved colonnade in the Piazza del Plebiscito.

As Josh and Tyler were leaving the room, Josh picked up an Armani bag.

"What's in the bag?" Tyler asked.

"A secret."

"Ooo-Kaaay," Tyler puzzled, drawing out the syllables.

When the four met in the hall, Billie noticed the bag and asked, "What's that?"

"A secret," Tyler said.

"Really."

"Guess he'll show us later."

They walked along the waterfront to the elevator up to the piazza, strolled up its wide slope, and rounded the north end of the colonnade, taking a right onto Via Gennaro Serra. Again, it was a warm night, and everyone was wearing what they had worn to Pompeii. Soon they stepped through a wrought-iron gate into the paved courtyard of Il Limoneto (The Lemon Grove) and looked around, waiting for someone to seat them. Lemon trees loomed over candle-lit tables, and music played in the background. The corners of the courtyard curved to form planters, blue with plumbago below and flecked with yellow hibiscus above. A young woman with long, black, curly hair came out of the restaurant, greeted them, and asked where they would like to sit.

"What about the table in the corner?" Josh asked, indicating a table for six with big, fat lemons like lanterns dangling over it.

Tyler slipped onto a weathered bench against the wall, and when he scooted over, making room for him, Josh sat next to him, standing the bag on the bench. Billie looked at them curiously, then sat across from Tyler, but Phil, instead of sitting across from Josh, took the chair at the head of the table between Billie and Tyler. A couple of red, wavering votive candles cast faint wine stains on the tablecloth, and a yellow hibiscus with a scarlet throat yawned from a small, ceramic vase.

"I really enjoyed what I had last night," Josh said deadpan. "Hope tonight's just as good."

"I'm sure it will be," Billie said slyly.

"Will you two let go of that meal metaphor?" Tyler chuckled. "I know what you're talking about."

"Don't know what *you're* talking about," Billie claimed.

151

"What?" Phil asked, forehead crimped.

"Nothing!" Billie chirped.

Everyone decided to order just antipasto and perhaps dessert later. So they shared platters of prosciutto, bresaola, shrimp, mozzarella, smoked provolone, grilled peppers, arugula with Parmigiano flakes, and so forth. Billie ordered a bottle of Lacryma Christi del Vesuvio Bianco just because she liked the name, a straw-colored wine which she said tasted fruity with a hint of licorice. Again, Josh said that drinking at night kept him awake, but ordered a Campari as did Tyler, a Campari convert, as Josh described him.

"Why do you like such a bitter drink?" Tyler asked

"Bittersweet," Josh corrected him, "with fruit and herbs."

"I see."

Phil carried the getting-in-touch joke forward by proposing a toast to getting in touch with Italy, and everyone clinked glasses.

"Rather ruddy faced," Billie said to Tyler.

"Am I the only one who didn't wear suntan lotion?" he asked, sipping Campari.

"It'll tone down by morning," Josh smiled, brushing something off Tyler's shoulder.

"What?" Tyler asked.

"I don't know. Little flower petals."

There was that tender, solicitous manner again, Tyler thought. Josh's physical coziness with him made him think of the compatible Trees and Odysseus' wish for Princess Nausikaa in *The Odyssey*.

> *May the gods grant your wish:*
> *a house, a husband, and pleasant dialogue*
> *with him....*

No mention of love, Tyler noted. Just compatibility.

"So," Tyler turned to Phil, "how long have you two been married?"

"Thirty-two years."

"Have children?"

"A son," Phil said, glancing at Billie. "Died five years ago."

"Sorry."

"Thirty-two years is a long time," Josh remarked. "What's the secret of your success?"

"Like-mindedness," Phil said with a tossing-away gesture, "and, ironically, hard times. Trial by fire has steeled our mettle, to use a couple of clichés."

"And puns," Tyler remarked.

"We have had some hard times," Billie said stoically. "Phil's an oak, a real oak. He's sheltered me through many a storm."

"If I'm an oak," he replied, touching her hand, "then you're a linden."

"Linden?" she puzzled.

"A gentle ornamental," he explained. "You add even more beauty to my life."

"Thank you, sweetheart," she said, leaning to kiss him. "If I had a wreath of oak leaves, I'd crown you with it."

The rhyme *gentle ornamental* made Tyler think of how Phil and Billie rhymed in other ways. He glanced at Josh leaning forward, elbows on the table. When Josh faced him, blinking, Tyler took a second to enjoy his pink pout, his pale-green eyes, his frank expression of passive desire. You sexy little saint, he thought. When Billie cleared her throat, Josh glanced at her and sat up straight. Then something caught Billie's attention.

"What a lovely song," she remarked, head cocked. "Te voglio bene assai" ("I Love You A Lot") was sifting through the sieve of branches.

"Sounds like Pavarotti," Phil said, dipping a shrimp in a cream sauce.

Billie savored the music, then looked at Josh. "How's that scratch on your chest?"

"Just a scab," he replied. "Tell Tyler about Seaweed."

"Seaweed?" Tyler asked.

"Phil and Billie's house."

"Uh, three-bedroom, three-bath," Phil said, elbow on the chair arm, hand up, finger pointing into the dark foliage and lemons.

"Chilly mornings, cool evenings," Billie brooded.

"Big windows," Phil added. "You won't believe the sunsets: red, pink, purple, gold."

Tyler noticed that Josh gave Phil a strange look when he mentioned the sunsets.

"There's a garden terrace with a hot tub, grill – " Billie began.

"And a beach!" Josh blurted. "Sixty feet down to the beach, right?"

"Right," Phil said somberly.

"There're stairs," Billie said, sipping wine, "but as I told Josh, try getting up them at our age."

"One of the strangest miracles in our life," Phil remarked, "how the house was restored."

"What do you mean?" Tyler asked.

"Well," Phil said, tapping the table, "we took in a pair of what appeared to be homeless guys, and they wound up doing just about all the work for us."

"That *was* a miracle," Billie stressed. "One of them. We've had hard times, but we've also had good luck."

"Good karma," Tyler said, winding a red pepper around a fork.

"Beautiful location," Billie mused, staring at her plate. "The house looks like it's growing out of the rock."

"Like the cottage I've rented in Amalfi," Josh remarked.

"The area's called Passion Point," she said, glancing up, an odd undertow to her look.

"Passion Point!" Tyler blurted. "I'll have to visit."

"Anytime," Phil said, holding a fork with mozzarella and arugula. "We'd love to have you, both of you."

"Speaking of Amalfi," Josh paused, glancing at Billie, then Tyler. "Listen. We were wondering if you'd consider going to Amalfi with us tomorrow." When Tyler did not respond, Josh continued. "We're staying at a little hotel just west of town, Il Piccolo Sogno. That is, they're staying at the hotel. I saw this – this apartment online and just fell in love with it. Set off by itself near the hotel. Big balcony. Very romantic."

"Romantic," Tyler smiled.

He was grateful for the offer, but his feelings like filings were repelled magnetically by the idea. He guessed the reason was that he was afraid his bad luck would rub off on Josh. In Atlanta, the purple Japanese maple was usually so eager to bloom that its tulip-like blossoms got burnt by the cold. Tyler didn't want to burn Josh's naïve affection for him the same way.

Then he thought of himself. Detached, he felt safe, so he was resistant to getting involved with him or, for that matter, them. On the surface, the request was trivial, under the surface, though, important as a shark. First, it meant he was consenting to a sort of short marriage with Josh, a man, a young man he didn't really know, except intuitively.

"As Blanche says to the nurse from the sanatorium," Tyler said, "'I don't know you.'"

"What?" Josh laughed.

"For all I know," Tyler said, "you could be secret agents sent by one of my enemies to wreak vengeance on me."

"And you could be the god of wine," Billie said, rolling some arugula in a slice of prosciutto. "We've had this conversation."

When Billie glanced at Josh, Tyler could easily see her emotional investment in him. She studied Tyler with concern, then bit off half of the prosciutto.

"The god of wine wasn't married, was he?" she asked.

"Ariadne," Josh said. "Don't you remember? He's slumped in her lap in the Villa of the Mysteries."

"Your point?" Phil asked.

"Nothing," she said. "Just wondering."

"Moving right along," Phil said, making a move-on gesture.

"I'd just gum up your plans," Tyler frowned.

"We don't have plans," Phil replied. "All we know is we're going to Amalfi."

A smart Adonis with peach fuzz on his lips was asking him to accompany them to the Amalfi Coast, someone who prized his company, his opinions and feelings. What was wrong with that? He also knew that, if he went, sex was inevitable. How could he resist the young man's complaisant overtures, such accessible warmth? In a cold world, he added. Besides, there were worse problems than getting a hand job. He was a feather in the wind, an oar-less boat pushed sideways by a breeze. Another irresistible current was carrying him forward, but this time actually toward something, a port, not out to sea. Perhaps, at least for a while, as an experiment, he would just let it. In the spirit of adventure – and psychological curiosity – he was willing to wing it with Josh for a few days. Who was he kidding? he asked himself finally. The conflict was resolved. Why was he acting as if it weren't?

"We'd love it if you tagged along with us," Phil said. He slipped a slice of provolone into his mouth and chased it with a sip of wine.

"There's a huge king-sized bed," Josh claimed. "If that's too close, there's a daybed. I'll be glad to take the daybed."

"Said the spider."

"Come on, please," Josh pleaded.

Tyler slumped on the bench, heels together, knees spread, hands on the table. "If it makes you happy," he conceded, the same phrase he had used in Josh's room last night.

"It would!"

A smiled bloomed in Josh's face mirrored in Tyler's.

"It would make us all happy," Billie added.

"At least till you grow tired of me," Tyler said.

"No way," Josh swore.

"We find you very companionable," Billie said.

Liked not only by Josh, Tyler thought, but also by the Trees, intelligent people with artistic sensibilities, and, for some reason, he wanted to please them more than he wanted to be left alone. Traveling with them surely would be more fun than traveling alone.

"I need to be distracted," Josh chuckled, resting his hand on Tyler's knee. "I could use something to look forward to."

Fire with fire, Tyler thought, squeezing Josh's hand. He held it, and touching him casually this way was sensual, of course, but also affectionate, merely friendly. It was also as if someone else were holding Josh's hand, as if he himself hadn't taken it consciously.

"Besides, Ty," Billie said, "you need to see Amalfi and Positano." Billie glanced at him, then Josh as if aware of what was going on under the table. "Tourist musts."

"I've heard," he said.

Perhaps he would do well in their balmy climate, as he thought of it, the way the abundant tree above him was thriving in the sultry air of Naples. He, like Josh, could use some R and R, that is, healing, if, in fact, his wounds could heal.

"Here's to lifelong friends," Billie said, lifting her glass.

"Who visit each other often," Phil added, lifting his.

When everyone touched glasses, Tyler smiled, tilted his glass, and glanced up. Here and there among the maze of leaves glowed the huge, lopsided lemons, bloated with rich, acidic juice, he knew, but also chock-full of many small, young promises.

Chapter 18: A Black Silk Shirt

Instead of having dessert at Il Limoneto, Josh suggested they stroll up to Bar Gambrinus in Piazza Trieste e Trento. He wanted to show them what he called the faded grandeur of Naple's most famous café. After coffee and pastries, they headed back to the hotel, but at the main entrance to the Galleria, the south portal on Via San Carlo, Josh leisurely started up the steps, and everyone followed. Since Josh was carrying the shopping bag, Tyler assumed that he wanted to browse some display windows.

The wide marble floor made Tyler think of a glassy pool in an enormous grotto; the arched dome, the nerve-like branches of a magnificent pine. A white pine's bark, he knew, was deeply furrowed like fractured glass, and he wondered if any of the thousands of roof panes had fallen and injured or killed anyone. The detail in the place was overwhelming, more than the eye could take in: pillars, pilasters, plaques, festoons.

Billie and Phil lagged behind, looking in boutiques, and Tyler stopped to stare at a wide-winged angel staring down at him, but when he looked at Josh, Josh was smiling at him tentatively, as if worried about something.

"So," Tyler said, "what would Wright have thought of this?"

"Guess the dome would've impressed him," Josh replied.

"Reminds me of the Guggenheim's spiral."

"And some of his cantilever work," Josh said, "like the Johnson Tower in Racine. Of course," he admitted, "the dome's basically ugly, a big steel spiderweb."

In the cavernous light, Josh's sweet, green eyes looked pale, washed out, as if from crying.

"You like everything Wright did?" Tyler asked.

"I appreciate it all," Josh said, "but don't necessarily like it all. The Millard house in Pasadena looks like a creepy mausoleum, an overgrown Mayan ruin. On the other hand, he's managed to make concrete blocks interesting with some great geometric patterns."

When Billie and Phil caught up, everyone strolled on.

"Someplace we can get a gelato?" Phil asked.

"You don't need a gelato," Billie said. "And Josh," she added, "hold your shoulders back. You look like a puppet with a couple of strings cut."

"Yeah, Ma." The building was like a cathedral in that it had a nave and transepts, and when they reached the zodiac mosaic in the center, Josh patted his thigh nervously and said, "Uh, would you mind waiting here a minute?"

Everyone looked at him quizzically.

"I, uh, I have to go to the men's room."

"You can go to the bathroom in your room," Billie stated. "What are you up to?"

"Just do me a favor and look around for a while," he blushed. "OK? Back in a minute."

Josh strolled off, but when he was out of hearing, Billie said, "It has something to do with that Armani bag."

"What great mosaics," Phil commented, staring at the one at their feet.

Tyler glanced at Sagittarius in the form of a centaur-dolphin about to let fly an arrow. The brawny male had pulled the bow string taut with his right hand, which, in the tile work, simultaneously looked like a big fist and, since it was held in front of his chest, also like a big, muscular heart. Tyler noticed the figure's modern hair style and loved the way the eye's fierce focus was suggested by a single black tile.

"I think it has something to do with the bag too," Tyler said. "Let's spy on him."

# # # # #

If the Galleria were a temple, Josh thought, then it was definitely a temple of commercialism, and the young men loitering outside were a Philistine commodity of sorts, a contemporary version of the viable dolls he had seen in a book of Wilhelm von Gloeden photographs. He was curious, though, about the judicious absence of police.

Valerio was treading the edge of a large step as if walking a tightrope, one foot directly in front of the other, hands floating up and down slowly like the pans of a scale. But tonight, despite his antics, he was not the Happy Hustler, it seemed, his expression stone sober, as if he were, in fact, walking a tightrope and could fall to his death.

He was wearing jeans, a jean jacket, and Nikes, his long hair shiny with amber highlights, and as Josh, standing at a corner, watched him, he wondered again about the affective dimension of tricking. Valerio had a wonderful equine masculinity about him, and men, especially butch types, suppressed feelings. Valerio, obviously, had them. At the moment he was frowning.

At this point in life, naively or not, Josh still believed in three things. The first was a natural bond between two people, any two people. Second, despite his pain over Owen, he still believed that the heart was a kind of seed pod that, when ripe, would burst with joy, scattering it everywhere. Though he did not know why, he had apparently been so desperate for Owen's – or, for that matter, anyone's – affection that he mistook an exciting form of emotional exploitation for it. Third, he believed in an innate balance of body, heart, and mind, that is, the whole person. Just as men couldn't have babies, wasn't living on a purely physical level sterile in other senses as well? The proper order of things was out of whack, character was destroyed, and the fruits of such labor, in Valerio's case, risked violence, VD, and jail. If you cut yourself off from who you were, like a severed branch, Josh thought, you were dead.

He did not know much about Tyler, but what little he did know still left open a number of promising doors. As for *body*, Josh was certainly attracted to him sexually and hoped that the hand job, though one-sided, was a sample of the sensual feast to come. As for *heart*, Tyler was amiable enough alone with him and at dinner with the Trees. Josh interpreted his divorce as somewhat similar to his own first, disastrous sortie into love. He was no more culpable than Josh was with Owen. But more importantly, he saw it as a failure at playing straight, probably the tipping point where Tyler had tilted toward gay. As for *mind*, he was a successful writer, which, by definition, meant he had intellectual interests they could share, drama, movies, Frank Lloyd Wright, Pompeii. In short, Tyler was balanced, a whole person, and Josh would definitely try his best to pique Tyler's interest in him. He had already replaced Valerio in Josh's sexual fantasies and would, at least for the next couple of days, replace him in life as well. Josh would give Valerio his gift, then simply not cross paths with him.

When Josh started down the steps, Valerio noticed him out of the corner of his eye and, turning, lost his balance, taking a couple of steps backward down the steps.

"Josh," he said, lighting up as he had the other night. "Come stai?"

"Bene," Josh smiled. "E tu?"

"Bene, molto bene."

When Josh saw that Valerio was not wearing a shirt under the jacket, his body flushed with pleasure. Valerio's chest was smooth and tan, burnt Siena, Josh decided, since it was Italy. Light hair, like a light bruise, darkened the sternum, and the brown eyes of his erect nipples peeked from the denim. Josh took a step down and Valerio one up so that they were standing on the same level, and then they just stood there, grinning at each other. Rollo and the others turned to see what the fuss was about.

"Oh, I have something for you," Josh said, remembering the shirt. "I went to the Armani shop in Piazza dei Martiri, the one I mentioned. You go there?"

"Not yet."

After an awkward moment, Josh handed him the bag. "For you."

Josh knew that the Greeks would make an offering to a deity on an altar at the east end of a temple, so he thought it was appropriate that he was giving Valerio, a sex god, a gift at the Galleria's eastern portal.

"Grazie," Valerio said, taking the bag. He bit his lip, looked into the bag, and took out a black silk shirt. "Grazie mille!"

The shirt had been folded in gray tissue, so he sat the bag on the step, shook out the shirt, and admired it. It the lurid light, it had the sheen of a black pansy, the aura of something rare.

"Bello!" Valerio smiled. "May I ask you something?"

"Sure."

"Why black?"

"You don't like black?" Josh asked, unconsciously touching the cut on his chest.

"Oh, yes," Valerio stressed. "Very much. Thank you."

"I don't know," Josh said. "Thought it would look good on you."

"Know about the Black Shirts?"

"No," Josh admitted.

"Fascists."

"I'll take it back."

"No, no," Valerio said, unbuttoning it. "Means nothing now."

The phrase *fashion Fascist* popped into Josh's head. Then he noticed that Valerio's expression had changed from cheerful to puzzled, and he looked in the direction Valerio was looking. Emerging from the Galleria were the Trees, arm in arm, and Tyler, hands in pockets, focused on Valerio. The three just stood there, quietly watching the scene, as if from the top of an amphitheater, and Josh wondered what, from their vantage point, they must have been thinking about the little nocturnal drama spread out before them. He knew he wasn't living in Henry James' oppressive milieu. He was no Daisy Miller flouting convention with a charming, young coquet. Still, he was confused and embarrassed. He didn't want Tyler to know he'd consorted with hustlers, yet he'd led them there.

Phil sat on the top step, and Billie sat across his lap, an arm around his shoulder, squinting at Josh. Tyler glanced down to his left, then bounced down the steps.

"Hey," Josh said. "This is Valerio. Valerio, Tyler."

"Tyler," Valerio said. "A pleasure."

Tyler took his hand out of his pocket, and they shook hands, gazing at each other.

"Josh's boyfriend?" Valerio asked.

"Uh, no," Josh jumped in. "Actually, we just met."

"Sorry," Valerio said. "You look like a couple."

Josh decided not to ask why he thought so.

"I was putting on this beautiful shirt Josh gave me," Valerio said.

"I see," Tyler said.

Valerio handed Josh the shirt, slipped from his jacket, and swapped the jacket for the shirt, and during the exchange, Josh could not help taking in Valerio's flat abs and groin, the sharp crease between his waist and his thigh. Despite himself, he imagined his tongue in the crease. The jacket also had the same rousing scent of aromatic foliage he had smelled on Valerio the other night.

"I, uh – " Josh began. "I was thinking of recommending Valerio to Phil. Valerio's a masseur." When Tyler gave Josh a blank look, Josh turned to Valerio and gestured toward Phil. "Phil has back problems."

"Anytime," Valerio said, slipping the shirt on.

"Valerio would also like to model," Josh added.

"You certainly have the looks," Tyler said.

"Grazie."

"Wouldn't you be better off in Milan?" Tyler asked. "I mean, *the* fashion center."

"One day," Valerio said.

Valerio had not shaved around his mouth and chin, and Josh wondered if he were going for what Josh thought of as the satyr look, an Italian variation on the Vandyke. He could imagine him even more desirable as a satyr.

"Know a good gay club?" Tyler asked.

"Club?" Valerio buttoned the two buttons over his navel, smiled, and held up his hands to show off the shirt.

"Nightclub," Tyler explained.

"There's the Seventh Circle," Valerio said. "Not too far away. Piazza Portanuova. Have an Arcigay card?"

"What's that?" Tyler asked.

"Uh," Valerio hesitated, glancing to the right. "A membership card, but more. The fee pays for health initiatives like condoms, and Arcigay fights for civil rights."

"Where can we get one?" Josh asked, folding Valerio's jacket.

"At the door," Valerio said. "But night life here starts late. The doors open at eleven, and no one shows up till twelve."

Josh picked up the bag, stuffed the jacket in it, and sat it down.

"Civil rights," Tyler said. "Any progress in that area here in Italy?"

"Well," Valerio began, "we have an openly gay regional president, a Communist, in a conservative area, Puglia. A couple of gays, a lesbian, a bi in Parliament."

When Valerio slipped his hands into his pockets, Josh knew what he was up to.

"For the first time in history," Valerio said, "we had national, state, province, and city governments for Gay Pride sponsors in Rome."

"In Rome," Tyler repeated. "Within sight of Vatican City. That *is* progress."

"The slogan," Valerio chuckled, "was 'More Freedom, Less Vatican.'"

Josh wondered if Tyler had noticed what Valerio was doing.

"A Cabinet member," Valerio said, "the Minister for Social Solidarity, he even participated in the parade. So," he concluded, "we've come a long way, particularly in the area of employment, but we still have a long way to go to catch up with the rest of Europe."

"You'll get there," Tyler said optimistically.

"Well," Josh said, head bobbing. "We should get back to Phil and Billie."

He traded stares with Valerio, but looking into his eyes was like looking into the dark, a warm, inviting dark where anything could happen.

On cue, Tyler extended his hand. "Pleasure to meet you."

"Piacere," Valerio said, shaking hands.

Josh hesitated, then carefully leaned forward to hold Valerio's arms and exchange air kisses with him.

"Go by the Armani shop," Josh said, stepping back.

"I will," Valerio smiled.

Josh glanced at Tyler, and as they trudged up the steps, Billie and Phil got up, and Phil dusted off the seat of his pants. As Josh was about to join them, he glanced over his shoulder at Valerio, who smiled, pinched the shirt over his nipples, and shook it as if airing it. Josh waved subtly, then turned to the others.

"Lucy," Billie said, addressing him, "you have some 'splainin' to do."

Chapter 19: Sea Smoke

"See!" Karen blurted, pointing to Peeve. "That's what you did to me."

"Sorry," Tyler smiled gently. "The damn cat looked like it was going to...."

"Tormenting me with your violence and threats and games."

"Oh, my."

"Trying to isolate me from everybody."

Alice rose with a disgusted look, lifted a riled Peeve off the table, and carefully slipped the cat to the floor. She watched it slink through the maze of baskets and buckets. When it sprang gracefully onto a rocker, the chair rocked quietly, then stopped as if a hand had touched it. When the cat curled into a sullen heap, Alice, satisfied, sat back down.

While this was going on, Linda, obviously annoyed, reached a box of matches, stood, and lit the chandelier, then the lanterns to either side of the arch into the kitchen. The house had grown oppressively dark and surprisingly cool and scented with balsam, and as the lights from the lanterns and candles opened up, they cast a warm, Romantic spell on the room – the dreamy flames reflected thousands of times in miniature in the small mirrors of the glass containers.

"Criticizing every friend I tried to make," Karen went on. "Thank God Cindy stuck by me. Otherwise, I really would've killed myself."

Tyler had slapped Cindy after she had swung a vintage Samsonite suitcase at him. He could not remember the cause of the skirmish, but the sharp slap had put an end to suitcase assaults.

"Killed yourself?" he scoffed. "Karen, we were famous for our rowdy parties."

Their parties were memorable because of the great cross section of people they knew: academics, Bohemians, hippies, bikers, nurses, blacks, even a gorgeous male cop.

"I made all the money," she said, "but couldn't go anywhere, do anything because you wouldn't let me spend any of it."

"You didn't make *all* the money," he corrected her.

"As if I were some sort of financial retard," she groused to herself.

"We lived on cokes and bologna sandwiches," he said. "Face the facts. We were poor."

"The only thing you ever let me buy for myself was a pair of maternity shorts. Maternity shorts! In all the time we lived together. God!"

The temperature was dropping, and he was so drugged that the cool air on his face was about all keeping him from drifting off.

"When I was carrying Alice," she said, "I was sick with pneumonia, but you made me wait to see a doctor. I had so much trouble breathing that pains shot down my arm, but again I thought that – crazy me – I was just imagining it."

If he were a student, he wondered, couldn't she have gone to the health center? If she were working for the phone company, wouldn't she have had insurance? If she were pregnant, wouldn't she have been seeing a doctor? He could see being reluctant to see a doctor over some minor ailment, but not pneumonia. He had had pneumonia three times as a child. Again, it was too long ago. He'd have to do research.

"But I wasn't imagining the times you hit me and threw things at me."

"I never hit you," he sighed. "Slapped Cindy, yes. Never hit you. Girls?" he asked, turning to them.

Alice, like an audience, watched from her chair, nervously fondling the neckline of her blouse. Linda was standing by the arch, pigeon-toed, observing the scene as if from the wings. She gazed at Karen, kicked one foot with the other, and, again, smiled an almost smug smile. Then a shadow dimmed her face, some dark, serious concern. When they did not respond, he slumped over, eyes closed, completely exhausted, but when he realized he was going to faint, he jerked himself up, head back, struggling to keep his eyes open.

"I lived in fear that, at any moment, you might explode over some little nothing," Karen swore, "an inmate in the cell of my life, and you had the key!"

"Enough," he said. He glanced down, smiled affectionately, and tried his legs against the plasticuffs. Again, he foolishly thought he had discovered some supernatural powers deep within himself and could, at will, somehow miraculously free himself from the ties. "Cut these damn things off me. Please. Cut me loose, damn it!" he laughed.

He leaned forward, stood up the best he could (bent over like a hunchback), and jumped back so that the chair landed hard on its back legs, breaking the right one like a bone.

Alice stood, Linda stepped forward, and Karen, hands up, yelled, "Stop that!"

"Untie me," he said. The chair hopped like an insect.

"Stop that," she repeated. When he stood again, she commanded him to "Sit down. Sit!" as if addressing a dog.

"You lure me out here to this desolate island like some Venus Flytrap," he said, stooped, "and expect me just to sit here like some meek catch. I won't."

Again, he jumped back hard on the back legs with a crack, and the chair tipped toward the fractured one.

"Stop it!" she insisted.

He looked her straight in the eye: "No."

The chair hopped a few inches.

"Stop!" she barked.

They traded looks, his dull, yet amused, hers bright, yet furious. Her fist came at him out of a 3-D movie. When he turned his face, she missed his nose, punching his left eye. The room heeled like a boat, and he realized he was balanced on the chair's back legs. Time slowed, and as he went over backward little by little, the last thing he saw was the red, ceramic rooster and a gush of purple peonies.

He felt as if he were falling from a great height – body clinched, head bowed, fingers spread – and when the chair banged the floor, he chuckled, "You bitch."

His weight pinned the back of the chair against his arms, pressing his hands into the harsh, sandy floor. Straight up, dark, surreal stalactites of herbs were hanging from the rafters, wavering in the tepid light from the candles. On the mantel stood the stuffed crow, clock, and duck. On the daybed, the quilt skirt smelled musty, and when he kicked against one of the ties, the chair, as if injured, wobbled slightly, then stopped. Then the women's faces crowded in, hovering over him like mourners at a casket.

"I lived in fear," Karen claimed, "and when I'd finally had enough and asked for a divorce, you threatened to kill me. But you're not going to kill anyone now, are you?"

"Kill you," he murmured.

He wondered, if he extended his legs, if the ties would just slip off the chair. But would he have to try that slowly, hoping they wouldn't notice, or all at once before they could respond?

"Yes, kill me," she growled in his face. "A warning I considered so dangerous I kept a cook's knife in my purse."

"She must've thought you really meant it," Linda said, rocking vaguely foot to foot.

The motion reminded him of a sick dog.

"I paid her lawyer so she could divorce me," he told Linda calmly. "Is that the action of an angry man?"

When Alice noticed Linda's rocking, she took Linda's arm and stopped her.

"When you left, it was worse," Karen squawked. "You put this plastic bag over my head."

"Plastic bag?"

He had to quit repeating her, he told himself. It gave him time to think, yes, but it sounded stupid.

"This financial plastic bag over my head," she complained. "I couldn't breathe for all the debts. I'd strain for a breath, but all I'd get is plastic in my mouth, no air. No air! For years! Just debts. Nothing but debts for years. You fucking prick." As she spit out the words, a small bubble appeared at the corner of her mouth and popped. "Know what it's like being smothered, huh?" she asked, shaking both fists at him.

Like a horse stomping a snake, he thought. That's what she reminded him of.

"Know what it's like not being able to draw a breath?" she asked. "Huh? Know what it's like?"

He studied the troubled face looming over him, a face warped with hate, but all he was hearing was a rabid snarl, not words.

"No one who knew us back then will corroborate any of this – " He smiled. All he wanted was to get it over with, no matter how, whatever was going to happen. After all, he was in quite the position for it, he thought, on his back with his legs in the air. Despite the pain in his arms, he knew that by softening his mental focus just a little, he could lapse into a calm, agreeable void. "Craziness," he said finally. "Yes, craziness, Karen. No one."

"Crazy!" she snapped. She squinted at him as if trying to figure him out. "I'll show you crazy. Wanna see crazy?" She lunged for the daybed. "Here's crazy," she said, pressing a pillow to his face.

# # # # #

Karen knelt over him, holding the pillow down on both sides of his head so that he could not turn it.

"Alice!" she called.

Alice, in reflex, knelt by his head and braced on the pillow, smiling at Karen childishly. The foam pillow muffled his gasps. His legs twitched, his shoulders rocked, his hips bucked off the chair in a strange sexual rhythm, making it hop.

"With us or not?" Karen asked Linda.

Linda slowly, as if hypnotized, crouched near his head, biting her lip, then, arms stiff, leaned on his face.

When he continued to struggle, Karen shouted, "Stop it. Stop!"

When he did stop – his feet turned out as if broken – she seemed to come to and sat on her heels, releasing him. Then Alice and Linda sat back, and they all stared at the pillow as if at some big, puffy sea creature that had washed ashore. Linda touched it tentatively, then pinched it and pulled it off his face slowly, revealing what looked like a grayish-blue Tyler asleep with his mouth open.

"He's wet himself," she said, noticing the stain in his crotch.

"Is he dead?" Alice asked.

"He's not breathing," Linda observed.

Karen pressed two fingers to his neck. After a while, she said, "No pulse." She leaned over him and slapped him, turning his head to the side, and as she waited for a response, a great hush fell on the room. Then she took hold of his shoulders and shook him. "Tyler! Ty!" she cried in his face.

His head bobbled, and when she let go of him, his mouth closed. When she thumbed his eye open, she thought she saw his pupil contract, but was not sure. When his eye closed again, she did not know if it would do that if he were dead.

"What about CPR?" Linda asked.

Karen glanced to the side, thinking. "No telling how he'd use this against us. We'd wind up in jail. That what you want?"

Linda stared at her curiously.

"We could cut him up and eat him," Alice suggested deadpan. "Like they did in *Fried Green Tomatoes*."

"Have you lost your mind?" Linda asked in disbelief. Then she turned to Karen. "What do we do?"

"What we have to do," Karen said. "Get rid of him."

They snipped the ties off his ankles with scissors, pushed him onto his side, and snipped the ties off his wrists, and in a few minutes they were lugging him headfirst, like a big rag doll, across the yard in the light of the full moon, Karen and Linda by his hands, walking backward, Alice his feet, forward. When that arrangement did not work, Karen and Linda faced forward, and they stumbled through the hedge and down the path through the firs, his head upside down, mouth open, the seat of his jeans scraping the stone and dirt.

One of Alice's pumps caught a root, and she tripped, falling awkwardly. When she let go of his feet, his heels thumped the ground, and Karen and Linda lurched forward, almost falling. Alice got up, slipped her shoe on, and then just stood there, tired, peering into the dark. She fondled a bristly twig, and in the lull as she rested, again they all seemed aware of the curious hush that had fallen on the island, on everything, in fact, the bay, the world. Alice stooped to take hold of his ankles, and, without a word, they took up the path through the bushes and weeds.

As they came out of the boulders onto the beach, sea smoke was rising around the pier as if the sea were smoldering. They stopped for a second, startled by it, then proceeded down the shore. When they reached the boat, they lay him gently near the edge of the pier and caught their breath. Linda took a flashlight from her back pocket and turned it on, running the light along his body head to feet and back. Spread-eagled with his arms above his head, he looked as if he were surrendering to someone. The salmon Izod rode above his navel, revealing his groin, and even dappled with shadow, he looked as young and spare as ever, she thought, so striking, in fact, she knelt beside him, switched the flashlight to her left hand, and ran her right over his brusque hair.

When she kissed his forehead, Karen asked, "What are you doing?"

"He was my father," she said, gazing at him.

"A fake," Alice said, correcting her. "A fake father." But there was something rash and puzzled in her tone.

Linda studied him as if to remember him, then rose, rubbing her left arm. Then she glanced from Alice to Karen. When no one said anything, she pointed the flashlight toward the boat, then into what looked like flimsy sheers twisting in slow motion on the water.

"We'll have to be careful," Karen announced. "If we drop him in the water here, we'll never get him out."

The impromptu plan was crude at best. Linda got in the boat and wedged the flashlight between a thwart and the hull while Karen and Alice sat him up and faced him toward the boat, swinging his legs off the pier. When they lifted him by his armpits, Linda pulled his ankles, slipping him over the edge, and as Karen and Alice lowered him, Linda guided him down by his waist so that soon he was more or less standing, head bowed, directly in front of her.

When Linda embraced him, Karen groaned, "Got him?"

Linda muttered, "Think so."

"OK," Karen said, bent over the edge. "Here we go."

She nodded to Alice, and they let go of him, but when Linda tried to sit, she fell backward with him on top of her nearly upside down in the bilge. With effort, she heaved him onto his side, and when she managed to slip from under him, he wound up draped facedown over the thwart.

"Jeez," she exclaimed, panting.

Karen and Alice climbed into the boat, cast off, and sat on the stern bench. Karen started the motor and, as Linda pointed the flashlight forward, eased the boat through mist toward the yellow buoy. Out of the cove, the sea smoke cleared, drifting west, and the sea opened up in big, black swells glistening with moonlight. Linda turned off the flashlight, and when Karen spotted the seal rocks starboard, she slowly shoved the throttle forward, and the boat began rolling over the crests and down the troughs of the waves with a languid, if ominous, pulse. She steered for the lights at the inn for about ten minutes, then pulled back on the throttle, finally killing the motor, and they simply sat there awhile, riding the waves and taking in the night: the sea all crimped, black satin, the cool air honed with salt, the sporadic slosh of a wave against the hull strangely prominent in the peaceful hush. One by one they noticed, in the distance, the gray curtain of sea smoke gliding toward them.

"Let's do it," Karen said.

Linda turned on the flashlight and scooted against the side to give Karen room to step across the thwart across which Tyler was slumped.

"What if he washes up somewhere?" Linda asked.

"Well," Karen replied, "we'd better get our stories straight, hadn't we?"

First, Karen and Alice turned him over. Karen clutched his left hand and, with Alice pushing, got him into a drooping sitting position. Then, with Alice's hands in his armpits, Karen took hold of his feet, and they rolled him overboard with a splash.

# # # # #

He was a disembodied voice talking to himself rationally in space. Then he was being sucked violently up a long, black tunnel like a tornado. He woke, choking and coughing, clinched in the fetal position from the bitter shock of the water. He could not move his arms or legs. They were tight against his body as if defending it against some hard, fatal cold that could reach into his chest. The first thing he saw was a liquid, illusory darkness streaked with spectral moonlight and strung with shiny bubbles. The first thing he heard was padded splashes and gurgles as he righted himself, broke the surface, and gasped his first deep lungful of brackish air. When he sensed the faint glow and sounds behind him, he turned and saw a sad dream of Karen and Alice standing and Linda sitting in the boat, everything silhouetted against a billowing veil of sea smoke.

"Oh, my god," Karen exclaimed. "He's alive."

"What the fuck are you doing?" he cried, spitting out brine.

The women waited, frozen, mute.

"Where are we?" he asked, swimming toward them. "I don't understand."

When the boat swayed with a swell, Karen and Alice half squatted for balance and grabbed each other's hand momentarily for support.

"How did we get here?" he asked. Then he remembered his last drowsy moments at the house.

As he neared the boat, Karen picked up an oar, and as he reached for the gunwale, she pushed him away with it so that he wound up floating on his back.

"Let me in the boat," he insisted, treading water.

When he swam toward the boat again, she raised the oar above her head and started hitting him with it, his shoulder, his head, his arm. She tried to hit him again, but he grabbed the blade, and when she lost her balance, Alice grabbed her hand, losing her balance, and both fell in, sending the boat sideways. When they surfaced, they caught their breath and began flailing and screaming, Karen hysterically, Alice with concern for her, and their screams and splashes, with a short delay, began echoing off the fog as if several women were screaming and splashing.

Meanwhile, Linda dropped the flashlight onto the floor with a clunk and began touching the air as if blind and feeling for something. She tilted her head back, mouth open, as if trying to catch raindrops, and when she fell backward, all he could see was her legs stiffening and kicking in some strange upside-down dance. A seizure, like an electric current, was shaking her violently.

Tyler sensed something to his right. Something immense swam past him, making a massive, shimmering swell, something leisurely and horrifying and wonderful. When a huge fin rose from the water, followed by a taller fin, his body clinched in the fetal position again, and when the shark hit the prow with a thud, the boat started revolving slowly, fading into the mist.

One honest, if lenient, way of describing what happened to Tyler was that he divided into his body and the rest of him and that his body (the primitive, intuitive animal in him) took control. He was sedated, yes, but though he wanted to swim to them, to get them into the boat, to save them, his body refused, literally paralyzed with fear. Instead, he only floated, as still and calm as possible, his arms and legs as close to his body as possible. If he didn't move, his survival instinct dictated, perhaps the shark would forget him.

His physical paralysis, in turn, required an attendant emotional paralysis, and he felt his heartstrings, his natural, affective connections to the women, trailing off in the water like so many broken fishing lines. Instinctively, he realized that he wasn't the kind of hero who was willing to die in vain trying to save them. If he had not been willing to sacrifice himself for them in life, why would he in death? Besides, he thought without consciously thinking it, what could he do? Nothing. His options were clear. Pain, death, no. Pleasure, life, yes. Continued existence.

Alice's screams became choking and gargling slipping into slaps and sprinkles. One of Karen's screams was cut off abruptly as if she were pulled under. Or, rather, he thought he heard her screaming underwater. Sea smoke, like ghosts, rose around him. Then nothing: water, silence, mist, and an overwhelming, almost unbearable horror of being, all at once, clamped in a huge vise of razor-sharp teeth.

Chapter 20: Amalfi

Tyler spent the night with Josh again, but this time they simply undressed, went to bed, and, still exhausted from jet lag, fell asleep quickly. The next morning, they had breakfast as soon as the dining room opened, then took the funicular up to Vomero for Tyler to check out of his hotel. Despite Tyler's objections, Josh wanted to go along, and Tyler had a pretty good idea why.

"You're so much trouble," he smiled, packing.

"I wasn't sure you'd come back," Josh blushed.

"You know me so well," Tyler joked.

"I know you come when I jerk you off."

"Actually," Tyler frowned, zipping his bag, "that's a lot."

# # # # #

Soon, they were boarding the boat to Amalfi. Tyler was carrying Billie's suitcase as well as his own and went ahead of everyone to the upper deck. Using the bags, he saved seats on benches on the port side, the side he knew would be facing land, two against the rail for Phil and Billie and, behind them, two against the rail for Josh and himself.

"Better view," he said, insisting that Josh take the rail seat.

Everyone stowed the luggage under the benches, and when everyone was settled, Tyler slouched on the seat, his butt on the edge, his arms spread along the back, his feet on the back of the bench in front, a few inches from Phil's shoulder. Josh was loose too, draped over the railing like a shirt. Phil and Billie, though, sat upright, holding hands, quietly taking in the harbor. As the boat pulled away, a cool breeze whipped up, and the small Italian flag on the stern unfurled and fluttered. The four had worn something extra for the trip: Phil a blue blazer, Billie a dark-gray cardigan with clusters of dark-red grapes embroidered on it, Tyler his shirt with the floral print over a salmon polo, Josh a red windbreaker open over his yellow polo.

"What a great color on the lighthouse!" Tyler remarked, his voice loud over the noise of the boat, waves, and wind. "What color is that?"

"Dark tan," Billie said over her shoulder.

"Tan?" Tyler scoffed. "I expected something like ochre or burnt sienna."

"Orange," Phil joked.

"Speaking of tan," Josh said, "your burn's toned brown. Brings out the olive in your skin."

"It'll peel in a couple of days."

Tyler noticed a massive structure in Vomero.

"What's that building up there?" he pointed.

"It's called the Certosa di San Martino," Josh said, "an old monastery, now a museum. Actually, that's a castle behind it."

When they got onto open sea, the boat began to ride the slow, momentous swells, which, after a while, had a lulling, almost undetectable hypnotic effect. The boat stopped at Sorrento and Positano, letting off and taking on passengers, and as they got underway again, Josh stood as if in response to the beauty of the coast, reached under his shirt, and seemed to be absently touching the scratch on his chest. Tyler stood behind him, enclosing him with his left hand on the rail and his right foot on the seat. He was not sure how sharing the trip with the three would make it more enjoyable, but he knew he could enjoy it and getting to know them at the same time. Two pleasant experiences for the price of one, as he thought of it.

"Are there great whites in the Mediterranean?" he wondered, staring at the sapphire rush of the water.

"Don' know," Josh replied.

Tyler imagined a gray shadow running beside the boat, a huge snout breaching the surface, but, strangely enough, was not afraid of it. In fact, he even felt an odd impulse to strip and jump overboard, to immerse himself in the lucid blue. He'd curb himself, though. There'd be plenty of time for a nude swim later.

"Once," he said, "at a writer's conference in Seattle, I was staying at this hotel on a pier over Puget Sound, I guess, and while I was sitting on the balcony, I saw this large, white shark slowly weaving through the water. I was surprised to see one so far inland or what I thought was far inland."

Josh moved his hand next to Tyler's on the rail so that his pinkie was just touching Tyler's thumb.

"There's no point to the story," Tyler said. "Guess I was just struck by the contrast between the serenity of the scene and the danger lurking in it."

"Can you swim?" Josh asked.

"Yeah," Tyler said. "I swim like a fish."

"I love to swim."

"The only way I'd drown – " Tyler hesitated. "I'd have to be unconscious."

Josh leaned back just enough to brush Tyler's chest.

"Good lord," he smiled. "The road up there." He was looking at the winding road carved from the cliff. "Glad we didn't take the bus."

"Me, too," Tyler agreed. "I get motion sickness."

"The boat doesn't bother you?"

"No."

They passed, to starboard, a schooner with four masts, then, to port again, the huge cave above Il Saracen Hotel and talked about how scary it must be to live above or below it. Then Josh suggested that they were traveling not only to Amalfi, but also back in time. Tyler also thought of the trip as traveling toward a little more self-awareness. In Amalfi, he could let himself go and see where he went, so to speak. His conflict between trust and paranoia, he knew, was a kind of break in his personality that anyone could see if he only looked close enough, a subtle chink which belied the deep seismic fault running through him. At first, he'd thought he could find some sort of mental or emotional glue to hold himself together, then realized that gluing himself together like a broken vase wouldn't work. His imagery of himself then took the form of two Tylers disconnected inside him, the old suspicious one which he associated with his purely straight life and the new, confident one who would have to kill the other.

"That's it!" Josh exclaimed.

As they passed a promontory, Josh pointed toward a bungalow wedged high in the rock face. A wrought-iron railing wrapped around the terrace, and beyond it Tyler could just see the top of a pair of French doors under an overhang and, to the right, a shady, vine-draped pergola purple with flowers.

"A cave?" he asked.

"Yeah," Josh smiled, obviously excited. "The wall behind the bed is solid rock."

Actually, a roof of terra-cotta tiles projected from the cliff about twenty feet, but Josh's excitement was catching. Despite himself, a great swell of well-being was slowly rising in Tyler. He was eager to see the interior.

"What do you think?" Josh asked, gazing at him happily.

"Couldn't be more secluded."

From the cottage a path ran east along the cliff and curved around a corner. When they had rounded the promontory, however, the rest of the path swung into view, leading to a hotel, an old, picturesque palazzo set above the sea. Vintage Italy, Tyler thought.

Amalfi was a steep waterfall of ancient structures spilling down a gorge, tile roof over roof, building on top of building, some colored in as if with pastel pencils – yellow, ochre, pink – all the way down to Piazza Flavio Gioia and the picture-book sea. As the boat docked, Tyler tried to take in as much as he could: sky, cliffs, greenery, villas, umbrella pines, date palms. To the left, boats crowded the calm harbor, reminiscent of Maine, he thought, flashing back. To the right, rows of beach chairs and umbrellas daubed splotches of color on the black, volcanic sand.

"Fabulous," Billie said.

Fabulous, Tyler thought. They haven't stepped off the boat, and Billie's already speaking Gay.

"You'd think Italians could come up with something prettier," he joked.

Despite the fact that the piazza was a bustling parking lot, he loved the fact that it was named Gioia: Joy. How appropriate. From the spellbound look on everyone's face, they were about to enter Paradise. If he couldn't be happy here with these people, he told himself, he was hopeless.

# # # # #

They could have walked from the piazza, but took a cab to the promenade that led from the highway out to the hotel at the end of what Tyler thought of as a phallic peninsula. The promenade was paved with flagstone and lined with umbrella pines shading them as they strolled along with the luggage trundling behind them. The path rose slowly and eventually segued into a high, breezy loggia with huge terra-cotta pots, one almost covered by the trailing fronds of an asparagus fern, one with a luxuriant spider plant trailing offshoots, and one with a fan palm with a big display of fans. Wrought-iron lanterns dropped from the tie rods between the wall and arcade, metal grilles clutched the massive windows like bars on a rustic, yet elegant prison, and big wire birdcages fluttered with green and yellow canaries singing and echoing off the loggia, like hundreds of little bells.

Three sprightly terriers came scurrying out of the entrance, barking playfully, a Cairn, an Australian, and a Norfolk, followed by an attractive brunette, shouting, "Vassoio, Bianca, Tesoro!"

"Come si chiamano i cani?" Josh asked. He seemed uncertain of the names.

"Vassoio, Bianca, e Tesoro," she smiled.

"Tray, Blanch I guess, and Sweetheart," Josh repeated.

"Oh, my god!" Tyler laughed. "The three dogs from *Lear*."

"I'm impressed, Tyler," Billie said. "Only you would've known that."

"'See, they bark at me,'" he quoted thoughtfully.

"What language would you like to use?" the brunette asked.

"English," Josh said.

"Ebbene," she said, turning to the others. "Benvenuti. Welcome. Come in."

"I think we've found the Enchanted Hotel," Billie said to Josh. "Thanks so much for suggesting we come here."

Tyler smiled at Billie's innocent pun on *come*.

# # # # #

After everyone checked in, the plan was to unpack, rest, and meet at Josh and Tyler's cottage in a couple of hours. Then a handsome man with curly,

174

flaxen hair appeared and led Phil and Billie to a small, wrought-iron elevator cage. The brunette led Josh and Tyler back to the loggia and pointed toward a large, rough-hewn door at the end.

The door was marked "Vietato Entrare," forbidden to enter. Josh unlocked it and held it for Tyler, and when they stepped outside, they just stood there, taking in the view: below, over a stone wall, a sheer drop to rocks and surf; above, a gray precipice splotched with dark-green mastic trees, mock-orange, giant fennel, rosemary, cacti. They smiled at each other, then strolled along the path, Tyler first, suitcases rattling over the stones.

When they arrived at the cottage, the granite molding around the door was bossed with bunches of grapes, the door's upper panel painted green with Bacchus in a grape arbor with bunches of black grapes. Above the door hung a small, wrought-iron lantern with rippled, amber panes. A few feet to the right was a small window with bars in a diamond pattern and a yellow shutter inside.

When they stepped inside the cottage, the room smelled of crushed juniper. Tyler's first impression of it was that it was safe in a snug, uterine, grotto sort of way. Here, he knew, they could be themselves without worrying about what anyone else had thought or would think of them, without, in fact, worrying about anything. Period. They were above it all literally, accessible only by the cliff path and two heavy, locked doors. And the apartment, of course, was the honeymoon suite with all that such a romantic name implied: uninterrupted and uninhibited nuptial bliss. Though he had never intended it, he could clearly see them nestled in bed, pink, panting, and glistening with sweat after some ecstatic cannibalistic rite.

"Well, here we are," he said, looking around.

"No drafting board, no file cabinets," Josh remarked. "Wright would appreciate all the rich textures."

Except for the bathroom, the apartment was one big open space with the living room to the left and bedroom to the right. Tyler glanced through the bathroom door and saw himself, flushed, yet pliant, in a mirror, the mirror to the old dressing table below it, but separated and hung on the wall with little, wire, Fifties-looking lamps to either side. The table had a sink, and on the floor to the side sat a tall cane basket with flimsy towels hanging from the rim, everything framed, like a big modern painting, in a lime-washed panel of olive green. When he realized that Josh was watching him looking at himself, he smiled, then ventured a few steps farther into the room.

Behind the bed, as Josh had said, was moon-like rock face, but the other walls were plastered with stucco and color washed the hue of honey-colored sandstone. Balancing the austere cave effect was the noon light blazing through the French doors and sheers. Linen curtains were drawn, and the

Mediterranean light bouncing off the walls, rugs, and beams filled the room with an airy, amber glow. A happy place, Tyler thought.

"You can see why I went to some trouble to reserve it," Josh said, parking his suitcase at the foot of the bed.

They stared at each other with sly smiles, then broke into laughter. The *suite nuziale* had certainly lived up to its name.

"Let's act on impulse here," Josh said. "No hang-ups, no beating about the bush."

"Fine with me," Tyler agreed. "We'll get to know each other fast." Then he added, "We'll get to know ourselves."

"So we're agreed?" Josh asked.

"Agreed," Tyler smiled.

He thought of the décor as Bohemian chic, perfect for them, unique, artsy, comfortable, a love nest for free spirits. The living room was rustic with exotic touches. To the left stood a big, stuffed sofa upholstered in a colorful kilim. In front of it, end to end, were a couple of hand-made trunks painted with mythological motifs and coated in a gold lacquer. One pictured Perseus and Medusa; the other Achilles and Patroclus. In the corner was an old, electric-cable wheel with a watering can with wheat and a bust marked "Eros" on a plinth. At right angle to the sofa and table, a huge window looked out on the shady part of the terrace under the pergola. In front of the window were a couple of wrought-iron arm chairs with claw feet, brass finials, and fabric striped in burgundy and an earthy yellow. The chairs looked straight out of the Renaissance. Between them sat a small, metal table with a wire-mesh top.

But the most striking piece in the living room was the light fixture. Over the trunks hung an antique bronze and glass chandelier in the shape of a large flying cupid, feet together, arms and wings spread as if in a swan dive. Balanced on it were eight glass candle holders with a skirt of glass teardrops and a flame-shaped light bulb: one on its head, in each hand, on its back, on the tip of each wing, on its buttocks, on its soles. It was suspended from a beam by a chain and strings of crystals – dusty icicles, as Tyler thought of them – the heavier ones smoky purple. He flipped a switch to see it lit up and strolled over to admire it. Around the cupid's neck hung a crystal, pear-shaped lavaliere. He reached up and rested the pendant on the tips of three fingers. When he touched the cupid, it felt hollow and light.

"Never seen anything like it," he said.

"How apropos," Josh remarked. "Cupid."

Tyler turned toward the sprawling platform bed. "My god," he said. "Phil and Billie could sleep with us, and we'd still have room."

"Room," Josh replied, "but not much fun."

As Tyler strolled toward the bed, he noticed the bamboo clothes rack and luggage stand to his right and parked his suitcase there. On top of the rack was a stack of plump Pakistani pillows embroidered with complex geometric patterns in muted earth tones: sienna, umber, rust. They reminded him of feed bags, but felt silky.

He stood next to the bed, arms akimbo, and took it in. The expansive bed, of course, required an expansive spread, in this case one in light cotton with bands of various sizes appliquéd with designs in strong colors – yellow, violet, white, green – all against a chestnut background. He thought the spread would have made a beautiful tapestry over the bed, but why hide a feature as unique as a cave wall? Propped against the wall were big, deep-rose, velvet pillows sewn with all sorts of imaginative floral figures. The side tables were squat urns with circular slabs of marble on top, the lamps converted candlesticks with small, burnt-orange shades. One table also had a phone. At the foot of the bed crouched three multicolored Moroccan ottomans. He was sure that, with the French doors open, the room would be perfect for sleeping: dark and calm, especially with the soothing lullaby of the surf.

He glanced around. Angled in the far corner was a lumpy, camel-back arm chair covered with a skirted, cranberry slipcover. Very comfortable looking, he thought, a good place to relax and read. To one side was a little table with a braided-bronze lamp; behind the chair, on a pedestal, a small statue of Athena: helmet, breastplate, and shield. Near the chair was a wide, nondescript chest of drawers.

"This is the best part," Josh announced, brushing a sheer aside. When he opened the doors, the diaphanous fabric lifted lazily on a breeze.

When they stepped onto the terrace, Tyler was blinded by the sun. As his eyes adjusted, he looked around and, by force of habit, began taking notes on the oddly shaped, pentagonal terrace. Inside, the terra-cotta tiles were waxed to a glossy finish; outside, worn and faded. Three old olive jars with geraniums sat just far enough from the house for the indigo shutters to swing flat against the wall. A basket of fuchsia hovered over each, dripping hundreds of blooms. Straight ahead sat a couple of rustic chairs with sloped backs, a cross between arm chairs and chaise lounges. Beyond them, two sturdy, wrought-iron railings met at a point over the ocean. The rails were twisted into the shape of thick ropes and looped like mooring lines around the support posts, the top rail thicker than the bottom. To the right, strung between the railing and a ring in the cliff, hung a cotton hammock with fringe and blue pillows.

To the left, a couple of fat white columns propped up a pergola mauve with bougainvillea, a dappled Bower of Bliss, as Tyler thought of it. Under the pergola were an L-shaped banquette, a weathered picnic table, a bench, and a farmhouse chair. Latticework, thick with foliage, hid the area from the view of anyone on the path.

"Amalfi's where the Evans boy reserved a modest pleasure suite," Tyler recited, parodying the first lines of Coleridge's "Kubla Khan." "A pleasure pavilion," he remarked. "A very cozy pleasure pavilion."

They strolled to the point where the railings met. Tyler grabbed each, leaned over, and looked down, slumped in a comfortable S Curve, elbows bent, one foot in front of the other. Josh heeled beside him like a faithful dog, lay a hand on a rail, and looked down. Below, the cliff plummeted to a ledge mottled with what looked like tarnished marigolds growing in the cracks. The sea was a clear teal. It surged against the rocks, burst, and leapt up as if trying to toss them diamonds. The diamonds floated for a second, then dropped through mist to the lacy froth below, everything accompanied by an undertone of sibilance. Tyler felt as if he were literally listening to the Tyrrhenian Sea breathing.

As they stood there, he looked out to sea and thought of Josh and himself as ancient sentinels on one of the Saracen towers strung along the coast. However, today there was only a sleek yacht plying the waters, not Arab invaders. How private, he thought. Just them. Now. They could sunbathe nude if they wanted, do anything nude if they wanted. He was sure Josh was up for just about anything. After all, they had just agreed to follow their instincts, to toss their hang-ups overboard.

"Think I'm going to really enjoy myself here," Josh said, a hand on Tyler's shoulder. "Here in Amalfi." Then he added, "Here, too."

"Yeah, me too," Tyler agreed. "Can't tell you how grateful I am for inviting me."

Tyler stood up straight, and when he smiled at Josh as if waiting for him to kiss him, Josh took Tyler's arms and did, a fun peck on the lips. Then they embraced and stood there, holding each other.

"You know," Tyler joked, "you're really got to stop being so cold and distant."

"If you were only more attractive," Josh smiled, stepping back.

They laughed.

"Let's unpack," Tyler said.

He put his arm around Josh's shoulder, and they strolled toward the room.

Chapter 21: The Hike to Atrani

Around noon, Billie called Josh and Tyler, and Josh walked to the hotel to open the door to the cliff path. The Trees loved the suite, but Billie's response to the sunny terrace struck Josh and Tyler as odd. She strolled to the railing, and when she looked down, gulls were hovering below them, floating up slowly on an updraft, and farther out, a school of dolphins was bounding east, curving smoothly in and out of water. Billie, however, did not seem impressed. She just took in the scene, turned away, and said she was ready to go into town.

In Amalfi, they strolled through Piazza Gioia again, and when Josh pointed out that it was named after the man who invented the compass, Tyler tried to think of how to make something poetic out of the two: the compass and joy. Joy invented the compass.

"What is the compass that points to joy?" he asked.

"That one's easy," Josh replied, walking beside him.

"Really?"

Josh glanced over his shoulder at Phil and Billie trailing out of hearing.

"Ty," he said, "it's your dick. Your dick is the needle that points to joy."

"Right."

As they passed through an arch into Piazza Duomo, the town was so picturesque Tyler felt he was stepping into a painting. The piazza was surrounded by shops, signs, and awnings, and scattered in front of the cafés were umbrella tables and chairs. Directly ahead, Via Lorenzo slowly wound uphill into a narrow ravine of colorful buildings with geometric designs, shuttered windows, and wrought-iron balconies decked with potted palmettos and draped with flowering vines. Above it loomed towering cliffs, dark greenery, and a sky splotched with small, puffy clouds. To the right, a bride and groom were carefully inching down the steep steps of the Arab-Norman Duomo Sant'Andrea. To either side, the wedding party was throwing confetti on them. Tyler glanced at the pediment's mosaic of Jesus in blue encircled by kings and angels in white.

"Check out the mermaid," Phil suggested, referring to a figure in a fountain.

Water was trickling from her nipples, which, in fact, looked like big, dark penises.

"How bizarre," Tyler laughed.

Josh, as tour guide, mentioned that the doors to the duomo dated back to 1066 and started the craze for such in Italy. He also mentioned that there was a

Moorish cloister above the church, the Chiostro del Paradiso with St. Andrew's crypt and a courtyard with a hundred and twenty marble columns.

"Someone who touched Jesus is buried up there," he said. "Wanna see?"

"No," Tyler frowned.

"Why?"

"I believe in facts, and I'm rational. Or try to be."

"Well," Billie said, "if you don't want to see an apostle, I don't either."

"Fine with me," Phil said, making a throwaway gesture. "Someplace for lunch?"

# # # # #

They lunched at La Perla, then strolled back through the piazza and arch onto Corso delle Repubbliche Marinare, the road running along the beach. There, Phil and Billie went into the tourist office while Josh and Tyler went into the post office to mail postcards Josh had written in Naples.

When they met on the street, Josh asked, "Up for a hike to Atrani?"

"Could use the exercise," Phil said.

"You'll get that," Josh claimed. "There're a lot of steps."

"Go slow," Billie advised.

Josh got out his notes and led everyone at a leisurely pace down one *via* and up one *salita* (ascent) after another, right, straight ahead, down, finally leaning on a low wall to take in the view: the road curving below, pendulous clusters of buildings spilling down cliffs, coastal towns faint through a white chiffon of haze, mountains blue, then lighter blue in the distance. Phil and Billie were standing against a wall a few yards behind them, gazing at the scene, but propped beside Josh, Tyler thought of the haze as his own lack of mental clarity compared to Josh's self-transparency. Josh was comfortable in himself, Tyler thought, already knew who he was, a blond idol for Tyler to worship. As if reading his mind, Josh smiled, took his hand, and led him up a flight of steps to a bare rooftop where he backed him against the parapet, knelt before him, and mouthed his crotch.

"Have you no shame, young man?" Tyler joked, running his fingers through Josh's glimmering hair. Tyler was wearing cargo shorts but could feel Josh's warm breath even through the thick twill, warm breath which inspired in Tyler a warm thrill, so much, in fact, Tyler's cock grew and squirmed for freedom. Tyler glanced down at Phil and Billie, and when Billie glanced up, he smiled and waved.

"Come on," Tyler said, lifting Josh. "This is what our room's for."

Josh stood, rouged with a blush.

# # # # #

Josh found steps leading down to the quaint *piazzetta* in Atrani, Piazza Umberto I, with its wrought-iron balconies with planters and pots of geraniums. There were cane tables and chairs near an old-fashioned, three-pronged streetlight, and when Billie sat as if she meant to settle in, the others followed suit. A waiter came out, dressed in black pants and shoes with a blue, short-sleeved shirt and a black apron. He was somewhere between ordinary and handsome, and Tyler wondered what it was like to be him and live in a small town, albeit a tourist town, on such a beautiful coast in Italy. Phil and Billie ordered white wine, Josh and Tyler Campari.

"You academic types," Billie groused, meaning Josh and Tyler, "all of you have such poor posture."

"Billie, really," Phil protested.

"I'm just relaxed," Tyler said in self-defense.

When the drinks came, they drank and talked for a while. Then Phil said he wanted to wade in the Tyrrhenian and asked if anyone wanted to come. Josh said he would, but Billie wanted to rest, and Tyler said he would be happy to sit with her.

Chapter 22: Joshua Tree

Josh and Phil strolled under one of the huge arches holding up the highway and stepped out onto a small parking lot, then down onto a taupe beach, light where dry, dark where wet. Sand near the water was roughed up with glistening stones and pebbles, which Josh thought of as sea change, shiny coins of the sea.

"Guess we need to slip out of our shoes," Phil said, scuffing gravel the purple of grapes.

Josh glanced toward the rocks at one end of the beach, then toward what looked like a flock of colorful boats at the other.

"Over here," he said, headed for the boats.

They sat on a gunwale and took off their shoes and socks, Phil loafers, Josh sneakers. Josh was wearing his khaki shorts, but Phil had to roll up his slacks. As they set off toward the water, the smooth stones and wet sand massaged Josh's feet. A ribbon of surf wound along the waterline, and the subtle breakers, almost inaudible, reminded him of his sound machine. Here, he thought, was the real thing, and as they waded into it, the shallow clear-blue water gradually deepened to sapphire. Josh stopped beside Phil. A salt breeze blew up, the smooth water chopped, and a boat at anchor bucked like a colt.

"She wants to adopt you," Phil said, gazing out to sea.

"Adopt me?" Josh asked.

"Not legally," Phil explained, facing him. "She feels a connection, the name, I guess, Joshua."

"Your son." Then Josh put the two names together: "Joshua Tree. Were you thinking of the cactus?"

"Yucca," Phil corrected him. "We were young – young hippies, to be exact, young, anti-war, Summer of Love, nature-loving hippies." Then he smiled. "We'd smoked a lot of pot."

"Well, it's a great name," Josh joked, "if I do say so myself."

He wondered why Billie was so prudish about his pot when she had smoked it.

"Tyler keeps quoting *King Lear*," Phil said, flapping his hand. "Well, Billie's not so much interested in replacing our son as replacing our son with a good son, an Edgar for a Edmund, Gloucester's good son for the bastard."

Josh was surprised to learn that a couple as civil as Phil and Billie would have a bad son.

"It's almost as if there's a pun involved," Phil remarked. "To her, you're the difference between a sunless day and a sunny day."

Josh puzzled over the statement.

"S.U.N for S.O.N," Phil explained as if typing with his index finger.

"Oh," Josh exclaimed.

"By the way," Phil pointed, "you're the sunny day."

"Got it."

When a few higher waves rolled in, they stepped back to avoid getting their pants wet.

"Let's see," Phil said. "He was twenty-two when he died. You're how old?"

"Twenty-six."

Phil slipped his hands into his pockets and gazed into the water as if looking for something. Then he seemed to wake up.

"OK," he said. "That's enough. I can say I did it. I'm baptized now, born again."

They waded ashore, strolled to the boat, and sat on the gunwale in silence, Phil upright, Josh bent over, elbows on knees. When the sky cleared, the beach brightened, and Josh pulled off his green polo, soaking up the sun. When Josh touched the scratch on his chest, Phil glanced at it, then gazed down the beach.

"What happened to your son?" Josh asked.

"Hmph," Phil grunted. "Most people have two sides like the moon. The bright side was he played tennis for Stanford. He was on a sports scholarship, and it was a good thing he was. We never could've afforded Stanford. A champion, a great athlete with a career high singles ranking of forty-seven. A grunter. Grunted when he hit the ball, would drive opponents crazy, throw them off game. A few protested, but he couldn't help it, wasn't even aware of it. He also liked surfing, longboards. So he was not only in perfect shape, but tan, a California icon. He liked the Beach Boys, Chris Isaac, the Doors. "

"Must've been a girl magnet," Josh remarked.

"He was," Phil affirmed. "He definitely was. Incredibly good-looking. But he was set on one girl, Sheila, whom he'd known a long time and loved deeply. At least at first." He lay an ankle on a knee and unrolled his pants leg, then unrolled the other. Then he planted his feet in the sand and sat bolt upright, hands on thighs. "There's a side to most people that's never known, like the dark side of the moon. He destroyed himself with petty revenge."

"Revenge," Josh repeated, sitting up, hands on the gunwale. The gunwale was hard on his buttocks, so he shifted position.

"She was unfaithful, but asked him to forgive her, and when he wouldn't, she dropped him for someone else, someone less – naïve, let's say. To get even, he became a philanderer, a party boy. 'Women are a feast with many courses,' he said. And somewhere in all the partying, he got his hands on coke and something called Obedrine."

"Obedrine?" Josh asked.

"An amphetamine, I think," Phil said. "He always drank a lot of coffee and took a lot of No-Doze. Stimulants were the next step up. Guess he thought the buzz would help his game, his stamina. It didn't. In fact, he lost his game, plummeted in the rankings, was teetering on the verge of losing his scholarship." Phil wiped his feet with his socks, shook the socks out, and pulled them on one foot, then the other. "He was on speed with a girl and some friends at a nightclub one night. She said he snorted coke and danced for an hour, but when he started to come down, he snorted some more, but, this time, got a sudden, severe headache. He also said his neck was stiff and the lights hurt his eyes. Then he fell down, and they called 911."

"He had a stroke," Josh surmised. He finally understood Billie's concern about drugs, even pot.

"Yes," Phil said, brushing the sole of his sock. He slipped into a loafer, brushed the sole of his other sock, and slipped into the other loafer. "Quote unquote: 'a cerebral accident precipitated by the ingestion of cocaine and amphetamines.'"

"So sorry," Josh said, glancing at him.

"Coke, speed, they raise your blood pressure and up your chances of having a stroke, but what we didn't know was that Joshua had an AVM, an arteriovenous malformation."

"AVM?"

"A little knot of irregular blood vessels."

Josh wiped his feet with his socks.

"Sheila visited him once in the hospital," Phil said, "then never saw him again."

Josh slipped his foot into a sock, then the other.

"Of course, he couldn't play tennis," Phil said, hands open in an *obvious* gesture. "He was paralyzed on his left side, blind in one eye. He could barely talk, confused and angry, terribly angry. Can't tell you how angry he was. Imagine having a stroke at twenty-one."

Josh, in fact, did try to imagine what it must be like. You tell your arm to move, he thought, but it ignores you.

"The doctor said that with the abnormal vessels, if he'd had the stroke any later in life, it would've killed him. The only reason he survived, in short, was that he was young, ironically at the peak of health."

Josh slapped his sneakers together to shake the sand off, brushed the sand off one sock, and slipped into the sneaker. Then he repeated the process with the other foot and bent over to tie his laces.

"Well," Phil said, gripping the boat, "he tried therapy for a year and got back most of his speech, which gave him hope, but after a while he realized that he was never going to walk again, that he was always going to be confined to a wheelchair. Late one night, I got up to go to the bathroom, and when I looked in on him, he wasn't in his room, so I looked around and found him sitting on the terrace in the fog."

Josh imagined the dim silhouette of Joshua in a wheelchair.

"The nights are pretty cold there," Phil said, "so I went out to check on him, and, at first, he looked fine. He was just sitting there, staring at the fog, but when I felt his hand, it was ice cold, and I realized something was wrong. I wheeled him in and called Billie, then called an ambulance. Billie thought he was tripping."

"Tripping?" Josh asked. "LSD?"

"No, tripping on speed, but he was doing more than tripping. He was trying to kill himself. Apparently, he had a stash in the house, but just by chance, we'd found him in time. It sounds like a stupid, loser thing to do, but he was a very smart boy. He was trying to spare us the burden, the financial burden, the emotional burden...." He trailed off, staring at the sand, then looked up. "Sometimes I wonder if we should've just let him do what he wanted to do. I mean considering how it turned out."

"What do you mean?" Josh asked.

A shallow channel cut into the beach where a stream trickled into the sea, and Josh watched a gull there pecking a clump of seaweed.

"We didn't have insurance, and about that time, I was incurring some medical bills myself. We thought we'd lose the house, and we totally misjudged how determined he was. We never left him alone, but one day, when Billie was gone, I took a nap, and when I woke, I found his chair on the terrace. He'd crawled through the plants to the edge of the cliff."

Phil clunked the boat with his hand to indicate what happened.

"And fell," Josh whispered. He wondered if he could direct his hand to take his life, but figured he could if he were suffering chronic pain or nausea.

"He didn't understand we'd always love him, come what may. Sports star, physically impaired – he was our son."

"Forgive me for asking," Josh began.

"Sure."

"Did he leave a note?"

"No," Phil said. "No note."

186

Josh glanced at the huge arches holding up the road and the huge boulders cropping out of the cliff under them, also emblems of strength. He thought of Phil and Billie as a kind of arch, too, halves of a curve that, without the keystone, where they touched, would fall. Each was the other's strength. Each leaned on the other, held the other up. And now, at least for a while, Phil could lean on him, too. High above it all loomed three yellow domes with a green, diamond-shaped pattern in tiles, the biggest and highest with the garnish of a cross on top, like parsley. A church, he assumed, interesting architecture to someone like him, little more.

"Ready?" Phil asked.

When they stood, they stared at each other, and when Josh hugged him, Phil rocked him slightly like a tree nudged by a breeze. Then they headed back.

"It shook us to the core," Phil said, stepping up onto the parking lot. "An earthquake couldn't have shaken us more. But we did what all good Californians do. We rebuilt. We're fine. We know that's what he wanted, and if that's what he wanted, we're fine. And art has the power to soothe," he added, apparently referring to their painting. "Great therapy."

"I'm sure the trip's a great diversion."

"And you," Phil said, glancing at him. "Can't tell you how much Billie enjoys your company."

"Glad to be of service," Josh smiled. "So," he pondered, "all I have to do, really, to make her happy is hang out with her."

"Think so."

"I'd be glad to be her son." Then he added matter of fact, "I don't have a mom."

They strolled across the parking lot toward the entrance to the piazza.

"Tyler's lost a child, too," Josh confided, slipping his shirt on. "A daughter. Boating accident. Along with his ex-wife."

For the first time, he wondered about the fact that he and Tyler had lost family members in boating accidents, in Josh's case his mother.

"The common denominator of humanity," Phil remarked, "death."

Chapter 23: A Rock He Could Swim To

While Phil and Josh were at the beach, Billie and Tyler discussed Phil's health. They had ventured onto the subject when Billie said she was glad that Tyler and Josh had taken it easy on the hike over.

"So many steps," she said, toying with her silver necklace. Josh had told her it was safe to wear it in Amalfi.

"What's wrong with Phil?" Tyler asked.

"He's been overwhelmed with health problems over the last year or so," she began, "an emotional seesaw, let's say, of slow progress and disappointing setbacks. The positive side is that his cancer was curable – "

"Cancer?"

"Yes, prostate cancer," she explained. "And we've found a solution to most of the problems associated with it. The sheer number of them, though, almost wore us down, well, did actually, but we're on the mend. He had BPH, benign prostatic hyperplasia, but his PSA – "

"Prostate specific antigen," he interjected.

"...went up more than a point in a year, a sign, his urologist said, there might be a more serious problem. So Phil had a biopsy, and one of the aftereffects jarred him a bit, peeing blood, fresh blood, then brown blood, old blood. His masculinity, to him, was dependent on his sexual performance. He also didn't want to give up what he considered life's greatest pleasure, sex. So he masturbated occasionally and ejaculated blood, he said, again fresh blood, then brown blood. The biopsy, of course, exacerbated all of his BPH symptoms. In other words, his prostate swelled, squeezing his urethra shut, and he had to take Flomax to pee. Flo-max," she said, drawing out the word. "Says it all, doesn't it?"

When Tyler crossed his legs, he accidently banged the table with his foot. The glasses hopped, but none spilled.

"Sorry."

"Then we got bad news and good news," she said. "On Valentine's Day of all days, the doctor called with the diagnosis, microscopic prostate cancer. Two out of three pathologists said it was cancer. One wasn't sure. Eventually, we got a confirmation from Johns Hopkins. Yes, the problem was serious all right, serious as a Wyeth painting. Friends circled the wagons, and, to me, it was appropriate that we received the news on Valentine's Day. The diagnosis, of course, only deepened the bond between us. I was there for him, always would be, 'for better or worse,' a rock he could swim to. And," she stressed, "the prognosis was good. We had caught it, so to speak, in its earliest stage. It had a Gleason score of six, meaning average rate of growth. There was no perineural invasion."

"Meaning?" he asked.

"Apparently, cancer can use the nerves as a path out of the prostate, but it hadn't. Dr. Braude, our internist, and Dr. Cornell, his urologist, gave him a 100% cure rate. Dr. Merlin, his oncologist, a 96% cure rate. So, despite a lot of worries, Phil's initial attitude was positive. He researched the topic, looking up words like *malignant, tumor, metastasis*. But he worried about how in the world we were ever going to pay for everything. He worried about having to have a spinal instead of general anesthesia because of a drug reaction he'd experience during a colonoscopy. But most importantly, he worried about telling Joshua, our son."

"Why?" he asked.

"Joshua had had an aneurysm, was paralyzed on his left side, was severely depressed."

"I see."

"Phil could have done nothing about it, the cancer, that is. Said nothing about it. A lot of men take a wait-and-see attitude."

"It's so slow growing," he remarked, "most men would probably die of something else first."

"Right," she agreed. "Some men are so afraid of it, though, they have a prostatectomy, which, as you probably know, has some serious side effects."

"Like impotence."

"As Phil likes to joke," she smiled, "'I'm not impotent, I'm not incontinent, and I'm not incompetent.'"

He laughed.

"He never would've considered the prostatectomy."

"His machismo."

"Exactly," she said. "He was not going to do anything that would deprive him of his precious erection."

"I understand," he smiled.

"Thought you would. In any case, he'd done his research, and he chose the treatment with the lowest odds of affecting his sex life, a combination of iodine seed implants followed by a month or so of external beam radiation. Cornell said, 'You're going to be amazed how easy this is,' and Phil talked with a patient who'd had the procedure, someone whom the clinic must've paid to lie about the pain. Of course, on the spectrum from pain to no pain, Phil may have been just one of the 'lucky' ones on the pain end. Once he'd made his decision, he was eager to schedule everything. He read the packets the clinic sent him, read the emails, made phone calls, filled out forms, signed consent agreements. And phase one of the process, the implants, was, as Cornell called it, a success."

"Good."

"Then things started going wrong. Three hours after we got home, his catheter clogged."

"Clogged, why?"

"Clogged with blood. We went back to the clinic, where a second catheter was put in, and, again, after we got home, it clogged."

"Poor Phil."

"At that point in the day, the clinic was closed, so we had to go to an emergency room, where we waited for five hours before a nurse got to us. Imagine having to pee, but having to wait five hours. He actually wound up peeing around the catheter."

Tyler went from open mouth to burying his face in his hands.

"The nurse showed us how to irrigate the catheter ourselves, and it was a good thing she did because, around midnight, the damn thing clogged again."

Tyler slouched in his chair, fingers to mouth. Billie stared into space, absently fiddling with one of her silver earrings.

"After the catheter came out, the problems kept coming. He peed blood again," she stressed, "and sometimes his bladder would clog, and he'd have to strain to pass the clot. So he began drinking a lot of water to dissolve the clots, and gradually they became fewer and smaller until they went away. His ejaculate cleared up."

Tyler smiled.

"He was in pain when he peed, clot or no clot, so he began taking Oxycodone. His old BPH symptoms were worse, as you might expect. He was going every hour and still had to strain to pee. His balls were sore and swollen. Of course, he liked that, big balls."

"Never would've guessed Phil was such an old lech."

"Let me assure you, he is, cancer or no cancer."

"More power to him," he said, scratching his neck.

"Then we come to phase two," she said, "radiation. He got a CT scan just to map where things were, but he was scared during the scan because thought he could feel the radiation. Irrational, of course. He said it was all he could do to relax and keep still. Then he said he started fantasizing about fucking me hard in some Tuscan barn, and everything was fine."

Tyler laughed heartily.

"What?" Billie asked.

"That word from *your* mouth," he said. "Less of a shock from Queen Elizabeth."

"You'd be cursing too," she claimed, looking tired from the weight of the problems. "Going all night, getting the urge to go, but not being able to, stopping and starting." Then she added, "Wearing Depends. There's nothing less attractive than a man in a diaper."

Tyler reached across the table, squeezed her hand, and let go.

"He was caught up in a vicious circle," she said. "Peeing was so painful that his crotch would clinch so that he couldn't pee and would have to go again in a little while. God!"

"Thought you said he was taking Oxycodone," he asked.

"So much, in fact, he worried about becoming a narcotics addict. He was so unhappy." She stared at her wine glass, then glanced up. "We watched a lot of romantic comedies. Movie therapy."

"But things got better," he said.

"Better?" she scoffed. "Worse. He suffered a series of setbacks. First was a drug reaction. He began taking Pyridium and Rapaflo on the same day, Pyridium to soothe the urethra, Rapaflo as an experiment instead of Flomax. His feet swelled, a rash broke out around his toes, and Merlin ordered a barrage of tests just to make sure the problem wasn't something worse. Apparently, swollen ankles are a symptom of all sorts of dire things. Well, everything was fine, but he had taken an antihistamine, which, as it turns out, constricts the urinary tract. So he had to go back to Flomax to open it up again. Then he discovered Viagra."

"Viagra?" Tyler puzzled.

"He took half a Viagra one night – old lech that he is – and after it kicked in, as he put it, he peed like an eighteen year old."

"Really?"

"It gave him twelve hours of relief. Eureka! What a fluke! Merlin said another patient had said the same thing. Only problem was: Medco, his health company, allows only six pills per month. Cornell faxed Medco a prescription for more. Rejected. Phil called Medco and talked with a pharmacist. Rejected. Phil appealed. Rejected."

"They couldn't dispense it for something it wasn't approved for," he observed.

"Phil had made this amazing discovery, but no one would listen to him. He and a Pfizer rep just happened to be in Cornell's waiting room one day, and Phil told the rep about it, but the rep just looked at him as if he were crazy. So the only alternative was to find an alternative. Cornell gave him all his samples. A friend got a prescription filled and gave him the pills. Phil ordered it online from what appeared to be a legitimate Canadian company that required a prescription. He also ordered it from Mumbai cheap. The question was: Was the online stuff real? Were the online sites scams? You have no idea how broke we were. Desperate. The choice was simple: Viagra or pain."

"And Phil chose Viagra."

"Hell, yes. He worried about the side effects of taking so much of it, though. He emailed Pfizer. He talked with a Pfizer pharmacist on the phone. The pharmacist said the main concern was low blood pressure. Low blood pressure, ha," Billie laughed cynically. "After all he'd been through, Phil's blood pressure had shot through the roof. Which brings us to his second setback." Their table was sitting on a point of a big, eight-pointed star in a circle superimposed on the piazza's overlapping wave pattern of pavers. She seemed to focus on a wave, then glanced up. "He came to me one day and said he couldn't remember the passwords on his computer nor the names of the cities in Italy he wanted to visit. In other words – "

"You thought he'd had a stroke."

"The same thing that had paralyzed one side of our son, our big, beautiful son who was now wasting away, morose, in his room." Her lip quivered, and she started to tear up, but stopped herself. "It was back to the emergency room. A cat scan, an MRI, $10,000, and seven hours later it was decided: no stroke. But we had forgot his meds, and by the end of the day, his urinary tract had shut down. He was taking Lisinopril for blood pressure, and the ER doctor added Antenolol. But, of course, no one would give him Viagra."

"What caused the amnesia?" he asked.

"Well, we had a friend who experienced something called transient amnesia, and the MRI did show some spots on his brain, spots which no one seemed worried about at the time and spots which had gone away on an MRI three months later. No one knows what they were, but whatever they were, apparently his immune system took care of them. We had the house tested for mold, carbon monoxide, even radon. We had the heater, AC, and ductwork cleaned. But here's the kicker."

She paused.

"Yeah?"

"When I got home one day, Joshua's wheelchair was parked at the edge of the terrace. While Phil was taking a nap, Joshua had killed himself, thrown himself off the cliff."

"Oh, Billie," he said, sitting up straight. "I'm sorry."

"Three days later," she said matter of fact, "Phil had what he likes to call a brief emotional breakdown, not a mental breakdown, mind you. He gets angry if you call it that. A brief emotional breakdown," she repeated. "Even before Joshua's death, Phil was simply overwhelmed with anxiety. We were drowning in a sea of debt from Joshua's stroke, and here comes another tidal wave of it. He saw Viagra as fake relief, that is, temporary, not a permanent solution, and he was caught up in another vicious circle: his fear of a stroke would send his blood pressure up. My oak," she sighed, "toppled to the ground."

"He seems fine," he observed, elbows on chair arms, fists closed. "How'd he get going again?"

"He saw a shrink a couple of times," she smiled, "but it really wasn't the shrink that helped him. It was his preparation for the shrink."

"Preparation," he mused. "What kind?"

"An outline," she said. "He made a two-page outline divided into four categories: pain, discomfort, fears, and stress factors. He tackled one issue at a time until he had resolved them all. Most importantly, he addressed the irrational nature of his greatest fear."

"Which was?"

"That he would never recover. And he did that by forcing himself to accept the fact that he'd actually made progress. First of all, he was cured. Second, every organ in his body had been checked that year. They were fine. Third, he was, in fact, in less pain. And fourth, he had me. No matter how awful he felt, he had me, always would. Love makes up for – "

She shook her head as if searching for the word.

"Everything."

"Yes, Tyler," she said, staring at him. "Everything. Remember that."

"I will," he nodded, staring at the veins in the back of his hand. Suddenly, he was aware of the transience of everything on his bones.

"After the first visit, the shrink wrote him a prescription for Remeron, which, when Phil researched it, turned out to be an antidepressant, an antianxiety drug, and an antihistamine."

"Which constricts the urinary tract."

"So he never filled it. After the second visit, the shrink wrote him a prescription for Gabitril, an anticonvulsant. We have no idea why he prescribed it. To say the least, we didn't fill it either. Phil had Valium. Can't remember who prescribed it. But he took it because, when he read about it – "

"It didn't affect his sex life."

"As far as he could tell."

"What a dirty old man!"

"We can't swim in the ocean off our house. There're sharks, and the undertow's too strong. But he likes to hike the trails on the cliff. He likes the Douglas firs, their citrus smell, as he calls it. He jokes about them. He says, 'I like Douglas firs,' in a mock-crazy tone of voice. 'Firs are com-fort-ing.' And he makes this mock-crazy, wide-eyed face when he says it."

"Like Blanche in *Streetcar*," he said. "'Something wrong with me?'"

"The bracts on the cones look like the tails of mice sticking their heads between the scales. An Indian myth says the tree let the mice hide there during a forest fire. That's sort of what Phil's doing on his walks."

"Hiding in the trees?"

"He's safe there," she murmured, sipping wine. Then she brightened. "He has an elliptical machine when the weather's bad, and he rides that, watching TV."

"Exercise is great therapy," he said, sipping Campari. He swallowed it wrong and coughed to clear his throat. "Studies show it." He stood, leaned over, and hugged her, then lingered, a hand on her shoulder. "Is he still on Viagra?"

"Oh, no," she said. "He weaned himself off it. He takes it now for what it was meant for. He just takes Flomax and Doxycycline, an antibiotic."

"So he's OK?" he asked, strolling around her.

She looked at him as if considering the question.

"OK, yes," she said. "Apparently, you can't kill the old goat. He just comes back to life. The trip is such a distraction he hardly ever focuses on the fact that it still hurts to pee. At least, that's what he tells me. The bottom line is his PSA has dropped from 4.5 to 0.4. Cured is defined as .02 for a long time."

"Almost there," Tyler grinned.

He took her hand, and as he rubbed it, the modest princess-cut diamond in her wedding ring sparkled.

"He has this plastic urinal," she said, holding on to him, "and he doesn't know it, but sometimes I watch him sit up on the side of the bed at night to pee in it. He seems so lonely, but, of course – "

"You're there."

She patted his hand, then let go of it.

"I would never abandon him just because he's sick. All the more reason to stay."

"I'd really like to have what you have," he said, "that kind of rock-solid relationship. Believe it or not, I'm romantic at heart."

"Well, as far as I can tell," she said, looking at him askance, "Josh is a hot flame waiting to set you on fire. If you stand too close...."

"Flambé."

"Or has he already? Are you already burning with lust?"

"My mental capacity is diminished dramatically around him. I just want to give in."

"And you should."

195

He thought of Blanche in *Streetcar* again. "Death," she says. "The opposite is desire."

Billie was right. He was already burning with a slight amorous fever, aching all over with a stiff, poignant soreness that only the young man's assiduous massage could relieve just as he had massaged the kink out of his neck back in the hotel room in Naples. Tyler knew he could easily die of such fever. Or was it: would willingly die?

"Promise you won't hurt him," Billie asked. "You mustn't let your missteps and failures make you bitter."

"What makes you think I can't be hurt?" he asked.

"You're right," she said, relenting.

"Besides," he reminded her, "I've known him all of three days."

Despite the age difference and theoretical difference in maturity, Josh seemed more like a guardian angel to him than the other way around, a Hermes, a handsome messenger sent from Zeus to tell him the truth about himself.

"What happens with the iodine seeds?" he asked, slipping his hands into his pockets.

"They stay inside him," she explained.

"Forever?"

"Yes. Dead now, of course, inert, but he has a card about them in both English and Italian just in case he sets off an alarm at airport security. The trip is his reward for surviving," she paused, "for surviving all the pain he's been through."

He glanced around the piazza: a fountain, sandwich boards with menus, terra-cotta urns with geraniums. Then Phil and Josh strolled into view, Phil's face soft with a triste smile, Josh's literally shining with a playful blush.

Chapter 24: A Sprig of Rosemary

Valerio slouched, hands in pockets, in a pew near a confessional, idly fondling himself while waiting for the last penitent to exit. The confessional was built into a stone wall with two doors, one for the priest, one for the penitent, a pair of lights above the space between them, one green, one red. There was no third door, as in a double confessional, an auspicious fact that added to what Father Dorato called "the beautiful privacy" of the sacrament. High above the doors loomed the shattered mirror of a stained-glass angel holding up a white cross radiant with the late Neapolitan sun behind it. Valerio thought of the blasé expression on the angel's androgynous face as the same blank look a harpy might have just before swooping down on a victim. He imagined the angel coming to life amid the colorful panes and gliding down, like a crazed aerialist, to snatch the sunglasses hooked in the neck of his sleeveless T-shirt.

In the corner of his eye, he noticed the red light go off, the green on. The penitent opened the door and stepped out, a coarse, heavyset woman in a black dress, brogans, and stockings with a black kerchief wrapped around her head and tied beneath her chin. As she shuffled away, Valerio rose, took his hands from his pockets, and strolled over, his spotless Nikes hardly making a sound on the marble floor.

Inside the booth, he shut the door, slumped on the seat like a dog in a doghouse, and, knees spread, began unbuttoning and unzipping his jeans. After the stocky woman, the muggy confessional smelled of vinegar, and it certainly was not the most comfortable nor private place for tricking in La Nostra Donna di Sincerita. There were rooms which could be locked, including Dorato's office. But sex in the sacred booth was much more exciting than in a cozy office or even a toilet stall in a public men's room mainly because of the great taboo, and Dorato, Valerio knew, was definitely hooked on what must have been for him the incomparable thrill of such an utterly profane violation.

The little problem of the lattice screen between the booths had been solved long ago when a number of the congregation had fortuitously expressed a desire to confess face to face. Clever as he was, Dorato had conveniently come up with what he called "a decent solution" and had seated the screen on a sliding track so that the penitent could open it if he or she chose and Dorato or another confessor could close it so that the next penitent could make up his or her own mind. It was, in fact, a glory hole in church clothing, and the padded kneeler and arm rest were a minor physical obstacle that Valerio had quickly learned to overcome. Of course, the fact that he was well endowed helped considerably. The bronze crucifix over the grille was not much of a spiritual obstacle either. Valerio had always seen it more as the warped image of some sick sadomasochistic torture that had gotten out of hand, a stark symbol of self-mortification that ironically aroused him.

"Would you like to pray for the spirit of repentance," the priest asked, "in order that you see your sins for what they are and – "

"Father," Valerio began, freeing himself from his jeans. "We may as well be praying to one of those polished skulls the Death Cult names and talks to."

"Valerio," the priest sighed, making the sign of the cross. He sat up straight to gird himself for his role. "My son," he murmured, "are you here to admit your guilt and be absolved of your sins?"

"No, Father," Valerio replied, fondling himself. "I'm here for my Wednesday blow job." He always gave the priest bulk rate since they had been having sex so long, in fact, in one form or another, since he was nine.

He began slapping his cock gently until it stood up straight, and when the priest heard the quiet slaps, his posture immediately dissolved, and he leaned against the wall between them, resting his head near the little lattice sifting his loved one's voice.

"And how many times have you committed this sin this week?" the priest asked, touching the latticework tenderly.

Valerio rolled his foreskin between his thumb and index finger, smiled, and wondered if the priest wanted him to tell a pornographic anecdote to arouse him.

"It's not a sin, Father," Valerio stated, noticing the priest's stout fingers. Stuck to the crosshatching, the pale hand reminded him of a spider caught in a Venus Flytrap. It also reminded him of a prisoner's fingers resting on bars. "You have to choose to sin," he explained, "and I didn't choose. I am. I just am. No choice, no sin."

The priest pressed his forehead against the wall: "We both have the power to denounce this sin and walk away from it."

"It's not a sin," Valerio stressed, bored with the priest's remorse. He stood, lay his sunglasses on the seat, and looped the front of his T-shirt behind his neck. Then he faced the little window and began slowly stroking himself. "And I'd like to see you walk away from this."

Occasionally, the weary priest, Valerio knew, would lapse into a bout of doubt and depression, deluding himself into thinking that the frail saint in his mind had the upper hand over the virile lech in his robe who, when younger, had preyed on nubile boys, but who now, as age rushed in like a cold front, had managed to limit himself to this furtive and troubling release once a week. It was his way of keeping the lid on what he thought of as his simmering passions.

"After all," the priest whispered, "it's a venial, not a mortal, sin."

Valerio could hear the thin resolve thawing in his voice, breaking up into delicate, see-through plates of ice floating down the minutes.

"Not a sin, Father," Valerio countered, noticing the small, awkward valentine that he, as a teenager, had scratched into the panel with a pocketknife. Someone had darkened it with furniture polish so that it was almost impossible to see it in the gloomy booth. "An act of pleasure. Anything that feels good is good. See for yourself."

The priest knelt as if to pray and, as he watched Valerio intently through the grille, began unbuttoning his cassock below the sash. Then he reached inside it and began pulling himself.

"I'm sure rape feels good to the rapist," the priest breathed.

"Would you like me to rape you?" Valerio asked, a palm on a pec. "In the booth? Now?"

"No," the priest replied, disturbed. "No, Valerio. Don't do anything foolish, please."

"Feels good to both, Father," Valerio stated, irritated with the priest as with a fly. "Christ, Father. Sad that I have to spell things out."

When the lattice slid open, Valerio could see how servile the priest was, lips parted in anticipation, eyes fixed on him with fervent desire, even adoration. Because of the black robe, the handsome face in the small frame looked as if it were floating in the dark, a strange, middle-aged portrait of sensual, if not spiritual, torment that had magically come alive.

"You have the freedom to make decisions," the priest said, jerking himself casually. "You can will yourself to lead a better life."

To Valerio, the priest looked as if he had stuck his hand inside a ruptured suture and were manipulating an internal organ.

"Nothing's better than getting a blow job," Valerio said, "especially when I'm getting paid for it, especially by a priest. And even if I did will myself to fuck a woman, I'd still be gay. You are who you are, not what you do. I could fuck a woman the rest of my life and still be gay."

The priest took his hand out of his cassock and reached through the window to hold Valerio. Valerio stepped forward to accommodate him, then just stood there, legs spread, hips thrust forward, quietly watching the hand closed around him. Then Valerio began lightly fingering the fuzz around his cool nipples, pubescent wisps of hair as fine as the white down on a plant.

"I've known many proud gay men deeply involved in the gay movement who have renounced this – " The priest searched for a word. "This practice…and went on to marry and raise a happy family."

"Father," Valerio smiled, enjoying the familiar touch of the man's big hand, all the sweet, warm sensations it was giving him. "Gay men don't turn straight, and if one thinks he did, he was never gay to begin with. He may have

199

engaged in gay sex, even exclusively, but he wasn't gay. More likely, though, he's lying to himself and everyone else for that matter, the way you're lying to me now and the church and everyone else who walks through the door and kneels before you for communion. I know how you feel when a boy sticks his tongue out. I know how you feel when you place the wafer on it. I know how you feel now."

The priest withdrew his hand, stuck it in his cassock again, and pressed his face, like a man in a pillory, into the window, mouth open, tongue out, as Valerio had described, for the blissful blessing. A starving chick could not have looked more solicitous, straining for the worm.

He teased the foreskin with the tip of his tongue, making the member snap to attention again and again like a coil, but when he actually went down on him, Valerio stepped back, slipping out of him, and said, "Money first."

The priest retreated into the shadows, and Valerio could hear the witchy rustle of the cassock as the priest rummaged through it.

"Thirty this time," Valerio added. "I need thirty."

"Thirty?" the priest balked. "Why?"

"I want pants worthy of the shirt an admirer gave me. I want to look my best for my friend."

He knew how much to take from the priest both in Euros and emotionally. As his father once said, "To remove the bark in a circle would kill a tree." But today he was asking only a little more.

"No," the priest stated, stunned with jealousy. "The usual."

"You'll give me thirty," Valerio said confidently.

"You threatening me?"

"I don't need to threaten you, Father. You'll give it to me."

"Why?" the priest asked, pondering the Euros in his hand.

"You're in love with me," Valerio smiled. "You love me even more than that fictional god you say you believe in."

"May God forgive you, my son."

"There is no God, Father. Your faith's a lie." Humiliated, the priest handed over the money, which Valerio counted and stuffed into a pocket. Then Valerio stepped forward and grabbed the priest by his forelock. "Open your mouth, Father," he said calmly. "Time for communion."

As the priest blew him, Valerio tweaked his left nipple with his left hand and unconsciously touched the soft, sensitive area behind his right ear with his right. The latter gesture had something of a surprised element to it, a curious puzzlement over the priest's sporadic foolishness about sin and guilt and penance. Valerio wondered what had spooked him during the week. He also wondered if the body of Christ, especially a small, wheaten wafer, had ever given the priest as much consummate solace as he himself did now or the grape juice of Christ in an ounce of semen.

Whatever the case, once the priest had surrendered to him sexually, he had given himself up entirely, heart and soul, sucking him off in such a slavish frenzy that he brought him off rather quickly for Valerio, who could usually hold out as long as a client wanted. Through the years, Valerio had become programmed to the booth erotically, and when he came, ecstatically sighing, his pecs and palms lit up as if pressed, not against a wall, but someone's back and the back of someone's hands.

On the other side of the wall, the priest looked as if he were punching himself in the crotch. Then he gagged on Valerio such a loud gag that he startled himself, jumping back onto the seat and furtively coughing and gasping.

"Are you sorry for this sin?" he asked, buttoning up.

"Sorry?" Valerio smiled, pulling up his jeans. "I enjoyed it."

"Do you intend to commit this sin again?"

Valerio laughed to himself. "Yes, Father, I do. Here with you next Wednesday." Then he added, "And if you call it a sin again, I'm going to drag you by the hair down the aisle and fuck your lame ass on the altar."

"You must do some good to make up for this – "

Before the priest could finish, Valerio snapped, "I do a lot of good. I give men pleasure. It's the only thing I can do that's good, and you should thank me for it. In fact, I insist. Thank me for it. Now. Father?"

"What?" the priest asked, sprawled against the seat.

"Thank me," Valerio said. "Now." When the priest failed to speak, Valerio kicked the wall and shouted, "Thank me!" and his voice went echoing down the nave.

"Thank you, thank you," the priest whispered nervously. "I'm grateful for this favor you do me once a week."

"More like it," Valerio said, zipping up.

Then a lull ensued. On one side of the wall, Valerio adjusted himself in his jeans. On the other, the priest tugged, unconsciously, on the small, white square at his throat. He looked as if he had just been locked in a solitary cell.

"I forgive you, my son," the priest said, casting about the booth.

"Nothing to forgive, Father," Valerio replied, straightening his T-shirt. "Forgive yourself for being such a fucking hypocrite." Then he added under his breath, "Such a fucking mess."

As Valerio picked up his sunshades, the priest murmured, "Ego te absolvo a peccatis tuis in nomine Patris et Filii et Spiritus Sancti. Amen."

"And six acts of contrition for you," Valerio suggested, slipping his shades on.

He stepped out of the confessional and squinted toward the glare of the entrance. To him, stopping by the church on Wednesday was like stopping to smell rosemary on a walk. He would rub the tip of a sprig between his thumb and index finger, sniff the clean, refreshing scent on his fingers, and stroll on.

Chapter 25: The Crystal Ball

Tyler and Josh sat on opposite sides of the bed, slipped off their shoes, and propped against the pillows.

"You're not going to believe what Phil told me," Josh said, hands clasped on his chest.

"Wait until you hear what Billie told *me*," Tyler replied, hands clasped behind his head.

They traded stories peacefully, then dozed off to the hush of the surf.

# # # # #

Josh had given Billie his key, and about an hour and a half later, she and Phil knocked on the cottage door, Phil with a wine cooler cradled in his arm, Billie with wineglasses. Everyone sat at the table under the pergola, sipping prosecco, and during a lull in conversation, Phil looked around the terrace.

"Reminds you of home, doesn't it?" he asked.

"Yes," Billie confessed.

"Seaweed," Josh said.

"The terrace," Phil explained. "Similar."

"Except for the vast difference," she smiled. "No firs and fog. As we said, you two should visit us. I already think of you as family."

Family, Tyler thought, in the sense of kindred spirits, for sure the same tribe culturally with culture in the broadest sense of the word. He could see the four of them gathered around a stone hearth in the living room of the handsome house he imagined in California, a ménage a quatre of sorts. No, ménage was too suggestive. A commune, an art colony. Mom, dad, son, and son-in-law.

"It's Prairie School," Josh said to Tyler, "low roof, windows turning corners, open space that continues outside."

"But not Wright," Tyler said.

"Right," Phil punned. "He built a lot of houses in California, but not ours."

"Who did?"

"Eichler maybe," Phil suggested.

"Probably not," Josh said. "It's not a tract house, is it?"

"No," Phil said, facing Billie. "We'll have to look it up."

"Familiar with the Hollyhock House in Hollywood?" Josh asked. Phil shook his head. "Wright built it for an oil heiress. Looks like something out of the old *Flash Gordon* serials."

"Why's it called the Hollyhock House?" Billie asked.

"Owner's favorite flower," Josh said. "The motif's in the carvings and stained-glass windows, actual hollyhocks in the planters."

# # # # #

Around seven thirty, they headed into town for dinner and, since they had not made reservations, wandered into the first restaurant they saw, Il Chiostro, the dining room of an old hotel off Piazza Duomo. In the foyer, a pair of sofas faced each other across a rustic coffee table under a big, tarnished chandelier, and they waited there in silence for about fifteen minutes before being led to a table. Tyler noticed a big aesthetic discrepancy between the contemporary tables and chairs and the elegant room itself with its coffered ceiling, brocaded walls, and heavy, carved sideboard. The worn brocade was a warm, lustrous gold with a swirling acanthus pattern, but, to him, it also looked allergic and unhygienic. "Con te partiro" was playing in the background barely audible over what he thought of as the aviary of voices, china, silverware, and glass.

"Don't think I'm up for the wild-boar sausage," Billie joked, scanning the menu.

"What about the roast suckling pig?" Phil quipped.

The meal was another epicurean delight: red tuna from Cetara for Josh, blue fish Chianti style for Tyler, linguine with seafood for Billie, and chicken lasagna for Phil. Again, Billie ordered a bottle of local wine simply because she liked the name: Olivella.

"One must yield to one's desires," she said cryptically.

When Phil asked Tyler if he'd made money off his screenplays, Tyler said yes, first off *Drains*, a "brilliant" script about mutant coyotes living in the storm drains under Atlanta, but most importantly off *The Crystal Ball*, what he considered an art script, the prize winner they had talked about in Naples.

"My main source of income. Not for you two," he said, meaning it was probably not Phil and Billie's cup of tea. "Kim, the main character, cuts a woman's throat and scares a burn victim to death, and her love interest, a porn star, shoves a dildo up a killer's ass."

"Cut throats and burn victims and dildos," Billie recited. "Oh, my."

"My God!" Josh blurted. "I've seen that. The porn star hangs the killer from a trapeze, right?"

"A suspension bar in an S and M dungeon."

"S and M," Billie gawked, eyeing Josh. "When he ties you up, don't say you weren't warned." She turned to Tyler. "I knew you were a risk."

"One worth taking," Josh said, coming to his defense.

Tyler glanced at him sitting up straight and knew that Billie still wasn't sure he was suitable for Josh, her new son. Suitable, he thought. The word made him think of a suit. Apparently, she was shopping for an eligible bachelor like a fine linen suit, a Zegna, let's say, that would fit Josh perfectly, that would match his class and looks.

"Some of it was hard to watch," Josh declared. "But I loved the ending."

"The ending?" Billie asked.

"You actually get to fill in the ending yourself," Josh smiled.

"Why did you make money off that one?" Phil asked, hand up, open.

"Well, one," Tyler said, "it's a cult hit, and, two, I negotiated a good contract. It was a new production company. They never dreamed the film would take off, let alone become, as they say, a cult classic, so they were willing to give me just about anything I asked. First, I got an option, then the purchase price. A certain percentage was deferred, but I got it eventually, as well as compensation for first rewrite and some additional writing. Thank God I had the sense to ask for not only a substantial basic agreement, but also what's called profit participation. I'm a gross participant, as they say. I have profit participation along with the director and producers. Then there's the publication fee when it went to DVD, credit and parity with the director and producers, and so forth."

"What are you good for?" Billie asked.

"Financially?" Tyler smiled. *Now she's checking my financial qualifications.* "I'll send you my portfolio."

As usual, Tyler slouched in his chair, legs spread under the table, and when he felt Josh's leg touch his – Josh's right under Tyler's left – he could also feel all the intricate vessels and nerves in his crotch growing like roots in a rich, warm excitement. The way to his heart, he guessed, was through his fly.

"What about you two?" he asked. "You're in Italy. You must be solvent, right?"

"Don't worry about us," Phil said, shaking his finger. "Some god saw fit to save us from our debts."

"Oh, how?" Tyler asked.

Phil looked nonplussed.

"Let's chalk it up to working hard and finally being discovered," Billie suggested.

"OK," Tyler said, mystified. According to Billie, they "were drowning in a sea of debt" a year or so ago. Now they're yachting across it.

"Room for dessert?" Josh asked.

He and Tyler shared lemon peels in chocolate; Phil and Billie a santarosa, a custard pastry with black cherries.

"Why are horror films good?" Phil asked, flicking a flake of crust off his lip.

"Why are horror films good?" Tyler repeated to himself. "Let's see. Well, they entertain people, get their minds off their problems. It's a form of catharsis in a couple of ways. The audience gets to face its worst fears without really being in harm. Practice for the real thing. You know, the old question, 'What would I do?' The audience is also purged of certain emotions, fear and pity in classical tragedy, violence, I guess, in the gladiatorial games. A sport like football is the modern gladiatorial game. People leave it civil, allegedly, since they've experienced the violence vicariously and in that way vented it. It's cathartic for me, too. Writing's therapy. I solve the problem on the page instead of paying a shrink. The films made the producers a lot of money, which means they'll probably fund more of 'em, mine that is. And," he stressed, "those horror pictures paid for this trip, where I just happened to sit next to you."

Chapter 26: The Joy of Blow Jobs

After dinner, the couples returned to the hotel and said goodnight in the loggia, sniffed and verified by the three Shakespearean terriers. Tyler and Josh strolled along the cliff path, and when Josh paused in the lantern's orange glow, calmly unlocking the cottage door, the moment, to Tyler, was sad and sweet. He felt like a trick Josh was bringing home, a lonely man pairing up with another lonely man for the evening. Because of the devilish Bacchus on the door, he also felt as if he were about to be introduced to some lurid secret rite, some psychic revelation initiating him into the next more gratifying phase of his life. A derelict was being towed into port, a scruffy waif taken in. As he stepped inside, Tyler knew he was one step closer to finally being himself.

Josh turned on the lights, stepped into the bathroom, and, from the squeak of the shutter, apparently opened the window. Then he strolled across the room, and when he opened the French doors, the sheers billowed like sails in the cross breeze. Meanwhile, Tyler had wandered to the camel-back chair in the corner and, a little confused with himself, was waiting for him. Josh faced him, smiled wide-eyed, but hesitated. He looked both eager yet uncertain. Then he stepped forward, carefully embraced him, and rested his head on Tyler's shoulder. Tyler wrapped his arms around him and leaned his head against his affectionately.

Obviously, something more than mere sex was going on between them, Tyler thought, or they wouldn't be just standing there, holding each other quietly. Apparently, Josh wanted to go slow, to compose himself in close contact with him, with the tricky intricacies of the situation, before shifting gears into a direct sexual approach. Did Josh think groping him would scare him off? How would they actually pull off the change from companions to lovers? Would it be natural, awkward?

In the past, Tyler knew, when it came to blow jobs, it pretty much did not matter who was giving him one. It was more a question of compatibility than the sex of his partner, that is, whether he was able to relate to the person or, put another way, to the person's "soul," though he did not mean *soul* in a religious sense – perhaps spiritual, not religious. Though the hand job in Naples was great, his developing relationship with Josh was satisfying certain basic emotional needs as well, for example, belonging with, if not to, someone for whom he had great respect and affection. Josh was a beautiful young man in ways other than as a sex object. If Josh wanted to blow him, blow jobs felt good, and if he (Tyler) were enjoying himself, then technically he was happy. He couldn't argue with that. He was also attracted to what he considered the alternative, individualist nature of the act.

Josh stepped back and studied Tyler's face. Then he pulled Tyler's polo shirt from his shorts and, when Tyler raised his arms, over his head. He dropped it onto an ottoman, held Tyler's sides, and began seductively biting his chest. When he, cheek to pec, tongued Tyler's nipple, Tyler cupped the back of Josh's head and mashed his face against him. Josh gnawed him hungrily, and when he began licking his way down Tyler's abs, Tyler felt some final vestige of reluctance surrender to him unconditionally. Well, not so much to him, Tyler thought, to himself, to certain frank, indisputable desires. He wanted to be deep inside the young man one way or another.

"Get undressed," he said, grabbing Josh's shoulders. When he tried to raise him, Josh resisted, playfully chewing Tyler's crotch through his shorts. "Get undressed," Tyler chuckled, stepping back.

Josh glanced up, stood, and unbuckled his belt.

When they were naked, Josh said, "Have a seat," indicating the camel-back chair.

He had left his sneakers on and stepped to the chest of drawers, where he took out a soap dish, a paper clip, his yellow Bic, and the half joint they had toked in Naples. When he lit up, Tyler noticed the thin scab on Josh's chest, and when he passed the joint, Tyler realized that he felt as comfortable around him nude as he did clothed, as comfortable as he did, slumped, legs spread in the lumpy chair. They were half aroused, but the moment, strangely enough, had the straightforward, casual air of a locker room.

Josh, with the soap dish, sat cross-legged on the glossy tiles between Tyler's feet, and they traded hits, holding the smoke in their lungs, then exhaling in slow, fragrant clouds, all the while staring at each other mischievously. When the joint had burned down to a roach, Josh twisted the paper clip into a roach clip, and they traded a few more hits, but when it was too short to toke, Josh tapped it out in the dish, pinched it from the clip, and swallowed it. Then he handed Tyler the dish, which he set on the side table. At that point, the pot had worked its magic, along with the suggestiveness of their positions, Tyler dominant, Josh submissive, but namely, as Tyler thought of it, the velvet valentine of Josh's mouth in the vicinity of his erection.

When Josh took hold of it and began jerking it leisurely, Tyler slid farther down in the chair, relaxed completely for the first time in a long time – knees spread, hands clasped behind his head – and just let himself enjoy being loved by someone, someone making love to him in a way in which the expressive physical aspect of the experience, for a change, was almost inseparable from its intimate, emotional aspect. Because he was high, he guessed, the room assumed an exquisite, timeless quality, and when the sheers slowly billowed again like sails, he imagined that he and Josh were floating off to some quiet, fire-lit scene where two men, thousands of years ago, were doing exactly the same thing, Lucanians, he fantasized, a pair of local Italians.

Josh changed position, half kneeling, one foot on the floor, one knee. Then, jerking him, he leaned over Tyler, licking his chest, his abs, his groin like a cat, so much, in fact, his tongue became pleasantly dry and raspy.

"Oh, my god," Josh whispered, straightening up. "You're so fucking hot."

"So are you," Tyler smiled, drowsy.

Josh's pink erection was standing up, the purple crown resting near his navel, the young plums of his testicles drooping one slightly lower than the other.

"Hot abs!" Josh said, his hair winged out on his temples. He licked Tyler's abs for emphasis, painting a broad swath with his tongue. "Can't believe I've had such good luck."

"Luck?"

"I have a good-looking man with his pants off in the honeymoon suite of a hotel in Italy. If you let me, I'm going to enjoy you as much as I can."

"As I said," Tyler replied, gazing at him complaisantly, "'If it makes you happy.'"

If it makes you happy, Tyler thought, all dreamy and sentient.

In that sense, his cock was a gift, a generous, swollen gift of himself and candid pleasure. Commensurate with Tyler's willingness to explore him sexually was Josh's apparent eagerness to please him in return, and when Josh finally went down on him, he swallowed his cock all the way down to his pubes, then choked it with his throat a few times, staring up at him with bright, roguish eyes. When he let it slip from his mouth, it was a vibrant, glistening red, and when he kissed the sensitive area under the head, it tingled with excitement. He seemed curious about it, experimental, licking the shaft, the neck, flicking the "helmet," sticking the tip of his tongue into the slit. He paused, holding it, looking at Tyler as if for some cue. When none came, he went back down on him, closed his eyes, and began lightly stroking himself.

The massage in the hotel room in Naples had been a kind of physical therapy segueing into sensual pleasure. Here, Tyler also saw the sex as Rolfing, physical and emotional massage therapy. Pleasure was certainly the antidote for pain, indisputable solace for everything from petty troubles to his grievous past. They had stepped out of their lives for a moment, were devoting themselves to just making each other feel good, so good, in fact, his body was now turning against him in a sense, giving itself up to all the pure animal lust it could stand without coming.

"Too much of a good thing," Tyler said, lifting Josh's head off him.

"Never too much," Josh grinned, staring at Tyler's thigh.

When Josh went down, Tyler tried to focus on giving him, as well as himself, as much pleasure as possible with his cock: lifting his hips, spreading his thighs even farther, thrusting himself up and into his face as deeply as possible, again a form of symbiosis, the emotional pleasure of giving physical pleasure. Then his mind went blank, and he came, gushing in his mouth. In response, Josh jerked himself faster and shook his head slowly to work Tyler's cock around in his throat, jamming it into it hard when he came, shooting onto the chair. He kept him in his mouth, milking himself of the last few drops of come, then straightened up, his hands on Tyler's knees.

"Were you a porn star in a former life?" Tyler asked.

Flushed and sweaty, he felt himself slipping beneath the flickering surface of what may as well have been a black, oblivious ocean. He had to push himself upright in the chair to keep from losing consciousness.

"Found my G-spot," Josh said, touching the dimple above his sternum.

He blushed and wiped his mouth with the back of his hand, his lips bright red from sucking.

"Best head I ever had," Tyler said, shaking his head to clear it.

He leaned forward and gently brushed Josh's hair off one temple, then the other. Then he caressed Josh's neck, pulled him forward, and looked into his eyes as far as he could. All he could see, though, was how happy he was.

"Let me get a towel," Josh said, rising.

When he stepped into the bathroom, a neon-green gecko appeared on the windowsill. They stared at each other, then Josh pulled a couple of the thin towels off the cane basket. When he returned to the room, he handed Tyler one, knelt in front of him, and wiped the skirt of the slipcover.

"Were you close to your father?" Josh asked, standing.

"My father was as warm as an ice cube," Tyler said, dabbing his crotch.

Josh just stood there.

"Think having a son would've satisfied some desire you had to replace the relationship you never had with your father?"

"Wouldn't know," Tyler said. "Never had one. Had two daughters."

When Josh stuck his hand out, Tyler handed him the towel.

"I'll turn out the lights," Josh said.

He walked to the door and flicked the switch, plunging the room into a deep, sensuous blue-print blue. He waited as if for his eyes to adjust, strolled to the bed, and dropped the towels on a night stand. Then he sat, unlaced his sneakers, and slipped them off.

Meanwhile, Tyler had shuffled to the bed and, when Josh was ready, helped him turn down the sheet and spread. They slipped under the covers, propped against the pillows, and stared at the sheers billowing and folding. From the hush gradually emerged the womblike mother's breath of the waves. At the same time, they faced each other and held hands. Tyler pulled him next to him and put his arm around him. Josh slid his hand under the covers and cupped Tyler's thigh.

"Tell me," Tyler began. "Why do you like to suck cock? I mean, why does anyone do it? I know what I got out of it. What did you get out of it?"

"Sex," Josh stated as if it were obvious. "I wanted to have sex with you, and there are only a couple of holes you can stick your dick in. The lips, the mouth, the throat – they're erogenous zones."

"You said you found your G-spot."

"Sort of kidding," Josh smiled, "but I really do seem to have this spot deep in my throat that, when a cock bumps it, lights me up with all kinds of good feelings. In fact, sometimes I get so excited I think I could come from just giving head."

"No hands."

"No hands," Josh claimed. "Of course, my other G-spot's deep in my ass. I have this warm, wonderful walnut wedged in there."

"Your prostate."

"Right," Josh laughed. "I can come, for sure, having it banged."

"No hands."

"No hands," Josh swore. "And let me tell you, nothing feels better."

Tyler knew he could make men come by fucking them, and some could come only when fucked hard.

"But I have a couple of biological and psychological theories about it," Josh said. "Giving head. They have to do with the womb, early infancy, and the idea of nurturing."

"Really?" Tyler yawned. "You've thought about this?"

"I think one of the reasons guys like to give head is that, on some level, it harks back to the womb, which, of course, is associated with security and pleasure. From the very beginning, the mouth is an erogenous zone to insure that the fetus sucks its thumb as training for breast sucking. Thumb sucking is nothing short of necessary for survival, and it's associated with one of the first things the fetus experiences, rhythm. In the womb, the fetus hears not only the beat of its own heart, but also the bigger, stronger, louder beat of its mother's. The same's true not only for the mother's breathing, but also the fetus's."

"The fetus's?"

"The sibilant ingestion and expulsion of amniotic fluid into and out of the lungs. The rhythmic nature of cock sucking, as well as that of any sexual act, for that matter, goes back to the pleasant, assuring rhythms of the womb."

Tyler was tired heavy, but still, palpably settling into the supple bed, just letting himself rest. The male music of Josh's voice was soothing.

"Another reason why guys like to give head," Josh said, "is that it subconsciously reminds them of their infancy, which again is usually associated with security and pleasure. The thumb or anything like it, like a cock, is, in this light, a breast substitute, even though thumb sucking comes first chronologically. To an infant a nipple is as big as a cock is to an adult. Sucking a male nipple is like sucking on Mom's. Sperm even looks like milk. And sucking sounds about the same whether you're sucking a thumb, a breast, a bottle, or a cock. Of course, to a man a cock is not a substitute for anything. It's the real thing."

When the sheers drifted apart, Tyler gazed across the terrace – past the rustic chairs and railing – at a cluster of stars almost eye-level with the bed as if the room were on Olympus.

"Point is," Josh stressed, "everyone gets a whole lot of practice sucking other things first, things associated with a sense of well-being."

A breeze like a wave flowed into the room, flooding it with a faint salt smell.

"A third reason why cock sucking's fun," Josh said, "is that it's, let's say, psychologically nourishing. Since the cock replaces the breast and sperm replaces milk, cock sucking, on one level, is a sort of nursing. Sperm is a form of food that sustains a guy not so much physically as mentally and emotionally."

"Sperm's milk," Tyler smiled, "and my cock's a kind of emotional salami."

"Right," Josh laughed.

Tyler thought of Ariel's line in *The Tempest*: "Where the bee sucks, there suck I."

His cock was the flower that gave up the pollen to make honey. Honey, he thought, as in pleasure.

"Just as someone becomes hungry physically," Josh said, "he becomes hungry emotionally, too. Without food, he dies physically. Without love, he dies emotionally. A cock and sperm taste good not only because of the erogenous zones involved, but also because of the mental and emotional satisfaction. Looking at it this way, the guy who gets sucked off becomes the mother."

"The emotional-nourishment provider," Tyler joked, rubbing his right eye with his fingertips.

"The guy who sucks him off," Josh said, "the contented child. The physical climax of one is the emotional climax of the other."

"Let's see," Tyler summed up. "You like giving head because it feels good, it reminds you of the womb and early infancy, and it's a form of emotional sustenance."

Josh squinted as if checking the statement's accuracy. "Right," he said, squeezing Tyler's thigh. "I tell you. Once you try it, it's hard to give up."

Tyler knew that from the number of men who did it and did it compulsively. He imagined taking Josh's cock in his mouth and knew from kissing that his lips were, as Josh said, an erogenous zone. There was no reason to believe that blowing him wouldn't feel good, and if the experience were enhanced, as Josh claimed, by subconscious memories of superimposed heartbeats and surf-like breathing, even breasts and nipples, so much the better. Come in the mouth, though.

"What does come taste like?" he asked, half asleep.

"Well," Josh chuckled, "actually, you were so far down my throat, I couldn't taste you. It's just a gob of warm, salty goo. To a gay, of course, it's an aphrodisiac. You've just ingested the essence of your man. To put a romantic slant on it, he's part of you."

"I'm part of you, huh?" Tyler scoffed.

They stared at each other curiously, kissed intimately, then insistently, and stared at each other again. Then, as if on cue, they rolled onto their sides, Tyler's front to Josh's back, fitting together like spoons.

"We should sleep well tonight," Tyler said.

"Guess so," Josh agreed. "I shot a pint on the chair."

Chapter 27: Considea (Fear of Pillows)

Tyler's dream took place in two places at once, on the sofa of the cottage in Amalfi and on the sofa in the living room of his house in Atlanta. It was also about two subjects at the same time, his daughter Linda and Samantha, his cairn terrier. In the year before Samantha's death, she had been having seizures, and in the dream, Tyler was petting her and telling her telepathically that he loved her, and she was telling him telepathically that she loved him, too, and in the dream there was absolutely no doubt that they loved each other.

Then, in Linda's most tender childhood voice, the dog said, "Daddy."

When he woke, he felt as if he'd heard the word as clearly as if Linda were there in the room. The sheers lifted like a veil, and when someone stepped through the door, Tyler gasped and sat up. The figure appeared to be the slim silhouette of a woman with a pillow walking toward him ominously. As she crossed the room, she assumed the slim, muscular build of a young man, and Tyler realized it was Josh. Tyler shook his head slowly, and his hand went up as if fending him off. Tyler's legs twitched, and his shoulders swiveled slightly as if he were dancing. His hip lifted off the bed as if he were about to get up. Then, thanks to some determined inner gimbal, he righted himself emotionally and calmed down.

"What are you doing?" he demanded, absently pulling the covers over his lap.

"What do you mean?" Josh asked, stopping near the bed.

In silhouette, Josh's face was a black mask. He was holding the pillow as if holding a tray, and his shadow stretched like a ghost across the tiles. Far below, waves like bulldozers bumped the cliff, breaking against the rocks so hard Tyler could feel the bed tremble.

"With the pillow," Tyler said.

The room seemed unreal, the walls washed in moonlight, devoid of color as an ink sketch. He felt as if he were still dreaming.

"I woke up and couldn't go back to sleep," Josh said. He let go of the pillow with his right hand, letting it hang by his side. "So I went out and slept on the terrace. Got cold. Thought I'd try the bed again." Tyler heard him yawn, and Josh seemed to be scratching his chest. "What's wrong?"

"You weren't going to try to smother me with the pillow, were you?" Tyler asked, his voice deadpan.

"What?" Josh asked, his voice soft, but incredulous. "Smother you with the pillow?" When Josh stepped toward the bed, Tyler backed against the wall. "Whoa," Josh said, halting. "Tyler, look. Sorry I spooked you. Just slept outside awhile."

At that point, Tyler noticed, over Josh's shoulder, what looked like someone standing in the corner, someone even Josh was not aware of. Because of the helmet, it came into focus for Tyler the way a soldier on night watch might emerge from the dark. Then he realized what it was: the bust of Athena.

"You awake?" Josh asked. "It's me, Josh. It's about 1 A.M.," he said, holding his watch up to read it. "We're in the *suite nuziale* in Amalfi." When Tyler failed to respond, Josh said, "I'll just stand over here."

He started to turn toward the chair in the corner, but stopped, looked at the pillow, and tossed it like a life preserver onto the bed. As he did, Tyler could see his plump dick bobble in the gloom, and the little bobble echoed lightly in everything eccentric in Tyler attracted to him: a nude male. Tyler's mind was telling him one thing, the young man's sensual appeal another, pulling him like a magnet helplessly toward his sculptural outline, his petal-white skin.

"So you're not going to try to smother me with the pillow?" Tyler asked.

"Uh," Josh muttered. "No, I'm not."

"Thanks," Tyler groused. "I appreciate it."

"Tyler, why would I want to do that? Well, smother you with kisses maybe, but.... Siamo amici del cuore. [We're buddies.]" He laughed sadly. "Man, you must've had a bad dream."

God, Tyler thought, slumped forward, abs crunched. *She's poisoned everything.* He uncurled, leaned against the wall, and planted his soles on the sheet, knees bent.

"OK if I get in bed?" Josh asked solicitously.

"Get in bed," Tyler said, cupping his hands over his crotch as if modest.

"Should've bought some bottled water while we were out."

Chapter 28: The Lunar Eclipse

Tyler knew he couldn't panic. There was no choice about that. Screaming and splashing like Karen and Alice would attract the shark. He would have to regain his composure like Odysseus. Odysseus, he knew, would, in fact, experience fear, then compose himself and think. And where was that delusional sense of invulnerability he'd been enjoying all evening, that amazing trick of amused detachment? He would simply have to delude himself again, block out all the terrible thoughts from his mind. He'd often fantasized about going to Italy. He'd think about that: a rustic villa, an olive grove, a big, embossed terra-cotta pot with a single, lush lemon tree basking in the sun. Going to Italy – he'd reward himself if he lived.

As far as he knew, Karen had never learned to swim, but he had always felt perfectly at home in water. He could swim for miles, even in open seas, especially floating on his back. Once, house-sitting for a friend, he had the swimming pool to himself and experimented with floating vertically, just his face above the surface, legs and arms dangling comfortably like a puppet's. When he would breathe out, he would start to sink, but when he breathed in through his nose, he would rise again effortlessly. Only floating in the womb, he thought, would have been more relaxing. As long as he was conscious, he knew, he could swim. It wasn't water he was afraid of, but what was in it.

When the sea smoke cleared, there was no sign of the boat or oar, just swells, stars, the slosh of a cresting wave. His impulse was to swim quietly in the direction the boat had drifted, but he didn't. He wanted to call to Linda, but couldn't. No. At least, she was in the boat. She'd be OK. She'd come to, start the engine, head for lights.

When a wave washed over him, he gulped water, but was afraid to spit it out, letting it spill from his mouth. He wondered if the shark could hear him breathing. Then he realized that he had to do something, could not just float there. Slowly, he unclasped his shiny watch and let it sink in the water, then removed his wallet, keys, and change, watching the bright coins flicker, like moths, down into the dark. He had an irrational fear of removing his clothes, though. Naked, he would feel more like a big piece of bait. He knew he had to start swimming, but with the swells as high as they were, which direction? The ocean was a shattered black mirror; the sky, a drop curtain spangled with stars.

The lower left rim of the moon was tarnished, the beginning of the eclipse, but though the moon had washed out a lot of the sky, he could still see the Big Dipper, and when he located the Pole Pointers, he knew where north was and, thus, west and Bailey Island and, on the crest of a wave, when he looked in that direction, saw the handful of lights there twinkling like diamonds. He looked for the boat one last time, but, not seeing it, started dog paddling quietly, then swimming smoothly for the inn.

After about fifteen minutes, the lights seemed no closer, and he sensed he was not making headway, at best marking time. The tide was probably bearing him backward, he guessed, east, out to sea. He turned over and swam on his back, bobbing to the soothing lilt of the waves, gazing patiently at the diamond dust of an astonishing, dreamlike Milky Way. The moon was half white, half tarnished, like a silver platter half uncovered over time. He was trying to save energy, paddling, unhurried, with his hands and feet, but knew he had to keep swimming to generate heat, to avoid hypothermia. He rolled over and, riding a wave, fixed on the lights at the inn. He wiped away the water stinging his eyes, and when he started swimming again, he accidentally sniffed some water and blew it out as softly as possible.

During the next hour, he would swim prone or sidestroke, but when he swam on his back to rest, the moon would be in a new phase. First, it went from half black to what looked like a misshapen zygote undergoing mitosis. Then it looked like a dark eyeball with a white cornea, then a bright sickle as if a sharp fingernail had pressed into the night. By midnight, it had achieved red totality, a blood smear set off by a vague, romantic-blue corona.

At that point, everything paused. The breeze dropped, and the sea went flat. The term for it, he knew, was slack tide, and he knew he should take advantage of it, making as much progress as he could, but waited, resting, treading water, awed by the wondrous universal calm. He glanced around at the whole world plunged into shadow, the sea and sky one darkness, various shades of black, with only the stars twinkling and the string of lights blinking on the horizon, easily seen now, brighter in the dark. Then a breeze ruffled the water, and waves began to swell. The world began rolling the other way, and, borne by the tide, he began swimming toward the inn.

During the next thirty minutes, as the moon waxed, his abilities waned. The grim grin of the rim reappeared, beaming from the dark. Then the moon looked like a bright skull peeking around a stone. When it was half itself, the veined, blue corona, like an iris, flashed around it again. While this was going on, he could feel his heart racing faster, and his strokes became slower and more clumsy, slapping the water at times.

Then a bank of sea smoke overtook him, blotting out everything, and he lost his bearings. He stopped and treaded water, waiting it out, and, as he did, he thought he heard the leaden knell of a bell buoy clanging and echoing in the distance, but, because of the fog, could not tell from what direction. Even if he saw the buoy, he wouldn't go near it, let alone try to climb up on it and wait out the night – he had such a terrible fear of what would be circling beneath it.

One fear led to another, and he was suddenly afraid of being upright instead of flat in the water as if his submerged feet would attract sharks. Was it better to see the fin slicing through the water directly toward him or be bitten with no warning? If he saw the shark, there was certainly nothing he could do about it. He would simply suffer what would seem like an eternity of horror before passing out. If he were going to be attacked, he decided, he didn't want to know about it. When he began shivering, though, the shivers brought him back to the moment, and he realized how much his toes and fingers hurt. He had to start swimming, he knew, and when the sea smoke cleared, he did.

During the last thirty minutes, the moon rounded out, and when he reached the cove under the inn, the lobsters buoys, like hundreds of heads, stuck up darkly from the water. He entered the maze, trying not to touch them, but as he swam through them, the seaweed trailing from them, like ghost hands, would caress his arm or foot, and occasionally, as on the way out, the tangled ones would bump together, clicking like teeth. Instead of swimming to the boat ramp, he decided to head for the boulders below the inn porch, and when he felt the first slimy edges of rocks underwater, he was filled with such horror and revulsion it was all he could do to keep from screaming. As he tried to climb out of the water, he realized he could not move his fingers. His hands had become flippers, and he crawled up on the rocks on his elbows like some new, inept amphibian. Out of the water, his first impulse was to find a hole in the rocks where he could curl up and hide, but when he could not find one, he simply sat on a ledge in a kind of soft, smooth stupor, staring at the porch light of a house across the cove.

When he came to, he could not remember anything: what had happened, where he was, how he got there, nodding on a rock.

When he tried to call for help, all that came out of his mouth was a low "El," then a louder "Elp," then a blunt "Help!" He gazed curiously at his shriveled fingers in the moonlight, at his salt-caked clothes. "Help!" he cried, glancing up over his shoulder. "Help meee! Anyone there?"

A window rattled up, and an old woman asked, "Someone down there?"

"Here," he shouted, "under the porch. Help me! Please!"

The muscles in his lower back stiffened, and he started shaking uncontrollably, gripped by a chill.

Chapter 29: The Most Beautiful Hell

There was no car-rental agency as such in Amalfi, but Josh had sweet-talked a tour guide into letting him rent his silver Mercedes for the trip down to Paestum the next day. At breakfast, however, when Phil and Billie said they were going to pass on Paestum, Tyler and Josh assumed they were giving them time alone and insisted they come, but Billie said she'd rather spend the gloomy day shopping instead of trooping around ruins in the rain.

"I'll arrange a nice place for us all to have dinner tonight," she said, "and you can tell us all about it."

Tyler had seen a weather map on TV that morning and knew that a cool front was moving out and that the skies would be clearing that afternoon, but now it was drizzling, so they wore jackets and brought umbrellas. They strolled to the tourist office to pick up the car, and though Josh drove slowly on the wet road, Tyler got car sick and cracked a window for fresh air. Everywhere he looked: spectacular vistas, village-dappled mountains plunging to the sea, everything seen through a sour haze of nausea. In Minori, he asked that they pull over and switch drivers, but switching did not help, and in Maiori they switched back and Tyler put a plastic bag inside another in case he had to throw up.

"I brought Dramamine for the boats," he said, "but didn't think about driving on such a narrow, winding road. Swinging out over cliffs doesn't help much."

"Sorry," Josh said, obviously concerned.

The nausea began to fade when they came down off the cliffs, and by the time they passed the Gaudi-esque Solimene ceramic factory in Vietri sul Mare, Tyler was beginning to feel better. After Salerno, the road was flat and straight, and he enjoyed the drive, slumped in the seat, gazing at the endless barrier of cropped eucalyptus trees that lined the coast.

It was still drizzling when they arrived at Paestum, but he was so excited to see the Temple of Athena come up on the right that he did not care about the weather. He felt as if Josh had, in fact, transported him back in time to a Grecian city.

When they pulled into a parking lot next to a restaurant, he was still a little queasy, and it was good to step onto solid ground instead of floating in the car, good to feel the cool, damp air on his face. There was also the clean, refreshing smell of mint in the air.

"Some of the best preserved Greek temples in the world," Josh said, locking the car.

"And they're in Italy," Tyler quipped. The place was quiet as a cemetery – because of the weather, Tyler assumed – and as they walked down the middle of the road, he asked, "What's the history? I mean, how did Greeks wind up here?"

"Some Achaeans drove some Dorians out of Greece, and they wound up here. Something like that. They called the place Poseidonia."

"After Poseidon."

"The same sort of story as Aeneas leading the refugees from Troy to Italy," Josh said. "Only in this case, it actually happened. The Romans took over in the third century BC and named it Paestum."

"What does Paestum mean?" Tyler asked.

"Don't know," Josh smiled. "Pesto sauce?"

"That's it," Tyler laughed. "Pesto sauce."

When the drizzle turned to rain, they popped open their umbrellas and stepped through an entrance to the archeological zone, face to face with a couple of magnificent temples. To Tyler, they looked like immense mushrooms.

"Let's start with the one on the left," Josh said, heading toward it. "It's called the Basilica, but that's a misnomer. A basilica was a high court, a place where transactions were carried out. It's definitely a temple, though a little different than the usual temple at the time. The *cella*, the inner sanctuary, was usually divided into three aisles by stone columns, but this one is divided into two. It's the only temple in Italy divided this way."

"Why?" Tyler asked, stopping at the low, x-shaped fence.

"Well," Josh said, propping his foot on a rail, "the statue of the god could not have been placed at the end of or between the columns, so the place must have been a double temple, one dedicated to a pair of gods, and the most probable pair is – "

He glanced at Tyler, waiting for him to fill in the blank.

"Zeus and Hera."

"Right," Josh said, pensive. "Two gods, one house."

Tyler noticed the ground lights pointed at the building and thought of how grand it must look at night, lit in the dark.

"A lot of votive statues of Hera were dug up around it," Josh said, "so the theory is that the cult of Hera overcame that of Zeus."

"The way one partner becomes dominant in a relationship," Tyler smiled.

"And about a century later, this other temple was built," Josh said, nodding to his right, "and dedicated to Hera. It's called the Temple of Poseidon, but again it's a – "

"Misnomer."

"A lot of terra-cotta statues of Hera were dug up around it, too, and a shield with the inscription: 'Dedicated to Hera. Make our arms invincible.'"

"Amazing how something so simple can be so beautiful," Tyler remarked, glancing up at a tapered column.

"Proves we like things in order," Josh said. "My theory is that orderliness makes us feel safe."

"Chaos threatens us," Tyler mused. "I believe it."

"Part of the Greek concept that what's right is beautiful, and if that's true – "

"Then what's beautiful is right."

Josh smiled slyly: "I was hoping you'd see it that way."

Tyler puzzled over the remark, then laughed and changed the subject.

"What's the date on it?"

"550 BC," Josh said, taking his foot off the rail.

Tyler felt as if he were trying to avoid some latent issue by asking about details, but didn't know what issue or why. Maybe he should avoid it, he thought, until he could figure it out.

"Why do the columns slope up like that?" he asked, referring to the way the columns narrowed toward the top. "I mean, it's beautiful, but I wouldn't think there'd be a structural reason for it."

"No," Josh thought. "It's just aesthetic. It's called entasis, a design technique used to counteract an optical illusion. When a column is straight, it looks weak. It appears to have an inward curve, something to do with the eye. An outward curve makes it look strong."

"So straight appears bent, and bent appears straight," Tyler laughed.

Josh's face bloomed into a big smile: "Right."

Again, Tyler felt as if they had inadvertently wandered off into some mysterious subtext.

"I've never seen capitals like that," he said. "They look like big cushions. Doric, right?"

"Archaic Doric," Josh agreed. "They're rare." At that point, the rain dwindled to mist, and Josh stuck out his hand to test it. "Rain's let up."

They closed, shook, and fastened the umbrellas.

"Just think of how rational the architect must have been to design something so harmonious," Tyler commented.

"I read somewhere," Josh said, "that you can infer the entire temple from a section of a column."

"Or a person from a glance," Tyler quipped.

"Hope to have my name on something someday." Then Josh added, "Other than a tombstone."

They laughed, looking down, poking the grass with the umbrellas. Then Tyler looked around to see if anyone were watching. When he did not see anyone, he smiled at Josh, and they stepped over the fence, strolled to the temple, and tramped up the steps to a column. When Tyler touched the rough, mottled stone, Josh did too, their hands just a few inches apart, and from the blank check of Josh's lonely look, Tyler knew that Josh, by touching it, felt as if he were also somehow connecting with him. Tyler also knew that he himself was touching something that someone else had touched twenty-five hundred years ago, someone from an uninhibited society that gloried in beauty and pleasure, the culture of Hebe and Adonis. In other words, he was directly connecting with joy. He thought of what ol' Puritanical America would do with Aphrodite these days if it could get its hands on her. First it would rape her. Then it would accuse her of provoking the rape and nail her to a cross.

"Let's get out of here," he smiled, "before we create an international incident."

Instead of going through the temple, though, they went around the west end, stepped over the fence, and headed toward the second temple. As they did, the sun broke through clouds, and Tyler surmised that the cool front had passed.

"How did they build them?" he asked, meaning the temples. "The stones are so heavy. How did they get them here?"

"A few pairs of oxen could haul them," Josh said.

"They must weigh tons."

"Two to three," Josh agreed.

"How did they lift them?"

"Ramps," Josh explained. "Ramps and a lot of patience, hoists and a lot of care. The hoists were like big scales."

"So you keep putting weight on one side of the scales till the other side goes up."

"The way the past lifts the present," Josh stated.

"What?" Tyler laughed

"Sorry," Josh said. "Guess you'd have to have a heavy past to get that one."

"Look," Tyler smiled. "I'll put my past on the scales with yours any day. I can assure you – mine'll send yours through the roof. Speaking of roofs, what kind of roofs did they have?"

"Wood with terra-cotta tiles," Josh said. "Try to imagine the temples with statues and bas-relief, the frieze painted, everything stuccoed to look like marble."

"Makeup," Tyler quipped.

"The decorative elements made this severe style more graceful, but even with makeup, they were handsome, not pretty."

"Well, they sure built 'em to last."

"Yeah," Josh agreed. "No mortar or cement. They even made it through the great earthquake of AD 62, the one that destroyed the temples in Pompeii."

They walked to the west end of the second temple and looked through it to the opening at the other end.

"460 BC," Josh said. "The columns look more slender because they have more flutes, twenty-four instead of the usual twenty."

"Same, yet different," Tyler thought.

"More graceful," Josh said. "A paradox, graceful strength."

All at once, Tyler realized how male the temples were. There was obviously a masculine aesthetic to them, an architectural parallel to the myth of Hercules. He thought of how strong they were and how attractive strength was. The strength of the pinkish stonework suggested the strength of a muscular body, and he thought of the pun in the word *build*.

"Also," Josh said, "the flutes of the corner columns lean toward the center slightly to make it look sturdier."

"How so?" Tyler asked.

"If the lines tilted out, the building would look as if it's about to collapse."

"Again, straight appears bent, and bent appears straight," Tyler chuckled.

"We're seeing it with the roof off, of course," Josh said, "but imagine a mysterious dark interior with the statue of Hera lit with flickering braziers and torches. The heart of the temple is like the heart of a body, the place where the soul resides, the direct link to the god, in this case Hera."

As they stepped onto the Sacred Road, the clouds started breaking up, and shafts of sunlight shot out of them like spotlights, polishing the ruins to a slick sheen. As they approached the forum, Josh pointed out the residential area to the left.

"There's a bit of analogy between the temple, the house of a god, and a Greek and Roman house," he said, "except that the atrium, the heart of the house, was open to the sky."

"To catch rain," Tyler speculated.

"Another earth-sky connection," Josh said. "To the right is the forum, Roman, third century BC, larger than Pompeii's. Lasted about five-hundred years."

"And the United States is only two hundred years old," Tyler mused.

Josh pointed out an Italic theater. Then they strolled to the gymnasium.

"Pieces of pumice from Vesuvius were found in the swimming pool."

"Just to remind us of the vanity of things," Tyler commented.

"And the base of a statue was found with an epigraph to the fencing master of the Paestum Youth Association."

"Do I detect a gay fantasy?" Tyler joked.

"They did compete naked," Josh smiled.

"Like all good Greeks."

"And greased their bodies with oil. Speaking of gay fantasies."

"Why'd they do that?" Tyler asked. He knew why body builders did, to highlight muscles, but wondered why any other athlete would, for example, wrestlers. Oiling themselves would certainly make the struggle more difficult.

"Smooth skin?" Josh joked. "Haven't thought about it."

"A lubricant does have sexual connotations."

"Dozens of shiny athletes," Josh smiled. "Does make the dew drip."

"Dew drip," Tyler laughed. "Guess athletics were more of an aesthetic experience than I thought."

"Speaking of aesthetic experience," Josh said, "let's walk over to the amphitheater. That's where the gladiators and wild beasts fought."

"Oh, my."

They walked by the ruins of the Temple of Peace and an open-air theater, then through the vaulted entrance to the amphitheater. Half of it had been cut off by the road on which they drove in, Via Magna Graecia, Highway 18. The remaining half formed a crescent moon of big weathered stones.

"People watching people kill each other for entertainment," Josh pondered. "Right here," he said, scuffing the moist dirt with his shoe. He glanced at Tyler.

"I've had to fend off a few wild beasts myself," Tyler said, his tone serious.

They stared at each other. Then Tyler glanced at the glossy leaves of an oak growing near the stands. He somehow saw it as a symbol of good growing out of violence.

"Let's head back to the Sacred Road," Josh suggested. "One more thing I want to show you."

The Sacellum was a small stone structure, mostly belowground, with a roof of large, red tiles.

"Sixth Century BC," Josh said. "Discovered in 1954. No one's sure exactly what it was. Could have been a temple or a cenotaph."

"Cenotaph?" Tyler asked.

"Tomb without a body," he said. "A memorial. The amazing thing about it, though, is that contained nine vases, eight bronze, one ceramic. The bronze ones were sealed with wax and contained soft honey."

Tyler gaped. "You mean, edible?"

"I think. There's a chunk of it on display in the museum."

"Just as sweet now as then."

Josh smiled: "Like sex."

"That hasn't changed," Tyler laughed. "We're still sticking it in the same place."

"Places," Josh corrected him. "The ceramic vase," he explained, "was carved and painted Attic style, black figures on a red background, Heracles arriving on Olympus on one side, maenads and satyrs on the other."

They followed a path to the Temple of Athena, and Tyler stopped to look at it framed by a couple of picturesque pines. The thick clusters of needles were dark underneath like the bottoms of storm clouds, but glassy with sunlight on top.

"About 500 BC," Josh said. "It's called the Temple of Ceres, again a misnomer." They said *misnomer* at the same time. "A lot of small terra-cotta statues of Athena were found around it, along with a vase fragment with Athena's name. Somewhere I read that the pediment probably contained a frieze with life-sized figures from the Trojan War with Athena in the center with armor and the aegis, the shield she used to panic enemies."

"Actually," Tyler said, "I'm very familiar with the aegis from Homer."

"What's different about this temple," Josh said, "is that it's a mixture of two styles, Doric and Ionic. Inside were eight columns with Ionic capitals."

"Guess you could say it was bi," Tyler remarked

"Bi, huh," Josh said, glancing at him curiously. "Let's have lunch."

They returned to the restaurant where they had parked and had lunch at a table among puddles under a big, green awning. Both had the special, a big plate of insalata caprese with a glass of Aglianico Paestum.

Afterward, they strolled to the museum and slowly worked their way through the exhibits to what Josh described as "Why we really came, The Tomb of the Diver, La Tomba del Tuffatore, 475 BC, discovered in 1969, the greatest find of the century, as far as I'm concerned."

"Really," Tyler said, focusing on the blue fabric in one of the frescoes.

"Other than vase painting, it's the oldest Greek painting in existence," Josh claimed. "Nothing like it."

Propped on Lucite stands, as if floating, were the four limestone walls and cover slab of a tomb, all covered with frescoes mostly of muscular males wearing garlands. On an end wall, a nude ephebe was pouring a libation from a wine cup with wine from the krater on a table hung with faint-green festoons. On a side wall was a funeral banquet with a lyrist, a flutist, and singers with garments wrapped around their waists, all reclined on couches with blue cloth and brown or white pillows.

"That's how I'd like my funeral to be," Tyler said. "New Orleans-style, one big party."

On the other end wall were an older man with a cloak and walking stick and a nude ephebe with a blue cloth draped across his arms like a shawl. The ephebe was dancing to the music that a young girl in white, the only girl, was playing on a flute as she lead them off. Tyler saw the scene as allegory – youth, age, death.

Then he noticed the other long wall. The composition of the fresco was similar to that of the other side wall: a banquet scene with five males on three couches, one, then two, then two. But the two on the right were gazing amorously into each other's eyes, the clean-shaven ephebe's expression calm and pleased with a Mona Lisa smile, the bearded man's expression excited, cheerful, and eager, his mouth open in sensual anticipation. The man's right hand caressed the back of the ephebe's head as if to draw him in for a kiss. The ephebe's right hand was extended toward the man's chest in an ambivalent gesture that could have been interpreted either as reaching for him affectionately or fending him off playfully. The fingers of his other hand were woven among the strings of the lyre held against his side.

"Wow," Tyler smiled. "And this is how old?"

"About twenty-five hundred years."

From Josh's obvious pride, Tyler realized that Josh had pilgrimaged here the way that Muslims pilgrimaged to Mecca or gays to Michelangelo's *David* in Florence. Quite an accomplishment, he thought, to validate yourself with proof positive of the universality of gays.

"Look at that one," Josh said, indicating a figure on the middle couch. "He's supposed to be playing a game called *kottabos* with the others, but he's distracted by the lovers."

"Bit of mischief in his look."

"The three playing the game are holding their wine bowls," Josh pointed out, "but the lovers have set theirs down."

There was a festooned table by each couch, but the only one with kylixes, or wine cups, was the lovers'.

"Notice how rosy the ephebe's lips are," Tyler said.

"Hmmm," Josh hummed, gazing at them.

Tyler walked back and forth in front of the frescoes, comparing mouths, and decided that the amorous ephebe's was definitely the rosiest. However, he did not know what to think of it: youthfulness, the flush of love, lipstick, the only pigment that hadn't faded.

The tomb's cover slab was spectacular in its simplicity. Josh's theory about pleasure in order again, Tyler thought. Slender willows framed a scene in which a male nude was diving off a platform into a blue pool.

When Josh saw that Tyler's attention had turned to the cover, he stepped beside him and said, "This is a tomb, right?"

"Right."

"The subject is death," Josh said, "but look at his attitude. He's happy. He's looking forward to it. The others are having a party, and this one's dancing to the music of a pale figure in white leading him off to whatever's beyond the edge of the fresco."

Tyler suddenly saw a parallel between the scene with the dancing figure and the one with the amorous pair. In both, an older man was interested in a younger man. He and Josh, to some extent, were reflected in the wall paintings. The man with the walking stick following the dancing youth also struck him as sad. Was he himself trying to relive his youth through Josh? Not that there was that much difference in their ages. Their sensibilities were certainly similar.

"They couldn't have thought of death as the end," Josh said. "They must have thought of it as a new life, something to look forward to."

"As I said," Tyler said, "New Orleans-style, one big party."

Then he thought of Alice's funeral and Karen's memorial service: not exactly one big party, more like hell, a strange New England hell of bitter disgust and acidic recrimination.

"What about you?" he asked. "You believe in an afterlife?"

"No," Josh said, shaking his head. "This is it. If we don't have fun now, we're never going to have it. Why waste your life on anything else?"

"I agree."

As they were leaving the museum, they stepped into the gift shop, where Tyler bought postcards and Josh a couple of prints, all with scenes from the Tomb of the Diver. They strolled through shops on the Via Magna Graecia, but did not buy anything, then decided to head back to Amalfi.

"Maybe we can find a chemist," Josh suggested, using the British term for pharmacist.

But when he asked a clerk, she said there was none in Paestum, and when they got to Salerno, it was siesta time, and everything was closed.

"Shit," Tyler blurted. "Well, at least I'll get sick the last half of the trip." And he did, "nature being oppressed," as he called it, referring to *Lear*.

He felt so good after lunch that he thought he would not get sick, but by the time they had gotten even to Vietri, he started sweating and, at every turn, could feel the nausea swelling in his stomach. He threw up in the plastic bags near Maiori, and near Minori his body started clenching hard with dry heaves.

"Nothing feels worse," Josh said.

"You're wrong," Tyler replied, panting. "Pain's worse." After another loud retch, he spit into the bags.

"Should I pull over?" Josh asked.

"No," Tyler said. "Keep going. Let's get it over with. Besides," he smiled, "this is the most beautiful hell I've ever been in, and I've been in a lot."

Within sight of Amalfi, they were halted by two buses stopped head-on at a turn. The bus driver from Amalfi was too afraid to drive around the other bus, and cars were lining up behind each. The woman tour guide from the Amalfi bus got out and was cursing the second bus driver in Italian and making lots of emphatic gestures. Finally, cars started backing up, and the bus from Amalfi swung out over the cliff just enough to get around the other bus. When Josh and Tyler got to the hotel, Josh dropped him off and returned the car to the agency. By then, Tyler was so weak that when he got to the room, he stripped, dropped his clothes on the floor, and fell into bed.

# # # # #

He fell asleep immediately and in about thirty minutes began dreaming about a sacrificial rite in front of the Temple of Athena. He was wearing a purple chiton and gold cape and officiating over an altar scattered with variously colored roses. It was a bright summer day, and a festive procession was winding through a broad field, then crowding around him, playing music, singing, and dancing. Chariots with warriors brought up the rear, parting to reveal Josh, nude, leading a black bull by a rope. Josh pulled the bull's head by the rope, stretching its neck over the altar, its big eyes crazed with fear. Then Tyler picked up a double-edged axe and, filled with an incredible sense of power, raised it over his head. When he started to swing it down, the intense thrill of the dream was simply too much for him. He woke.

# # # # #

It took him a moment to remember where he was. The room was dim, but the soothing surf reminded him. He sat up slowly and, still nauseated, noticed Josh sitting in the chair in the corner, staring at him like a guard dog. Without saying anything, Josh moved to the bed, sat near Tyler, and offered him a joint.

"It'll cure the nausea in a minute."

"What a panacea," Tyler said, taking it. "Sore shoulders, nausea."

Josh lit him with the yellow Bic, but, when Tyler had a puff, took the joint and tamped it out on the marble top of the side table. Then he licked the tip of his index finger and rubbed out the ash smear.

"A puff'll do," he said, laying the joint and Bic aside.

"Just had the wildest dream," Tyler whispered.

"Tell me about it," Josh murmured, looking all care and affection.

"Later," Tyler smiled. "Have an idea for a poem."

"Poem? Great."

"Need to write it down."

"First things first."

Josh strolled to the bathroom, where Tyler heard a can of soda pop open, ice cubes clink in a glass, and the fizz of carbonation.

"Here," Josh said. "Sip this."

"7-Up?" Tyler smiled. "Where'd you get Diet 7-Up?"

"You can probably get anything here," Josh said, "for a price."

Josh opened a pack of butter cookies. "Start nibbling these. You need to get some sugar in you, get your energy level up." Then he returned to the bathroom, ran water, and came back with a folded damp cloth. Tyler was lying on his side, sipping the soda, and eating the cookies.

"Where do you want it?" Josh asked. "Forehead?"

"Neck," Tyler said. "Behind the ear." When Josh carefully laid it on Tyler's neck, Tyler set the soda down and pressed the cold cloth into the hollow behind his ear. "Boy, that feels good."

"Ready for light?"

"Yeah."

Josh drew the curtains and sheers and opened the doors. In a gush, bright light, the cheerful splash of surf, and a refreshing breeze swirled into the room. Then Tyler noticed that his clothes had been put away.

"Think you'll be ready for dinner at eight?" Josh asked.

"Hope so," Tyler said. "A big plate of pasta is just what I need to get back on my feet."

Josh lingered by the doors, arms akimbo, looking around the room. "What do you write with?"

"Clipboard and pen," Tyler said. "My laptop's at home."

"Where are they? I'll get 'em for you."

Chapter 30: The Kindness of Strangers

At eight that night, the four went to dinner at Il Teatro, an unassuming restaurant with tile floors, white plaster walls, and a high, Saracenic vaulted ceiling that bounced light around like the lens in a lighthouse. The place reminded Tyler of both a church and a white-washed catacomb. "Maria, Mari!" was playing in the background, barely audible over a quiet resonance of voices, china, silverware, and glass, as well as the pots and utensils from the open kitchen in back. The room was full of old Windsor chairs and tables with white tablecloths on the bias on top of white tablecloths. Rustic wrought-iron chandeliers hovered over the tables, and a basket streaming creeping jenny was hanging from a pulley from the ceiling. A plump, matronly woman showed the four to a table and, when everyone was settled, presented them with menus.

"Acqua?" she smiled, turning the wine glasses up.

"Si," Josh responded, shaking out his napkin. "Minerale non gassata."

"Goodness," Billie exclaimed, scooting her chair to the table. "This place is bright as Olympus."

Tyler noticed that everything was so over-lit there were no shadows in the room.

"Heard you weren't feeling well," Billie remarked, glancing at Tyler.

"Josh had an herbal remedy which cured me right away."

"Herbal remedy?" she asked.

"Puff of pot," he stated.

"Pot?" Her disapproval was as clear as cellophane.

"Billie," Josh smiled. "Not the way your tone of voice implies. As I said, you have a sip of wine, right? We have a puff."

"Anything else?" she asked.

"Pot, not coke," Phil scolded her, touching her arm. "OK? He doesn't have to fill out an affidavit swearing he doesn't abuse drugs. You can trust him."

"OK, OK," she complained. As she fondled her necklace, it glimmered in the bright light. "You're prickly as a raspberry patch."

The woman returned with a bottle of mineral water, four glasses, and a bread basket. Phil poured water, and Tyler unwrapped the bread and passed it around. When he took a bite of it, it was soft, warm, and buttery, and he looked forward to a delicious meal and, despite their idiosyncrasies, the pleasant company of his new friends.

"So why is everyone here?" Phil asked, elbows on the table, hands clasped.

"You've asked that before," Billie said.

233

"Have I?"

"Yes," she claimed. "That restaurant in Naples."

"Oh, well," Phil sighed.

"You said we're here to enjoy ourselves and Italy."

"We're here," Josh joked. "I'm queer. Enjoy yourself." He was playing off the protest chant: I'm here. I'm queer. Get used to it.

"We're here," Phil began. "We're straight. Let's – " His forehead creased as if he were thinking of a rhyme. "Let's celebrate!"

Billie turned to Tyler: "Your turn."

Tyler laughed, eyes fixed on the creamy rose in the budvase. "I'm here, sincere, but bruised a bit." Everyone chuckled. "Sorry. Only rhyme I can think of."

Actually, he had thought of *I'm here. I'm bi. My alibi.* But he wasn't sure what it meant.

"There's a line in the song 'Hotel California,'" he said. "'Some dance to remember. Some dance to forget.' Well, I'm here to forget a recent debacle associated with a play of mine and that so-called Protest Theater in New York."

"Oh," Phil said. "What happened?"

"Forget, I said, not conjure up the dead."

He could've used the money, of course, but refused to make changes suggested by DeWitt Dill, the artistic director, and Christopher Queen, the resident director. The fiasco may have put a dint in his professional reputation, but he was at a point in his career when he was relatively free of what others thought. In other words, he didn't give a damn. As for Dill, he couldn't type a literate email. As for Queen, he was that all right, Tyler thought, a queen.

"I'm here to forget what's his name," Josh joked. "Talk about drama. Only mine was real."

Tyler felt himself unlatching himself from the scene, observing everyone as if from the audience. Everyone wanted happiness, he thought, each in his or her own exclusive way, despite the nihilistic transience of things, the knowledge that the play ended, everything faded to black. Then, through will, he fought his way back to the literally bright moment. He didn't want to devalue it by drifting away from it, by not savoring it.

"Can't believe you didn't take advantage of a study-abroad program," he said to Josh.

"Yeah," Josh said, staring at the tablecloth. "I wanted to get my degree and get out, to start making money. I'm here because my dad wanted me to travel some before settling down at the office."

When the woman returned, Billie ordered *scialatielli* (a local pasta) with tomato and eggplant, Phil wine-steamed mussels, Josh a seafood pizza, and Tyler penne with carbonara sauce. Phil and Billie ordered a bottle of Furore, and Josh and Tyler decided to try a cocktail, Cynar and orange juice.

"We're here," Phil said, "because we finally had the money to come here. I'm a little hesitant to talk about it because you'll probably think we stole it. You might believe me more if I told you a suitcase packed with cash fell out of the sky."

"Yes," Billie laughed to herself. "A lot came out of very little: Jeff and Herman."

"Jeff and Herman?" Josh asked.

"One day we picked up a pair of hitchhikers near San Gregorio," Phil said, "an older man and a younger man, who we assumed were father and son. They were a bit bedraggled, but had such great smiles we thought we'd help them along the way, in fact, all the way to Full Moon Bay."

"Great smiles, huh," Tyler questioned. "You know, you can't go by appearances. They'd could've cut your throats."

"I don't know," Phil said. "People so obviously happy can't be up to much."

"If they were going to rob us," Billie said, "they certainly weren't going to get much with all our medical bills, but they could probably tell that from the old Mercury we were driving."

"In any case," Phil said, "when we asked if they were hungry, they said yes, and we took them home and fed them, and when we asked if they needed a place to stay for the night, they said yes too and wound up staying a month. The house wasn't much, but it was cozy and clean, and the terrace, of course, has that spectacular view."

"We were so entranced by them," Billie said, "they were more like sons home for the holidays than strangers in a spare room. And it didn't take long to figure out that what we saw in them that was trustworthy was what we had ourselves."

"A good marriage," Josh said.

"Right."

All at once, Tyler noticed three things about Josh: that the blond highlights in his hair glistened in the bright light, that he was sitting up straight, and that he hadn't brought his backpack. Without it, he looked less like a tourist. Then he realized that he himself was slumped in his chair and sat up.

"Herman, the younger one," Billie said, "either cooked or helped me cook, and Jeff, the older one, did a lot of landscaping, especially near the cliff, something I really didn't want Phil doing, and at night we'd sit around the fireplace and sip wine and talk."

"But it was always about what you'd think people would want to avoid talking about," Phil said, "politics, religion, the economy."

"Never about them," she said, "which, of course, puzzled us. Were they escapees? Were we aiding and abetting some California version of Bonnie and Clyde?"

"You see homeless people with those work-for-food signs on the street," Phil said. "Well, Herman had a proposal for us. He said he knew an art dealer and if we let him bring him a canvas or two, he could get us the money to fix things up around the house. They'd do the work, he said, to pay us back for our hospitality. The only stipulation was we couldn't ask questions. The dealer, the buyer, everything would have to remain anonymous. Well, we certainly needed work done on the house."

"We were curious as hell to see what they were up to," she added.

"What happened?" Josh asked.

"The artwork started disappearing," Phil said, "and good things started happening around the house. They fixed a leak in the roof, the stairs to the beach, reinforced the doors, lay new floors in the kitchen, changed the fireplace to gas, bought a termite inspection, put a new medicine cabinet in a bathroom, put in new lighting inside and out, stripped some siding from the house. You name it. Jeff even fixed my computer when it crashed, updated everything."

"Certainly earned their keep," she remarked.

"And then some," he stressed.

"And then this weird thing happened," she said. "One day, a boy from the liquor store showed up with several cases of Santa Christina and said we'd won a random drawing. We'd discovered Sangiovese at a little Italian restaurant in town and shared a couple of bottles with the guys. But when the free wine showed up, well, we really began to wonder. Who the hell were they?"

"And then this other weird thing happened," Phil said. "Every night, Herman would go down to the basement to fetch a bottle of wine for dinner, but one day, when they were down at the beach, I checked the wine myself and, as far as I could tell, we had just as much as when it arrived."

"I don't know if this is related or not," she said, "but one day, Herman and I drove into town to get a goose. I wanted to cook *oca arrosto*, roast goose, something special, but easy to make, but when I went to pay for it, the card didn't work, but before I could say anything, the clerk said not to worry about it. He'd start a tab."

"Well, we halfway expected to overhear them whispering in some secret language," Phil said, "and then I did hear Jeff on the phone one day, telling someone to tell the board that, if he wasn't back in a week, the CFO should quote unquote 'give the plenary speech at the shareholders meeting.' The mere fact he had a phone proves they weren't who they claimed to be."

"Beggars," Tyler said.

"So we think they were, in fact, just mysterious humans," Billie said, "not supernatural beings."

"I picture Jeff sitting in a marble office on the top floor of some software temple in San Jose," Phil said.

"And Herman was his partner," Josh said, "life partner."

"It was just a lark," Phil explained, "a game, the way they'd decided to spend a vacation, testing people."

"So," Tyler squinted, "how did it end?"

"Well," Phil paused, flicking his hand in a puzzled gesture, "we came home one day, and there was a note on the table, telling us how much they appreciated our hospitality. Later, we found out that the house was paid off, as well as our medical bills. I'm too embarrassed to tell you how much they put in our bank accounts."

Tyler and Josh gaped at each other.

Then Billie said: "And we still don't know who they are."

Chapter 31: The Garden
of Handsome Men

That night, as usual, Valerio and friends were loitering outside the Galleria, gossiping, and furtively cruising cars as they crept by. Valerio was wearing his signature jeans and Nikes, but a different shirt, a black pullover with a set of tan stripes down his pecs, as well as a small, crumpled, red and black backpack. When someone asked about the backpack, he gazed toward the dirty moon brooding over the bay and, hands in pockets, said shrewdly, "Gifts from admirers." When the others laughed, he smiled to himself and, unconsciously, kept groping himself.

Despite his injuries, Rollo – black eye, red nose, puffy cheek – was back on the scene, scolding Claudio, a new boy from Paestum, for going cheap and driving down prices. He held him by one shoulder against a pedestal and was shaking his finger in his face, but when he was finished with him, he limped over to Valerio, lit a cigarette, and grunted, "What a little *checca*," or queen.

If Rollo were to be out, as it seemed he must, Valerio thought, then Valerio wanted him with the flock so he, like a shepherd, could keep an eye on him. Rollo had not been able to defend himself against the detectives, and now that he was bruised and sore, he was even more vulnerable. Valerio had uncanny instincts when it came to johns and cops, what he generally thought of as the hungry wolves lurking in the woods around them, and if Rollo hooked up before he did, then he wanted at least to get a good look at the john.

Rollo thought that he remembered the detectives' names from the booking, but Valerio had called a hot cop named Stefano Vincolo and asked him to quietly look into the incident. Stefano, as he had discussed with Valerio, thought of the world as a garden of handsome men and, more horticulturalist than whore, liked to pick as many flowers as possible, yet was cautious to the extreme mainly because of his job, that of *poliziotto*, a member of the Polizia Municipale. He was young and cute and obviously did not have to pay for sex, but he also had a hustler fantasy that he liked to indulge from time to time and with who better than Valerio, the best looking and most adept exotic in his collection. Besides, Valerio had made him an offer he could not refuse: in exchange for some information, Valerio would let him fuck him.

A older john in a silver Alfa Romeo Spider pulled up and eyed Valerio, but when Valerio subtly shook his head, the john drove on. Then a midnight-blue Vespa came buzzing around the corner, slowing to a halt at the curb. Stefano turned off the motor and rocked the bike onto the stand. He was wearing a matching blue helmet, and standing there, a leg on each side of the bike, he looked up and down Via Verdi as if paranoid about something, then turned the black mirror of the visor toward Valerio.

"You can take off the helmet," Valerio said, strolling over, hands in pockets. "After all, you do have a license plate."

"That's OK," Stefano said, his voice muffled by the helmet. "Let's go."

Even through the visor, Valerio could see how pleased he was to see him.

"You can always say you're undercover."

When Stefano shushed him, it sounded as if the helmet, like a space helmet, had sprung a leak.

"Why didn't you wear your uniform?" Valerio smiled.

Stefano touched Valerio's arm and shushed him again. "Come on."

Valerio had certainly blown cops before and had, thus, developed a fantasy about men in uniform, in this case the white cap, epaulets, grades on lapels and collars. Tonight, however, the only part of his uniform Stefano was wearing was his tall, shiny boots. Except for the sleek helmet, the rest of his clothes was soft materials: worn jeans, a white, canvas belt with a buckle with two catches, a gray cotton hoodie with a silver eagle on the back.

"Take me where they took Rollo," Valerio said sotto voce. He knew it was not far away, among old warehouses on the port.

Stefano's helmet rotated an inch toward Rollo leaning against a wall.

"That him?" Stefano asked.

"Yeah," Valerio nodded. "The one with the black eye."

The helmet rotated back to Valerio. "You crazy?"

"What about Villa Comunale?" Valerio asked.

"Valerio, really," Stefano chuckled. "You're a shameless exhibitionist. Tell you what. I work security at Stadio Collana. Let's go there."

"Take me there, and we'll fuck," Valerio said.

"No problem," Stefano said, stepping off the cycle. He unlocked the back compartment and took out another blue helmet for Valerio.

"In fact," Valerio smiled, "you can fuck me on the way. I've always wanted it riding a motorcycle. The bumps."

"Bumps, huh?" Stefano laughed, rocking the bike off the stand. "No, no, no. No public fucking." He straddled the saddle, motioning Valerio to get on.

Valerio fitted the helmet over his head and snapped the chin strap, and when he sat on the passenger seat, his feet on the pegs, the scooter settled a little under their weight. When he wrapped his arms around Stefano's waist, Stefano scanned the hustlers, then looked up and down Verdi. Again, he seemed suspicious of something. Then he grabbed the handlebars, started the bike, and sped off.

As they buzzed through the streets, Valerio rested his chin on Stefano's shoulder and could smell, even with the wind whipping past them, the rich forest-spicy scent of the young cop's freshly bathed body, the soothing essence of valerian, and comforted there, hugging him in the middle of such a large city, he felt a strange sense of accomplishment, as if nothing were finer than this, and remembered the wonderful moment when he rode a bicycle for the first time and realized that he was going to stay up. His father had shoved him off down a dirt driveway that seemed miles long at the time, an exciting adventure between gigantic cypress at the remote villa where his father worked as a gardener.

The rattle of the bike segued to the drone of the scooter, and soon Valerio found himself strolling, helmet in hand, toward the goal at the north end of the dark, dreamy stadium. Stefano, helmet in hand, rolled the Vespa to a stop between the goal and a large, blue, high-jump mat. Then he rocked it onto its stand and, true to form, looked around suspiciously. Valerio looked around as well, but more from the delightful novelty of the place. He had never stood on a professional soccer field. The goal, to him, was the heart of a temple, an exclusive inner sanctuary where only priests and the pick of the gods could go. It thrilled him that he was just a few feet away from such a sacred place, in this case, one with three balls. Beyond it stretched the green field striped with lime, bordered by the clay track, and surrounded by the cyclopean walls of the stands, the colors washed out, almost lost in the night. The ends of the field were also bounded by various buildings with gyms, rinks, and pools, as well as the vague shapes of trees and giant light towers. The complex was ringed by office and apartment buildings dotted with a few lights. Valerio felt comfortably out in the open and hidden at the same time.

When he turned to Stefano, he recognized his warm smile as more than one of just sexual interest. It was softened with a pure, kind sadness which stemmed from two sources, he knew, romance and, since Stefano was a cop, the hopelessness of romance. After all, Valerio was a gay prostitute, one that realized that they should enjoy themselves while they could, but that their genuine affection for each other was certainly doomed, little more than what could happen between any hustler and john. He thought of Stefano's tristesse at such moments as a teaspoon of sugar in espresso. It sweetened the fun.

"So," Valerio said, breaking the mood, "what do you have?"

Stefano opened the storage compartment, took out a flashlight and a Manila folder, and stowed the helmets. Valerio, meanwhile, slipped from his backpack, unzipped it, and took out a bottle of wine, a Dolcetto.

"This has pictures of the two," Stefano began, the folder in one hand, the flashlight in the other. If anyone in an apartment building had noticed it, the light must have looked like a tiny star in the void. "Adolfo Pelosi," he said, aiming it, "and Alberto Citti. It's a program from a charity benefit for a big-brother organization, one concerned with rehabilitation of at-risk Catholic boys." He had circled their pictures and written their names under them with a black marker. Then he turned to a picture of a soccer squad. "They played in a tournament dedicated to the memory of some restaurant owner who donated often to police funds."

Valerio uncorked the bottle and poured a drop of wine onto the track.

"What are you doing?" Stefano smiled.

"Libation to Bacchus," Valerio said.

He took a drink, then traded the bottle for the folder and slipped it into his backpack.

"What's this about?" Stefano asked, taking a drink.

"Don't ask," Valerio said, looping the pack over a rear-view mirror. "The less you know, the better."

"They always take them to the same place," Stefano said, sharing the bottle, "a dead-end between warehouses between Molo Immacolatella and Molo Piscane."

"Rollo told me," Valerio said, corking the bottle.

"You can't tell anyone I gave you this," Stefano said solicitously. "I'd not only lose my job...."

"I understand," Valerio said, standing the bottle on one of the Vespa's floorboards. "Believe me, I'd never do anything to risk the life of such a handsome, young cop." He took the flashlight from Stefano, turned it off, and stood it next to the bottle. "You never gave me anything."

"Thanks," Stefano grinned.

"Thank *you*."

Stefano looked around, gave Valerio a quick, impulsive kiss, and just stood there, staring at him. He reminded Valerio of Tony Perkins in *Psycho*, but only his looks. He was simply too much fun to have many hang-ups, let alone dark, horrendous secrets. His sweet brown eyes were black in the night with thick, black brows and lashes to go with his thick, black hair, a long, narrow nose to go with his long, narrow face, and a mouth shaped like wings with full, impatient lips just pink in the ambient city light.

When Valerio stepped forward, they embraced and kissed voraciously, Valerio's lips parted for the phallic substitute of Stefano's slick tongue. As far as Valerio was concerned, Stefano may as well have just eaten a spoonful of honey. His breath was so nice. The only problem was that Stefano's face had a day or two more stubble than Valerio's and was rubbing his lips raw. Panting, Valerio stepped back, unzipped Stefano's hoodie, and spread it, exposing his long, sinewy torso down to his groin. Besides his beauty, Stefano's most distinctive physical trait was that he had lots of body hair – across his pecs, down the midline, over his abs – but it was always trimmed close, a sexy

242

badge of virility. In short, he looked both hairy and smooth at the same time. Valerio ran his hands all over him and, sucking a nipple, undid and reached inside his pants.

"Where are all those beautiful locks I love to hold when you blow me?" Stefano asked.

Valerio paused long enough to say, "I'm sure you'll love my buzz cut just as much."

When Stefano was hard, Valerio, catching him off guard, backed him up until he tripped and fell into the goal, caught in the web of the white net. Then Valerio went down on him, a sort of voluptuous spider eating a pleasure-stunned fly. The spice added to the meal, of course, was that he was doing him in sight of a dozen apartment buildings.

When he glanced up to see his effect on him, Stefano was watching him and nodding, "That's it. Yes." But when his excitement was just about to boil over, he grabbed Valerio's head and lifted him off him. "Want it on the bike?"

And soon they were nude from the waist down, coupled on the bike. Stefano was sitting on the saddle, his feet on the ground, his hands on Valerio's hips. Valerio was vigorously bouncing on his lap, his feet on the floorboards, his hands on the handlebars. When he started the motor, Stefano put his feet on the floorboards too, and they rolled into the dark, tilting around the curve in the track. Valerio steered off and on the track, trying to find bumps, and when he would hit one, thrusting Stefano even deeper into him, they would laugh heartily and veer in another direction, trying to find another. When he discovered the pit for the long jump, he bounded over it several times, but when Stefano said he was getting close, Valerio parked in the middle of the field and bobbed on his lap until Stefano leaned back and – legs spread, feet on the grass, hands on the grab rail – cried out in ecstasy. Anyone hearing him would have thought someone was stabbing him to death, the groans were so raw and primal. Then Valerio leaned back and started to rapidly jerk himself off, but Stefano reached around and took over, bringing him off, in contrast, with a string of violent, but quiet spasms. An 8.5 on the Richter scale could not have shaken him more.

# # # # #

A few minutes later, they were dressed and lying near the goal line, sharing the Dolcetto, and staring into the sky's smoggy void.

"You drive a taxi, right?" Stefano asked.

"No," Valerio laughed, hands behind his head. "Where'd you get that? I clerk at Bella Capri, the hostel across from the Maritime Station. You must have me mixed up with some other trick."

Instead of responding, Stefano faced Valerio and slipped his hand under Valerio's shirt, resting it on his ribs. The gesture was that of a gentle doctor feeling for something.

"You bored with your job?" Valerio asked. "I can tell you're smart, smart enough for more than traffic tickets."

"I'll get promoted," Stefano said, his fingers playing on Valerio's ribs like piano keys. "Of course," he joked, "I'm grossly underrated."

Valerio faced him and picked grass blades from his hair, and then they just lay there, smiling at each other, enjoying each other's young, male beauty, Stefano's hand on Valerio's side, Valerio's on Stefano's shoulder. To Valerio, sex with him there had been a secret alternative rite which refreshed and sustained him. He had sacrificed himself for Stefano's pleasure, but fulfilled himself as well. He had experienced the physical contact, sense of freedom, and emotional warmth he needed to feel good about himself again. Even his faith in humanity, like the growth of a weed, had actually melted the cynical crystals covering it, mainly due to his intuitive, if foolish, faith in Stefano, its representative.

Then Stefano's smile began to fade, not dropping to a frown, but a blank expression, as if the young cop no longer knew exactly how to respond to him or even to himself, as if he once again had given in to the highly addictive futility of his feelings. His look became pensive, concerned, the mope of a ripe adolescent's fall from grace. He tried to smile, but the smile was forced, a defeat. Embarrassed, he sat up, ankles crossed, arms crossed on his knees, and stared down the field.

"When we're together," Stefano said, "I enjoy you as much as I can. Hate the thought of something happening to you."

"Such a romantic officer of the law," Valerio smiled, noticing Stefano's imprint in the flat, matted grass.

One blade, then another sprang back up, and as if taking its cue, Valerio sprang up and kicked the balls, one by one, out of the goal. As if taking Valerio's cue, Stefano sprang up, and he and Valerio began dribbling the balls with their feet, manipulating them like a hacky sack, and working them down and up the field, Stefano less skillfully in boots. When Valerio assumed the aggressive posture of a forward, Stefano retreated a few steps and assumed a defensive stance near the goal. Valerio began his charge slowly, picked up speed, and zigzagged, kicking the first ball to Stefano's left. Stefano lunged for it, arms stretched, and caught it, landing on his side.

"Be careful, Valerio," Stefano said, getting up and brushing himself off. "I don't know what you're up to, but I do know that if you fuck one of them," meaning the detectives, "two of them will fuck you." He tossed the ball casually into the goal. "The thing with Rollo, let it go. He knows who to avoid now."

"They think we're a big zero, nothing," Valerio said, his foot on the second ball.

"They're right," Stefano replied. "They control you like puppets, even if you don't see the strings. You're dumb to think otherwise."

His fondness for Valerio, like a sacred statue, was locked safely inside the box of his heart, a secret place where, he thought, Valerio would never see it. He had done his best for him.

"Revenge is a game two can play," Valerio said, stepping back from the ball. "Blow for blow, so to speak."

"Exactly," Stefano stressed.

Valerio began his second charge with a few careful steps, then accelerated, kicking the ball hard. When it flew into Stefano's stomach, Stefano wrapped around it, as if protecting it from someone, and stumbled backward a few steps.

"Valerio," he pleaded, drop-kicking the ball into the goal, "just enjoy yourself. You can't threaten them. You can't climb on their backs. You can't push them or pull them." He sighed audibly in frustration.

"Not my nature," Valerio said, setting up the third ball. "Can't help myself. Couldn't stop myself if I wanted to, anymore than I can stop wanting to suck cock, any more than you can hide how you feel about me."

Stefano crouched and stuck his hands out, set for the ball. "I don't feel a thing for you, you idiot."

"I can see it in your eyes," Valerio claimed, taking a few steps back, "hear it in your voice. It's real."

"You're a fool," Stefano claimed. "You're a fag."

Valerio actually felt as if he were on the brink of doing something especially good in his life, something that transcended even the only thing he could do that's good, as he had explained to Father Dorato. He would defy the gods, he told himself. He would tend his little flock.

"They'll tear you to pieces," Stefano said, bouncing from foot to foot. "They'll eat you raw like a pack of hounds."

Valerio was, in fact, familiar with the myth of Actaeon. Actaeon was innocent, he knew. He wasn't, but he'd be careful.

"Think you're a god?"

"I'm not naïve," Valerio said, rocking front to back. "I know they're a pack of hounds." Then he made as if to kick left, but when Stefano jumped left, kicked right, sending the ball sailing through the dark into the net with a zip. Joyous, he raised his fists above his head and shouted, "Goal!"

Chapter 32: The Tomb of the Diver

Josh dreamed that he was in the silver Mercedes stuck in traffic in the Piazza Gioia at sunset and that when he tried to get around the traffic by driving over a concrete median, he broke the car's axle. He was late for dinner with Tyler, Billie, and Phil, so he grabbed a loaf of bread from the seat and hurried along the waterfront toward the restaurant. When he got there, the lights were out, and the maitre d' held a torch and led him to a table, where the three were waiting with saucers of olive oil and balsamic vinegar. In the shadows, a woman was singing and spinning a spinning wheel which played beautiful harp music. Toward the back of the room, couples were dancing in the dark.

Tyler, Billie, and Phil were smiling as if there were something funny about him, and when Billie said, "Here. Let's take that off," she reached across the table and pulled off a piece of mosquito netting which he had been wearing over his head. When it came off, Josh realized that the lights were on and that the restaurant was a converted church.

"How stupid of me," he laughed, slumping in the chair. "Won't do that again."

"When we get back to the room," Tyler said, "how 'bout a nice long bath?"

# # # # #

When Josh woke, Tyler was sleeping next to him, but when they had gotten in from dinner at Il Teatro, instead of going to bed, Tyler had stayed up to write, taking up residence in the corner chair with the bronze lamp and Athena looking over his shoulder. He had joked that good sex like they had the night before always inspired him to write and that he wanted to get something about the tomb in Paestum down on paper.

Josh had joked in return: "Why don't you write about a gay man coming out in his thirties. Thought he was bi, but really likes cock."

"Go to sleep," Tyler said, slouched in the chair, ankle on knee, clipboard in lap, pen in hand.

"I'd also like to read a novel in which a gay man cries," Josh said. "Never read one. Gays must think it's unmanly. To me, it only makes a man human."

"As I said – "

"Yeah, yeah, yeah," Josh smiled, snuggling down with a pillow.

Now, he was slipping from bed quietly, trying not to wake Tyler. As he neared the chair, he saw crumpled paper scattered on the floor in the moonlight, then spotted the clipboard on the seat in shadow. He took it to the bathroom, closed the door carefully, and turned on the light. Then he lowered the toilet seat, sat, and read what looked like a neat final draft.

247

The Tomb of the Diver by Tyler Lynn

The rich perfumes have evaporated, the washed skin vanished,
as well as the blush on the roses in your cheeks. The honey pie
in your hands – vanished, eaten by Cerberus. The gold coin
on your tongue – vanished, paid to Charon. The handsome musicians
who led the procession – vanished, too, on the path
to the tomb, but not the tomb, a box laid open like a gift. In the museum
at Paestum: The Tomb of the Diver decked with frescoes
twenty-five hundred years ago.
On one long wall, a banquet where, on couches draped
with blue (the color here of happy pleasure) lovers gaze
into the sensual mirrors of each other's eyes – the ephebe's, calm,
the bearded man's, content – the ephebe's head caressed
to draw him near, the man's mouth open in anticipation of
the delicious lips, the delicious moment when the olive leaves
in their wreaths mingle as the young man's slender fingers mingle
with the quivering strings of his lyre.
Three others play kottabos, flicking drops of wine
from cups into a vase floating in water, but one has turned
from the game to look at the lovers with mischievous lust.
On the opposite wall, you host (not there) a funeral banquet:
music, dances, games – a lively party with lyres and flutes.
Here, as before, two couples on couches draped in blue
and a single man to grace the others' joy.
On one short wall, an ephebe, nude, is pouring out a cup of wine
from the big, ceramic vase on a table hung with green festoons.
There is no blue here since he is alone.
On the opposite wall, a man
with a cloak and a walking stick, a dancing ephebe,
blue cloth draped on his arms, and a girl
– the only girl – in white, playing a flute.
On the cover slab, the eponymous scene. In a clearing framed
by willows, a nude, midair, is diving joyfully into a pool.
Since you had to die, I hope you were asleep
and, dreaming sweetly, dove into death
the way he –lightly bearded, genitals lifted – dove into blue.
What better way to balance death than life? The strum
of harmonious strings, the strum of youthful skin

that plays the lovely song, the delicious kiss
that's all the lavish banquet that we'll ever need.

Chapter 33: Sea Cliff

Six weeks after the catastrophe on Casco Bay, Tyler opened the outer blue door to Linda's room at Sea Cliff, a mental health facility. There were, in fact, two thick doors, each with a foot-square window with wire mesh embedded in thick glass. The outer door opened into the wide, sunny hall, where Eddie, Linda's sweet husband, waited, the second into the cool, dust-less room, where Linda, in a white hospital gown, was dozing, drugged. The auburn snakes of her disheveled hair crawled Medusa-like across a white, wrinkled pillowcase. Eddie had institutionalized her after she had overdosed on Xanax, and there she was – with the bed tilted up – supine and limp as if poured into the bed and pale, in fact deathly pale. Her arms draped across the sheet like those of a mannequin or, worse, a corpse. Though she resembled Tyler, she was an emotional mirror of her mother before "the accident," as it was referred to, a broken mirror, as he thought of her now.

He held the door knob in one hand, a bouquet of banksia roses in the other, and when he looked around the room, the fact that there was no window made it feel like a cave, not claustrophobic – the ceiling was too high – but a morbid, concrete cave. The second thing he noticed was that, except for the daisies on the side table, the room was devoid of the cozy, colorful details he associated with a home. The bed, rails down, had a faux-wood headboard and footboard. The side table was faux wood as well with a plastic, mustard-colored pitcher and clear, plastic glasses, the plastic vase of childlike daisies that Tyler assumed were from Eddie, and a big bottle of Tom's of Maine Mouthwash "Wicked Fresh!" On the other side of the bed was an over table on wheels with a plastic dish and spoon smeared with what looked like chocolate pudding. Across the room, in the far corner, was a black faux-leather lounge chair. The plot-like fluorescent panel in the ceiling was on dim, and the soft, dreamy twilight made everything look as if it were glowing from within. The room was so quiet he was sure it was soundproof, and, despite the flowers, a subtle, adhesive fume gummed up the air.

He shut the door carefully, but when he let go of the handle, it clicked, and Linda stirred, opened her eyes, and squinted at him.

"Hey," he smiled, head down, looking at her from under his brows. "How are you?"

She just lay there, eyes cast down to her right. Then she sat up with effort and looked at him. "How do you think I feel?"

"Right," he nodded.

Why was he there? he asked himself. In what role? For himself as a father who wanted just to be loved by his daughter, despite what she had done. For

Sea Change

her as a father who wanted just to see if he could make her feel better, even in a priest-like role to see if he could help her (and himself) spiritually, too, though, again, he certainly did not mean *spiritual* in any Christian sense. Actually, nothing mattered to him except that she was there, alive. He didn't care about what happened on the island and the bay. When he strolled toward her, she backed up as if he were approaching her with a shiny butcher's knife, not creamy roses, and he realized that, despite himself, he was there in another role, as threat. He was a little paranoid about their conversation being taped or overheard. After all, Karen had tried to kill him, and Linda was a *de facto* accomplice, though, he felt, a hesitant one.

"Linda, sweetheart," he began. He started to say something, but changed his mind. "Where should I put these?" he asked, meaning the roses.

"Over there," she whispered, glancing toward the over table. "I'll ask a nurse for a vase."

He crossed the room as if walking on ice and lay the bouquet on the table. Something about the gesture reminded him of the weird moment when he lay the calla lily on Alice's casket.

What he had, in fact, told the sheriff's deputy the night of the incident and the medical examiner the day of the inquest was that Linda had a seizure as they were returning from a day trip to the island. Karen stopped the boat, but when she tried to go to Linda's aid, lost her balance and fell overboard, pulling Alice in. He dove in to help them, but before he could, a huge shark attacked them, and during the attack, the shark apparently hit the boat, sending it spinning off into the sea smoke. At that point, he said, he lost sight of everyone, but, when the fog cleared, could see the lights on Bailey.

When Linda came to, the flood tide had carried her northwest past Haskell Island within sight of a cluster of lights, which turned out to be South Harpswell, where she put in and asked someone to call the police. An ebb tide would have taken her due south onto open ocean. Tyler tried to imagine what it had been like when she opened her eyes and saw the moon and Milky Way bobbing above her. Linda's story was that she could not remember anything because of her seizure, and the mere fact that she said she had one was enough, it seemed, to corroborate Tyler's version of things.

Alice's body was found floating off Great Mark Island a couple of weeks later, and the medical examiner reported her death as by accidental drowning. Even though only Karen's left hand washed up on Haskell a few days later, it was apparently enough, along with Tyler's testimony, for the medical examiner to report her death as due to a shark attack. Tyler didn't want to think about what her last moments had been like.

When he turned toward Linda, she was rocking slightly the way a sick dog would, and though he moved toward the bed as cautiously as he could, she still shied away from him.

"Anything I can get you?" he asked, deferential. "Tea, soft drink? How's the food here?"

She shook her head. Up close, he could see that the young pinkness of her cheeks had been cured like a rash by all the strange grief she had suffered.

"We can break this awful spell cast on us out there," he began, pinching the sheet absently. "We can redeem ourselves from this awful curse on the family."

"What are you talking about?" she slurred.

"She did this to you, too," he said. "You're a victim, too."

"Of your neglect."

To Tyler, it was obvious that she was still proud with affection for, even blind with obedience to, her mother.

"If you shut me out, your father, you're shutting out part of yourself, who you are. You have to know and accept yourself if you ever want to be happy. If you don't, you're a lost dog who never finds her owner."

He noticed the leather straps of the wrist restraints dangling off the bed.

"Owner," she said wearily. "Dog. No, I don't want to go on with this absurd charade of a relationship."

"I just want to help you get – "

"You never caused me anything but hurt and rage," she snorted, interrupting him. "You contacted me more in the month before your visit than you did in all the years prior to it. And that made me think, 'God, I have to have brain surgery for him to be concerned.'"

As a writer, his other role, he wanted to know what had happened while he was passed out, the part of the story only Linda knew, and he knew that the magic portal, like a god's eye, through which he could see the truth – that is, the moment, now – was quickly closing on him.

"What happened?" he asked. "You know, when I was unconscious. It would do you good to talk about it, right?"

"Get out of here," she snapped, hard with hate.

"Linda, for your sake," he faltered, "despite what happened – "

"Get out," she insisted.

"Linda, my writing's my therapy," he explained. "I can work things out on the page. You need to work things out with Dr. Oswald here and Eddie and me."

"Which brings up another point," she snarled. "Don't mail me any more of your vile, revolting writing. How could you send me that disgusting *Crystal Ball*?"

The second time she had called the script disgusting. Over the years, among other manuscripts, he had sent her the script for *The Crystal Ball*, his

253

horror film in which Kirby, a handsome psychopath, kidnaps, rapes, and tortures women. Kim, the protagonist, outwits him, manipulates him emotionally, and finally manages to kill him and escape. Tyler saw the script as a tribute to Kim's heroism; Linda, as abuse of women. But then there were Kirby's cruel lines about barren women: "I can tell how worthless you feel. You can't even get pregnant." What was he thinking? He assumed she'd be all right with the script, that she could distinguish fiction from reality, but apparently Kirby's taunt had hit home, not a little too close to home, but home.

"It's a horror film, Linda," he said, head bowed. "It's supposed to be disgusting." Then he faced her head-on, studying her. "It was just a small dream of mine that you'd like my work, my movie, in fact, anything about me."

When he noticed something faint in her eyes, he grabbed her arm, pulled her near, and stared into her as only he could, as far as he could, to the core, as if his eyes were, in fact, the alien eyes of a god who could see the terrible truth inside her and judge her objectively. Caught out, she jerked her head away, covering her face with her hand in the melodramatic way a vampire would flinch from a cross.

"I don't want to see you," she cried. "Don't ever contact me again!"

When he let go of her, she fell against the pillow, and he feared she would have a seizure. Besides, since he knew their nature, he knew, since they would act true to nature, how they had reacted at any given moment. He could make up the practical details of how they had carried him down to the boat.

"I'm sorry," he said, penitent. "Calm down."

"If I never hear from you again," she stated, lunging toward him, "I will be even happier than the joyful, lucky, amazing woman I am now."

They were in a gloomy room in a mental institution because she had tried to kill herself, and she had just called herself joyful. He was simply astounded.

"I hate you most truly and earnestly and joyfully," she sneered. "Get out!" She tried to slap him, but he leaned back. "Get out, get out, get out!"

Linda had told him how the Androscoggin River behind her and Eddie's house would freeze over in winter and how fishermen would build dozens of little "ice shacks" on it. As she had written in a letter, "It's like having a little village in the back yard." Then, in spring, the ice would thaw, break into chunks, and slowly slide away. Well, that was the way he was feeling now, he thought. His irritation with her and coldness toward what he considered her senseless, purely self-destructive hate was strangely and slowly melting and sliding away, though not toward love: indifference. He was grateful to have seen her, but knew that he was never going to see her again, that nothing would ever come of trying to reconcile himself with her.

"OK," he said, patting the bed. "I won't bother you. You know where to find me. Sorry. Bye."

She threw herself against the bed in a fit of exasperation, and as he leaned toward the door, something inside him like a ship's mast tilted away from her as well and everything with which she was associated. He was turning not just from his daughter and the room, but also yielding to an entirely new direction in life, as naturally repelled by pain and drawn to pleasure as filings to a magnet. At first, he had thought that the life she represented had needed fixing or broadening to accommodate him. Now he realized that he needed to adjust himself, and he would.

As he reached for the doorknob, he turned and said, "I know you love me."

A nurse opened the door and rushed in, and Tyler stepped into the hall and faced a concerned-looking Eddie.

"She's all right," Tyler assured him. "I'm sure she relaxed as soon as I left the room."

Eddie was wearing a gray, wool turtleneck sweater, dark-green jacket zipped halfway up, khakis, and penny loafers. He was a big, kind, Nordic type with a blunt nose and a mop of mussed red hair kindled by the sunlight streaming through the window. His faint eyebrows faded into pale skin, brows so light he looked as if he did not have any, just one large forehead. In fact, despite Eddie's rosy cheeks, Tyler was a little put off by his paleness, his skin glowing with a soft luminescence.

"My usual effect," Tyler sighed.

Eddie's eyes glittered like sapphires, but he wore thick, almost circular glasses in tortoise-shell frames, and the big glasses made him look as if he were constantly surprised. He had a natural wide-eyed expression which contributed to the effect, but at the moment he was peering from his lenses with a subtle, analytical look as if trying to figure out, Tyler thought, if he were, in fact, the evil monster everyone said he was.

"What happened out there?" Eddie asked finally.

"I told you what happened," Tyler said, caught off-guard.

Eddie stepped closer and whispered, head down, "I don't know who's protecting whom from what."

"Would Linda protect me?" Tyler asked.

Eddie paused, then nodded knowingly. "Right."

Tyler glanced down the hall. The shiny white and gray squares of linoleum funneled in a checkerboard pattern toward a gurney with a green sheet and a cart covered in white canvas.

"At least she has you," Tyler said. He felt tired and weak, his sinuses padded with emotionally black cotton, as he thought of it. "You're the perfect compensation for my immense failure as a father. Words can't express how grateful I am for you."

"Believe it or not," Eddie said, poking the bridge of his glasses, "she still needs a father. It's never too late to re-invent yourself. The best do it every day."

"Tell *her*," Tyler said, glancing at him. He put a hand on the wall, leaned against it, and studied a big rectangle of light, a blank canvas sectioned off by the shadows of bars. The bars on the window reminded him again that they were not in a careless hotel or even a general hospital, but a special hospital, as he had heard someone whisper. "By the way," Tyler added. "Something occurred to me."

"Yeah?"

"What happened to Peeve?"

"Peeve?"

"The cat," Tyler explained. "I didn't want to mention it to Linda."

"What are you talking about?"

"Did anyone get the cat off the island?"

Friday, October 6

Chapter 34: Positano

Though the day began with a glitch, Tyler, Josh, Phil, and Billie had a lot of fun playing tourist at the Grotta Smeralda and in Positano. In Amalfi, in a small office off Piazza Gioia, Josh thought he was buying tickets for a day-trip to the grotto and Positano, even pointing to the excursion in a brochure, but as it turned out, he was wrong. They boarded a motorboat at one of the docks, and as they puttered along the coast, a young faun, as Tyler thought of him, kept pointing here and there and reciting a narrative in some local dialect even Josh could not follow. When they got to the grotto, the faun helped Phil and Billie out of the boat onto the rocky shore, where a tour guide led them into the cave, helped them into a wobbly rowboat, and paddled them slowly around the gloom. There was a hole underwater where light from the sea entered the cave, fanning out in long, bottle-green, wavering beams like a weird undersea sun, a beautiful, natural effect, Tyler thought. What trivialized it, though, was the fact that the guide felt he had to play the buffoon. He sang a corny rendering of "O sole mio." He asked everyone to imagine a certain tall, ghostlike stalagmite as Tony Blair or, if they were American, Georgia Boosh. And he when he pointed out a tacky, sunken nativity scene, he declared, "Eet's a meeracle!" a bit of irony which served as a running joke throughout the rest of the trip.

After the grotto, everyone got back in the motorboat, but, when the prow pointed east, realized they were not heading to Positano. However, when they got to Amalfi, they bought tickets for the next ferry to Positano and were soon plunging west again along the coast, whipped by a brisk breeze. On arrival, they paused on the wharf to take in the sights: the Saracen tower; grounded boats and swarms of sunbathers idling on the black sand; the glistening majolica tiles of the church dome; cliffs, hotels, foliage rising in terrace after terrace up to the faint blue mountains, glowing sky, and high clouds. The town looked like one big, euphoric birthday cake, Tyler thought.

Since Josh forgot his map and notes, they had lunch at La Zagara, where they decided to split up, do some shopping, and meet in a couple of hours at Le Tre Sorelle (The Three Sisters), a restaurant on the beach. Josh and Tyler slowly strolled up a road to an overlook with a great view. Boardwalks and long lines of chaise lounges and teal and yellow beach umbrellas formed geometric patterns on the beach far below, and boats of various shapes and sizes were scattered on the crystalline water. An orchid tree was in bloom, and on a low wall across from an antique shop, someone had set a bronze copy of the *Dancing Faun* from Pompeii.

As they passed a hair studio, Josh decided to get a haircut, and when the stylist said he could take him, Josh asked Tyler to wander around for a while. When Tyler returned, Josh was standing outside with a dramatically new look and a sheepish smile that seemed to be saying, *Like me, please.* His hairstyle had gone from a feminine wedge to a fauxhawk: close on the back and sides, but thick on top and pitched forward like a wave.

"You look hot," Tyler said, eyeing him. "Fucking hot. Ow!"

When they joined Phil and Billie at Le Tre Sorelle, Billie said, "Better, much better."

"Billie, really," Phil sighed. "Josh would look good bald."

They took a table, had a round of limoncellos, and watched the beach scene. Then they ambled over to the wharf and caught the ferry to Amalfi. Back in their room, Josh and Tyler helped each other do sit-ups, then took a nap.

Chapter 35: Protest Theater

That night, the four dressed up and went to dinner at Eolo, a posh restaurant with tables on a terrace with a wonderful view of Amalfi. There, Phil brought up the topic of Protest Theater again.

"Won't talking about it help sort it out?"

"I guess," Tyler said.

"Just pretend we're a panel of shrinks," Billie suggested.

"And I'm the nut case."

So Tyler told the tale of his stage production which never took off.

"It was a theatrical version of my screenplay *The Crystal Ball*," he said, "and I was grateful they liked it. At least, I thought they did. I was looking forward to working on it, an excuse to be in New York. I can write just about anywhere, and while some friends, a painter and a writer, were apartment-sitting for someone out of the country, I stayed in their apartment on East 4th in the Village, an old, roach-infested studio with a loft bed, where I kept hitting my head on the ceiling. The theater was in this creepy abandoned church in Soho. I halfway expected to see a stray dog trotting across the apron, bats flitting in and out of the rigging."

"The ghost of a murdered choirboy wandering around backstage," Josh joked.

"I was so naïve," Tyler confessed. "I was willing to workshop it for unforeseen production problems, inconsistencies, errors, but, at the first reading, they went at it like a school of piranhas. Should've known what was coming. When they greeted you, no one shook hands."

Gathering his thoughts, he gazed toward the picturesque town: the gigantic waterfall of sparkling night lights cascading down the steep cliffs to the beach and docks, the fringe of ghost-white surf.

"The moment I set foot in there," he said, "I was an outsider, the playwright as outsider in the theater. Jeez! It was me versus them, the playwright versus what I call 'theater people,' people you'd think would nurture a play. They had a lot of experience producing plays, granted, but were grievously lacking in what I call 'literary skills.'"

"The artistic and resident directors you mentioned," Phil said.

"Right. Or as I like to refer to them: Christopher Queen, the maniac, and Dewitt Dill, his spaniel. Dill must've been his sex slave before they began their professional relationship. Man, what a psych ward!"

The menus were big, the pages soft like fabric, and Tyler noticed that Billie's menu did not have prices.

"The basic assumption," he said, shutting the menu, "was that a new play, no matter how good, always needs change. The notion that I might possibly know what I was doing was foreign to them. They would say something like 'We're your friends' or 'We just want to help you make it the best play possible,' when I didn't need their help, at least not in the sense they meant. Even the cast had an opinion. They thought that writing a play was supposed to be some sort of group effort, play by committee. By definition, play by committee is the opposite of original."

"Isn't that the way Hollywood works?" Phil asked.

"Of course," Tyler agreed. "Hollywood is completely different. In Hollywood, I understand that what I sell is a first draft. The script is totally at the mercy of the producer and director. As it turned out, though, the screenplay for *The Crystal Ball* fared fairly well. It wasn't 'developed' into something that wouldn't recognize itself. To my great surprise, a lot of it actually made it onto the screen."

"You were making money," Billie suggested, "not art."

"I'll probably be getting residuals from it," he said, "for the rest of my life. I wouldn't be sitting here with you right now without it. Let me tell you. Horror pays."

"Why did you say you got a good contract?" Josh asked.

"They didn't think it would go anywhere," Tyler said, "and my agent's one of those totally amoral Hollywood attack-lawyers who'll make your balls jump up in your chest."

"What did Queen and Dill object to?" Phil asked, turning the conversation back to New York.

"Well," Tyler mused, "they kept saying it was difficult to stage, which I found mind-boggling since it had one simple set. The scene changes are practically instantaneous. Lights fade. Lights rise. All you have to do is walk from one area of the stage to another. In Shakespeare, characters walk on and say where they are. Sometimes they don't even do that. In some scenes, it doesn't matter where they are. Queen was absolutely dumbfounded by the fact that I wanted the lead to change clothes on stage. There are eight major costume changes on stage in *M. Butterfly*."

The waitress, an elegant, middle-aged woman in black, appeared at the table with a carafe of wine, again something local Billie had ordered simply because she liked the sound of its name when Josh had pronounced it, drawing out the syllables: Sciascinoso (Shah-she-no-so). The Riedel decanter had the longest spout Tyler had ever seen, and as she poured his wine, the glass became a large, vivid ruby.

"The second problem, according to Queen, was that, because of short scenes, the actors had to keep 'resetting' themselves. That was the term he

260

used: reset. Dill objected to the quote unquote poetry in it, squinching his face as if poetry, of all things, were something distasteful. Said he had to make sure the audience could follow what was going on. At one point, he took all the metaphors and similes out of it. I promptly put them back. They also objected to the narrative in the play, as if there weren't narratives in *The Glass Menagerie* or *Our Town* or even *M. Butterfly*. Hell, half of *Oedipus Tyrannus* is narrative, and that play's lasted a couple of thousand years. To say the least," Tyler summed up, "I was surprised at how anti-intellectual and downright unimaginative they were."

"For theater people," Josh joked.

"The biggest problem, though, was Queen's baffling hate. I'd never met the guy, and he hated me, I guess, from reading the script. I've had students like that. I walk into a classroom, and a student projects someone he hates onto me, or a student hates authority figures, which I'm not. And let me tell you. I'm well acquainted with irrational, out-of-control hate. I know it when I see it."

He sniffed the wine's pleasant vinous odor.

"Queen had a lot of acting experience and Off-Broadway productions of his own, so you'd think he'd be more sympathetic, but he was the worst, and you may not believe this, but I think he was jealous. There's no other logical explanation."

He tasted the dry, "soft" wine.

"He'd stare at me aggressively as if we were in some sort of staring contest, so much so that I began to question his mental stability. How could someone harbor so much animosity toward a play he himself wanted to direct? One of the characters in the play thinks he's possessed by a devil. Well, when I stared into those jaundiced green eyes of Queen's, I halfway expected to see a pair of devil eyes behind his staring back at me. To say the least, it was disconcerting. I couldn't tell if he wanted to fuck me or kill me."

"Or both," Josh suggested.

The lotus in the budvase on the table reminded Tyler of the orchid tree in Positano, a thorny, spindly exotic with boughs of pink, floppy stars.

"He couldn't have been more condescending," he said. "His notes on the play were in big print with underlining and exclamation points. He may as well have been yelling at me. All these pompous, dogmatic assertions based on false assumptions which, I guess, came from not really reading it or not making the effort to get it or not being smart enough to get it. He certainly didn't approach it as literature."

He focused on the colorful ceramic the waitress had given Billie: a shiny, flower-like fish with many fins.

"He didn't just raise questions or suggest things. He used the word *should* a lot, which I never do without thinking about it first. Or he'd issue an imperial command. 'Cut that character. The narrative has to go.' And my favorite: 'Let it be what it's really about, Satanism.' That was the greatest arrogance of all: that he knew what the play was about better than I did. Basically, it was my play versus his, some play in his head he wanted me to write. He said a play about a real blood-thirsty demon was far more interesting than a play about a psychotic who thinks he's a blood-thirsty demon, and, for some strange reason, he thought I'd write it. Of course, when I refused, when I refused to write *his* play – "

"You were a conceited bastard impossible to work with," Phil said.

"If he wants a play about Satanism," Tyler said, "let him write his own play. That's not mine."

"What is yours about?" Billie asked.

"A heroic woman," Tyler stated, "a deeply flawed, but heroic woman scarred by trauma, one who overcomes it and decides to do something good with the rest of her life."

"How did you deal with all this – " Billie hesitated, "antagonism?"

"At first, I tried to defend things, tried to explain why some scene or character or line was important. Then I just shut down, locked all my windows and doors."

"What's the status of the production?" Phil asked.

"Oh, there's not going to be a production," Tyler said, "even if they wanted one, and they don't."

"Can they sue?" Billie asked.

"Let 'em," Tyler assured her. "I had an air-tight contract with final say and an exit clause. They had to produce the play by a certain date, or all rights reverted to me. I had the option of either extending the date or terminating the agreement. I terminated it. As soon as the date came and passed, I hopped a plane to Rome. Needed a vacation, something to distract me, get my mind off it."

"Disappointed?" she asked.

"Yes, but, you know, in the great scheme of things…" he trailed off. "And I have my successes: screenplays, stage plays. Let me tell you. Even with the successes, I only enjoyed watching other people enjoy them. The productions themselves were work. Besides, I've done what I always wanted to do, sold scripts. I can call myself a writer. I don't need to get a play produced to be happy."

"What do you need?" Josh asked.

"Friends, intelligent conversation, food, wine," Tyler said. "We're booked in the Piccolo Sogno, a beautiful hotel in a beautiful place, Amalfi. And I was pretty happy to begin with."

"So what have you learned?" Phil asked.

"To try fiction," Tyler laughed. "One fool to do deal with: an editor. I need to try something literary anyway, that is, if I want to leave a mark."

# # # # #

On the way back to the hotel, Tyler supposed that Phil was right. Talking about the mess had been cathartic, if bitter. It had, in fact, helped him sort it out, but left him in a funk, emotionally tired. Then, as they leisurely strolled along the waterfront, suddenly they heard a whoosh off the end of a dock, and rockets started arcing into the night, trailing long, bright tails like comets. At the apex of the arcs, they disappeared, then exploded in the intense white bursts of gold and silver fireworks, the gold ones shimmering like champagne bubbles, the silver ones sifting down in a flurry of incandescent flakes. Loud reports echoed off the cliffs and over the sea.

Everyone sat on a bench and watched, heads tilted back, mouths open, as the display went on and on, each dazzling flash lighting up the drifting smoke of the one before it. Tyler wondered what the occasion was or if there were always a fireworks display on Friday night in Amalfi. When he smiled at Josh, he realized that Josh's arm was around him, resting on the back of the bench. He also realized that Josh's affection had wiped away the funk. As always, it was nice to be liked by anyone, desired by someone of the same sex, a compliment.

The finale came in a barrage of bomb-like blinding explosions and deafening bangs, and when it was over, Billie shouted, "Yay!" and, childlike, clapped her hands.

"How 'bout a gelato at the Caffee Royal?" Josh asked.

Chapter 36: Test Drive

When Tyler and Josh got back to their room, Josh suggested that the perfect end to a romantic evening would be a good, long fuck.

"Have condoms?" Tyler asked. He wondered just how protective of himself Josh had been if he'd played second fiddle to someone's wife.

"Of course," Josh said. "Give me a few minutes in the bathroom."

Tyler stripped, wandered onto the terrace, and watched the waves crashing. Toward town, he could see wiggly trails of light on the water, not Amalfi itself. Then he reclined on a chaise lounge, listened to the surf, and gazed at the stars and almost full moon. He noticed that the light from the room dimmed and heard the chest of drawers open and close. Only when he heard the flick of the Bic did he smile and get up. When he brushed the sheers aside, Josh, nude, was sprawled in bed with the soap dish and lighter, smoking a joint. He looked like a male odalisque a la Ingres or Delacroix, Tyler thought, his very own harem of one.

On a side table, a lamp was on, and its small, burnt-orange shade cast a warm, cave-like glow on everything. Near the lamp were a bottle of water, a little bottle of lube, a torn condom packet, and one of the flimsy towels. Tyler shuffled over to the bed and stood, feet spread, hips thrust forward as if offering himself. Josh sat on the side of the bed, drew on the joint, and handed it to him, and as they traded hits, the proximity of Josh's velvety mouth had its predictable effect.

When Tyler was aroused, Josh tamped the joint out in the dish and set it and the lighter on the side table, but when he started to drape a pair of black briefs over the lampshade, Tyler stopped him, tossed them aside, and said, "Seeing's part of the fun."

And see he did: the pink scratch on Josh's chest, the stacked plates in his abs, his firm, smooth thighs like dolphins curving around his legs. His pubes, like a Rorschach test, reminded Tyler of a monk's hood, and Josh's flaccid cock looked like a plump mouse peeking shyly out of its foreskin. When Josh went down on him, Tyler held Josh's head with one hand, leaned forward, and sighed.

"I'm getting sort of fond of your mouth," Tyler said, stroking Josh's hair.

"Good," Josh said, leaning back. He stared at Tyler, brows raised as if for approval.

"I like what you do with that skilled tongue of yours."

Josh's tongue felt slick and complaisant, a mouthful of steam.

"Better to please you with, Sir."

He traced the crease between Tyler's crotch and thigh with his tongue, and as he stroked himself, his cock stood up, and his glans bulged to a big, elliptical berry.

"What position?" Tyler asked.

"Whatever you like."

"No," Tyler insisted. "Tell me."

"Well," Josh said, stroking Tyler, "deepest penetration is missionary. Most submissive, dog style. Easy entry, fastest thrust."

"Hands and knees," Tyler said. "Face the wall."

Josh promptly assumed the position, and Tyler grabbed the lube and condom, crawled into bed, and knelt behind him, cock erect and pointed at Josh's buns.

First, Tyler rimmed him, burying his tongue deep in his ass till Josh pushed back against him and groaned, "Oh, man!"

Then Tyler lubed him and finger-fucked him, massaging the soft, warm lump of his prostate. When he felt Josh was ready, Tyler sheathed himself, held Josh's hips, and funneled into him slowly and smoothly, up to the hilt in exquisite pleasure. Seeing where they connected, groin to cheeks, sent a thrill like hot water streaming through his veins, and for the first time he felt as if he had somehow completed himself in him. If there'd been an erotic equation for it, he imagined it would have looked something like Bottom + Top = 1.

"Gotta warn you," he whispered. "I can fuck all night with a condom on. In fact, I can fuck all night without one."

"Not a problem," Josh replied. "Fuck me till I come. Then come. Fuck me all you want."

Fucking him was like riding a spirited colt that enjoyed the ride as much as the rider. Josh was relaxed and receptive, Tyler deep and relentless, a drop hammer bent on pleasing him as much as he could, as well as himself. With every thrust, Josh, in tandem, rocked back on him, back arched, butt hiked, assuming the perfect position to present himself to him, to line up the perfect fit.

"Man," Josh sighed, "feels good."

When Tyler quickened the pace, he could feel the eager strength in Josh's response, a vital, euphoric vigor of will that made fucking him just as much a physical as a sensual workout. It was actually more deeply satisfying because it was, in fact, a good, physical workout, good for his heart in a couple of ways. More of this, Tyler knew, and he'd be better mentally as well. The room, of course, was a harbor of sorts, but then so was Josh, and Tyler was anchored in him, a handsome haven of genuine affection, slavish devotion, immunization against the disease of remorseful memories. How could he dwell on an angry past, jammed in such a sublime present?

He moved his hips so that his glans swabbed Josh's rectum, massaging its silky folds. Then he leaned over him and worked the supple muscles in his shoulders, back, and loins, and as he did, suddenly he became aware of the white noise of their breathing, his on Josh's on top of the surf. Again, he felt as if he were listening to the surf breathing. He figured that the sound must be like, as Josh had explained, what a fetus hears in the womb, the mother's hypnotic breath ebbing and flowing, a hush, then a sigh. Why the sound is so soothing. Why people always find their way to the sea. Why, later, he would easily fall asleep to the lilt of its regularly irregular lullaby. The sea was singing the same lullaby for them that it had sung for the lovers in the fresco in the Tomb of the Diver. It had always been singing it, always would, and he felt deep comfort in the fact that he was one small part of the world's sensuous continuum.

When he cupped Josh's cheeks, the touch of his skin flooded his body with a rich, libidinous bliss, so much so that he had to start fucking him again, calmly slapping against him in a natural, easy, heartbeat rhythm. He thought of what they were doing as taking Josh out for a test drive. He wanted to know how gay he was, that is, how much he liked getting fucked, if he liked getting fucked hard, if he could take it, his size. He was done with cool, inert lovers.

When Josh slipped prone, Tyler whispered, "Up against the wall," and Josh crawled forward and, half upright, braced on the stone.

Tyler crawled behind him, grabbed Josh's thighs, and slipped into him again.

"Fuck me," Josh murmured. "Oh, yeah, fuck me."

In the heat of the moment, the words sounded magic like trance speaking and thus weirdly exciting, as if spoken not to him, but to some lost spirit hovering over the scene. With his forehead pressed against his arm, was Josh even conscious of him?

"All of it," Josh breathed. "Harder, yeah. I want just you inside me. Fuck!"

Tyler held Josh's hip and casually picked up speed till Josh's ass began squeezing him hard over and over again, filling him like a glass with pleasure till, brimming, he spilled over and came, too, shooting what felt like ecstatic stars into the condom.

"Fuck, that felt good," Josh panted, slumped against the wall.

Tyler pulled out and dropped onto his back on the pillows, and when he clasped his hands behind his head, his biceps like plump snakes wound around his arms. Josh lay beside him, peeled the condom off, and dropped it onto the floor. When he leaned over him again, Tyler spread his knees and thrust his hips, plugging himself into the warm, wet socket of Josh's mouth. Josh ran his finger along Tyler's urethra, perineum to slit, pressing the last drop of come out of him and into his mouth. Then he rested on Tyler's chest, gazing into his eyes. He seemed to be inviting Tyler to look around inside him, to see for himself he had nothing to hide, but Tyler glanced away pensively. He did not want to search Josh's eyes any more than he wanted to shine a flashlight into his own, especially into the dark places in his soul where he kept all those terrible secrets about Karen, Alice, Linda, and Erin.

"Certainly got the job done," Josh said, swinging his legs off the bed.

"The principle's pretty simple," Tyler replied, reaching the towel.

"Back in a minute."

Josh picked up the milky condom and strolled to the bathroom. Tyler wiped a pillow, dabbed his crotch, and lay the towel aside. Then he just lay there, limp, eyes closed, feeling his body cooling, savoring their warm musk smells. In a few minutes, he heard the toilet flush, and when Josh came out of the bathroom, Josh sniffed and wiped his eyes with his fingertips. Then he turned off the lamp and slipped into bed.

"What?" Tyler asked, taking him into his arms affectionately.

"Nothing," Josh whispered.

"Tell me."

"Well," Josh said, face to face. "You've made up for everything."

"Everything?"

"Everything I went through with Owen."

Tyler nodded slowly, something he meant as a valid form of commiseration. Josh kissed him, separated from him, and lay supine, hands at his sides, like a mummy. Tyler carefully rolled onto his side to watch him in the gloom and, when Josh's breathing deepened, knew he had dozed off. Josh's body glowed with a phosphor-like blue, like a sensual source of light in the dark. Watching him turned on another kind of light in Tyler's chest, one that filled all the corners of his body with a soft, light-blue pleasure. Moonlight in a mirror could not have been more of a solace.

Tyler rolled onto his back and – hands clasped on his chest, staring at the ceiling – began to take stock of his present situation. He knew he could always meet his basic needs through his own ingenuity and others' altruism. For starters, he was eating well, in fact too well. Perhaps he should add a good, long swim to the daily agenda. Drinking well, too, lots of good local wine. He definitely had comfortable accommodations. Kalypso's cave couldn't have been more comfortable. How could he help but sleep well here with the surf and breeze?

At the moment, he was certainly living his little dream of peace and happiness. He didn't think anyone was after him, no tragic exes, no drug-altered mental patients. The Italians were friendly, despite the Bush administration, and he loved the Italians. He wished he knew the language. Josh could teach him. He would've liked more order in his life, but, as he had told everyone, could write anywhere and felt at ease drifting around. He could write in one place, too, say an apartment with Josh in Atlanta. And speaking of his sex slave, he joked, his needs in that area, without doubt, were being met. He knew that one of the best ways to achieve happiness was sex. It was based on beauty and satisfied a number of physical, emotional, and mental needs. And there were the companionship, attention, appreciation. His Sparky Award and first place at the Austin Film Festival paled by comparison. As he told everyone at dinner, he didn't need a play produced to be happy. And despite what others (from daughters to stage managers) may have said about him, he knew one thing for certain: he didn't need to hate anyone, not even them, not even himself. In fact, he liked himself. He had to. How else could he go on?

Liked himself, he mused. Had he really accepted himself? Did he really respect himself? Did he even know himself enough to? Did he take this side of himself seriously, the indefinite "dark" side he was scouting at the moment? Was he condescending toward Josh? Did he take *him* seriously? Everything seemed so right with him: their lover-like rapport, the magical suite, what he thought of as his inner silence around him. How did he get the rest so wrong?

Their ability to connect well physically was just a corporal image of how they connected emotionally. Despite his test-drive approach to the sex, there definitely had been an emotional component to it that wasn't there with women. Or did they connect well because he finally wanted to? He'd joked that his penis had a nondiscriminatory policy. Sex with anyone was sex and satisfying. He'd always distinguished act from nature, that is, the mechanics of what he was doing from something innate. What we do is not who we are. A gay can act straight. A straight can act gay. Now his reasons were beginning to sound like rationalizations: sexual experimentation for the sake of his writing, gayness as an antidote for Puritanism, bisexuality as a broadened definition of love. And what could be wrong with love?

Again, he thought of the end of *Women in Love* where Ursula tells Rupert, "You can't have two kinds of love." Neither Rupert nor Tyler had believed it. Now he wasn't sure. If Rupert were a double for Lawrence, had Lawrence been fooling himself? Then Tyler thought of the lines in *Lear* when the Duke of Albany tells Goneril:

> *That nature which contemns it origin*
> *Cannot be bordered certain in itself....*
> *perforce must wither*
> *And come to deadly use.*

Tyler had always thought of the cryptic quote in terms of his daughters' not accepting him as their father (their origin) and of what pernicious psychological effect such a denial would have in their relations with other men. Suddenly, he realized that it also applied to him in terms of his denial of what now seemed more than just a compartment of his personality: his sexual enjoyment of and fondness for men, especially young, vibrant, engaging men like Josh. What did Josh have to offer which was in any way inferior to what a woman did? He was companionable, affectionate, obviously willing to please. What was there to object to?

The fact that Tyler had not been "bordered certain in itself" had truly "come to deadly use," the loss of his ex and, in different ways, both daughters. It was as if his mental self had been, for the most part, unaware of his sensual self. He had always enjoyed sex with women just as much as with men. How could he have known that there was some inherent, emotional deficit that could be reduced only with revenue from men? Life was exploration, he thought, inside and out. He guessed he was simply finding himself in some slow, natural way, but wondered why it had taken so long. On the other hand, everything in his life had led up to that moment in that room with Josh. Perhaps he (Tyler) hadn't been slow, he conjectured. Perhaps right now was, in fact, the right moment to discover the obvious: who he was.

Suddenly, he felt it like a calm. Emotionally, everything inside him that had been going one way *paused* and was now about to go the other, like the slack tide off Maine.

But what's it like? Tyler smiled. Submission, his limbs as well as his heart like a lily opening up to the light of someone. Could he do it? Josh made it look easy. Then he realized that he and Josh were the same person just as tops and bottoms were the same person, a reverse image in the sexual mirror.

"Gay."

Chapter 37: Silver Gulls

Valerio and his friends were chatting at the east entrance to the Galleria that night when his cell phone chimed a few notes of the "Nessun dorma." When he pressed the phone to his ear, he recognized the big, deep voice of a long-term, dependable john named Silvio Castelli, a rich businessman and well-known member of the Naples Municipal Council. Valerio knew without looking that Silvio was watching him from his shiny Ferrari a block away, near the corner of Verdi and Brigida, as inconspicuous as a Ferrari can be, parked in public at night, yet liable to be recognized since it was also about a block away from Silvio's office in the Palazzo Municipio.

"Valerio," Silvio said sadly, "it's me."

Valerio slapped the phone shut, smiled at his friends, and strolled down the hill, his white Izod disappearing into the dark.

In the streetlight, the cherry-red Enzo gleamed like the polished armor of an enormous ant, and when the passenger door noiselessly arched open, as if to take Valerio under its wing, he slid into the small, luxurious cockpit next to the incongruous giant at the wheel. When he closed the door, sealing himself in the car, he could still smell the new-car smell of the carbon-fiber surfaces, as well as the new-clothes smell of Silvio's tailored Dolce e Gabbana and the fresh citrus and vetiver scent of his Armani Privé. Instead of shaking hands, Silvio clutched Valerio's thigh with the iron grip of a hawk. He squeezed him so hard, in fact, that the sensation was somewhere between the erogenous thrill of being touched in an intimate place and the dull pain of being crushed under a bear paw.

"Ciao, Bello," Silvio said, relaxing his hand. "How are you?"

Silvio was wearing sunglasses, a ridiculous attempt, Valerio knew, at being incognito, a red flag to any passerby.

"Fine," Valerio smiled gingerly, relieved of the ache. "And you?"

"Tired," Silvio sighed, "but restless. Missed you, my little horse. Thought I'd swing by."

When Valerio did not respond, Silvio faced forward, apparently mulling over something. He was much too big for a sports car, and Valerio wondered if he had paid the fortune for it because of the unusual way the doors opened, allowing him, in a sense, to fall into it. Also, since Silvio filled the interior, Valerio sensed that the car was somehow a robotic extension of him, a sleek "man machine," as in the ads for it, like a series of elaborate prosthetics attached to his arms and legs. The car was a misfit in another sense as well. Valerio thought of it as the kind of flashy car a wealthy, young playboy would drive. In other words, Silvio looked foolish in it, like the wretched married man he was in the midst of an extravagant mid-life crisis.

271

Likewise, Silvio's silk, pin-striped suit was a misfit too. Valerio admired it and thought of how good he would look in it, the kind of fun, trendy outfit a tall, skinny teenager should be wearing, not Silvio. On Silvio, as with the car, it looked silly. The glossy trousers were baggy enough to accommodate him, but the coat's long, narrow, satin lapels, the shirt's small collar, and the skinny, lambskin tie made him look, by comparison, even larger than he was, a huge, older, overweight man trying to look youthful and desirable.

When Silvio pushed the red start button, the various LEDs lit up, and he pulled onto Verdi, making his way methodically downhill toward the docks and the road toward the southeast along the harbor.

"Do the honors," he said, referring to the wine bottle on the floor.

Valerio opened the glove box and took out the corkscrew.

"A Sangiovese," Silvio said. "I know how you like an earthy Sangiovese."

Part of their ritual was to share a bottle, no glasses, and as they drove, they passed it back and forth.

"So," Valerio began. "What have you done for gay rights since I've seen you? What cutting-edge initiatives have you introduced to the council?"

He was partly joking, of course, egging Silvio on, an outspoken, homophobic, if hypocritical, champion of the conservatives on the board. On the other hand, Valerio was well acquainted with the kind of kinky scenario that turned Silvio on and eventually got him off. First, they would have to argue civilly, then heatedly, and so, to oblige him, Valerio never missed an opportunity to bring up leftist political issues. Gay politics, strangely enough, had become an integral part of Silvio's sexual fantasy. Valerio also wanted to enlighten Silvio about himself, and that was where they were, at the beginning of the argument. The question was: Was Silvio really aware of the stock scenes they acted out each time?

"None," Silvio sighed. He took a swig from the bottle and handed it to Valerio.

"No DiCo on the agenda?" Valerio asked, meaning civil unions, *de facto* partnerships. "Pensions, health insurance, hospital visitation." He sipped the strong, dry wine. "Graveside rights, inheritance." He corked the bottle and stuck it in his crotch so that it looked like an erection.

"How come a common street hustler like you is so knowledgeable about such controversial subjects?" Silvio asked somberly.

"I may be a hustler," Valerio replied, "but I'm not stupid. I can read. And I'm not common."

Silvio was a perverse father figure to him, and he knew that the man, like Father Dorato, loved him in his own warped way. A natural affection existed between them, a "bias of nature" as between Gloucester and Edgar in *King Lear*.

"I know, my lamb," Silvio said, taking off his shades. "Just kidding. You're actually hot stuff in this world of trade, the hottest, that is, I've ever had or heard of."

"Right," Valerio chuckled. "And a hot hotel clerk by day." When Valerio slouched lower in the seat, the tilted bottle stood up straight. "Back to my question. There are civil unions in the UK, Belgium, France, even Catholic Spain. I thought we were supposed to comply with EU standards."

"As you well know," Silvio began grimly, "the power structure is against the normalization of homosexuality: Casini, Berlusconi, the Vatican."

"And you?" Valerio asked.

"Berlusconi says it 'devalues the meaning of family.'"

"Benito?" Valerio joked.

"What?"

"Benito Berlusconi? The media dictator?"

"He attacked legislation to register with local authorities and receive rights: property, inheritance, employment. The Vatican says it would destroy the family, calls it 'the approval or legalization of evil.' Officially, the church, though, doesn't interfere."

"Ha," Valero scoffed. "If a legislator votes pro-gay, some Fascist bishop threatens him with excommunication. What nonsense," he smiled, impressed with the hum of the powerful car. "How do you destroy a family by wanting one? How do you destroy marriage by wanting to get married? How do you destroy traditional values by living according to them? Wanting something means you value it. As if gays are against family," he said to himself. "Just because we're not likely to have children doesn't mean we're against them. That's a conservative myth, mere propaganda. You don't agree with it, do you?"

"Quite honestly," Silvio began, "gay marriage seems like a mockery of the institution. I can just see some tacky transvestite and a burly leather number setting up house."

"Yeah," Valerio laughed, "and your little boy should see how well you suck my cock."

Silvio jerked his head around to face Valerio.

"What's his name?" Valerio asked himself. "Romano. Yes, Romano should see with what pleasure you swallow my delicious come."

Silvio faced forward, visibly relaxed, and sighed heavily. "You do have a sweet cock, Valerio, yes, and I do love sucking it. I miss it when I'm away, my little wolf. Not as much as your sweet ass, of course."

"Is it that you just can't imagine two men loving each other?" Valerio asked. "Loving each other so much they want to live together?"

"Strange sentiment from a rent boy."

"Well," Valerio insisted, "is it?"

"No," Silvio admitted, squeezing Valerio's thigh. "It's not that. You know it's not that."

"And I don't mean one of them setting the other one up in an apartment," Valerio snickered, "like a mistress."

Silvio caressed the neck of the bottle suggestively and began stroking it for Valerio's amusement. When Valerio grinned, Silvio uncorked it, took a sip, then corked it and slipped it into a pocket behind Valerio's seat.

"How unnatural you are," Silvio said, touching his forehead as if he had a headache. "I've been very generous with you."

"I know," Valerio smirked, cranking the window down, "and I'm sure you'll continue to be."

He leaned out, letting the hot wind whip his face till his cheeks felt flushed. The city lights had thinned out, and at the late hour, the shimmering pairs of headlights were as rare as dewdrops in the oppressive bay air. When he looked across the hood to the north, Vesuvius was as dark as the starless sky, a black stone weighing down everything.

He settled in his seat again and smelled the intensely aromatic smell of the long eucalyptus grove that, on his right, followed the road, a wind barrier of sorts, he figured. He was not sure how, but he could sense the sea beyond it, something about the dark sky and the way the trees were cropped at the same height as if nature were allowed only so much freedom near a beautiful, wide-open place that, as yet, could not be controlled by the prudery of people.

Silvio slowed to turn right at a big billboard with a big seagull, wings spread, painted in silver metallic paint. The banner across the bottom read: "Gabbiani d'Argento: Una Spiaggia Privata [Silver Gulls: A Private Beach]." He drove through a tunnel of trees to a glade where the road split around a ticket booth with a red and white barrier on each side. Silvio reached a remote control from the glove box, and when he clicked it, the thick, metal arm went up and, after they drove through, dropped behind them. They came out of the grove and turned left onto a long, paved parking lot bordering the beach. Sand filled cracks in it, swirled in small drifts across it, and, in the headlights, lit up white against the black asphalt. The headlights also lit up, in the distance, a couple of shacks: a concession stand and a storage shed.

Silvio pulled into a space facing the sea, and when he killed the motor and turned off the lights, a warm stillness closed in on them. Valerio could hear a soft surf, and the fact that they had the run of the beach, dark and isolated as it was, sent a wet thrill through his groin. He enjoyed the idea that, if that was what Silvio wanted, he could strip and swim and walk around nude on the sand.

"Yours?" Valerio asked, breathing the stuffy sea smell.

"Yes," Silvio said with a sad voice, a hand on the steering wheel, the other on Valerio's thigh. "Romano loves to come here."

On the beach, various objects like retinal images were fading to only the faintest impressions of themselves. Close to the car, the beach was spiked with big, folded umbrellas like birds of prey poised on sticks. They also reminded Valerio of so many cloaked, faceless, levitating nuns. In the dark, their deep, rich blue looked black. Wood and canvas chaise lounges were scattered here and there, some open, some on their sides, some folded and stacked on top of each other or leaning against the umbrella poles. The canvas was striped with blue, and the backs had big, blue pillows, but again, in the dark, the blue had dimmed to black. Then, as his eyes focused, he saw what appeared to be rows of skinny, frail frames painted in alternate bands of white and a faint color, which he assumed was red, like the arms at the ticket booth. They were frames for tents, the skeletal remains of a ruined holiday, but for him, they also brought other images to mind: abandoned market stalls, the brittle bones of giant fish, and the most childish, the imaginary crash site of a balsam airliner.

When Silvio's hand strayed to Valerio's crotch, Valerio said, "First, tell me what you think of the proposed anti-defamation law."

"What?"

"You heard me."

"What if I left you here and drove back to town?" Silvio asked, removing his hand.

"What if I let you?" Valerio asked, fingering the signature on the console plaque. "Besides, I can't think of anything I would enjoy more than spending the night here, curled up in one of those cozy lounge chairs. It's certainly warm enough."

"Guess you don't need the 300 Euros."

"Not any more than you'll miss spending them."

"You'll rim my ass," Silvio said, "but you won't kiss my ass. That's what I like about you, *amante mio*. [My love.] You're tough as a donkey."

"Well," Valerio said seductively, "if you want to ride this donkey tonight...."

"All right," Silvio conceded. "Hate speech. Uh, it's absurd to criminalize someone's opinion."

"Even when someone's opinion causes violence?"

"Mastella said he'd work for an anti-violence clause," Silvio said, meaning the Minister of Justice. "Besides, it's totalitarian, telling people how to think."

"And feel and act. What hypocrisy," Valerio said, unbuttoning and unzipping his jeans. "What's totalitarian is suppression of rights."

"Exactly," Silvio agreed. "We have freedom of speech. We can speak ill of Muslims, blacks, and gays if we want, even the children of gays."

"Silvio," Valerio laughed, surprised. To Valerio, Silvio had obviously detached himself from gays mentally, from his own sexual orientation. Didn't he realize he had just referred to Romano, his son?

"Four years in prison?" Silvio balked. "With no exemptions for religious groups? For priests? The Pope could be thrown in jail for anti-gay decrees."

"As he should be," Valerio said, lifting off the seat to shove down his jeans. "There's a direct link between the Pope's homophobia and gay bashing."

"And what would that be?" Silvio asked.

"He causes it," Valerio said, waving his dick around. "He may as well be beating gays to death with his crosier." He slapped his dick against his thigh to stress the point.

"If a priest says homosexuality is a sin, it's his right to say so, just as it's his right to speak out against pedophilia or incest."

Valerio thought of Father Dorato and laughed, "You just don't get it, do you?"

Silvio turned to him and said, "No, but you will."

Valerio pushed his thumbs into his pubic hair, making his erection stand. Then he smiled at Silvio shrewdly as if the gesture were more of a lewd, puerile way of sticking his tongue out at him. In any case, the taunt had the desired effect. In a few minutes, Valerio was nude, knees bent, elbows propped on the rear hood, butt cheeks pressed against the logo's rampant stallion, and Silvio – pants down, shirt open, tie slack – was on his knees in front of him.

"Heard about the swastikas in Piazza Bellini?" Valerio asked, casually fucking Silvio's mouth. "'La Napoli fascista non vi vuole,'" he said, quoting graffiti. The Naples *fascista* does not want you.

He was trying to work him up with their weird version of dirty talk, but gazing into the maze of eucalyptus, he was also immensely enjoying himself and the night, just being, and getting his cock sucked.

Silvio sat on his heels and spat the word, "Skinheads."

Valerio's depilated scrotum looked like big brook stones slung in a leather bag. Silvio moved one around with the tip of his tongue, then the other, and as he did, he reached up to palm Valerio's pecs, each about the size of a spread hand.

"What about that article in *Il Giornale*," Valerio asked, a hand on Silvio's shoulder, the other on a jet-like taillight, "the one about the Matteo boy? Sixteen, and his father almost beat him to death for being gay. Family values."

Silvio sat back again, and a small bottle of lubricant materialized from the dark.

"You don't know the details of the story," he said, lubricating Valerio's anus. "For all you know, he may have needed a good beating. He may have been a bad boy, a very bad boy, like you."

When he said the word *you*, he penetrated Valerio with his index finger, went down on him again, and began leisurely finger-fucking him. In response, Valerio drew a deep breath, grabbed Silvio's silk collar with both hands, and pulled Silvio's face against his groin as hard as he could.

"There were a hundred and fifty attacks against gays in Napoli last year, Silvio," Valerio said, warming to the deep, rhythmic strokes of Silvio's plump finger. "More than ever." He let go of the shirt, letting his hands ride on Silvio's neck. "And you know they weren't all reported."

Since Silvio, in fact, had no logical response for the statistic, he, instead, finger-fucked Valerio even harder with two, then three fingers, and when Valerio was apparently loose and juicy enough, Silvio began slowly stroking himself instead, getting himself hard enough to take him.

Valerio, on the other hand, was well acquainted with what was gathering strength near the license plate, what he thought of as the fat, glossy cherry of Silvio's dickhead. Silvio's priapic member was uncircumcised, like his, and slightly convex in the middle like the swollen column of a Greek temple. Exhilarated, Valerio knew instinctively that they had arrived at scene two in Silvio's erotic conflict-fantasy, the part in which Silvio would put on the condom and they would actually struggle physically.

When Silvio labored to get up, placing one foot under himself and grabbing the edge of the hood, Valerio shoved against his shoulders to hold him down, but he may as well have been trying to knock a Sumo wrestler off balance. Silvio rose above him, like an island rising from the sea, clutched his shoulders, and, with brute strength, forced him to turn around, bent over the car.

Valerio braced himself for what would have to be a talented minute or two of great, voluptuous pain before his ass, as it always did, would magically turn to a warm, bittersweet syrup, but as Silvio pushed into him slowly but surely, his huge hands holding him firmly in position, a strange thing happened, distracting Valerio for a moment. At that point, the sky cleared, and a dramatic, nearly full moon, bright as a searchlight, came out, coating the scene the bluish white of the wax on bayberry. The color of the sea changed subtly from a dull black to a gleaming black, the surface broken, like a hole in the water, by the blooming of the moon's reflection. Framing the view, about twenty-five feet offshore and about twenty-five feet apart, were a couple of piles topped with what looked like silver gulls, and farther out, some kind of oddly shaped, silver buoy was bobbing in place. The shore became luminous, a rumpled fabric flecked with little shadows. Three catamarans were beached near the water, and in the center of everything stood a tall pole with a little, wilted flag, black in the moonlight. The flag flattened into a flutter, and soon Valerio felt a fresh breeze blowing over him.

A particularly deep, uncomfortable thrust brought him back to the moment, and though he strained every muscle he could against Silvio, the big man kept slamming him, without restraint, against the car. Valerio's erection was prodding the logo, but when Silvio lifted him so that he was butt up, chest on the hood, his feet no longer touching the ground, it rubbed the name Ferrari to the point that, as Silvio kept punching his prostate, he oozed pre-come. From the rear, it looked as if Silvio were fucking the Ferrari, and when he mashed Valerio's face against the hood, Valerio rolled his head sideways to keep from breaking his nose, and his cheek, clean-shaven, smarted against the hot surface.

Silvio picked up the pace, leaned over Valerio, and, panting and grunting, gradually lowered himself onto him. Valerio tried to push up against him, but again the effort was like trying to dead lift an ox, and as Silvio's overwhelming size inevitably bore down on him, he collapsed, helpless, suppressed against the car. Now they had arrived at the third and most dangerous scene in the scenario, the one in which Valerio lay crushed beneath him, squirming and pleading, thrashing about like a fox in a net. Only then could Silvio come, as he did, wallowing on him in ecstatic waves of weight. Cock slick, Valerio knew, despite himself, he could not hold back.

"Silvio," Valerio gasped, squirting on the car, "I can't breathe. Silvio."

Over the years, Valerio had developed an inherent immunity to emotional and, to a great extent, physical pain. He knew how deer would roll in mud to keep insects away, and he had coated himself in cynicism in much the same way. Those uninitiated in the mysteries of life – what he considered real life, the sensual, passionate life – would never enter the cella of his heart. Silvio could fuck him all he wanted. He could even crush the life out of him if he wanted. He could not, however, crush the life out of his fierce will.

# # # # #

The next thing Valerio remembered was Silvio's chest hair, like sand paper, scratching his back as he lifted off him.

"You cut your hair," Silvio said, rubbing Valerio's head playfully.

"You noticed," Valerio quipped, standing unsteadily, trying to catch his breath.

Silvio peeled off the come-filled condom and tossed it away. Then he pulled up his underwear and pants and began fastening them.

"When are you going to let me – "

"Set me up in a nice apartment in the Vomero?" Valerio asked, interrupting him.

Then a strange thought entered his head: My god is Cupid, not Minerva. No matter what you do, I'll never love you, even if you, by some remote miracle, brought about gay rights in Italy.

"There are so many oranges on the tree," Silvio mused, buckling his belt. "Which one to eat? Yet I picked you. My little David."

"David?" Valerio asked, a hand on the car. "Oh, David." Then Valerio looked him straight in his sad eyes. "Ever thought of coming out and actually living with a young lover? Not me. Someone else."

"When the courts consider gay marriage," Silvio said, buttoning his shirt. "When public figures come out."

"Mieli says you should come out," Valerio said, referring to the leader of the 70's gay movement in Italy. "Dario Re and Giuseppe Archiletti are out," he added, referring to the Naples bank director and his accountant partner.

"Coming out would ruin me, and you know it," Silvio said, stepping around to the passenger door. He reached through the window and grabbed Valerio's clothes. "It would destroy my family, let alone my political career, even the slightest suspicion of...." He returned and set the clothes on the hood. "People still think gays are monsters who murder people to come. In the same basket with goat fuckers and corpse fuckers."

"Or so the Vatican would have you believe."

Slowly Valerio's breath came more easily.

"What would Italy be without the Vatican?" Silvio asked, poking his shirt in. "Atheist, secular, demoralized."

"Able to think clearly," Valerio countered, "to reason from facts."

"Save it for next time."

As Silvio adjusted his tie, Valerio, yet again, saw him for what he was, a bored, tragic failure of a man who, for any number of reasons, was deeply closeted and would always remain so.

When Valerio headed for the beach, Silvio asked, "Where are you going?"

"To wash up."

As Valerio stepped onto the sand, his prostate hummed, and his body sang with afterglow and the pleasant stress of actually taking such a large man. He strolled among the chaise lounges and umbrellas, past the flag pole, and into the cool, bluish surf, stopping about knee deep, where he crouched and splashed water into the cleft of his buttocks, cleaning it with his finger. Then he stood, shook the water off his hands, and gazed into the simmering expanse of sea and stars, every tiny, dream-like detail adding up to a consummate sparkling beauty mischievous, if not downright licentious, in the temporary privacy and freedom it offered.

When the wind whipped up, the silver gulls swiveled into it, facing southeast, paralleling the shore, and he realized that they were, in fact, weather vanes. Farther out, the oddly shaped, silver buoy hove to as well, and now he saw that it was a big, toy ship riding at anchor. He smiled at the whimsicality of the ship and gulls and, childlike, stood there, mesmerized, watching them bob and veer. Magical totems could not have had more of a vulnerary effect on him. His deepest wounds healed, at least for the evening. Then, over the sly whispers of the surf and breeze, came the bass voice of Silvio calling him.

Chapter 38: The Vortex

Tyler started dropping by the Vortex Bar and Grill for a burger around five o'clock on Monday and Wednesday before driving down Euclid Avenue to the community center, where he was teaching a continuing-education creative-writing class. The Vortex was a gray and red building with red awnings, the façade a giant skull with big eyes with fanatical red and black spirals, the door a pair of bones and a row of teeth. Above the teeth, the nasal cavities drooped like melted holes. As he approached the "mouth," he smelled the delicious odor of greasy burgers grilling.

Inside, the smell changed to that of fresh sandwiches, and as he navigated the room, a surf of incessant voices broke over him with Candye Kane's "Who Do You Love?" playing in the background. The crowd was a sampling of what he considered the sexually confused Bohemian types kinking up the area. He thought of them as "uncreated," a term he had picked up from reading D. H. Lawrence. And here, the uncreated were divided into three areas. A skeleton riding a motorcycle hung over the pony wall between the bar and restaurant, and in the restaurant, a red-and-black, wrought-iron railing with skulls set off a pavilion of sorts with glossy white columns and a cornice strung with red Christmas lights. The skulls glowed red inside, and a row of beer cans ran along the top of the cornice, punctuated, like an exclamation point, with a huge carving knife. The pavilion, he noticed, created a perception problem. It was inside, but looked outside.

Tyler did not see a table available. Then he spotted a squat Latino busboy clearing one, went over, and stood near it. When the table was ready, he took off his leather jacket and draped it across the back of a chair, but when he grabbed the chair to pull it out, it was heavier than he thought, and he scraped it with a screak across the floor. He sat and scanned the table's worn surface, a glass lantern, a plastic basket of condiments.

When he looked up, what he was seeing was as cluttered as what he was hearing. It did, in fact, look like the surreal vortex of a tornado, a freeze-frame explosion of hundreds of objects stuck to the walls and suspended at various heights from the dark beams of the ceiling. But was there a theme, he wondered, a unifying central idea behind it, such an overwhelming visual experience? Certainly, a lot of objects had to do with the dead, the taxidermy, for example, a stuffed fox, a mounted fish, a deer hoof, a dusty pheasant, a boar's head, a bat, a gull. If you looked long enough, he realized, you saw several explicit death symbols: a black flag with a skull, a skeleton standing on a shelf over the bar, a flying skeleton with wings, another skeleton flying with its hands straight out like Superman. The skeletons emerged from the details the way someone suddenly sees the hidden figures in a picture-puzzle game.

The rest of the objects seemed chaotic, everything from a big Gulf Oil sign to a framed print of Andrew Wyeth's *Black Water* – hubcaps, model airplanes, a tuba, a knight's helmet, even a big, gold, Styrofoam eagle – all lit or silhouetted from various angles by neon signs, industrial pendants, an old-fashioned streetlight, a revolving barber pole, a flashing green "Restroom" sign. There was no unifying principle behind it. It was irrational, he joked, like life. Behind the chaos of life lies death, he concluded, a philosophy which, he guessed, fit the barbarous biker image the place affected. He didn't know. Despite everything, he was still working on a more optimistic outlook. For instance, he hadn't ruined his life for revenge.

Across the room, a waiter started to hustle over, but a waitress calmly touched his arm, said something to him, and strolled over, moving much more slowly than the rest of the staff buzzing around like bees. As she approached, she stared at Tyler seductively, her expression tough, yet hurt, mentally burnt out for someone as young as she was. If she were a flower, he thought, she was already wilted and browning, for whatever reason. Past bloom.

Part of her appearance was, to Tyler, standard lesbian fare: loose, faded jeans with white, threadbare patches, a blueberry-blue T-shirt, and old, soft Keds tennis shoes. Her belt was an ammunition belt. He assumed it wasn't real. Her narrow, pale face set off her pink lips, and her flat ears made her face look even more narrow. But it was her somber accessories that defined her, Tyler thought. They were the clues to what possibly made her unique. On the front of her shirt was an angel with huge, drooping wings and a hand to her brow as if to lament, "Woe is me." In her other hand the angel was holding a big circle with the letter *A*. The waitress was also wearing a thong with a shark's tooth around her neck, a big piece of leather on her left wrist, and string macramé with a snake pattern on her right. The clincher, Tyler thought, was the little feather fishing fly through her right earlobe. Clincher, that is, besides the horny gaze.

"How ah ya?" the waitress asked in dialect.

"Fine, and you?"

"OK." She stood next to Tyler an inch too close for a second too long, handed him a menu, and set the utensils on the table. Then she took an order pad and pen out of her black apron. "So what may I do ya fah?" she asked, crouching beside him submissively.

She had a surprising cherry odor, and Tyler could smell the peppermint on her breath.

"I'm hungry," Tyler announced.

Again, she groped him with her eyes. Me too, they seemed to say, staring at him from under thick, black brows. Me too. And Tyler, in turn, looked around inside her, so to speak, with his uncanny knack for sizing up a person, a personal curse that was, as it turned out, a blessing for a writer. What he saw wasn't much, he decided, and what little there was was as subtle as a snowflake, the first snowflake of an eminent storm.

"Ah you?" she asked provocatively. "Fah what?"

"Food," Tyler chuckled. "My usual, the Steakhouse Burger. Extra 'shrooms."

"Shuah ya wouldn't like ta try somethin' new?"

What feral eyes, Tyler thought, the eyes of a fawn, only bleary. He thought she was tired, the reason, as he thought of it, she was so cow slow. Then he recognized the look. She was "on something."

"Uh, no," Tyler smirked. "Just a big, juicy, mouth-watering piece of meat I can sink my teeth in."

"Side?" she asked, jotting down the order.

"Potato salad," he said, amused, friendly. "What's your name?"

"Erin," she replied, glancing up. "E.R.I.N. Yoahs?"

"Tyler."

"Tyla," she said, translating the name into her dialect.

"Your accent," he said, handing her the menu. "You have a lovely accent, Erin." When Erin looked down left, Tyler added, "No, I mean it. I like it. Nothing to be embarrassed about."

"Thanks," she said. "Guess wheah I'm from."

"Well, it ain't Missouri," he joked. "Up east?"

Erin closed her eyes briefly, then said, "New Hampshah. Yeah, in New Hampshah we drive a cah fah."

"Not a Mainah?" he asked.

She stood slowly, eyes wide. "Somethin' to drink?"

"Watah," he said, teasing her. "Just watah."

She smiled vaguely, pirouetted slowly, and strolled off. As she walked away, Tyler read the back of her T-shirt: "Stupidity should be painful."

The utensils were wrapped in a black napkin, and while he was waiting, Tyler unwrapped them and began unconsciously turning the knife over and over. Then he leaned back in the chair, knees spread, hands clasped behind head, and tried to see the tree in the forest, that is, to focus on a specific detail in the wreckage raining down on the room: a tray, sign, or mirror floating mid-air, a cooler here, a telescope there, a toaster, a giant plastic beer bottle, a fan, even a wolf trap.

In a few minutes, Erin strolled over as if afraid she would drop something. She carefully set down the glass of water and the platter with the huge burger and dish of potato salad.

"Need anythin'?" she asked, assuming her suggestive tone.

"No," Tyler said. "Looks good."

She stood there, gazing at him, and though Tyler knew better, he could not help himself, carried along by the irresistible current of his morbid curiosity. The sluggish girl intrigued him as a writer. He simply had to know more about her.

"So," he began, searching for something to ask. "How long you been here? In Atlanta?"

She glanced right, stirring her hair with her finger. Her hair was Goth, spiky with green highlights.

"Couple of months," she said.

"Why here?"

"Uh," she hesitated. "I just needed a place to stahrt ovah. Could've been any place."

"Really. What are your plans?"

"Plans?" she mused, rubbing her forearm as if it were sore. "Don't have any."

"No?"

"Guess the plans'll hahv ta come ta me." She stared at Tyler, licked her bottom lip, and with her finger tapped a beat on the edge of the table as if trying to summon her courage. "Whaht about you? Whaht do you do? Seen ya befoah. Mondays an' Wednesdays, right?"

"I teach in the community center down Euclid."

"Teach whaht?"

"Creative writing."

Erin nodded, her gaze fixed on the floor, then glanced at him tentatively.

"Creative writin'," she repeated. "I'd like to write."

"Oh, yeah."

"Whaht time's the clahss?"

"It's at seven, but it started a month ago."

"Could I sit in?"

"Well," Tyler paused, cagey, leaning back, "it's really not up to me. You usually have to pay a fee and register."

"How much?"

"$120," he said. "Erin, what other reason do you have for wanting to join this class?"

She squinched her face in an indecisive, warped expression.

"Well," she began, scratching her neck with her index finger, "maybe I could meet people. I don't hahv any friends."

"No friends," Tyler puzzled. "Someone as – " he wavered. "Accessible as you."

"Accessible?"

"Easy to get to know."

"I like to think of myself like thaht, but most men leave me flaht."

"Not me?"

Erin's response was the raw stare.

"Hmmm," he hummed.

Can't meet people at the Vortex? He balked at the idea. The placed served food, but the liquid social aspect of it took care of a lot of other basic needs as well. If Erin wanted in, figuratively, she had failed to give the correct password. Tyler could be kind and open-minded about her, he knew, but was suspicious of "her dark motives," as he thought of them, her strange behavior, her fumbling attempt at sultry seduction. On the other hand, finding out what she was up to would be an adventure, the kind of reckless mind-quest appealing to his analytical nature.

At that point, however, she suggested, "Bettah let ya get to thaht while it's hot. Enjoy yah food."

"Thanks."

About halfway through the meal, she glided over and asked, "Got everythin'?"

"I'm fine," Tyler chuckled.

"How is it?"

"Delicious, filling. Whatever the secret ingredient is in the potato salad, it's good."

"Good."

"Wicked good," he joked. "Tell me."

"Yeah?"

"What's that tooth on your neck?"

"It's a shahk's tooth," she said, touching it. "I cahl it my sweet tooth 'cahs I like chocolate so much."

"Really," he brooded. "OK. I'll remember that."

Tyler noticed that Erin noticed the burly, bearded man watching her. The man had thick, wavy hair and was staring at Erin as if irritated with her.

"The manajah," she explained. "I don't move fast enough, 'e says."

When Tyler glanced at the man, he glanced at Tyler, then walked off.

"He makes me work the late shift on weekends," she added. "Since I'm new, 'e says. I'll get even with him."

"Get even?" Tyler asked. "Would that make you happy?"

"Actually," she hesitated, staring at him coldly, "yeah."

"Ignore him," he advised. "You'll get fired."

"I'll let you eat."

When Tyler was finished eating, Erin was not in sight, so he sat back and waited, noticing a yellow pedal cab hanging from the ceiling. The cab reminded him of the red fire engine he pedaled as a kid. Somewhere there was a photograph of him and Jane Fredericks, the girl who lived next door, with him in the fire engine and her on a tricycle in his driveway. How innocent they were, he thought. Desire and disappointment years away.

When Erin appeared, Tyler raised a finger, and she strolled over.

"Would ya like dessert?" she asked. "Somethin' sweet?"

"Like what?"

"Well, theah's stuff on the menu and stuff that's not. I can be sweet."

Again, she gazed at him with what he considered an emotionally broke person's hapless look.

"You're a mess," he smiled. "No, I'm full. How 'bout the check?"

He knew that he didn't have the proper feelings for hooking up with her, mainly because of the age difference, he guessed about ten years. To him, she was nothing more than a cute curiosity, a possible trick. Still, Erin's difference did have its appeal: the interesting accent, her stab at being sensual and unconventional. Besides, he was already caught in some perverse psychological eddy. It was futile to swim against it. All he could do was float and flounder forward inevitably in a huge magnetic curve toward the bottom of something he knew would not end well. He had grown up in Baton Rouge, and driving over the Mississippi River bridge or standing on the levee, he had seen big, powerful whirlpools swirling like galaxies along the riverbank. Anyone trapped in one had drowned.

Erin left the check in a black-leather check presenter, glanced at Tyler gloomily, and walked off. When Tyler opened the folder, he noticed that she had written something on the customer's copy: *flexible*. He laughed, glanced at her across the room, and left fifteen dollars, more than twice enough for the tip. When she returned, he slid the folder over to her, but before he could remove his hand, she laid her hand on his and stared at him again. He returned the stare, but withdrew his hand.

"OK," he smiled cautiously.

"I get off at midnight."

"Get off?" he joked.

"Yeah," she said, squinting as if in glare. "How 'bout you? Wanna get off?"

"Uh...."

"Need a written invitation?"

"Think I just got one."

"I noticed you weren't wearin' a ring, and I thought maybe…."

Tyler still missed his wedding ring in a physical sense, sensing something odd about his ring finger at times and, for a split second, thinking, "My ring's missing," then remembering. He missed it at times the same way he missed a romantic relationship.

"Live around heah?" she asked. When Tyler failed to answer, there was an awkward pause. "I live aht the Hemlock. Right behind heah. You cahn throw a rock an' hit it. Gotta go through the gate at the pahking lot in bahk."

"Erin, you're about as subtle as a hash pipe."

"Shuah," she said with an uncertain smile. Even she seemed amused by her own ineptitude. "I'd give you my numbah, but I don't hahv a phone. You'd hahv to cahl me heah." She gazed at him. "You hahv a numbah?"

"Yeah, I have a number."

"May I hahv it?"

"Let's play it this way," he suggested. "I'm here Mondays and Wednesdays at the same time. I'll see you Wednesday. I'll ask for your table."

"OK," she said, swaying in slow motion.

"We'll exchange business cards then," he joked.

"Man," she blurted, "I'm all lathered up with your lahk of interest."

"That's what I'm known for."

She looked at him as if he had just confirmed something about himself.

"Erin!" the manager called.

Chapter 39: A Long Day's Journey into Night

On Saturday, Tyler, Josh, Phil, and Billie took a ferry to Capri, which, as they bounded west along the coast, rose out of the sea gradually like a big, pale-blue iceberg. The ferry docked at the Marina Grande, but when Josh tried to get a cab to Anacapri, the driver insisted on taking them on a tour. Only when Josh approached the second driver in line, did the first consent to drive them.

On the way, Josh kept saying, "Oh, my god," as the narrow, skewed road kept ascending, cutting back on itself, and rounding corners with spectacular views.

When they arrived in Piazza Vittoria, Josh left everyone to buy tickets for the *seggiovia* (the chairlift) to the top of Monte Solaro, the highest point on the island.

Billie had no idea what he was up to, and when she stepped around a corner into the station, no sooner had she said, "I'm not sure I want to – " than the chair scooped her up, the attendant snapped her in, and she lifted into the air.

Phil, Tyler, and Josh got on and soon were floating over trees and bushes up to the top of the mountain as if up to the sun. The ride took about fifteen minutes, and when they arrived, they strolled around and took in the endless views: the Bay of Naples, Mt. Vesuvius, the Apennines, the mountains of Calabria, and far below, white as icebergs, the three massive rocks of the Faraglioni. Sheer cliffs dotted with vegetation dropped 1,900 feet to the water, and from that height Tyler could see only the wakes of motorboats, not the boats themselves. He was high above everything literally, but also in another sense, the way he'd felt when he and Josh had first entered the *suite nuziale*: safe, proud, carefree, uninhibited, buoyant.

Colorful deck chairs surrounded small tables with blue cloths on the terrace of the café, and after the stroll, the four settled around a table in the sun. When a waitress came, they ordered cappuccinos, and as they waited, Josh mentioned some of the tourist sites on the island, first Villa Jovis, one of the many villas of Tiberius.

"Gay," he pointed out.

Next he mentioned Villa San Michele built by Axel Munthe, a Swedish physician.

"Gay?" Tyler asked, sprawled in his chair.

"Gay," Josh smiled.

It contained sculptures from Tiberius' villas on the island, and Oscar Wilde and D. H. Lawrence had stayed there. Josh also mentioned the Blue Grotto and the Faro (the lighthouse).

"Good for rosy sunsets," he said.

The waitress returned with a tray and set out the coffees. Tyler paid her, and since a light breeze was blowing, Phil pulled a rough-looking cigar from his shirt pocket, a Toscano Classico, lit up, and puffed on it, occasionally tapping the ashes into the clear, blue ashtray on the table.

"Why don't you take a picture of Tyler next to that amphora over there?" Billie suggested to Josh. "You don't have a picture of him, do you?"

"As a matter of fact," he said, "I do."

"You do?" Tyler asked. "When you take it?"

"In the Archeological Museum when you weren't looking," Josh admitted. "You were standing near the Farnese *Bull*."

"You little spy," Tyler laughed. "That was before I even knew you."

Tyler thought of the cliché of a snapshot as a moment frozen in time. He also thought of their moment there relaxed on the mountaintop as a moment out of time, but in a good way, not detached, as if the four of them could go on forever. Everything was OK, he told himself. The sunny interlude was probably what it was: a coffee klatch with friends. No irony.

The three had adopted him the way Billie had adopted Josh. Phil was an intelligent and interested father figure as opposed to Tyler's mythical father and his adoptive father, who was there just physically. Billie was a downright loving, if guarded, mother figure as opposed to Tyler's biological mother, a coarse woman muddled with ignorance and primitive superstitions. He had looked her up and visited her, but once was enough to know that being around her wasn't good for him. Likewise, his adoptive mother was about as sane as Mary in *Long Day's Journey into Night*, a vintage Eugene O'Neill character trapped eternally in a super-neurotic drama to which he was merely an audience member. Josh, on the other hand, was playing multiple roles. For the few days Tyler had known him, he was a good friend, a loyal brother, and the kind, attentive, and sensually uninhibited lover, male or female, Tyler had always wanted, even, in some sense, since Josh was younger, the son he never had.

"We should make a pack to come back here a year from now," he proposed.

"Fine with me," Josh agreed.

"Me too," Billie said.

After the coffees, they rode the *seggiovia* down to the piazza, had lunch at a sidewalk café, and caught a cab back down to Capri, where they split up and shopped for an hour. When they reunited, the funicular down to the marina and the marina itself were so crowded with tourists that Josh knew that getting to, in, and back from the Blue Grotto would be a bobbing, seasick Tourist Hell. He recommended they hop the next ferry back to Amalfi, and soon they were bounding east along the coast. Phil and Billie took seats on the upper deck. Tyler and Josh, shoulder to shoulder, rested on the railing on the lower, gazing at the waves. Tyler wondered how he would describe the color if he wrote about it, perhaps bright sapphire.

"Now I know where the Italian love for blue and yellow comes from," Josh said. He stared at the water as if he could actually see into its depths.

Tyler stared at it too, then glanced at Josh.

"Yellow?"

"The light on the water," Josh explained.

Tyler studied the swells rolling past. Then his face lit up. Once he saw it, it was obvious: a subtle fiery sunshine flickering on the surface.

"Oh, yeah," he exclaimed. "Now I see it. I would've never noticed it if you hadn't pointed it out."

"Well," Josh said, nudging him, "sometimes the obvious has to be pointed out."

Then something strange happened. When Josh touched Tyler's hand, Tyler glanced at the blue veins on the back of Josh's hand, then where he pointed with his other hand. Ahead, off port several yards, a patch of water turned such a radiant gold that Tyler halfway expected a mermaid to leap out of it. He squinted toward a cliff house with a molten-gold window.

"Sunlight reflected off that window up there," he remarked.

He didn't know what his train of thought was, but the miraculous sun in the water reminded him of the eclipsed moon off Maine.

"Eet's a meeracle!" Josh joked, imitating the guide at the Grotta Smeralda.

#

That night, the four had dinner at Trattoria da Boccaccio in a small square off the main one in Amalfi. The men were dressed in slacks and short-sleeved shirts, but since they were going to a nightclub later, Billie had put on a fun outfit: a red peasant skirt, a girly lace blouse, and cork wedge sandals. She had also put on her "party face" with mascara, eyeliner, eye shadow which she called vervain blue, and shiny scarlet lipstick. Three ordered pasta – ravioli, *scialatielli*, and linguine – but Phil ordered Caporalessa, a baked dish with cheese, tomatoes, and eggplant. He also ordered a bottle of Taurasi, a red. For dessert, the four split two orders of Delizia al Limone, a sponge cake filled and topped with lemon custard. The cakes were made with limoncello and peels and looked like breasts with perky nipples of cream.

"What a feast," Tyler said, laying his fork down.

"What a life," Billie said, touching her lips with her napkin. "And we're enjoying it, this delicious meal, this wonderful wine, the pleasant companionship we've discovered in each other."

"Reminds me of a quote from Homer," Tyler remarked. He held the table, tilted back in his chair, and glanced toward a sky washed out by the pink glow of the streetlight. "Well, a modern version would go something like this." Then he began reciting –

I tell you, friends. There's nothing better in life
than sitting at a feast in summer
and listening to a poet sing
while a waiter brings the wine and fills your glass.

"What else?" Billie asked.

Tyler took her question to mean what else better than what they were enjoying.

"It's summer," Phil said, gesturing. "We have food and wine. Too bad we have no poet singing."

"I just recited for you, didn't I?" Tyler asked, righting his chair.

"Oh, yes," Phil admitted. "You're the poet."

"You *are* going to Rome with us tomorrow," Billie asked, fondling her necklace. "He is, isn't he?" she asked, turning to Josh.

When Tyler glanced at Josh, he looked, Tyler thought, happy as a baby with a new toy. He guessed he was the toy and knew he could take it away. Earlier, when Josh had asked him about Rome, he'd said yes. Still, he didn't know Josh, and Josh certainly didn't know him, a renegade chased by the Furies. Had he evaded their violence by coming here? Was he protected from them by the good will of such apparently well-meaning people?

"Good question," Tyler smiled. "Let me think about it."

When everyone looked at him, he could see the emotional rope that linked them like mountain climbers. Phil was attached to Billie, Billie to Josh, and Josh to him. Did he want to cut them free or move on with them – or should he say *up*? – scaling the mountain, metaphorically speaking? Of course, in this case, the mountain was more a Solaro than an Everest.

"You look like the cat that swallowed the canary," Phil said.

"And why would I spit out such a delicious biiiiiird?" Tyler purred.

"He's going," Josh laughed. "Why would he give up such a good thing?"

Right, Tyler thought. Josh's sweet mouth, Billie's blessing, and, more importantly, his secret enjoyment in letting himself feel a certain euphoric tenderness for Josh, the first person he'd felt anything for in a long time.

# # # # #

Club Europa was a nightclub in a cave deep in a cliff over the sea. It reminded Tyler of the uterine *suite nuziale*. A disc jockey was set up on stage in an alcove set off with a string of white lights, and the arched walls, like a megaphone, funneled the resonant music toward the terrace and sea. The bar faced a dance floor with large Lucite circles in it, like sinkholes, through which guests could see the grotto below with its stalactites, stalagmites, and churning, iridescent water. Because the circles were lit with marine blues and greens, they looked like giant sapphires and emeralds embedded in the floor.

Phil and Billie had insisted that Josh and Tyler go by themselves, but Josh wanted them to see it, though he never intended to stay long. He knew that clubs in Italy opened too late for them and that it would be too loud for them, and, there, he also remembered, as Phil had told him, that their son had had a stroke in a club. Billie, however, seemed at ease there, even serene, and since they were early, they found a relatively quiet table on the terrace, one with a spectacular view of a bright moon suspended over a sparkling sheet of moonlight on the sea.

When a waiter came, everyone was taking so long to decide what to drink that Phil said, "Hell, let's all have Campari. Four Camparis and soda, please."

They drank on the terrace for a while, but when Tyler heard the disco beat and Goth chords of Poni Hoax's "Budapest," he grabbed Josh's hand and pulled him toward the dance floor. Josh took Billie's hand and Billie Phil's, and they wound, hand in hand, toward the middle of the crowd. At first, the men all seemed to be dancing with Billie. Then the two couples paired up, but when Billie let her guard down and started acting silly, as Tyler thought of it, the others followed suit. She tiptoed behind Phil, fingers arched like Nosferatu, and soon the four looked as if they were stalking each other in a circle. She changed direction, buried her face in the crook of her arm, and peered over her elbow at Josh the way Bela Lugosi peers over his cape in *Dracula*. When the music struck a number of harsh, minor chords, she opened her mouth as if showing her fangs and bounced her head to the beat. Tyler thought she was making fun of the music – the ominous voice, the staccato violins – but when she finally smiled, he knew she was having a good time.

The music ended with a cymbal crash, then segued to The Rapture's "Whoo! Alright-Yeah...Uh-Huh," a relaxed, funky song, to which everyone tried to dance as "cool" as possible. Billie rolled her fists as if showing off her muscles. In response, Josh shook his index fingers at her as if scolding her. She locked eyes with Phil and shimmied, shaking her breasts. When he shook

293

his hips, she moved close and groped him. She danced around Tyler, caressing his face, then Josh, who took her hand and twirled her a few times. She put her arms over Josh's and Phil's shoulders, and when Josh put his arm over Tyler's, Tyler put his over Phil's, forming a circle rotating clockwise, then counterclockwise.

"We're a four-leaf clover," Billie announced over the music. "Lucky."

"That we are," Phil agreed, and everyone started jumping in place like excited kids.

Then, for some strange reason, the DJ played Boris's "Farewell," what Tyler thought of as dreamy, psychedelic space music. Some couples slow-danced. Some drifted off the floor, but when Billie started melodramatically waltzing with Phil, Tyler took Josh in his arms and began waltzing. When Billie switched partners, dancing with Josh, Tyler waltzed with Phil.

"If I didn't know better," Phil remarked, "I'd think you're the gay one."

"You're dancing with a man, Phil."

"Right."

When Billie switched to Tyler, Josh and Phil waltzed. Then she swirled off on her own, swimming among them in a kind of ballet burlesque. She pointed her toe to the right, then ahead, then, with the other foot, pointed her toe to the left, then ahead. When she struck an arabesque, Josh held her foot, Phil her hand, and Tyler performed a couple of sautés behind her in a comic *pas de quatre*. Then they did what Tyler thought of as a hand dance. Everyone stood in place and copied Billie's moves as she stretched her arms, hands limp, toward the ceiling in various poses.

Then she called, "Four-leaf clover," gesturing for them to form a circle again, in which they slow-danced for the rest of the song, gazing at each other shrewdly, as if they knew something no one else knew, then with their eyes closed, resting on each other as if tired, yet happy. The music kept hypnotically repeating two notes in what Tyler considered the musical equivalent of a drug rush, one long, ecstatic cymbal crash of well-being. He felt as if he were about to erupt in some sense, to break through some last shell of sober staidness. He likened the feeling to wanting to sing. He just didn't know what song.

When the music ended, everyone opened their eyes, and Billie declared, "Well, I'm deaf now."

As she and Phil turned away, Josh eyed Tyler and made a subtle gesture as if throwing a kiss with two fingers.

Tyler understood that Josh wanted a puff, and when Tyler winked, Josh shouted, "Mom! Going to the restroom. Meet you on the terrace."

"You mean to call her that?" Tyler asked.

"What?"

As soon as they opened the door, the restroom smelled of lemon-verbena soap. The floors were stone, but the walls were stucco with a cardinal-red lime wash as if they had stepped inside some large internal organ. The red color made the shiny porcelain toilets and basins pop. When a stall became available, they stepped inside and locked the door. Josh took out the half joint, Bic, and a metal clip he got from the hotel office, the kind used to bind a stack of paper. He lit up and, as they traded hits, tried to make out the pentimento of snarled graffiti on the wall.

"Scivolare il chiavistello nel foro," he enunciated, flushed from dancing. "Something like *Slide the bolt in the hole.*"

"To the point," Tyler said.

"I gay sono piu divertenti," Josh read. "Either *Gays are funnier* or *Gays are more fun.*"

"Fun," Tyler said as if he knew.

"Oh, this one's easy," Josh laughed. "Maria é una zoccola. Mary's a slut."

"Could've told you that," Tyler joked.

When they had smoked the roach down to a butt, Josh stubbed it out on his watch crystal and swallowed it, and when they returned to the dance floor, Beirut's "Postcards from Italy" was playing, and they stood on the side and watched the crowd. Tyler liked the campy ukulele and trumpets, the sexy young male voice. He guessed it was the Campari and pot, but, to him, the crowd was a coven of "beautiful people" wallowing in some wild Dionysian rite, everyone laughing and swaying sensually, swept with colors, spangled with light.

When Junior Boys' "In the Morning" came on, he and Josh slipped into the crowd and danced slowly and calmly, perfectly in sync as a mirror image. He was so euphoric, in fact, he felt as if he were dancing on air. A sublime wave washed over him, and his heart became, as it felt to him, a small sun blazing with bliss.

"Manic high," Josh yelled. Tyler did not know why.

Josh was so handsome and affectionate, he thought. Then he thought of Miranda's line from *The Tempest*:

How beauteous mankind is! Oh, brave new world,
That has such people in 't!

Chapter 40: A Cliffhanger

When Tyler and Josh got back to their room that night, the reality of the situation finally hit Tyler: he'd decided to stick with Josh. He was going with him and the Trees to Rome tomorrow. Manifest Destiny, he joked to himself. He'd seized what he needed and made him his own. Or was it the other way around?

"Based on what I know so far," Josh said as they went to bed, "which admittedly isn't much, I could be perfectly content with you. Unless," he added, "some horrible truth comes out."

"Horrible truth," Tyler repeated, turning off the lamp. "My conscience, I'm afraid, is about as cluttered as a – as a – "

"Bulletin board," Josh suggested. They lay there, staring at the ceiling. Then Josh asked, "What are you talking about?"

"What if I told you that, while trying to kill me, my ex-wife was killed by a shark and my younger daughter drowned, that my older daughter is in a mental institution, and that a friend of hers tried to poison me with mushrooms? What if I told you all that?"

"I'd say you have a vivid imagination."

"You don't believe me."

"No."

"Don't say I didn't warn you." Tyler thought, then broke into a smile. "What if I told you, instead, that they tore me to pieces in a Bacchic frenzy, but, the very next spring, I came back to life?"

"Now that I believe," Josh chuckled.

Josh like a current had come along and was carrying him off to Rome, quite a long way from the Vortex in Atlanta, the neighborhood bar and grill where another irresistible current had drawn him rapidly into a deep, disastrous whirlpool. Or put another way, Tyler himself was no longer a slack tide, the "standing water" Sebastian mentions in *The Tempest*. Not only had his sexual scales dipped toward gay. He'd also selected a partner, fresh as their comfortable rapport was. The romantic moon was not eclipsed, but full.

# # # # #

Tyler dreamed about the Temple of Athena again. Again, it was a bright summer day. Only this time, he had horns and was walking nude at the end of a long procession winding through a field. Phil and Billie, to either side, were leading him with a rope looped around his neck. They were behind a row of chariots with warriors which, as it neared the temple, diverged with one chariot slowly turning to the right, the next to the left, eventually parting to reveal Josh standing over an altar scattered with variously colored rose petals. He was wearing a purple chiton and gold cape, and around him musicians were playing, singers singing, and dancers dancing. When he lifted a chalice, a hush fell on the crowd, Phil and Billie removed the rope, and Tyler hopped onto the altar and, with Josh directly behind him, sat smiling at everyone. With his left hand, Josh tilted Tyler's head back. With his right, he reached around Tyler's neck, touching his throat with the tip of a knife. When Tyler heard a baby crying in the distance, his heart filled with an incredibly joyous sense of love.

# # # # #

When Tyler woke, he noticed that Josh was not in bed and glanced around the shadowy room. There was no sign of him, only the tropical sound of the surf, the liquid dance of the ghostly sheers.

When he stepped onto the terrace, a damp, salt wind was whipping up the night, and Josh, nude, was leaning on his elbows on the railing, watching the surf. He was not sure how Josh became aware of him, but Josh slowly glanced at him over his shoulder, then out to sea. Tyler paused to admire him, his very own Ganymede waiting for him there in such a provocative pose, the right side of his body lit with moonlight, the left dark. A guard keeping watch on a Saracen tower would've looked like him, Tyler thought, that is, if he were keeping watch nude and, as Tyler finally noticed, wearing a wreath of bougainvillea tied at the back. Tyler strolled to him, put his hands on Josh's hips, and pressed against him, Tyler's erection caressed by the soft crease in Josh's pale buttocks. Like a hotdog, Tyler thought.

At first, he simply held the position, enjoying the exciting sight of him slumped over, submissive, resting his forehead on his forearm on the railing. Josh's waist flared to his shoulders, and his blond hair and the wreath's papery bracts fidgeted in the breeze. Tyler began bumping him playfully, enjoying the sweet pleasure the bumps spread though his body. When he bumped him hard a few times as a joke, Josh rested his chin on his arm.

"Let's not go over the railing," he laughed.

Over the railing, Tyler thought. He thought of Phil and Billie's son going over the cliff in California, and the image gave him an idea. He swung a leg over the railing, straddled it, and swung his other leg over, poised over the cliff with his feet braced against the terrace.

Josh gasped, wide eyed, grabbed Tyler's arms, and blurted, "Tyler, what the hell are you doing?" When Tyler only smiled at him, Josh said, "Get back over here."

Tyler looked down at the rocks and water, a view which sent an electric surge through his nerves. The wind was stirring up the waves, working them into a lather of surf.

"I'm testing you," he said, facing him.

"What?"

"Have to know if you're one of Linda's agents."

"Linda?" Josh cried. "Who's Linda?"

"My daughter," Tyler said, his face set in remorse. "Have to know I can trust you."

"Have you lost your mind?" Josh asked. "Of course, you can trust me. Get back over here. Now!"

"A favor first," Tyler said.

"What!"

"If you do what I say, I'll climb back over. OK?"

Josh stared at him in disbelief: "OK, OK, OK!"

"Hold my right wrist."

Josh grabbed Tyler's wrist.

"Both hands."

Josh grabbed Tyler's forearm with his other hand, then looked at him as if for directions.

"I'm going to let go with my left hand," Tyler said. "Now."

When he did, he swung out from the railing, his weight pulling hard on his grip. When he looked down, a big wave was working itself up to a roaring crash, and when it broke, the cliff shivered, and Tyler could feel the cool mist swirling up and moistening him.

"I'm going to let go of the railing," he said.

"Tyler, please," Josh begged. "Don't know if I'm strong enough."

"The only thing that's holding me up is you. Understand?"

Josh leaned back and placed a foot on the base of the railing: "I won't let go."

"Ready?"

Josh nodded.

When Tyler said, "Here goes," Josh's fingers dug into Tyler's arm, and Tyler let go, leaning back even more. "I'm going to count to three," he explained, "so if you're one of Linda's friends, here's your chance. You can say it was a suicide. No one'll know. Say it was suicide, that you really don't know what happened. You just woke up. I was gone."

"I'm not one of Linda's agents, Ty," Josh swore. "I'm not going to let go of you."

"One," Tyler smiled. "Two. Three. OK!"

He grabbed the railing with his left hand, then his right and climbed back over, landing on the terrace, but Josh would not let go of him, leading him to the room and, once inside, closing the door.

"What the fuck!" he demanded, glaring at him through the gloom. He wiped beneath his right eye.

"Had to know," Tyler said. "Had to know I can trust you."

"I'm your friend, Ty!" Josh yelled. "Don't ever pull such a stupid stunt again."

"I won't. Don't have to."

When Tyler touched him, Josh sighed and held his forehead. Tyler stared at him, dropped his hand, and threw himself into bed, spread-eagled. Then, as if changing his mind, Josh scrambled to him, wrapped himself around him, and held him tight. Tyler took the wreath off his head, tossed it onto the floor, and embraced him.

"Do I have to worry about waking up with a drafting triangle wedged in my chest?" Josh asked.

"A what?"

"Something sharp," Josh snapped.

"No, no, no," Tyler smiled. "Nothing like that." Being wrapped in his arms and legs was a kind of warm, exhilarating high, Tyler felt, the Achilles' heel of his Nemesis. "Haven't lost you, have I?" he asked, eyes closed. "Just found you. Hate to think I lost you on day five."

Josh held him tighter, burying his face in his neck.

"Good, good," Tyler cooed, stroking Josh's shoulder.

He couldn't believe he'd been depressed enough even to think about suicide, let alone actually risk it, in short, so dead from fear he didn't want to live. On the other hand, for the first time in his life, he'd handed over the reins of his life to someone else, Josh. He'd been literally dependent on him. He'd been willing to die, if that's what it took, to restore his faith in himself and his life, and as he drifted off to sleep, exhausted, he could hear, off Maine, the buoy bell the sea nymphs were ringing. He could feel, through death, his bones changing to coral, his eyes forming pearls, himself, as it were, transforming "into something rich and strange," the new him born miraculously from the sloughed skin of the old.

Chapter 41: A Flock of Satyrs

Just in town from Rome was Guillermo, a friend of Gianluca, a satyr in Valerio's flock. It was one in the morning, and he was hanging out near Hotel Continental on Corso Meridionale. He had dark skin and hair, a Roman nose, and a slim moustache which made him look common and, thus, exciting to certain johns. At times, his left eye turned in slightly, a quirk which gave him, strangely enough, an intense, assertive look. He smiled at the security camera to the right above the hotel entrance, then into a sky blotted out by yellowish ambient city light.

He had passed on a few johns over the last hour or so, but when an old Alfa Romeo pulled up with its windows down, he recognized the driver as Detective Adolfo Pelosi from pictures Valerio had shown him. When Pelosi leaned across the passenger seat, Guillermo winked and strolled over, hands in pockets, chewing gum.

"Looking for a trick?" Guillermo asked bluntly, stopping a few steps from the car.

"Get in," Pelosi said, opening the door.

Guillermo pressed the re-dial button on the cell phone in his pocket, spit out his gum, and got in.

"What kind of song and dance would you like?" he smiled.

"The usual," Pelosi said. "How much?"

"How much do you think this should cost you?"

"Twenty-five enough?" Pelosi asked, forehead creased

When Guillermo nodded, Pelosi drove off.

"You're a fresh face," Pelosi said, making a U-turn. "Haven't seen you around."

Soon they were parked in the dead-end alley with the lights off. When Pelosi handed him the money, Guillermo put it away, shoved his pants down, and turned, facing him as much as he could. Then he leaned against the door, spread his knees, and sniffed the rank fish smell in the air.

"You look happy," Pelosi said, cupping Guillermo's balls. "Enjoy what you do?"

"It's fun," Guillermo said. Then he cautioned, "Watch the nails," meaning Pelosi's long fingernails.

When Guillermo's erection was standing up, he put his hands at his sides, eyed Pelosi, and glanced at himself. The look was a way of directing Pelosi's attention to what looked like a big acorn glowing in the dark.

Instead of going down on him, though, Pelosi asked, "That all you got?"

"If you think I'm small," Guillermo laughed, "you must've been blowing elephants."

"Have a joint?" Pelosi asked, tugging Guillermo's balls. When he let go, Guillermo's cock sprang up hard as a spring board.

"Yeah," Guillermo grinned, "a big, fat, juicy one."

"The other kind," Pelosi said, unfastening his pants.

Guillermo shook his head, then glanced across the hood at a couple of giant cockroaches crawling up the wall.

"What happened to your eye?" Pelosi asked, shoving his pants down.

"It's always been like this."

"Have double vision?" Pelosi asked, rubbing his foreskin between his fingers.

"No," Guillermo replied archly. "I see things quite well."

"Does it change how you see yourself?"

"How I see myself," Guillermo mused. "No, why? Anyone could have it."

"Why don't you do something about it?"

"If you don't want me, take me back to Meridionale."

"I'm serious," Pelosi said. "Why don't you do something about it?"

"If I wore a patch, I'd look like a pirate."

"A pirate might be hot."

When a subtle shadow darkened Guillermo, he knew that Detective Alberto "The Bear" Citti was standing behind him.

"Look," Pelosi said. "The eye thing bothers me. You do me. I'll give you fifty."

"No," Guillermo said. "I'm the man."

"Seventy-five."

"No." When Guillermo smirked, "Your dick head's weird," Pelosi shot him an annoyed look. "You're fingernails are weird," Guillermo went on. "You're weird. You're a fucking weirdo. All this talk about my eye and joints and shit. You're here to suck the big one, fag. Blow me or drive me back."

Pelosi stared at him, leaned over, and cupped Guillermo's balls again. When he squeezed them hard, Guillermo shouted and tried to break his grip, but Citti reached into the car, wrapped his arm around Guillermo's neck, and strangled him so violently he was pulling him out of the window.

# # # # #

According to Gianluca, the two detectives began abusing hustlers when Gianluca said in court that Pelosi liked it up the ass.

"Must've hit a nerve," Valerio smiled.

"Yeah," Gianluca joked, "a gay nerve. They jumped a couple of boys before Rollo, but, of course, the boys didn't report them. No one would believe them. They feared for their lives. But I would like to even the score."

"Me too," Valerio agreed.

Besides Gianluca, there were two in the Galleria group that Valerio thought up to the blind bravado required, Otto and Totonno. Plus, they needed someone as bait, someone unknown like Guillermo, who could hop a train out of town. Otto, despite his name, was Arab, a dusky, dreamy, snub-nosed boy with a thick shock of black hair, dark, almond-shaped eyes with a sad, yet sweet expression, and pursed lips that looked as if a lily should be drooping from them. Totonno wore his hair with two locks twisted up like faun horns and a short ponytail like a faun's tail. He usually wore regular clothes, but tonight had on camouflage fatigues and undershirt and army boots and looked like a kind of fantasy combat satyr.

Gianluca looked more German than Italian with his fair skin and flaxen hair brushed forward into a splash of curls on his forehead. He often wore a black baseball cap turned sideways, and when he did, he looked like a big, mischievous delinquent, in other words, a boy who could get you to throw reason out the window and then jump after it. Because he was blond, he was the favorite of a seventy-nine-year-old, former neighborhood Camorra boss, Fausto Ferri, who, for three years during WWII, had been the secret teenage lover of a blond Nazi, Lt. Hans Kessler, stationed in Naples. Fausto liked to dress Gianluca up in a Nazi uniform and then have him abuse him in various sexually gratifying ways. When Fausto heard about the rogue cops, he gave Gianluca a couple of old Bernadelli revolvers, ammunition, and his blessing. When Gianluca held the Bernadelli, he felt so powerful he decided to fuck Fausto as long and hard as it took to make him come, and when he did, Fausto kept crying, "Oh, Hans. Oh, Hans."

Around midnight, the four walked to the port and waited for Guillermo's call. When it came, each put on a leather mask which covered the head with openings for the eyes, nose, and mouth. In a few minutes, Pelosi pulled up with Guillermo, and soon Citti showed up, sneaking up on the car like a wolf. Valerio and Otto leaned around a corner and watched Citti watching what was going on in the car, so caught up in the dark spell of the crime he was committing that he failed to notice them slinking along the wall. Then Citti attacked Guillermo, his face at his neck the way a vampire would attack someone. As Guillermo struggled and screamed, Valerio slowly rose behind Citti and pushed the revolver's muzzle into the back of his head. Citti froze, backed from the window, and put his hands in the air.

When he started to turn, Valerio said, "Move and I'll kill you."

Totonno lifted the gun out of Citti's holster, stuck it in the back of his pants, and frisked him. He took Citti's handcuffs, cuffed his hands behind his back, and swiped his wallet. Then he stepped back, taking out the gun.

"What's this about?" Alberto asked.

"You know what it's about," Valerio said.

Otto had crawled along the driver's side of the car, and at the same time Valerio rose behind Citti, Otto reached through the window, stuck his gun in Pelosi's neck, and said, "Move and I'll shoot."

"Motherfucker!" Guillermo blurted, rubbing his balls. When he punched Pelosi's balls, Pelosi grabbed his crotch and groaned. "Hurts, doesn't it?" Then Guillermo relaxed, sighed, and frisked him.

When Pelosi's left hand began to inch toward his ankle, Otto said, "Just try it." Holding the gun on him, Otto stepped more toward the front of the car. When he said, "Left ankle," Gianluca opened the door, knelt, and removed the gun from Pelosi's ankle holster. He stuck the gun in the back of his pants, stole Pelosi's wallet, and stepped back, taking out the gun. When Otto said, "Lean forward," Pelosi did, and Guillermo patted down his back.

Meanwhile, Valerio and Totonno led Citti to the back of the car and dropped his pants and boxers.

"What are you doing?" Citti protested, face squinched.

"Bend over," Valerio said.

When Citti started to turn, Valerio pushed the muzzle into the back of his head, forcing his face to the trunk.

"I'll cut your balls off," Alberto swore.

"I'll shoot you in the back," Valerio replied. "You'll never walk again."

When Valerio started thrusting him, Citti clinched his ass, but Valerio kept pounding him until, sticky with seminal fluid, he loosened up and took him deeper and deeper, at last to the hilt. Citti grimaced, panted, and grunted shocked little grunts of "Oh, oh."

Valerio watched himself going in and out of him, the gun in his right hand on Citti's back, his left on Citti's hip. Then he detached himself from himself mentally for a moment and looked around at everyone now in place, doing what he was supposed to do, he thought, fitting together like living pieces in a big, sordid puzzle, whose final image, if he had known Dante, was "the perfect contrapasso": rapists being raped, thieves being robbed, corrupt cops being dealt rough justice – a strange nocturnal vision of tragic choices.

Otto stepped around the open door and pushed the gun into the side of Pelosi's head, forcing him down toward Guillermo's crotch. Guillermo began stroking himself with his right hand and drawing Pelosi's head down with his left.

When Guillermo was hard enough, he said, "Open up," slapping Pelosi's mouth with his cock.

Pelosi glanced at him with a curious worried expression, then, mouse-like, took him in both hands as if about to bite a panino. When he went down on him, he just held him in his mouth as if he did not know what to do with him, but when Guillermo whispered, "Suck it, sweetheart. Suck it for your man," Pelosi began going up and down on Guillermo's cock and soon gave himself up to it, taking it deeper.

When Guillermo, holding Pelosi's head, thrust himself down his throat, Pelosi's neck muscles contracted a couple of times as if trying to swallow him. When Pelosi gagged and made a calf-like, dry-heave low, Guillermo let go of him, and Pelosi backed off, panting, to catch his breath.

"Man," Guillermo said confidentially, "you must've been starved. What you lack in skill you make up for in appetite."

Pelosi glanced at him, then, without being told, went down on him again.

"How long's it been," Guillermo breathed, "since you sucked a big one?"

When Guillermo noticed Pelosi's erection, he sat up, put Pelosi's left hand on it, and moved Pelosi's hand up and down. When Pelosi began jerking himself, Guillermo leaned back, closed his eyes, and rubbed Pelosi's buzz cut and rough face, simply enjoying the deep-throat head the man was giving him, so much, in fact, he lost control and came.

Otto had been watching from the door, and when Pelosi choked, stiffened, and shot onto the floor, Otto stepped back, and Gianluca leaned forward and began snapping pictures. The flashes lit up the alley brighter than lightning, and Pelosi broke Guillermo's grip, sat up, and, mouth and chin glistening, shot Gianluca a startled look. When he lunged toward him, Gianluca stepped back, and Otto shoved the gun into Pelosi's eye, knocking his head back.

When Gianluca had leaned into the car, Valerio hid the gun behind his back, grabbed a handful of Alberto's curls like reins, and held his head up so that, when Totonno, to their right, started snapping pictures, he caught Citti, eyes wide, mouth open, staring directly into the camera. When Citti threw up, his body squeezed Valerio's cock so hard he came, slapping against him more and more slowly until, finally, exhausted, he braced on Citti's back. Guillermo got out of the car, and when Totonno and Gianluca had taken enough pictures, the three ran off.

"I'll drink your blood," Alberto swore, drooling vomit.

"No, you won't," Valerio panted, pulling out of him. "And if you ever harm one of these boys again, we'll post the pictures on the Internet. The whole world will see you with me up your ass."

Valerio fastened his jeans, and when Citti stood and started to face him, Valerio struck him with the gun, knocking his head around. Otto stepped back, pointing the gun toward Pelosi, but when he reached Valerio, they ran.

Chapter 42: Creative Writing

Tyler had met Erin, the waitress, on Monday, and the following Wednesday, he had a burger at the Vortex as he did on the nights he taught creative-writing in the community center down the street. When he did not see her, he assumed, somewhat negatively, that she'd been fired and was, in fact, relieved that he did not have to deal with her and the erotic snare into which she seemed to be luring him, meat in a cage that she was. Life would be simpler without inane sex with someone as obviously unstable as she was. So he was happy just to have a good meal, then drive to an hour or so of what he considered intellectual stimulation.

Whoever arrived first would arrange ten desks in a loose circle with Tyler's near the chalkboard, and at 7:00 PM, when Tyler stepped into the room, he greeted the students, slipped his leather jacket over the back of his desk, and took a seat. He was a natural-born teacher, so he was comfortable teaching just about anywhere, and his room at the center, all things considered, was not that bad, old but big with a high ceiling, huge windows, and metal desks with wood tops shaped like droplets in paisley. Metal fold-up chairs were stacked in rows in the back, and a musty, shapeless sofa was pushed to the side. The walls were what Tyler thought of as a dirty, insane-asylum green, the floors so scarred and scuffed they reminded him of a soft, brown carpet of balsam needles – everything coated with a subtle layer of dust.

# # # # #

"You can concentrate as much as possible into as few words as possible," Tyler reminded the class, "by using diction, imagery, and figures of speech. First, do what, Wyse?"

When it came to talent, the class was a mixed bag, but Wyse, pronounced "Wice," was a big, bushy-haired lion of a man capable of writing great books, Tyler thought, fiction full of sardonic humor and deep compassion for the mob of humanity. The next Mark Twain, Tyler hoped.

"Try to choose words with connotations," Wyse parroted back, "as well as denotations that work in the context."

"Second, Reeve?"

Reeve was a talented gay playwright, the most academic and literary in the group. Tyler knew he would do well. When Tyler first interviewed him for the class, the handsome, young man had used figures of speech naturally in the conversation.

"Use a concrete approach to each scene," Reeve said. "Think of each scene as a word painting."

"And third, Meryl?"

Meryl was a petite, neurasthenic Goth who could write Oscar Wilde-like gems, but seemed incapable of stringing them together in more than a brief poem, a delicate orchid of a poet who would bloom, he feared, only under the most tropical conditions.

"Well," she smiled thoughtfully, "sprinkle some figures over it."

"Why?" Tyler asked, struck by her deliberately sickly complexion.

Her pale skin reminded him of Helga's in a Wyeth painting.

"Hmm," she mused. "A figure usually has an image associated with it, which makes the writing more vivid, and an image can affect us emotionally, like the single strand of hair on the pillow next to Homer. It's synecdoche, that is, part for whole for Emily, and it makes me think of how lonely she was." Then she added, "Since she's sleeping with a corpse."

The topic for the evening was "Language Devices in Faulkner's 'A Rose for Emily,'" and Meryl was referring to Emily Grierson and Homer Barron, the two main characters in the story.

"One more thing about figures, anyone?" Tyler asked, looking around the class. "One more thing they do."

"Convey information," John began.

John was a big, blond Viking whose stories were Southern and satirical like Wyse's. His duties as a college division chair, however, were eating him alive. If he didn't find time for himself, Tyler thought, he would lose himself as a writer.

"The crayon portrait of Emily's father," John said. "It's a symbol for his lasting influence on her. Though he's dead, he's still there in a very real sense."

"Perfect," Tyler said, adjusting his position in his desk. He didn't know how students had sat on such hard seats all day. "Well, since we seem to be slipping into a discussion of the story anyway, let's turn to it, starting with the title." Tyler had Xeroxed the story for the class, and the students had marked-up copies in front of them. "The story is a rose for Emily in what sense?" The format of the class was to start with someone in the circle and continue clockwise with each question, allowing, of course, for anyone to comment on anything at any point. "So, Reeve," Tyler began, turning left, "a rose is a traditional symbol for what?"

"Love."

"Who's the narrator in the story? Who tells it?"

It was Happy's turn. "The narrator keeps saying *we*," she began, "so I suppose he's speaking for all the people in the town."

Happy did not have many language skills, but enjoyed the class and the arts in general. The worst Tyler could say about her was that she was just having fun.

"And why do they love this murderer?" he asked.

Happy thought. "I guess it's ironic that they see her as a victim, too."

"Of what?"

"Her father's a control freak," she stated. "When her suitors call, he answers the door with a horsewhip."

"And she represents what else to the townspeople?"

Wyse shifted in his desk. "She's about all that's left of the old way of life," he said, "the old South. In the first sentence, she's called a fallen monument, like a Confederate monument. A metaphor." Everyone knew to name the language device as they discussed it. "So we have the image of a toppled shrine, and she's fallen in a couple of other senses as well. She's fallen on hard times, and everyone thinks she's a fallen woman in the sense that they think she's been compromised by Homer."

"Has she?" Tyler asked.

"I wouldn't put my money on it," Wyse grinned. "I noticed that the word *tarnished* is used several times. Homer's silver toilet articles tarnish from age, but the townspeople also think Emily's reputation is tarnished."

"Very good. Let's stick with diction for a while. Frank," Tyler said, glancing at him, "any other examples of good diction?"

Frank was wise beyond his years because of years of decadence, Tyler assumed, namely sex and drugs. Tyler thought of him as Dorothy Parker with lots of body hair, a languid aesthete just on the verge of converting his hilariously cynical insights into actual words on paper.

"Well, it may be just me," Frank began with a gravelly voice, "but when I read the line that her house 'had once been white,' I thought that wasn't the only thing that had once been white. The whole South had in the sense of whites having all the power."

"Anything that works in the context," Tyler agreed.

"Also," Frank said, "Emily is described as once being 'a slender figure in white,' white as in innocent virgin."

"What about black?" Tyler asked, glancing at Sonia. "Later she's described as – "

"'A fat woman in black,'" Sonia said, filling in the blank. "I guess black there has all sorts of death connotations."

Tyler thought of Sonia as the thinker in the group, a trim, introspective Italian who took everything he said very seriously. However, he was not sure why she was taking the class, other than to improve her writing skills for business-related projects.

"And she has 'black eyes,'" John commented, "two lumps of coal."

"And how do we interpret that?"

"Well," John smiled, "she hasn't been punched in the face, at least not literally."

"Bad reputation," Meryl suggested.

"Very good," Tyler nodded.

Then they discussed the three references to Emily's iron-gray hair.

"Iron in what sense?" Tyler asked.

"Iron willed," Mabel offered, an older, feminist dilettante with overly rouged cheeks, Harry Potter glasses, and reddish, disheveled hair.

As far as Tyler could tell, she had spent her life dabbling in the arts in a futile attempt to find some direction.

"'Like the hair of an active man,'" Mabel quoted. "She's compared to an active man because she has seized control of the situation instead of playing the traditional passive role of the genteel Southern lady."

"Excellent," Tyler remarked. "And how did she seize control?"

"By killing him," Mabel said. "Homer."

"Guess she showed him," Wyse joked.

They also discussed the words *skeleton*, *sick*, *pall*, and *rose* in the faded rose curtains and "the rose-shaded lights."

The room had a slight echo, and just as they were turning to a discussion of figures of speech in the story, Tyler noticed Erin sneaking into the back of the room. When he looked up, surprised, everyone else turned and looked, too. She was wearing the same outfit in which he had seen her on Monday: jeans, the blue T-shirt with the angel on it, Keds. Again, he could feel some interested, inquisitive current carrying him toward her, but intuitively, he knew her presence was disoriented and wrong. She was disregarding some basic rules of behavior deliberately or out of naiveté. The class was a place where he could enjoy the camaraderie of people with similar interests, sharing what tricks of the trade he had learned, the occasional piece of fine writing. What had she to do with any of it?

"Erin?" he asked, his tone more as to what she was doing there than her name.

"Sahry," she said, slowly touching the shark's tooth at her throat. "Mind if I sit in?"

"Uh, no," he conceded. "Drag a desk up."

Sonia and Wyse slid their desks apart.

"Uh, no, please," she begged, shuffling toward the sofa. "This is fine."

"Come on," he insisted. "I'm sure the class will find your comments interesting."

"I just wahnt to obsehrve."

"Class," Tyler announced. "This is Erin. From New Hampshire."

"Hi," she said awkwardly.

She took an order pad and pen out of her back pocket, sank into the soft cushions, and sat there, blinking, pad and pen in hand as if waiting for everyone's order. That she was there at all, he felt, was bad enough, but late worse, and the fact that she was sitting outside the circle, as if keeping guard on them, confirmed his idea that her presence was wrong. It also spotlighted her, he believed, in a way that wasn't justified or fair to his students.

"OK," he sighed. "Where were we?"

"The faded rose curtains," Wyse reminded him.

"Oh, Erin," Tyler said, handing a copy of the story to Reeve. "We're going over a short story called 'A Rose for Emily.'"

Reeve, Happy, and Frank passed the copy to Sonia, who leaned back and handed it to Erin.

"Thanks," Erin whispered.

"Familiar with it?" Tyler asked.

"The story?" Erin asked. She shook her head.

"Let's see," Tyler said to himself, trying to focus. "Faded rose. Mack," he said, turning right, "if a rose is a love symbol, then in what sense has Emily's rose faded?"

Mack thought. "Her last chance for love, Homer's dead."

Mack was a real-estate agent with a glass eye. When talking to him, Tyler still was not sure where to look, and, as with Sonia, he was not sure why Mack was taking the class: writing skills in general, social interaction – he wondered.

"What happened to her other suitors?"

"Her father ran them off," Mack said. "There's that sentence...." He flipped a couple of pages. "Paragraph 25, where he literally blocks the door, doesn't let anyone near her."

Tyler turned to the paragraph and quoted: "'her father a spraddled silhouette in the foreground, his back to her and clutching a horsewhip, the two of them framed by the back-flung front door.'"

"Reeve," Tyler said, "what does *spraddled* mean?"

"Legs spread. As Mack said, blocking the door."

Then they discussed why he was a silhouette, what dark meant in the context, why his back was to Emily, and why he was clutching a horsewhip as Homer does later.

"But I guess the most important question is," Tyler paused, "why does he run off her suitors. Why does he thwart 'her woman's life,' as the narrator calls it?"

It was Happy's turn: "He didn't think any of them were good enough for her."

"Class is a big issue here," Sonia said. "In the old South, there was a class system in the sense of whites and blacks, but also, even among the whites, the upper and lower classes. Emily was the last vestige of Southern nobility."

"Maybe heh fahthah wahnted heh fah himself," Erin said lethargically.

Tyler enjoyed the way Sonia reacted to the comment. She slowly turned her head and, with a blank face, glanced at Erin. What control.

"What do you mean?" Tyler smiled.

"You know," Erin hesitated. Her eyes looked from side to side. "Maybe he wahs abusin' heh."

"You mean – "

"I cahn say it, right?" she asked, her voice leaden, dull.

"Sure," Tyler assured her.

"Sex. Maybe the ol' hound plucked heh flawah."

"Well," Tyler mused, pursing his lips, "what do the rest of you think about that?"

"There's no evidence *for* that in the story," Sonia began, stressing the preposition. "However, I think you're right to a certain extent." Sonia stared at Erin. "You certainly can't say they have anything like a healthy father-daughter relationship."

"Some fahthahs do thaht, you know," Erin sulked.

"She keeps his body three days," Frank said, "which foreshadows how she keeps Homer, which makes a parallel between her father and her lover. Quote unquote lover."

"Whaht do ya mean: 'she keeps his body'?" Erin asked.

"She clings to her father's body after he dies," Frank explained, "the way she clings to Homer after she kills him."

"Kills him," Erin blurted. "Her boyfriend. Why?"

"He apparently was not going to marry her," Meryl said.

"She killed him for usin' heh," Erin concluded.

"No," Reeve stated. "At least not in that sense, sexually. Emily was a fag hag. Homer was gay."

Erin's mouth opened. Her eyes widened. Also, several in the class looked puzzled. Tyler knew that everyone trusted Reeve's interpretation, but some looked as if they were not certain what details in the story suggested it.

Tyler leaned back, knees spread, hands clasped behind his head. "You know," he said, "I think you're right, but perhaps you should explain how you came to that conclusion."

"Paragraph forty-three," Reeve said. Everyone turned to it. "It's rather explicit." He quoted: "'Homer himself had remarked – he liked men, and it was known that he drank with the younger men in the Elks Club – that he was not a marrying man.' And then the last part: 'Homer Barron with his hat cocked and a cigar in his teeth, reins and a whip in a yellow glove.' The last part may be subjective. Still it's hard to overlook the innuendos."

"The connotations of the words," Tyler paraphrased.

"*Cocked*," Reeve said. "'A cigar in his teeth,' and then we have his leather-fetish drag: 'reins and a whip in a yellow glove.' Even his name," Reeve claimed, "has a gay vibe: Homer Barron."

"Barron?" Tyler asked. He realized he had slipped out of his clogs and, thinking it un-professorial, slipped back into them.

"Well," Reeve explained, "one meaning of *baron* – B.A.R.O.N. – is a powerful man, and he is. But if you just hear the word, don't see it spelled, it could also be *barren* – B.A.R.R.E.N. – in the sense of their relationship not going anywhere."

Tyler was afraid to ask the next question, but did anyway just to see where it would lead. "What other connotation of his name, spelled whatever way you want, works in the context?"

"No marriage, no children," Mabel suggested.

"A baron is a nobleman," Happy said, "which is ironic in the story because everyone considered him a day laborer."

After a pause, Erin said, "Gays cahn't hahv children."

Reeve sat up and turned, but as he started to respond, Tyler stopped him with just a slightly raised index finger.

"Gays can, in fact, have children," Tyler stated, "if they want to, but that's another issue. Let's get back to the question of why she killed him. If not revenge, then what?"

"He dumped heh," Erin squinted. "He's a hahrtless bastad."

She sounded irrationally bitter, Tyler thought, as if the truth were obvious.

"Not exactly," John remarked. "She kills him to keep him."

Erin looked confused.

"I mean," John said, "look where he is, in a nightshirt in bed in a bridal chamber." John turned to the last page. "Paragraph 59: 'The body had apparently once lain in the attitude of an embrace....' And the last paragraph: 'in the second pillow was the indentation of a head.'"

"Erin," Tyler said, "what does that detail imply?"

"Whaht detail?"

"The indentation of a head in the pillow next to Homer."

She tilted her head and stuck her pen into her spiky, witch-green hair.

"Some people will capture a butterfly," Reeve said, "stick a pin through it, and keep it in a glass case. Emily pinned Homer."

"How did she kill him?" Erin asked, gazing at Tyler.

"Anyone?" Tyler asked.

"Rat poison," Mabel said. "Arsenic."

"Ahs-nic," Erin repeated sluggishly.

# # # # #

After class, when everyone else had left, Erin lingered near the door. Tyler slipped his jacket on, picked up his papers, and approached slowly.

"I suppose you need to be here," he said. "Otherwise, you wouldn't have crashed the class."

She briefly closed her eyes, then said: "I need to lehrn how to write, to express myself. Therapy."

He caught a whiff of her cherry smell.

"Therapy. And?"

"And – " she faltered, her eyes droopy. "I need to lehrn how to hahv fun in ways othah thahn how I hahv in the pahst. You know, sex."

"Meaningless sex," he joked.

"Right."

He did not believe her. "And?"

"I wanted to see you."

"Why?"

"You know," she smiled subtly. "Meaningless sex. As I said at the Vahtex, most men leave me flaht. I hahv to respond to," she hesitated, "what I respond to. Besides, whaht's wrong with enjoyin' ahselves? I know I cahn make you feel good. Whaht's bad with thaht?"

"Nothing."

Slowly she raised her eyes and engaged his directly, and everything – him, the room, the night – spiraled down them. Then he blinked and snapped back into himself.

"Bring anything for me to read?" he asked.

"Whaht do ya mean?"

"A writing sample?"

"Uh, no."

"What does the *A* stand for?" he asked, referring to the angel on her T-shirt. The angel was holding a big circle with the letter *A*.

"I don't know. Adult'ry."

As good a guess as any, he thought.

"Ever snag anyone with that?" he asked, lightly touching the garish feather on her fish-fly earring.

"No such luck."

He was not sure that she had understood him literally.

"If you'd like to come ovah," she said, "you cahn hahv some desseht."

"Chocolate?"

"No."

"You?" he chuckled.

"I cahn be desseht."

"Stop it."

"People need people the way people need food, right?"

"Very good," he nodded. "A simile."

"We kinda stahve, you know, without 'em."

He was already hooked, he knew, if not on the earring, then on the mystery she personified.

Chapter 43: Roma

Sunday morning, Tyler, Josh, Billie, and Phil were the only people standing on the dock in Amalfi, waiting for the ferry to Naples. Down the coast, the sunrise looked like a murky orange tincture, and as Tyler gazed at it, he realized that – despite his dangerous escapade on the balcony – he and Josh, for all intents and purposes, had become a harmonious, sympathetic couple. The honeymoon suite at the Piccolo Sogno was where they had consummated their attraction to each other, and he wondered if they would ever return.

Soon the boat appeared and, after stops in Positano, Sorrento, and Pompeii, deposited them on the wharf in Naples, where they took a cab to the Stazione Centrale, where they caught a fast train to Rome. There they checked in at the Albergo Marmolada – Hotel Marmalade as Josh called it – then had lunch at a sidewalk café, where Billie announced that she wanted to give Josh and Tyler some time alone. Tyler figured what she really meant was give Phil and herself some time alone. The plan was for Billie and Phil to head to the Colosseum, Josh and Tyler to the Museo Montemartini, then meet at eight at a bistro around the corner.

"She noticed, but didn't say anything about the bruises on your arm," Josh commented.

"If they'd been on *your* arm," Tyler smiled, "we would've certainly heard about it."

When Tyler and Josh emerged from the Metropolitana at the Garbatella stop, they heard techno dance music echoing through the neighborhood and, as they strolled toward the museum, passed a crowd of punk rockers outside a warehouse where a memorial to Renato, a murdered DJ, was being held. From the roof of the warehouse hung a huge banner with a big red heart and the words, "Renato, Sempre nel nostro coure." *Renato, Always in our heart.*

Il Museo Montemartini was an old electricity plant converted to a museum for classical sculpture, and the industrial setting set off the humanity of the marble figures, torsos, and busts and the moods they portrayed in a way that a traditional museum couldn't, Tyler thought, especially in the case of his favorite, *Dionysus with a Panther* with its relaxed S Curve. Josh, however, was more attracted to a statue of a youthful Roman general because it was less muscular and, thus, more graceful, an argument he won by comparing its slender physique to the "perfect symmetry" of Tyler's slim build. The portrait busts had impressed upon Tyler the transience of life, even the life of people of rank, and the cumulative erotic effect of all the ideal male beauty around him stirred his desire to actually seize it and enjoy it in the young man next to him as soon as he could, so much so that he felt an irresistible urge to bump into Josh just to have some physical contact with him, a tactile canapé, as he thought of it, until he could indulge in the full meal.

# # # # #

The general impression of Josh and Tyler's spacious room at Albergo Marmolada was that it was masculine in a simple, austere sort of way, the perfect setting for a round of satisfying sex between two handsome, active men. The oak bed was big, strong, and rustic with side tables with small lamps. Near it sat a long, squat chest of drawers. Behind the bed, the wall was paneled with stained, carved pine up to about seven feet. Above that, the arched wall was painted with an olive-green fresco with strange figures fading in and out of its faint bucolic scene as if in and out of mist. Except for fresh linens, the room smelled of wood and carpet fabric with a hint of dust, and the tile floor and vaulted ceiling gave the sounds and voices in it a hard, slightly resonant quality relieved to some extent by the rough, washed-out Oriental rugs scattered here and there.

When they got in that night, their affectionate embrace segued to an avid kiss, but even in the midst of it, as he crushed Josh's mouth, Tyler felt divided from himself: both bird of prey and prey, raptorial Tyler who wanted only to ravish his young fan and romantic Tyler who wanted only to protect him from him.

"You know," Tyler smiled, "a slice of watermelon is about as pink and sweet as that delicious mouth of yours."

"You don't have to seduce me," Josh said. "You had me when you smiled at me in the museum in Naples."

"Did I?"

"Let's get undressed."

Josh began what Tyler considered slowly unwrapping the gift of his beautiful body, and when Josh slipped his briefs off, his genitals popped out heavy and earthy, dangling like fruit. He left a lamp on, then struck such a shameless pose that Tyler could not help laughing at him. Josh faced the bed, put a knee on it, and pulled a butt cheek aside, exposing his anus. In some strange way, it reminded Tyler of a mouth, the tight, wet grip of Josh's lips, and his cock sprang up at the thought of a kiss from it.

"Such a slut," he smiled, pressing his thumb into the base of his erection. When he did, it stood up even stiffer.

"Worked, didn't it?"

He thought of Josh as an angel gone bad (in a good sort of way), a beautiful boy so versed in the sensual arts he could've been a king's courtesan, the well-kept bottom of a corrupt politician. And here he was, flashing his butthole. And how odd, Tyler thought, that something as generally off-putting

318

as that could be the source of someone's emotional, if not spiritual, redemption. "Love has pitched his mansion in," as Yeats said, "the place of excrement."

Tyler strolled over and gently cupped Josh's fuzzy, white cheek, the glowing bum which had given him so much passionate pleasure in Amalfi. He pressed his thumbs into each cheek, and when he spread them, Josh bent over and braced on the bed, presenting himself, as Tyler thought of it. The muscular mounds, the tight sphincter, the supple body – everything about him implied his great physical talents which, coupled with a total lack of inhibitions, assured Tyler of the young man's absolute ability to satisfy him. If love were anything like sex with him, it would be dangerous.

When Tyler said, "Missionary style," Josh climbed into bed and rolled onto his back, knees up.

Tyler crawled between his legs, pushed Josh's knees against his sides, and, snug against him, took in the inviting toys at his disposal: Josh's fleshy member lolling on his groin, his balls, as if sleeping, loose on his crotch, the perineal seam leading down to the vulnerable spot where Tyler positioned himself to plug into him. He spit on it, leaned over him – hands clamped on the back of Josh's knees – and began prodding him slowly. He did not expect to penetrate him so easily, but with each slick push, Josh's bottom, as if melting, opened up to him a little wider, Tyler entered him a little farther, until they were connected comfortably crotch to butt.

"Feels good," Josh breathed.

"Certainly does," Tyler agreed, sitting back, Josh's feet on Tyler's pecs.

Then Tyler simply enjoyed all the good feelings kindled inside him. He rubbed Josh's quadriceps, his palms lightly brushing the sheath of gold hair on his legs. He grabbed Josh's ankles and held his feet in the air.

"Patchouli?" he asked, smelling an ankle.

"Yeah," Josh whispered, holding Tyler's hips.

Tyler held Josh's ankles like ski poles and began rhythmically thrusting him. If he were the musician and Josh the sensitive, finely tuned instrument, he thought, they were playing beautiful music together, but Josh was an instrument that could intensely feel and enjoy its own music. How did music correspond to emotion? Tyler wondered. How did the sex act they were performing correspond to the tender way he felt about him?

Tyler noticed the clear drop oozing from Josh's cock, his balls drawn flat against him, and when Tyler leaned over him, gazing into his eyes, Josh gasped ecstatically as if entered mentally, too. Tyler lay on him and tongue-fucked his ear, then his nose, sticking the tip of his tongue up his left nostril, then his right. He pressed his mouth against Josh's so hard that Josh opened like a flower, letting him stick his tongue down his throat, and when Josh started sucking it, Tyler tongue-fucked the hole his lips made. It was as if he were, face mashed against face, trying to stick himself into him as far as he could as many ways as he could, fucking him at both ends until he finally came in a fierce, blacked-out moment, uniting with him completely, then came to and sighed, sprawling on him, shining with sweat. Josh, meanwhile, had wrapped his arms and legs around him and kept thrusting Tyler's slippery stomach till he came too, just as Tyler came, shooting into the warm, moist space between them.

When they quit panting, Tyler did a pushup off Josh and sat, legs splayed, with his back against the headboard. When Josh sat up, he glanced at Tyler mischievously, then settled sideways in his lap, and they wrapped their arms around each other, Josh's around Tyler's neck adoringly, Tyler's around Josh's back protectively as if holding a child. They kissed a sly kiss. Then, as a joke, Josh collapsed in his arms melodramatically, eyes closed, face serene, lying across Tyler's legs like a limb caught on branches.

"The scab's fallen off," Tyler said, fingering the pink scratch on his Josh's chest.

Josh opened his eyes, stared at Tyler, and caressed his face.

They really didn't need to say anything, Tyler thought. The reverent way Josh touched him said it all.

"Oh, my god," Josh said.

"What?"

"Guess what we forgot." He poked Tyler's pec as if making a point.

"What?"

"A condom."

"Fuck!" Tyler blurted.

"Exactly."

Again, Tyler wondered how protective of himself Josh had been, playing mistress for a married man. If he would "bareback" now, would he with someone else he'd had a crush on?

"Well," Josh said, "you don't have to worry about it. I'm the one getting fucked. If you say you're negative, I believe you. You *are* negative?"

"Right," Tyler assured him. "I'm negative. But I could be just saying that. So why would you believe me?"

"You're the only person I would believe," Josh stated. "We're too important to each other to lie."

"Over a year since I've slept with anyone," Tyler said, "and I've had the test a couple of times."

"Over a year?" Josh asked, brows arched.

"Thought I'd give it a rest. Besides – "

"Every woman you've slept with has tried to kill you. What you said in Naples."

"Yeah."

"My god, Ty, no wonder you're gay."

"Go clean up," Tyler said, "and bring me a bottle of water, would you?"

Josh got up, strolled to the bathroom, and flicked on the light, and while he was gone, Tyler realized that, for the first time in his life, he felt genuinely happy. The reason, he believed, was that Josh, his good-looking beau, was giving him pleasure in three related ways: sensually, emotionally, and mentally. A few minutes ago, fucking him had been a moment of such great, transcendent beauty that it compensated for the lack of it in the rest of his troubled life. Coming inside him was also a moment of such great, transcendent pleasure that he immediately became addicted to it, like heroin. Josh was his sensual heroin. The sweet heat of it, he thought, like a pyroclastic surge, had incinerated him to a body cast of himself. Now, like the complacent tourist he was, he could view it with compassion and move on to whatever they were now. He tried to think of apt metaphors for them: bookends, a pair of masculine rhymes, a team working to accomplish what? The most important goal in his life: loving someone and, in turn, being loved by him, and he had become one with him, his lover, in some Platonic, brotherly way, too, if only for a week, and, thus, in a sense, would never be lonely again, even separated. It was as if he had been a hand in a latex glove and the glove had been stripped off it so that now the hand finally felt things directly, precisely, suddenly aware of what it had never known. Up to this point, his life had been an endless string of personal investigations, and if he continued with Josh, he would be setting out on a radically new course to totally new areas of experience, perhaps even back to the past he should've lived. He could live that past again with him, this time maybe even get it right.

When Josh returned, he set the bottle of water on a side table, sat on the bed, and wiped Tyler's chest, stomach, and crotch. Then he lay the towel aside, opened the bottle, and handed it to Tyler.

"What's it like?" Tyler asked, taking a drink.

"What?"

"Getting fucked."

"Well," Josh smiled, "once you learn how to do it, it's easy. The anus and rectum are laced with erogenous nerve endings. The prostate's wrapped in 'em. Like a tea ball," he added. "Simple fact. And when they're stimulated, it feels good. The prostate climax is one of the world's best kept secrets. When you come having your prostate banged, these warm waves of pleasure flash through your body." He reached the bottle and took a sip. "What do you logically make of the fact that men have erogenous nerve endings in their butt?"

"Men are supposed to fuck each other."

"Why?" Josh asked.

"What do you mean?"

"Under what conditions? How does it help the species?"

Tyler chuckled. "Overpopulation. I don't know."

"I don't either," Josh admitted, "but I do know that men can satisfy every need a woman can, except, of course, the need for babies." He took another sip and handed the bottle to Tyler. "Back to your question."

"What's it like?"

Josh thought for a moment. "If you love someone," he said, "you want to please him, right? It pleases me to please you."

"As I always say – "

Together they said, "If it makes you happy."

They laughed. Then Tyler took a sip.

"When I open up to someone physically," Josh said, gazing at him, "I'm opening up to him emotionally and mentally as well. I'm giving myself to him."

"In every way," Tyler said. "Speaking of opening up."

"Yeah?"

"You know," he hesitated, "I don't think you believed me when I told you a shark killed my wife and my daughter drowned, but it's true."

"You're not just telling a story."

"No."

"The kind of story a writer would tell."

"No," Tyler stressed, shaking his head. "My daughter washed up on Great Mark Island, Maine, but only my wife's left hand – my ex-wife's hand," he corrected himself, "washed up on Haskell."

Josh covered his mouth and stared at him. "And your other daughter's in a mental-health facility."

"Right."

"Sorry."

"Thanks."

Josh stared at the bed, then glanced at Tyler sheepishly.

"And since I seem to be opening up to you," Tyler said, "what about this married man with whom you had an affair?"

"Owen?"

Chapter 44: Owen

Josh was sitting on a sofa in a secluded corner of the library one day when a cute young man, hands in pockets, strolled up to him and said, "Hi," in a crisp voice. The young man was wearing loafers, slacks, and a blue, oxford-cloth shirt.

Josh put his book down and said, "Hi."

The young man could have been an Abercrombie and Fitch model: tall, slim, good-looking, impeccably groomed. He was obviously in great shape. His waist could not have been more than thirty inches. The clincher, though, was the cute face framed in a cloud of dark curls. His face alone would have made him appealing, body or no body. He had sparkling blue eyes and boyish freckles sprinkled across his nose and cheeks. His rosy lips were a diamond among lips, Josh thought, and when he smiled nervously, the smile was gem grade.

"How are you?" he asked in almost a whisper. He acted as if their meeting were a prearranged secret.

"Fine," Josh said, "and you?"

"Didn't know what to expect," the young man said, shifting from foot to foot. "You're actually quite nice."

"Thanks," Josh puzzled.

"What about the john?"

"The john?"

"We don't have to," the young man said. He bit his lip and stared at Josh. "Now that I've seen you, what if we meet in my office?"

"Your office."

"Yeah, I actually have an office. Only place I can think of where we can lock the door."

Josh studied him. "What's the number?"

"B-321," he said. "Five minutes?"

"The Business Building," Josh said. "OK."

The young man left, and Josh packed his backpack, strolled to the B-Building, and ascended the stairs to the third floor. B-321 was at the end of the hall, and the name on the small plaque by the door read: "Owen Payne, Teaching Associate," a title, Josh knew, for graduate students paid a few thousand a year to teach a class or two each semester. The plaque also had his office hours.

When Josh knocked on the door, Owen opened it, let him in, and locked the door. Josh looked around the carpeted, makeshift office, then noticed where Owen's hand was, cupping his crotch.

"Owen, huh," Josh began, replacing Owen's hand with his.

"Look, I'm straight," Owen said, letting him feel him. "I just like a little action on the side."

"Sure," Josh smiled, letting his backpack slip to the floor.

Josh sat in a chair by the door, and Owen unbuckled his belt, unzipped his pants, and shoved them and his briefs down his hips, letting his erection pop up, pulsing, near Josh's face. When Josh took the head in his mouth, he knew he was in trouble. The young man tasted good, like almonds, and a sweet, balmy feeling went coursing though Josh's veins. When Owen unbuttoned his shirt to get it out of the way, Josh glanced up at the bow-shaped pecs and midline of his body pointing like an arrow toward his crotch. He breathed its rousing musk as well as the fresh, grassy scent of his Vetiver cologne, and when Owen held Josh's head, casually pumping his face, Josh's excitement jumped a quantum leap. The young man may as well have turned some emotional thermostat inside him all the way up.

After a while, Josh stood, dropped his pants, and touched the side of Owen's head, his hand over his ear as if about to kiss him, but when he leaned forward, Owen leaned back and said, "Not into that."

Josh nodded, sat down, and went down on him again. He jerked himself with his right hand and made a tube with his left so that he was jerking Owen off and sucking him off at the same time, and soon Owen came with a sigh, filling Josh's mouth with a gush of what may as well have been honey. Then Josh came too, pointing his cock to the side so that he would not shoot onto Owen's pants.

"Look at you," Owen said, stepping back, his cock hard and glistening.

They dressed quickly. Then Josh reached into a pocket, pulled out a handkerchief, and tried to wipe his come off the carpet.

"How'd you know I was gay?" Josh asked, folding the handkerchief.

Owen looked surprised. "You're not the one who wrote the note."

"Note?" Josh stuffed the handkerchief into his back pocket.

"In the john," Owen said. "You're not the one I was supposed to meet, are you?"

"No," Josh smiled sadly. "Sorry."

"You know," Owen hesitated, glancing to the side, "it's, uh – it's probably best if you leave. Not sure who'll drop by."

But Josh could read his face, if not his mind. Owen was eager to get back to the library to meet his trick.

Josh slipped his backpack over his shoulders, but before he left, he leaned over Owen's desk, picked up a pen, and wrote his name, address, and number on a yellow post-it note.

"My number," Josh said, facing him.

"Right," Owen said, eyes averted, nodding his head awkwardly.

Josh left, but stepped into the bookstore, where he could see Owen strolling through the cafeteria and out the door. When Owen went into the library, Josh exited the cafeteria, crossed the grounds, and followed him in, slipping into the stacks. He peeked around the end of a stack, spying on Owen, who, like a mirror image, was peeking around a stack, spying on the reading area where they had met. Then Owen stepped back, thought for a while, and left.

He must not have liked him, Josh thought.

Josh had been living in a pricey two-bedroom apartment, and after six years, the place had a comfortable, homey look. He had turned the bedroom with the best light into an office with his desk and chair, drafting board and stool, and file cabinets. Above his desk hung a framed travel brochure (circa 1935) for Frank Lloyd Wright's Imperial Hotel in Tokyo. On the windowsill sat three terra-cotta pots, one with violets, one with parsley, and one with a greenish-white caladium. He had painted the other bedroom what he thought of as cave brown and filled it with a king-size platform bed. Above the bed was a series of framed Wright floor plans and tree-like elevations, some of the Imperial Hotel, some of the Johnson Tower in Racine, Wisconsin. The geometric patterns looked like delicately drawn abstract art.

On a night table was a clock-radio and sound machine that projected the time in a soothing blue light onto the ceiling, and one night, about a week after he had tricked with Owen, he had gone to bed and just pushed the "ocean" button when someone knocked on the door. He got up, slipped into boxer shorts, and strolled to the door.

"Hey," he grinned. "Come in."

Instead of Owen's previous crisp, collegiate look, this time he was wearing flip-flops, long, wrinkled shorts, and a big, loose, long-sleeved shirt with the first couple of buttons unbuttoned.

"Like a drink?" Josh asked.

"No," Owen smiled, antsy. "Don't have much time." He told him what he wanted with a look.

"OK."

So they went into the bedroom, stripped, and got in bed.

"Roll over for me," Owen said, and Josh did, willing to give him what he wanted out of simple curiosity about him.

Josh lay face down, and Owen crawled between Josh's legs, spreading them with his knees. Josh could not see him, but knew what he was doing, slipping a condom on. When nothing happened, Josh became aware of the surf's calm breathing on the sound machine, part of what it must sound like in the womb, he had thought. Then Owen's hands pressed into the bed to either side of him, and Josh felt the blunt nudge of Owen's cock. Owen began humping him, and after a while, Josh started opening up to him, letting him in more and more until he was all the way in and prodding his prostate. He rode Josh's hips, then, when he came, slammed against him hard, holding the last thrust jammed deep inside him.

"You come?" Owen asked, relaxing.

"No," Josh said, surprised by the question.

"On your knees," Owen said, and as Josh rose onto his hands and knees, Owen, still connected, held onto his hips. Then he began leisurely fucking him again. "Jerk yourself off."

Josh grabbed the sheet with his left hand, braced his forehead against his arm so that he would not slide forward, and, as Owen fucked him, began jerking himself. When Owen caressed Josh's hair, Josh thought of the gesture as Owen's first sign of tenderness, but Owen grabbed a handful of it and held on to it, fucking him hard till he came. Then he pulled out, got up, and began dressing, still hard.

"Thanks," Owen said, his erection tenting his pants. "Gotta go."

Josh looked up Owen's class in the schedule, drifted past his open door one day, making sure that Owen did not see him, and lingered near the door, listening to what he figured was a lecture on business writing, but all he really heard was Owen's voice, not the words, a masculine music as soothing to Josh as the cool purl of a fountain.

A few days later, Owen popped up sweaty from jogging, but ready to fuck. This time, he wanted Josh on his back with a pillow under him.

"Lift your butt," Owen said.

Josh's bed had brushed-metal bars running across the headboard, so he grabbed hold of a lower bar, braced his feet against an upper one, and raised his butt so that Owen could stuff the pillow under it. If he had been a baboon, he realized, he could not have presented himself to Owen more.

After that, Owen would drop by once or twice a week, and each time they went through pretty much the same routine: the pillow, the condom, then the slow, but relentless penetration. Once Josh had relaxed, Owen would ride him with their eyes locked in a strange stare, but soon Owen felt so good inside him that Josh would have to jerk off, shooting onto his stomach. Then Owen would pin Josh's knees against his shoulders and fuck him hard till he came, too. After a last, few, slow, savory thrusts, he would pull out and roll out of bed. The final requirement was that Josh, like a slave, had to wash him in the shower, a voluptuous ritual nothing short of shameless idolatry. Then, as usual, Owen dashed off.

Over the semester, the sexual relationship gradually transformed into what could pass for a real, if one-sided, affair, but when Owen refused to tell Josh where he lived, let alone meet there, Josh assumed that he was living with someone, a partner. In short, Josh knew he was being exploited. He was someone's male mistress. But Owen was such a doll and the sex was so hot he could not help himself. He could not stop seeing him.

Then the affair took a strange, inexplicable turn when Owen wanted to have sex any place other than Josh's apartment. Owen took Josh to a party given by one of Owen's students and, after a few drinks, led him upstairs to a bedroom, where, with the door locked, he face-fucked him on the side of a bed. When they came out of the bedroom, a young man with the build of a linebacker was passing in the hall.

He stopped, sniffed them, and asked, "You guys doin' weed?" Josh figured he must have smelled Owen's Vetiver.

The university owned a secluded vineyard as part of its agricultural program, and somehow Owen got the key to the gate and drove Josh there one night, locking the gate behind them. Owen wanted a parking fantasy, so he undid his pants, and Josh went down on him in the car, but just as Owen was about to come, he made Josh stop, and they got out and stripped. Owen broke off a leafy vine, tied it in a chaplet, and put it on Josh's head. Then he made one for himself, dropped to his knees under a luxuriant trellis, and sat on his heels, knees spread.

"I'm the god of wine," he said, erect. "Suck me."

The next episode began similarly, but ended differently and served as a subtle turning point in their relationship, though Josh was not aware of it at the time, for, after it, something wild would go out of the spontaneous, Bacchanalian tone of the escapades. The university was on a lake, at one end of which was a peninsula, which students referred to as "the penis," and at the other end of which was a hill, which the students referred to as "the mound of Venus." To get to the peninsula, you had to hike up a bumpy dirt road to the university observatory, then strike out through weeds. One night, Owen wanted to go to the tip of the peninsula, "the head," and had Josh bring a blanket in his backpack for them to lie on, but hiking back, as they neared the observatory, a security car was slowly bouncing up the road, and they hid in the shadow of an air-conditioning compressor a few yards from the building. The car stopped, motor running, with its headlights turned toward the compressor, lighting up everything around them as if the security guards knew they were there.

327

As he and Owen crouched there, Josh whispered, "This is more suspicious than just walking right up to them."

"I can't," Owen insisted.

Josh, Owen, and the guards knew each other. If he and Owen had acted nonchalantly, he was sure the guards wouldn't question them, let alone their presence there, at least not openly.

"Why can't you?" Josh asked.

"Shut up," Owen hissed.

Even in the dark, Josh could see how much Owen hated him.

Then the car backed up, and the headlights swung round, lighting up the observatory, then the uneven road. As it moved off, they stood slowly and watched it disappear into the dark.

After that night, the affair turned as cold as the Campari Josh sipped one night in the bar of a Holiday Inn across town from the university – as cold and as bitter, for Owen would see him, but would not have sex.

In fact, Owen said, "Let's cool it awhile."

"Why?" Josh asked.

It was Owen's idea to meet there, to avoid the powerful temptation of Josh's bedroom, Josh assumed, though there were dozens of bedrooms available all around them.

"I don't have to have a why," Owen groused in a lower register.

"Someone new?"

Owen laughed to himself. "No, no one new."

Someone old, Josh thought. His partner.

"Besides," Owen said, softening, "you graduate this summer, right? It's not as if it could go on forever."

"Yes, it could," Josh claimed.

"No, it can't," Owen snapped.

Josh had wanted to take the relationship to the next level. Instead, like the wrong elevator, it was going down, not up. He was afraid that, if he pushed the issue, Owen wouldn't see him.

The next strange episode involved a drive in the country. Owen picked him up outside Josh's apartment, and when Josh asked where they were going, Owen said nowhere. He was just going to drive, as he put it, and see where they wound up, which, as it turned out, was at an old, abandoned house at the end of a gravel road. They explored rooms downstairs and upstairs, and when Owen leaned against the wall, staring out a window, Josh mistook his intentions and groped him.

"No, no, no," Owen sighed, bored. "That's not why we're here."

"Why are we here?"

Owen glanced at him contemptuously. "Let's head back."

Letting him be near him, but not touch him was a terrible torment for Josh, yet another mysterious issue he was too scared to broach.

Owen teased him again one night when they just happened to meet, leaving school. Owen suggested they walk to the mound of Venus, where they lay in the grass, Owen, hands under head, gazing at the stars, Josh, propped on an elbow, watching him.

"Let me do you," Josh said. "You can see if anyone's coming."

"Coming?" Owen quipped, nervously tapping his foot. "What a little nymph you are."

"Nymph?" Josh asked. "Don't you mean satyr?"

Owen laughed, but the laugh was only a breath.

"You love me, don't you?" Owen asked, his faced turned away.

Josh laughed, too. "Yeah."

Owen gazed across the lake. "Mine forever, right?"

"Right," Josh said. "Anything you want anytime you want it. Even here. Now."

But the words only deepened the black gloom between them. The bond between them, Josh knew, was a kind of heavy chain, the chain of shackled prisoners on the run. How much more of this frustrating sadism could he bear?

Outside of conferences with his advisor and research that could be done only in the library, Josh had become a virtual prisoner in the comfortable cell of his apartment, an open cell he was afraid to leave for fear that Owen might come to his senses and drop by. The sentence he was serving, however, he managed to turn to his advantage. His main academic goal that semester was to finish his doctoral thesis, and his cloistered existence gave him plenty of time to work on that. But then, after a couple of weeks, he couldn't take it anymore: the terrible pressure building in his chest. He had to see Owen, had to know where he stood with him, what was going on.

When he went to Owen's office, the door was open, and Owen was sitting at his desk, reading. When Josh knocked on the wall by the door, Owen glanced at him over his shoulder, stood, and slipped his hands into his pockets.

"A student is due any minute," Owen said, uneasy.

"Thought your office hours were over," Josh said, stepping into the room.

Josh noticed that Owen's fingers were moving in his left pocket. The effect looked as if something alive were squirming in his pants. At that point, Josh sensed someone behind him and turned to see a young woman and a little boy at the door. The boy looked about four years old.

"Oh, hi," the woman said to Josh. "You ready?" she asked Owen.

"Just a second," he said. "Why don't you wait for me downstairs?"

"Daddy," the boy asked, letting go of the woman's hand, "can we go to the park tomorrow? Mommy says there's going to be a fair!"

Josh glanced at Owen.

"One of those cheap, traveling fairs," she explained, "with stupid rides for kids. I'm Carrie, by the way," the woman said, extending her hand.

"Josh," Josh said, shaking her hand. "Good to meet you."

"And this little man is Casey," Carrie said. "Actually, K.C., short for Kenneth Collins Payne. Say hi to the young man, Casey."

Josh knelt on a knee. "Hi, there, Casey. I'm Josh."

Bashfully, the boy ran around Josh to Owen and hugged his leg.

"You'll have to excuse him," Carrie said. "I never know what he's going to do."

Casey rocked from foot to foot and raised his hands to be picked up, and Owen gathered him into his arms. Josh glanced up, noticed Owen's ring, and understood what Owen had been trying to do in the pocket: take it off.

"You OK?" Carrie smiled.

"Uh, yeah," Josh said, standing. "Tired. Uh," he stammered. "Have to run. Pleasure to meet you." As he stepped into the hall, he added, "Have a good time at the fair. Bye, Casey."

"Say bye-bye to the nice man, Casey," Carrie said.

Casey stared at Josh as if Josh were stark naked, then threw his arms around Owen's neck.

As Josh inched down the hall, he could hear Carrie say, "He looked dazed. You fail 'im?"

He heard the door close, a door, he thought, which may as well have been the one to their affair.

The next night, the weather turned cold, and Josh cranked up the fireplace for the last time. He used cedar and even threw on a bundle of thyme from the kitchen, and soon the apartment was scented with the pleasant smell of the wood and herb. He put on a CD of Pink Floyd's *The Division Bell* and was working at his laptop in his office – in fact, making changes to the floor plans of his dream house – when he heard the front door open and assumed he had forgot to lock it. He swiveled in his chair, and Owen appeared at the office door. Josh stood, went to him, and embraced him compassionately.

"Wine?" Josh asked, stepping back

"No," Owen said.

"Don't have time," Josh guessed. "Let's do it."

Like zombies, they went through the motions of their sex routine, Josh butt up with a pillow under his hips.

Afterward, they lay there, catching their breath, staring at the time on the ceiling. When Josh faced him, Owen stared back. Then Josh forgot himself and went to caress what he romantically thought of as the grape clusters of Owen's curls, but when he did, Owen brushed his hand away, sat up, and gazed out the window. He was staring into the woods as if stranded on an island, waiting for a sail to appear. When he covered his mouth with his hand and began to cry, Josh did not dare do or say anything. If they did not talk about the truth, perhaps they could pretend it did not exist, and maybe, somehow, it would go away. They could still go on seeing each other.

"You're not going to get even with me, are you?" Owen asked, pulling himself together.

And there it was, not stated, but implied. The end. Josh recognized it the way he knew the Greek gods always recognized each other, no matter how disguised.

"Of course not," he said. "Never. You don't have to worry about that."

"I feel as if I went hiking," Owen said, "and got lost. I don't have a compass. I don't have the slightest idea which way to...."

"You can do this," Josh said. "I can't. You can. We both know if anyone can, it's you." Josh got up and slipped into his boxers. "I have something for you." He went into his office and came back with the framed travel brochure for the Imperial Hotel. He turned on a table lamp, handed him the brochure, and sat beside him on the bed. "Frank Lloyd Wright's hotel in Tokyo," he said. "I want you to have it."

"Can't," Owen said, trying to hand it back.

"Yes, you can," Josh said, shoving it back with the back of his hand.

"How would I explain it?"

Josh thought. "Say some student gave it to you. You wouldn't be lying." Then he joked, "Students give teachers bribes all the time."

"Is it valuable?" Owen asked, suddenly interested.

"Um, not really," Josh lied.

The brochure was Josh's "guest gift," as Homer would put it, what ancient Greeks would give guests ready to depart.

The next day, Josh's dad called to ask how his thesis was going and, after the conversation, felt so concerned about him he asked Henry Moon, one of Josh's high-school buddies, to fly down and check on him. Josh picked Henry up at the airport and, driving home, told him about the affair and how he felt that he had saved Owen from a kind of personal shipwreck, if only for a few months, how he had loved him unconditionally no matter how humiliating such a warped romance had been. It just wasn't fair.

"Well," Henry said, "you may have saved him, as you say, but it's time to save yourself. Your degree isn't in jeopardy, is it?"

"No," Josh said, shaking his head. "Surprisingly enough, that's on track."

"Good," Henry said. "Your dad's really proud of you."

"Is he?"

"Of course," Henry scoffed. "Yes. He's looking forward to your joining the firm. You have to finish everything over here, pass your licensing exam, and then maybe go somewhere for a while, forgot all about this Owen character. I can't believe you deluded yourself into thinking that someone like that could really love you. Josh, he's a homophobic gay."

But how could he let go of him? Josh wondered. He couldn't. He didn't have the heart or the willpower to send him away. He was addicted to him physically and emotionally. Owen would have to end it, and he knew that Owen could and would, probably at the end of the semester. The only thing Josh could do was to go about preparing himself for it. First, he would not seek him out. If Owen wanted to see him, he would have to come to him. Then, after the licensing exam, he would go abroad. To Italy. His dad wanted him to travel. The final touch on his education, as he put it. One day, of course, Josh gave in, as any addict would, and went to see Owen, but when he dropped by his office, Owen's name was not on the plaque by the door.

Chapter 45: The Interview

Late Sunday night, lightning, crooked as a crack, connected the vaporous sky over Vesuvius with a spot low on the mountain's northwestern slope. At the Galleria's east entrance, Valerio was sitting on a step, wearing his signature Nikes, jeans, and tee with the small red bulldog. He looked up with interest when a huge wave of thunder raked the city.

"Where's Rollo?" he asked, feeling his bristly buzz cut.

"Don't know," Gianluca said.

"Hmmm," Valerio hummed.

When a white news van pulled up, Gianluca and the others faded like ghosts into the shadows, but Valerio lingered on the steps, elbow on knee, a hand on the back of his head. The van had "Secondo Canale [Channel 2]" printed on the door, a satellite dish folded on top, and a ladder on the back door. The driver remained at the wheel in the dark, but a striking, middle-aged man got out, approached Valerio, and, with a polite smile, extended his hand.

"Buona sera," he began. "I'm Dino Durante, journalist with Channel 2, Napoli Nazionale."

"A pleasure," Valerio said, standing. "I've seen you on TV."

As they shook hands, Valerio glanced not at Durante's right, but his left hand, and saw not only the strangely phallic microphone with the Channel 2 logo, but also Durante's simple gold wedding band.

"Good, good," Durante said.

Durante was tall and lean, almost gaunt, with a rugged face the tan of tarnished camellias. He had deep-set, dark-brown, intelligent eyes glittering like lapilli, brows slanted down as if his face had settled, and a thin mouth the smooth maroon of cherry bark. He was wearing wrinkled linen slacks with a side-pack on his belt, a dark-blue dress shirt with a loose, light-blue tie, and a plastic identification tag on a strip around his neck. His thick, graying, dark-brown hair was parted on the left and puffed up in waves as if he had been riding in a convertible, not a van.

"We're coming up on the thirty-first anniversary of the great Italian writer, critic, and cineaste Pier Paolo Pasolini's death," Durante explained, "and in honor of that occasion we're making a documentary on him and his effect on the gay-rights movement in Italy."

"Gay rights," Valerio repeated, slipping his hand into his pocket.

"Yes," Durante said. "Familiar with Pasolini?"

"I've seen some of his films and read articles about him."

"Great," Durante said. "Would you mind talking to us on camera?"

After sizing up the situation, Valerio, as usual, felt safe as a god, as protected from harm as he had been from mosquitoes when his mother would smear her fennel tincture on his arms and legs.

"How much?" Valerio asked, pulling out a pocketknife.

"You wouldn't do it for free?" Durante smiled, business-like.

"Would I have sex for free?" Valerio asked, making eye contact.

Durante laughed thoughtfully, glancing down.

"How long do you think it would take?" Valerio asked, opening a small blade on the knife.

"Depends on how much you have. To say, that is."

Valerio glanced down, cleaned a fingernail with the knife, and, happy with the nail, folded and put away the knife.

"What about 25 up front?" Valerio asked, glancing at Durante. "I'll give it back after fifteen minutes if you're not satisfied."

"OK," Durante agreed, meeting his eyes. When he called to the driver, "Tommaso!" a light-toned black stepped from the van, wearing cut-off jeans, a white, sleeveless tee like Valerio's, a red cap, sneakers, white socks, and, like Durante's, an identification tag around his neck. He brought Durante a clipboard, and Durante took out a pen, wrote 25 E on a line, and marked an X on another.

"If you would sign here," he said, handing Valerio the clipboard and pen. "It just gives us permission to use the interview."

"All right," Valerio said, signing. "I trust you."

Valerio clipped the pen to the clipboard, and when he handed it back, Durante wedged it in his armpit, took out his wallet, and counted out twenty-five Euros. When he handed them over, Valerio stuffed them into a front pocket. Meanwhile, Tommaso had gone to the back of the van, opened a door, and taken out a tripod and camera.

"What if we sit on the steps?" Durante asked.

Valerio nodded, and they took up positions, side by side, facing each other. Durante laid the clipboard aside, and Tommaso set up the tripod about a yard in front of them, attached the camera, and, eye to viewfinder, turned a dial to tilt the camera up towards them. Face to camera, Tommaso looked as if he had become one with it bionically, his left hand rotating the lens.

When a clap of thunder cracked in the distance, Durante commented, "Sounds like Pompeii is getting some rain tonight."

"Or Vesuvius is erupting," Valerio joked, admiring the deep dimple in the man's chin and the dimples in his cheeks. When Valerio smiled at him seductively with his eyes, Durante locked eyes for a moment, then glanced at Tommaso.

"Ready?"

"Ready," Tommaso replied, switching on the bright light on top of the camera.

Durante turned to Valerio. "Ready?" he asked, flipping a switch on the side-pack.

"Shouldn't we sit closer?" Valerio asked. "For the camera?"

"Well, all right."

When they slid closer, Valerio tightened Durante's tie, then pressed his thumb into the corner of Durante's mouth. "A smudge."

Durante had a day's growth of beard, and in the bright light, the gray stubble sparkled like mica. Just touching it briefly lit Valerio's groin with a familiar warm sensation.

In response, Durante, wide eyed, froze as if thinking, then asked again, "Ready?"

The cameraman tilted away from the camera, apparently curious about the intimacy, then tilted back.

"I'm here at the Galleria with – " Durante began, holding up the mike.

"Stop," Valerio said. "Don't mention the place."

"Cut," Durante said to Tommaso. He turned to Valerio. "People can see where we are."

"Perhaps," Valerio agreed, "but you don't have to give them directions."

Durante thought, then turned to Tommaso. "Again. –Good evening," he said to the camera. "I'm here with a young man whom we'll call Angelo, discussing the approaching thirty-first anniversary of Pier Paolo Pasolini's death on November 2. First of all," he said, facing Valerio, "what films by Pasolini have you seen?" He pointed the mike towards Valerio's mouth.

"Saló," Valerio said, staring at the mike. "Hard to forget Saló. Teorema, my favorite. Medea with Callas."

"Angelo," Durante asked, "have you seen what he called his Trilogy of Life?"

"Oh, yes," Valerio said, remembering. "The Decameron, Canterbury Tales, 1,001 Nights. All I remember from The Decameron and Canterbury Tales, I'm afraid, are big cocks. I can say that, Dino. Big cocks."

"Oh, yes," Durante assured him. "Whatever you like. We can always edit it out. But now, to the point. OK," he said to himself, apparently regrouping. "Where do we go with this? Angelo, what's your opinion of what Pasolini did for gay rights?"

Valerio thought. "I'm not sure Pasolini did anything for gay rights. He was before the movement in Italy, wasn't he?"

"Not entirely," Durante said. "After the war, there were the Radical Party, which was pro gay, and FOURI, il Fronte Unitario Omossessuali Rivoluzionari Italiani."

"He was a Communist, right?"

"Right."

While Durante took out a small notepad and flipped through it, Valerio leaned back on his elbows. When he spread his knees, exposing his crotch to the camera, he noticed that Tommaso rotated the lens slightly.

"Let me read you a quote," Durante said. "Then, if you would, respond to it."

Valerio nodded.

"'My homosexuality,' he wrote, 'had nothing to do with me.... I always saw it as something next to me, like an enemy, never feeling it inside me.'"

Durante tilted the mike toward Valerio.

"Sounds homophobic," Valerio commented. "Schizophrenic." When Durante just sat there, Valerio added, "Not sure a homophobe would do much for gays."

"Right," Durante agreed. "Even Tonuti, his second lover, denied he was gay."

"Sad," Valerio said. "Isn't it?"

"Did you know he frequented hustlers?"

Valerio glanced at Durante, sat up, and took hold of the mike, pulling it towards his mouth, but when he did, he was also touching Durante's hand.

"Who hasn't heard of how he died?" Valerio asked, letting go of the mike.

"He is said to have liked a specific type, tough guys with an olive complexion and dark hair."

"Well, Dino," Valerio grinned, hands up, palms up, "he would've been very happy here, wouldn't he?"

"In fact," Durante said, "he called the type Gennariello, an imaginary Neapolitan, and as he grew older, the type became an obsession for him, poor, ignorant, rebellious."

"Well," Valerio smiled, "maybe he wouldn't have been so happy. Young men today, even poor, are more middle class, at least mentally."

"With age, money, and fame, what once had been a source of – of energy, let's say, for him, became, more or less, a mere transaction. How do you account for that?"

"Well," Valerio scoffed, "you said it yourself. First, his age. Who would you rather trick with, Dino, a hot stud or an old man?" When Durante just stared at him, Valerio said, "And if someone's broke and knows you have money, he has just one thing on his mind, and it's not romance. Sex for hire is what it is."

"He said the boys had changed from brothers to thugs whom he hated and blamed the change on capitalism."

"You hate the lover who doesn't love you, eh, Dino?" Valerio asked. "He was deluding himself. He had changed, not them."

"The question is – " Durante hesitated. Suddenly, he looked alone as a saint on a column. "Do you, as a random passerby, let's say, personally know of anything he actually did to better the lot of the boys he patronized?"

"Me, no," Valerio laughed. "Let's hope he paid them well."

"Do you think he exploited them?"

"Exploited, no. As you said, he liked tough guys."

"I guess it's debatable who's exploiting whom," Durante commented.

"I guess."

Despite the immediate implications of the statement, Valerio felt strangely at home with Durante, as if the sinewy man were, in fact, a friend or even a father. He sensed a non-gay subliminal rapport with him the way that certain animals sense a presence or threat, a simple humane empathy reflected in the familiar way the man now leaned forward, elbows on knees, the bulbous mike clasped in both hands.

"Why do you think he joined the Communist Party instead of the Radical Party and FOURI?"

To answer, Valerio leaned in close as well, sharing the mike, his left knee touching Durante's right. "Well," he began, "he may have actually been interested in class struggle, but if he was as homophobic as he seems, then he didn't consider his sexual orientation worth politics. What he didn't realize is that sexual freedom equals individual freedom and that individual freedom equals class freedom."

"Sexual freedom equals individual freedom," Durante repeated thoughtfully, his face close to Valerio's.

Gazing into the man's attentive eyes, Valerio let himself imagine him as a lover nude in a huge bed. In the fantasy, the bed had a scalloped blue headboard, an elaborate blue and yellow bedspread, and, hung from the ceiling, a circular ring of gauzy mosquito netting. Durante was leaning back on his elbows, legs bent, an ankle on a knee, revealing his butt.

At that point, Durante sat up straight, and Valerio snapped back to the moment.

"Toward the end of his life," Durante began. He searched back and forth through his notepad, but looked as if he could not find what he was looking for. He glanced at the camera, then at Valerio, and apparently improvised.

"Toward the end of his life, when society became more tolerant, he saw the tolerance as false, in name only. In fact, he called it something like 'the mask of the worst repression.' What do you think?"

"'Mask of the worst repression,'" Valerio smiled. "Boy, was he paranoid. No matter how lukewarm it is, tolerance is still better than intolerance."

"You think Italian society is more tolerant?"

"Yes," Valerio mused. "Of course, Prodi's commitment to increased rights is an unkept promise, and Berlusconi's so-called Freedom People is the new Black Shirts."

"Black Shirts?" Durante laughed. "Tell me what you really think about Berlusconi."

At the sight of Durante's deeply etched smile, Valerio realized that he had seriously misjudged the man and was a little embarrassed about how he had been teasing him. Whatever Dino's back story was, Valerio thought, it had left its harsh effects on his face prematurely: the snarl of wrinkles under his eyes, the dark furrows in his coarse cheeks, the creased, slightly receding forehead. Plants had nipple-like scars where a leaf had broken away from a stem, and Valerio had somehow glimpsed all the hidden scars behind Durante's wistful laugh. The professional journalist, despite the wedding ring, was just a sweet, lonely straight man, benevolent as bread.

"Back to Pasolini," Durante said. "He thought that the sexual permissiveness of today's consumer society had traumatized young males."

"Traumatized them?" Valerio puzzled, sitting up. "In what way?"

"Having to perform all the time."

"Ridiculous," Valerio said. "That's all young men want to do. What nuns in boy drag was he talking to?" They laughed. "I think he was the one worried about performance."

"Do you think that Pasolini, in fact, did anything for gay rights?"

"Well," Valerio thought, absently rubbing his thighs, "he was in the news a lot, a queer to be dealt with. There's something to be said for actually seeing gays. It dispels the myth that we don't exist."

Valerio paused when he realized he had just admitted he was gay on tape, and during the pause, a tangle of lightning, like cracked glass, lit up the clouds over the city. The deafening percussion sounded like a bomb going off. Everyone flinched and looked up. Then Valerio and Durante glanced at each other, both faces fixed in an earnest smile.

"And it presents an image of gays different from the stereotypes," Valerio continued. "From what I've seen of his pictures, he was a butch."

"One of the reasons he was in the news," Durante said, "was his conflicts with the Communist Party. It saw his sexual orientation as decadent."

"Then it didn't understand it. You are who you are, and the party should've defended a person's right to be himself, just as the church shouldn't try to pit itself against people simply being who they are. In that sense, it's the church that's going against nature. First, we should try to show it the error of its ways, but if that doesn't work, then we can at least ignore it, live outside it as much as we can."

"As do the characters in Pasolini's early novel *Ragazzi di Vita*. Read it?"

"No."

"Think you'd find it interesting," Durante said.

Valerio studied Durante's sly smile. "How did he respond to the party?"

"As you said," Durante stated. "He lived outside it. He was a Communist, but his own Communist."

"That's a great image to project, gays as individuals. He valued his individuality more than party loyalty."

"You saw some of his films," Durante said on another tack. "Do you think they helped further gay rights?"

"Any exposure to sex, gay or straight, is a form of desensitization," Valerio began, "so I think that the films probably helped in the struggle for sexual liberation in general. A big cock on the screen is a form of liberal ideology, an attack on repressive bourgeois morality. And I read that he had to fight several censorship battles to screen his films. Freedom from censorship is another form of sexual freedom."

"A moment ago, you mentioned the church," Durante said. "Pasolini saw it as passé, but pernicious, and polemicized against it and its influence on government and the country. He called it something like 'the merciless heart of the State,' which he referred to as 'a clerical regime.' What's your attitude toward the church?"

"Yes," Valerio stressed, looking beyond Durante to the left. "The church has far too great an influence on government, and a harmful one at that. It's a giant slippery octopus with tentacles in the police, the judiciary, the press, and schools, all working to preserve its power and that of its political allies. It's the source of most of the sexual repression and homophobic violence in the country. So if Pasolini attacked it, Dino, he was right to do so." Valerio felt the strong tow of an emotional undercurrent carrying him off, but did not try to stop it. "It's directly guilty for the beatings, molestation, and rape in the schools and orphanages it runs. The victims are treated like prison inmates or slaves, made to feel corrupted and worthless with no safe way to tell authorities. Pedophile priests, nuns, and older inmates attack the young on a regular basis and are shielded by the church."

"How do you know this?" Durante asked sympathetically.

"Personal experience," Valerio stated, looking Durante straight in the eye. "My parents died in a car accident when I was nine."

Durante turned to the camera pensively, then faced Valerio again. "Sorry to hear that."

"And there's the indirect violence," Valerio went on, staring right, "the psychological violence when Pope John Paul himself says that being yourself is a kind of mental disorder, grave depravity, morally evil. Such an outrageous statement creates a hostile atmosphere in which people think it's OK to make jokes about gays, to bully them, to assault them."

Durante had listened attentively, but, when Valerio had finished, did not seem to know where to go.

"Well, Angelo," he said, extending his hand. "Thank you very much. It's been a pleasure talking with you. Very informative." They shook hands. Then Durante turned to the camera. "This is Dino Durante for Napoli Nazionale, signing off from Santa Lucia. Have a good night."

When he made the cut sign, Tommaso turned the light off and began dismantling the camera.

"We seem to have drifted off topic," Durante said, turning to Valerio. "But I'm very pleased with the interview. I think we can use just about all of it."

Durante switched off his side-pack, picked up the clipboard, and stood.

"Any connections with a modeling agency?" Valerio asked, standing. "I'd love to be an Armani model."

"Modeling," Durante pondered. "I'll see what I can do, but you're surely better off in Rome or Milan. Everything's in Milan: design, theater, TV. Like to be there myself." He appeared to be mulling over something, then glanced at Valerio. "Do hustlers have protectors?"

"Protectors?" Valerio asked. At first, he questioned his faith in the man, then recognized the sober concern in his voice.

"Pimps," Durante explained, gesturing with the clipboard.

"No," Valerio said. "Not here."

"Any cases in which the boys are beat up and robbed?"

They stared at each other.

"No," Valerio assured him. "No story here."

"Good," Durante nodded. Then he took a business card out of his shirt pocket and handed it to Valerio. "This is how to contact me in case you think of anything else on Pasolini or any other story you think newsworthy, OK?"

Valerio read the card. Meanwhile, Tommaso had stored the camera and tripod, locked the door, and climbed into the driver's seat.

"Mind if I have your number?" Durante asked. "In case I need to clarify anything in the interview."

When Valerio nodded, Durante handed him his notepad and pen, and Valerio wrote down his first name and number and handed it back. Durante put the pad away and extended his hand again, but when Valerio took it, Durante hugged him.

"Grazie mille," Durante said.

"Prego."

Chapter 46: A Plastic Container of Mushrooms

After class, Tyler drove Erin to her studio apartment at the Hemlock, a run-down, brick bastion of negligence with a tall, wrought-iron fence around the property and a big, chained gate at the front. He thought the gate said a lot for the safety in the area.

He parked in the lot behind the building, and as they strolled through the entrance to the back yard, she warned him, "Stay on the sidewalk. Lots of dog shit."

They trudged up steps to a small porch with a lattice railing.

"The terrace," she said ironically.

"With a great view of dog shit," he added.

When she stopped to unlock the door, he noticed the number 1-F, then glanced right at the two chaise lounges with broken straps and, between them, a tiny, rusted table with a citronella bucket. Metal bars clutched the windows. To make sure you die in the fire, he thought.

When she opened the door, she flicked a switch, which turned on a lamp on a nightstand to the right of the bed. The lamp had a crazed, black shade with a sheer, red scarf over it, coloring the room with a dim, placental glow. The low ceiling made the small, stuffy space even more claustrophobic, and when they stepped inside, he felt as if he were entering a tomb, a dusty cubicle in Pompeii locked up for centuries. Then he thought of Homer Barron's room locked up for decades. To him, there was something deeply erotic about the place as if its *raison d'etre* over the years had been the soft magnet of the sultry unmade bed with its nuptial sports. He took in the thin sheets, the sallow pillows propped against the headboard, the old-fashioned bedspread knobby with tufts. One step up from a sleazy motel, he thought.

He glanced around the room as if someone could be hiding in it: to either side, gossamer sheers and the pinched swags of burgundy curtains; to his left, a mauve sofa with deflated cushions, frizzy fringe, and end tables; near it, against the far wall, a Formica table with four chairs.

As Erin walked across the hardwood floor, it squeaked, despite the Oriental rug, and when she paused at the table, she unscrewed the fish-fly earring and laid the pieces on it. Then she moved to the kitchenette.

There was a long, cracked mirror over the sofa, and when he stepped into the middle of the room, he noticed his split reflection in it. The mirror struck him as an invasion of privacy. He did not want to see what he was doing.

In it, behind him, was also what hung on the opposite wall over the bed. He turned toward an old, framed picture puzzle of a duck decoy on a black lake with a crescent moon reflected as a silver necklace.

Erin was pouring a glass of wine at the little counter in the kitchen, and when she offered him the glass, he looked beyond it to the name on the bottle.

"Sangiovese," he said. "How'd you know I like Sangiovese?"

"Just picked a bahtle off the shelf," she claimed, striking what he considered a silly pose. She slumped – hand on hip, one foot resting on a toe – holding the glass as if selling it in an ad. "Sahry 'bout the glahss."

"Not a problem," he said. "Where's yours?"

"Bettah not."

"Why?"

"Why," she pondered, glancing down right. "I'm tired. I'll fall asleep."

"So?"

"Not what I had in mind."

He studied her shrewdly. "Look," he said, taking the glass. "I'll hang around if you drink. I'm leaving if you don't. Drink up."

Face forward, lips pressed together, he gave her a funny, assertive expression.

"Ooo-Kaay," she said slowly.

When she poured herself less than what was in his glass, he insisted, "More." When she faced him tentatively, he toasted, "To your writing career."

"Yeah, right," she smiled, tapping his glass.

He took a swallow, and when she only sipped hers, he said, "Drink for drink."

She swallowed more hesitantly.

"Have you ever written anything?" he asked, grabbing the bottle.

"What do you think?"

He set the bottle on the table. She followed. They sat, he backward in the chair, resting his arms on the back, she elbows on the table. He asked about the various jobs at which she had worked over the years – dress shop, head shop, movie-rental store – and when their glasses ran dry, he poured a second round.

"Thaht's wheh I met my lahst lovah," she slurred, already tipsy. "Cinema City. He was jealous and mean, slappin' me around if he thought I was...." She seemed to fade away.

"Cheating on him," Tyler said, touching the fishhook. "How'd you wind up in Atlanta?"

"Well," she said, sipping the wine casually, "to be pehfectly honest, to get away from him, my lovah. Well, *lovah* isn't exactly the right word. More like bully. You know, men."

"I do," he confessed.

"One night, when I thought he'd kill me, I just went to our little aihport and hopped a plane. It just hahpened to be flyin' heah, Atlanter."

"To get away from a lover," Tyler mused.

"But let's not talk about that," she asked. "All in the pahst. Leave it theah."

"Sure," he smiled sweetly. "All we have is the moment."

But there was something theatrical about her short narrative, Tyler felt, as if she were acting a part, something rehearsed. Again, he thought about her saying that she had not made friends in two months, plausible enough, he assumed, after being "burned." Still, how could someone as easy as she seemed not have friends? She must be a veritable Pandora's Box of psychological bats. How many mangy specimens of the male species would pass up free snatch?

"If you take a big swallow," he coaxed her, "I'll take off my jacket."

She downed a mouthful, then rocked back in her chair, glancing at him defiantly. He stood, slipped out of his jacket, and draped it over the back of his chair. As he was about to sit, he noticed the loose, faded wallpaper with its witch hazel pattern. Purplish red sepals were bursting with wrinkled, yellow petal-streamers. The pattern was so old and dark that he had to lean in close and squint at it before he realized what it was, as if seeing the flowers through dense fog. The water stains reminded him of a Rorshach test. He didn't want to think about the bugs that lived in it.

Meanwhile, she unlaced her Keds, slipped them off toe to heel, and peeled off her socks. Then she braced on the table, pushed herself up, and pulled her T-shirt over her head, clumsily revealing her plump breasts.

He turned, winked, and jiggled the front of his shirt, offering to take it off. She finished her glass, accidentally banged it on the table, and began dancing drowsily and singing the lyrics to David Bowie's "Rebel Rebel."

"Yah mothah in a whihl," she recited. "Not shuah if youah a boy ah a girl."

He stepped out of his clogs and, barefoot, started singing with her. Then he split what was left of the bottle between them and began unbuttoning his shirt suggestively as in a striptease. It was a big, blue, blousy cotton dress shirt, and he held it open, exposing an undershirt, then began sliding it side to side down his shoulders as if drying his back with a towel. He tossed it over a chair, picked up the glasses, and handed her hers.

She drank and slid the glass onto the nightstand to the left of the bed. Eyeing him, she unbuckled her belt and unsnapped and slowly unzipped her jeans, slipping them down her hips slyly as if performing a number, a burlesque of a burlesque, gradually molting to a new form, as he thought of it: Erin, the exotic butterfly. She stumbled out of the jeans, nude except for black panties so sheer he could see her pubic hair through them. She danced toward him languidly a la Marilyn Monroe and, face to face, mouthed the lyrics again, but, after a dozen lines or so, began humming the riff.

"Warm enough in here?" he asked paternally.

"In heh?" she asked, draping her arms over his shoulders.

"The apartment."

"I haven't been heh long enough," she said, pressing against him, "to know what it's like in wintah."

"Right."

When she nuzzled his neck, he thought, *This must be where the flexible part comes in*, remembering what she had written on his check. He imagined her on top, bouncing on his lap furiously as a way to vent some pent-up hate for her father or abusive boyfriends. As for him, the prospect was of a vigorous workout to achieve a self-abolishing ecstasy, not exactly a Neo-Platonic union with the ultimate being, he joked, more like an rapturous blackout due to a drop in blood pressure. Of course, he could use a blackout, he felt. A break from thinking, no matter how short, would give his brain a rest.

"*Where* you from?" he asked.

"Biddeford."

"Thought Biddeford was in Maine."

"Yeah," she agreed, squinching her face. "There's one in New Hampshah, too."

"On the coast?"

She hesitated. "Yeah."

They stopped dancing, and, staring at her, he stepped back and finished his glass. He set it on the nightstand and gave her hers. She downed it, staring back, and he set it beside his. Then they just stood there, eyes locked, hers droopy, his sharp.

"How did you wind up here?" he asked. "In Little Five Points?"

"I got off at the Five Points station, Big Five Points," she explained, "and ahsked this grunjah."

"Grunjah?"

"This grunge guy wheh Pearl Jam would go?"

"Really?" he smiled incredulously.

"Yeah," she said, putting her hands on his chest.

"Then you got the job at the Vortex."

"Getting a job was very impohtant."

"Doin' OK?" he asked. "Financially?"

"Enough fah rent and meals."

"What are you on?" he asked, taking her hands.

"On?" she asked with an odd, sidelong glance.

"Yeah, on. You're too relaxed."

"You're the one who got me liqahed up."

She pulled him to the bed. The rocks of her bed, he thought, like a Siren, as if the bed itself were the gruesome river bottom to which he was being sucked down all along.

"Let's cut the crap," she murmured, but when she pushed him backward, she staggered too, falling against him so that they wound up with him sitting on the side of the bed, knees spread, and her kneeling between them. He leaned back on his elbows in a comfortable, provocative pose, and she shoved his undershirt up and licked his abs and groin. Then she sat back, unsnapped his jeans, and began to unzip them. He knew there was some magnificent lie between them, an unspoken game in which each was slowly circling the other with caution. Peeling off his clothes was like peeling off dry bark to find some rotten, vice-ridden truth underneath.

"Oh, no," she groaned wearily, eyes closed, a hand to her head. "Dizzy."

When she started to pass out, he grabbed her shoulders to keep her from tilting over, but her shoulders felt gross and fleshy to him, a strange sensation for which he couldn't account. He stood and hoisted her to her feet, and when he lifted her, she was so light she felt hollow, a big, soft doll, all lurid skin and vague sighs. When he lay her on the bed, she sank into the nebulous linens, and he covered her to the waist, then just stood there, looking down at her curiously.

"Take me," she whispered, barely conscious, someone under hypnosis.

When she patted the place beside her, he asked, "Got a condom?" When he opened the drawer in the nightstand, he saw a book of crossword puzzles folded open to one with a lot of erasures and a few words filled in: *shadow*, *apple*, *snow*, *plum*, *gilt*.

"We don't need one," she breathed, slowly spreading her legs.

"And I don't need blisters," he said, meaning herpes. "Let's just talk. Let's get to know each other first."

"Ah," she cajoled him. "Whaht's the fun in thaht?"

As a writer, he was grateful for a subject to study, callous as that sounded even to him. But then he wasn't pursuing her. She was guiding him, and he simply had to know where, to see the end of the experiment and have it over. He couldn't help himself. Of course, he would enjoy fucking her. The range of sensations in pure sex, as opposed to love sex, would be simpler, he thought, focused to a plain, uninhibited drive to penetrate her and release himself into her entirely. He liked the attention, but knew from the start she wasn't interested in him for the right reasons, at least none that would lead to anything lasting and satisfying, perhaps nothing more than rough sex, something to which he could give himself up to explore her, to find out who she was, yet hardly worth the effort. How important was sex anyway? Whatever was going to happen wouldn't make him happy, so it was wrong. It was as simple as that. And since he was putting nothing into it, that was about what he expected to get out of it. Nothing. No wonder he balked to take her, like a horse at a jump, recoiled from someone so apparently willing to throw herself away, the waitress with no friends. Even when she turned on him, as he knew she would, he wouldn't really care. He cared for her only as far as he cared for anyone. He was autonomous, self-judging, maverick. If she came to a bad end, he was not taking responsibility for yet another sad fool's tragic mistake.

"Look at me," he said, sitting on the bed. "Look at me."

He held her chin and shook her head till her eyes opened, but they were obliterated with sleep, shiny black berries in which he could see nothing but darkness. Some mental light was turned off. She was gone. If he fucked her now, it was rape.

He reached her jeans, but when he took out her wallet, there was hardly anything in it: stamps, $52 in cash. The name on her expired Maine driver's license was Erin Lee Siemens. Other information included an address in Portland (Cumberland County), age (23), height (5'7"), and weight (135 pounds). Her picture looked more normal than her, he guessed, meaning prettier, happier, more bourgeois. Her mirror image, as he thought of it, the reverse of the freak. However, there was still a certain quantum of brightness missing from her eyes. Then he found the piece of paper slipped into a pocket, and when he unfolded it, he was surprised, but not quite shocked to find a black and white printout of his picture from his faculty page on the Georgia State University website. He folded the picture, slipped it back into the pocket, and tossed the wallet gingerly onto her jeans.

He sat, thinking, lulled by the dead quiet. Then he heard a car horn in the distance, got up, and tiptoed across the squeaky floor toward the kitchenette. A rag hung from the handle on the refrigerator, and when he opened the fridge, he saw a steak wrapped in cellophane, a box of crackers, and a couple of black, moldy bananas. He thought of the Freudian bananas as penises sacrificed in some voodoo ritual. In a bin in the door, he noticed three bars of sweet cooking chocolate. The first cabinet he opened was bare. A line of ants meandered across a shelf. In the second cabinet, he found a plastic container of mushrooms. The label on the container had been scratched off, and the dried pieces of mushrooms looked burned and tarnished: flat caps, phallic stalks, little broken fans of gills, bits of mushroom stuck to the walls of the container. They reminded him of the herbs and weeds in Karen's house on Ashe Island. He opened the container, sniffed the foul, sickly sweet smell, and, crinkling his nose, snapped it shut and set it back on the shelf.

Between the kitchenette and the dining area, a short, narrow hall led to a door on the right and left. He opened the one on the left, flicked a switch, and scanned a closet with Erin's clothes, mostly drab winter wear. Something stood out, however, because of its vivid color, a man's purple tie draped over the rod as if someone had forgot it. Forgotten like Peeve, he thought, the annoying cat, abandoned on the island.

"No skeletons here," he joked to himself.

He turned off the light, closed the door, and pivoted toward the door on the right. He opened it, turned on the light, and strolled into a bathroom cluttered with Erin's toilet articles. Several bottles of over-the-counter pain relievers sat on the toilet tank, but when he opened the medicine cabinet, he froze. It was chock-full of prescription bottles: Tramadol, Oxycodone, Diazepam, Alprazolam, Ambien, Dilantin, Quetiapine, Gabitril, Remeron, some with more than one bottle. At a glance, he saw that the name on the bottles was Erin Siemens and that the prescriptions were from various doctors and towns in Maine.

"I'm surprised she can walk," he whispered.

He opened the Remeron bottle and shook a pill onto his palm. The orange oval had the word *organon* stamped on it. The name made him think of *organ* and *orgasm*. He funneled the pill back into the bottle, screwed the top on, and set it back, but when he examined the bottles more closely, he realized not only that some of the prescriptions were from the pharmacy at Sea Cliff, the mental-health facility where he last saw Linda, his older daughter, but also that they were prescribed by Dr. Mike Oswald, Linda's psychiatrist.

"My God," he gaped. "She knows Linda."

Chapter 47: A Completely Disorganized Tour of Rome

One of the first things Tyler and Josh did Monday morning was to help each other do fifty sit-ups nude. Tyler held Josh's feet and enjoyed watching the young man's abs crease and stretch tight like fabric.

Then Josh held Tyler's, and when Tyler was finished, Josh took hold of Tyler's cock and, with a rosy smile, asked, "Wanna go again?" meaning sex.

"Allow not nature more than nature needs," Tyler quoted *Lear*.

He was pleasantly sore and swollen from the night before. Besides, he did not want their passionate sexual matches to become routine. Instead, he suggested pushups, what he called floor-fucks.

After breakfast with Phil and Billie in the hotel dining room, the couples set out on separate itineraries, the Trees to a day at the Vatican, Josh and Tyler to the Domus Aurea, what was left of Nero's villa, where, according to Josh, they had to buy tickets at least a day in advance. When they got there, however, it was closed for restoration.

Since they were near it, they strolled up to San Pietro in Vincoli (St. Peter in Chains) to see Michelangelo's *Moses*.

"Horns?" Tyler asked, referring to the two projecting from Moses' head.

"Based on a mistranslation," Josh said, "like glass slipper for fur slipper in *Cinderella*."

They took the Metro up to Piazza del Popolo to see the obelisk of Ramses II, which was shrouded for cleaning, and the church Santa Maria del Popolo with its Bernini sculptures, frescoes by Raphael, and a couple of paintings by Caravaggio, Josh's favorite painter: *The Crucifixion of St. Peter* and *The Conversion of St. Paul*. In *The Crucifixion*, Tyler was struck by the "awkward" composition with a man's butt prominent in the foreground and the fact that the workmen seemed to be hoisting Peter upside down. Josh loved Paul's receptive pose in *The Conversion*. The saint was flat on his back, legs spread, arms wide, completely open to the spiritual light focused on him.

From there, they strolled along the Tiber to the Ara Pacis, Augustus' Peace Altar. It was closed, but since it was housed in a glass building, they could see it through the windows.

They veered south away from the river and, as they strolled along the street, came to Bar Milano, a panini bar, and decided to have lunch. They ordered at the counter inside, sat at a bistro table on the sidewalk, and, as they relaxed, idly eating sandwiches and sipping coffee, watched an inordinate number of young, good-looking businessmen go in and out of the place.

"Good lord," Tyler laughed. "We've found where all the fashion models have lunch. Brioni must have a branch around here."

There were so many handsome young men the odds were that some were gay, and Tyler admired the ideal they represented, the value placed on youth and slim male beauty: smart suit, smooth skin, perfect hair, a certain stolid reticence. Even the ones butched up with stubble were spruce.

Then one broke the emotional mold. As he walked by, he caught Tyler watching him and, with a sly grin, said, "How ah you do-eeng?" with an Italian accent.

Tyler raised his cup and smiled. There was the twinkle of recognition in the young man's eye. He had seen them as the gay couple they were, and Tyler realized that, dressed up and well groomed, he and Josh would mirror the ideal he was envying. Gay couple, he thought. He'd certainly failed in his stint as part of a straight couple.

Out of the blue, he remembered Karen saying, "Even when you were there, you wouldn't help with the kids. I remember on one of Mom's visits, she asked why I was carrying both girls."

He thought and thought, but, for the life of him, could not remember her mother or father, for that matter, visiting them. And then he thought of the part impossible to remember, his blackout on the island. Linda looked like an angel, but caught up in rage?

"I don't think you've put two and two together," Tyler began.

"In regard to what?" Josh asked, squinting in the glare.

"My ex-wife's and my daughter's death."

"Actually, I have," Josh admitted, "and I got four, you and your family. I assume that's why your other daughter's in treatment."

"It's like what happened that night has these long, poisonous tentacles that reach into my life consciously and unconsciously almost every second of the day. The thought of what Linda may have done – well, take the sting of a jellyfish and multiply it by at least a thousand times."

"If anything were different, Ty," Josh said, "we wouldn't be here now, right?"

The memory of Maine – it wasn't an issue of a dark past versus a bright future. The past was obviously necessary for the present and a future. Light needed dark the way an old photograph needed a negative. Darkness set off light, the way loss, grief, and regret set off the happiness he was enjoying in the sunlight on a street in Rome, and he knew that only because of the great darkness in his life could he see the glimmer of hope in Josh's eyes guiding him back to himself the way the sprinkle of lights along the coast had guided him back to the inn.

"You don't know me." Tyler said.

"I know," Josh smiled. "You have a dark side."

"If you saw it, you'd be shocked. You wouldn't want me. You wouldn't want anything to do with me."

"Give me a chance to get to know you," Josh asked.

Tyler stared at the sidewalk, then looked up. "I'm no hero. When it comes down to a choice between me and someone else, I always choose me."

"Well, one, I don't believe that," Josh said, "but I'll keep it in mind. Everyone, of course, has to look after himself first. Then, when he's secure, maybe he can take on the responsibility for someone else. We work from ourselves out. Besides, I'd never ask you to sacrifice yourself for me. What real partner would?"

In regard to his daughters, Tyler thought, he was guilty of indifference, yes, but in an existential world, he was not only the accused, but also the judge. Question was: What verdict would he hand down? Should he try to rehabilitate himself or throw his life away? Throwing his life away. What good would that do? None. His sentence would be a strong belief in his possibilities with Josh, the priest who'd led him through the Gay Mysteries in their hotel rooms just as he had through the Dionysian Mysteries at the Villa dei Misteri.

"OK," Tyler decided.

"OK?"

"We're on," he said, standing. "Where next?

Next was the incense-scented San Luigi dei Francesi (St. Louis of the French) for its three Caravaggios. In *The Calling of St. Matthew*, Tyler was not sure which figure represented Matthew, the one pointing to himself, he guessed, and it took him a while to notice the thin halo over Christ's head. What caught his attention in *St. Matthew and the Angel* was the angel's boyish gesture of timidly holding his left index finger with the fingers of his right hand. Perhaps enumerating a point, Tyler thought. He also wondered about the angel's quizzical gesture in *The Martyrdom of St. Matthew*. As Matthew is being killed, he seems to be reaching for a palm frond handed down by a cherub on a cloud.

"If you're going to be stabbed to death," Josh joked, referring to the muscle-bound assassin in a loincloth, "he's the one."

The Pantheon was a few blocks away and around the corner from that, Piazza della Minerva with its Bernini elephant with an obelisk on its back. Facing the piazza was the church Santa Maria sopra Minerva with Michelangelo's marble *Christ Carrying the Cross*.

"My lord," Tyler exclaimed. "He's the sexiest Christ I've ever seen."

A nude Christ embraced the cross, one leg in front, one behind in *contrapposto*.

"Enough to make you convert," Josh joked.

"Why convert to Christianity when I can be a pagan with you?"

"The girdle was added," Josh remarked, referring to the bronze fabric across the crotch.

"Too bad about that," Tyler lamented. "Would love to see his cock."

From there, they strolled to the Museo Barraco, which was closed, then down to the Campo dei Fiori, sort of a modern equivalent, as Josh called it, for the *macellum* in Pompeii. The large, cobblestone square was filled with dozens of stalls under a cloud bank of big, canvas umbrellas with trucks, minivans, three-wheeled vehicles, and motor scooters parked among them. Throngs of noisy tourists in casual summer clothes and sunshades were slowly weaving through the aisles, browsing the flowers, produce, and souvenirs. One stall sold dresses, blouses, and T-shirts printed with *Roma*, *Italia*, and *I love Rome*.

"Something for your mom?" Tyler asked.

"Mom would not have been caught dead in anything from here."

"Would not have been," Tyler mused. "So, she's – "

"Dead."

"Sorry."

"You're not the only one with a boating accident in your past," Josh remarked, giving him an odd look.

"Really?"

"Not the only one with – " Josh paused. "Family issues." Tyler was not going to ask, but Josh said, "Mom and Dad – the marriage was mechanical, just going through the motions. She dealt with it with Scotch and prescriptions."

They strolled past the statue of a hooded figure.

"Who's this?" Tyler asked.

"Giordano Bruno," Josh said. "The Vatican used to hold executions here, and he was one of them, burned at the stake for claiming that the earth revolved around the sun."

"What heresy," Tyler joked. "Next, people'll say that gays are normal."

"He faces the Vatican."

"Someone needs to keep an eye on it."

They had started at the east end of the Campo. At the west end, they approached an old fountain.

"La Terrina," Josh said, "the Soup Bowl."

"Not much going on architecturally around here."

"Except the usual beautiful Italian-ness of it all."

Tyler glanced at the blue sky, the sun slanting across the creamy buildings, the balconies decked with potted plants and window boxes. When he faced the square, he noticed Buca di Bacco, an outdoor café.

"Like a drink?" he asked.

"Sure."

The seating area was marked off with wrought-iron railings with plant stands with palmettos at the corners. They sat at a table in the shade of a big, flat umbrella and ordered vodka tonics with lime.

"The square'll pick up again tonight," Josh said.

"You've certainly done your research."

"An academic skill."

Then they just slumped in their chairs, watching the stalls shut down.

"You've been therapy for me," Josh said finally. "Of course, I thought you'd be Italian."

Tyler started to say, *I thought you'd be a woman*, but knew it was just a line.

"Therapy," he said. "In what way?"

"Owen left me emotionally drained. I thought it would take me a long time to fill up again, let's say, like a lake."

"So I've filled you up," Tyler quipped.

"Yeah," Josh chuckled. "That way too." Josh stared at his glass, shook it, clinking the ice cubes, and took a sip. "Can't believe I was such a bimbo."

"Time you had a proper boyfriend."

Josh was not exactly what Tyler had imagined for a lover, but then he'd been wrong about it. Now that he was right, he wouldn't mind giving in to one person, his conqueror, and there was something in Josh which could, in fact, dominate him if he chose to let it. But what was it? Intelligence, thoughtfulness, kindness, love, beauty, sexual pleasure – those were qualities you could name, he thought. And then there was that incomprehensible, intangible chemistry that occurred perhaps even on a molecular level. Josh, he was sure, could master him with it, based even on a week's familiarity. It would even be an abiding joy, at last, to submit to it. As Tyler laughed to himself:

> 'Ban, 'Ban, Cacaliban
> Has a new master. – Get a new man.

"I'm weak," Josh confessed.

"Weak?"

"You're strong. Why I think we'd make a good fit."

"Josh," Tyler smiled sweetly, "you're not weak. Snap out of that foolish mind-set of yours. Don't let anyone use you ever again, even me, especially me."

"You can use me all you want," Josh winked.

"Yeah, yeah, yeah."

"Use me. Abuse me. Make me write bad checks. I'll even throw in a pair of terriers."

"What?" Tyler laughed.

It wasn't just sex that he needed to be happy, Tyler knew. It was the emotional connection that went along with a friendly kiss, a casual caress. He'd read a study about babies in orphanages. Those held and loved flourished. Those untouched grew sickly, even died. A heart like a plant needed the sunshine and water of affection to thrive, and he had starved his daughters. Someone much less seriously hurt had taken their place.

Sex, however, was at least a third of a relationship, he believed, along with love and like-mindedness, and in regard to sex, Josh also presented him, as a person and a writer, with a new area of experience and growth. Tyler was curious about the passive role in sex and with Josh felt safe to explore it. In fact, he felt that sexual experimentation with him would be fun, a form of exploration, not exploitation, a form of making love versus, for example, fucks with grabby tricks. What would it be like to taste Josh's cock, to swallow his come, to be punched in the ass? Wow, he thought. He couldn't believe he was thinking such things.

"So," Tyler began, "where are we going to raise these terriers, Atlanta?"

"Guess so," Josh said. "Stroke of luck there. Otherwise, we'd be just a fling."

"Or at each end of a long-distance relationship."

"Which never works."

"Actually, I can live anywhere," Tyler said, staring at the ice cubes gleaming in his glass, all the bright, fizzy bubbles. "Hope you don't have some bourgeois marital model in mind."

"We both know where that leads."

"You said you'll be working for your father's firm."

"Right," Josh said, "but I don't really care about the money."

"Because you've always had it."

"All I really care about is a good relationship," he claimed, finishing his drink. He set his glass down. "Look. Neither of us is materialistic. We have good taste, if I do say so myself. And we couldn't conform to some hetero marital model if our lives depended on it. Look at my newly acquired parents. They're bourgeois through divine intervention. Some Silicone Valley CEO has forced them into the middle class."

Tyler laughed.

"Instead of building Taliesin," Josh said, referring to the Wright house, "I could flip villas in Tuscany. You could write. I'm sure I could get my father's backing."

"Why does that still sound bourgeois?" Tyler smiled.

Flip villas. In the restaurant in Naples he had thought of Josh and the Trees as two piers, one lintel. What would be their architectural equivalent, his and Josh's? And then he laughed: two studs.

"And that would make you happy?" he asked.

"I am happy," Josh claimed.

"You'd smile in every photograph."

"The whole album," Josh swore. "You won't regret it."

"'He's mad that trusts in the tameness of a wolf, a horse's health, a boy's love,'" Tyler said, quoting *Lear*.

"Tyler, please," Josh scowled, "I'm not a boy."

"How long have we known each other?" Tyler teased.

"A week."

"Seems longer."

Josh closed his eyes and whispered, "Because we've been traveling around."

Maybe they would continue day by day, Tyler thought, till they not only finished the trip, but something much longer. He glanced at the old-fashioned streetlight high above everything. He wished he had the overview of the year ahead that the streetlight had of the square.

"Promise you're not going to get all mushy on me," he said, shaking his head, "living off my breath, sipping me like coffee in the morning."

"What?" Josh laughed.

"All that good Achilles-loved-Patroclus schmaltz."

"*The Iliad* doesn't actually say they were lovers, does it?"

"It's obvious," Tyler claimed.

"But he doesn't say it."

"If he did, it may have been edited out when everything was written down. For example, the Greeks edited out arrows with poison tips. They considered them un-heroic." He drank a mouthful of vodka, enjoyed its clean, bitter taste, and swallowed it. "In *The Odyssey*, when Odysseus addresses Princess Nausikaa, he doesn't wish her love. He wishes her compatibility."

Next, they took a cab to Piazza del Quirinale with its magnificent centerpiece: a large fountain with marble statuary to either side of an obelisk. The fountain had a certain homoerotic appeal, as Josh put it, not only because of the phallic obelisk, but also because of the powerful physiques of the giant statues of Castor and Pollux and their horses, a strength implied in the colossal size and strength of the stone. From the piazza, they strolled down Via del Quirinale past Bernini's church Sant' Andrea to the intersection with the Quattro Fontane (the Four Fountains). Josh bought hair gel at a drugstore. Then they waited outside the Convento dei Cappuccini until it opened for the afternoon. Inside, they saw what Josh called the Capuchin Crypts, an ossuary, a series of arched vaults decorated rococo-style with dead monks and tens of thousands of dusty human bones.

"Bone sculpture," Josh said, "works of art in human bones."

A new concept for Tyler. There were chapels of skulls, a frieze of vertebrae, altars of spines, festoons of vertebrae like white roses, pelvises like big bows of sallow fabric, intricate chandeliers of ribs and clavicles. Posed among the bones, like manikins in macabre display windows, were the corpses of monks in discolored robes with narrow ropes tied around their waists. One was laid out under an arch of femurs with a row of skulls on top. Some were resting half upright in bone niches along the side walls. Some were hiding in the shadows in corners, heads bowed, hands tucked into their faded sleeves as if lost in prayer. Three stood in niches along a back wall, one head down, one looking to the side, one staring from his cowl directly at Tyler, his skeletal hands clasping an iron cross. His noseless, eyeless, lipless grimace still somehow looked like a grin. Tyler could imagine him stirring into motion late at night.

Tyler kept saying, "Oh, my god, oh, my god," and as Josh watched him, Josh smiled guardedly as if the place were having some desired effect on Tyler.

"Jeez, Josh," Tyler exclaimed, touching the cool wrought-iron fence between him and the crypt. "You knew what we were in for?"

"Had a good idea," he said. "Catacombs."

"I'll never think of a cappuccino the same way again."

At another crypt, eighteen crosses tilted out of the dirt floor. Tyler pulled Josh to him and hugged him. Then they just stood there, arms around each other, gazing at the small, interior cemetery.

Suddenly, Tyler remembered the huge fin rising from the water, the shark hitting the prow with a thud, the boat slowly rotating into the mist. Again, he heard Alice screaming and slapping the water, Karen's scream cut off as she went under. He also thought of the plates with sautéed mushrooms sitting on the counter in Erin's grungy studio.

Besides being a sickly kid – pneumonia, asthma, flu – he had a history of near-death experiences. On vacation in Arkansas, his parents had considered taking a boat ride on a lake, but decided against it. Later, they learned that the boat had flipped and a man drowned. Similarly, after his father died, he and his mother went on vacation in Miami, and he asked if they could take a helicopter ride up and down the beach. She had considered it, but decided against it, and later they learned that the copter had crashed and killed three people. In high school, a group had gone into the woods to gather moss to decorate the gym in a plantation theme for the prom. They had filled the back of a pickup with moss and ridden on top of it on the way back to the high school. When they got there and lowered the tailgate, a huge water moccasin, amid screams, dropped to the ground and slithered off. And so on…. In short, he had long ago learned to savor the moment. The question was: What was he being saved for? Now it was clear: to make Josh happy and himself in the process.

Caravaggio may have been Josh's favorite painter, but there was a painting by him that had a profound influence on Tyler, too, his *Bacchus Crowned with Vine Leaves*. In it, the tipsy god is wearing a wreath of grapes and vine leaves. His cheeks are rosy, his eyelids slightly droopy. He is offering the viewer a glass of red wine with his left hand. On the table is a carafe with a small reflection of Caravaggio at his easel, but more importantly, there is also a small reflection of the god's face on the wine in the glass. The god in the wine, Tyler thought, like communion. He thought of the painting as life offering pleasure, and he was willing to reach into the painting and take it.

After the crypts, Tyler and Josh took the Metro to the hotel, rested while Phil and Billie rested, then escorted them to Trattoria Imperiale for dinner that night, after which, they discussed going to the Fontana di Trevi.

"Think a little night touring will do you in?" Billie asked Phil.

"I'm fine," he assured her. "Our little nap has brought me back to life."

As they approached the fountain down a side street, they began to hear, over the purl of the crowd, the incessant whish of a waterfall, and when they rounded a corner into the square, they saw the immense, illuminated fountain and smelled the fresh damp in the air. Hundreds of tourists were mobbing the fountain and milling in the square.

"Wow," Tyler exclaimed.

"Magnificent," Billie remarked.

They took steps down into the crowd at the rim and just stood there, taking in the view. Silvery streams were spilling down the various courses among the statues, sheeting over ledges into the coin-spangled pool. When seats became available, the foursome sat on the bench curving along the wall.

"So, what's going on here?" Phil asked, gesturing toward the sculptures.

"It's a celebration of water," Josh explained. "Tritons are guiding the hippocamps drawing the shell chariot of Oceanus, god of the waters."

"Hippocamps?" Phil asked.

"Horse monsters," Josh said. "See the wings and fish tails."

"Oh, yes."

"That's Abundance in the niche on the left," Josh pointed out, "Health on the right. Notice the snake drinking from her cup."

"I like the guy blowing the seashell," Billie said, "his puffed cheeks"

When a space opened at the rim, Josh got up and offered it to Phil and Billie, but when Billie said, "No, go ahead," Tyler stepped beside him and took in the magical theatrical effect of the underwater lights. Some shot up, illuminating Oceanus and the shell chariot, some the Tritons and hippocamps, the dynamic play of bright light and etched shadow accentuating their muscular bodies.

"Have some change?" Josh asked, digging a coin from a pocket.

"Yeah," Tyler said, digging one out.

"Ready?" Josh asked, poised to flick the coin into the water.

Tyler held his hand up.

When Josh said, "Now," each flicked his coin into a high arc, flickering into the pool with a tiny splash.

Chapter 48: A Bottle of Santa Christina

The day had been unusually hot even for Naples, the Bay flat and glassy, flashing with glare, the air over it a hot stew of brilliant haze. Then the thin, washed-out sky slowly dimmed to night, and the streetlights along Via Verdi bloomed into bright angels needling the street with a ghostly sallow glow. At midnight, Valerio appeared at the top of the steps at the Galleria's east entrance, dressed in his new Armani outfit, his left hand in his pocket, his right carrying a bottle of Santa Christina. Unnoticed, he stood there, fondling himself and watching his randy goats, as he thought of them, quietly grazing the scene.

He felt better about himself than usual that evening. He had worked out a couple of hours ago and literally sensed how toned he was. He felt as if the exercise had sweated all the disappointments and distractions out of him, and his intent was simply to have a good time tonight. He also thought that he looked like a model. He liked his butch haircut, and, as Josh had suggested, he had gone to the Armani boutique to ask for a job, but also to buy slacks, belt, shoes, and socks to go with the black silk shirt. Because of his confidence in his "hot," polished look, he even decided to increase his fees.

His attitude had taken wing at first hint of the expectant spring dawning inside him. For whatever reason, he was no longer satisfied with the present situation, clerking and tricking. He was bored. He wanted something different, something to share like wine with someone like Stefano Vincolo, the cute cop. He had even asked Silvio Castelli, the politician, to help him. It was as if he had finally become aware of what he had been feeling and living all along, finally noticed the happy spirit hovering at his side. It was difficult for him to put into words exactly, but he knew it had something to do with his personal well-being and how that would enable him to help others like Rollo.

Rollo had been standing to the side of the steps, leaning against a wall. He was wearing frayed cargo shorts, a yellow tee, and sandals, and Valerio could tell, even from a distance, that his acne had flared up.

Rollo checked his watch, and when Valerio called, "Have a date?" Rollo fluttered like a pigeon.

"I wish."

When Rollo hobbled up the steps, Valerio saw a pink Jim Morrison on the front of the tee. He also saw that Rollo's cheek had gone down and that his nose was not as red. The bruise around his eye, however, still looked like a big, livid pansy. Valerio pulled the cork from the bottle, took a swig, and handed the bottle to Rollo.

"Thanks," Rollo said, looking down.

Valerio took Rollo's chin and lifted his face. "You're eyes are bloodshot."

"Allergy," Rollo claimed, his eyes darting left and right. "Something in the air."

"The smog's terrible," Valerio agreed. He looked at Rollo curiously. "You haven't smoked?"

"For once, no."

Rollo drank and handed the bottle to Valerio, who was sure he was lying. Perhaps he had been crying, Valerio thought. He would have to be especially attentive tonight.

"Me without grass," Rollo joked, briefly closing his eyes. "Bad trip."

"Why didn't you smoke?" Valerio asked. "Oh," he said, thinking Rollo, since the beating, was trying to be more cautious.

When Valerio sat on the top step, Rollo sat beside him, his body turned to the left, his left foot over his right. They shared the bottle in silence. Then a particularly rough-looking customer drove up in a noisy, banged-up Fiat and motioned broadly toward them.

"Let Totonno have him," Rollo suggested, squinting at the man. "He can handle him. Besides, Totonno's short on funds."

Valerio smiled at Rollo with his eyes, then called, "Totonno! Your father wants you."

Totonno strolled to the car, leaned on the door, and apparently came to terms with the john. When he loped around to the passenger side, he looked at Valerio and Rollo and yelled, "Babbo wants to suck his son!" When he got in the car, the man scowled at them, shifted gears, and squealed off.

"He looked like a bulldog," Rollo frowned.

"I'm sure Totonno's bone is big enough," Valerio joked, corking the bottle.

He sat it beside him, and when he glanced at Rollo, Rollo was apparently lost in thought, pinching his lower lip as if trying to squeeze something off it. He tentatively touched his bruise, then, just below it, a patch of moist acne. He checked his watch, and when he realized that Valerio was watching him, he began shivering as if with a chill, then crying. When Valerio opened his arms, Rollo embraced him and sobbed into his neck.

"Rollo," Valerio asked, "what's wrong?"

"What's to become of me?" Rollo cried. "Look at me."

When Valerio tilted back and tried to, Rollo coughed, sniffed, and slowly lifted his eyes, revealing a strange, crazed look. Then he kissed Valerio with a deep, receptive, no-holds-barred kiss radiant with emotion.

When Valerio broke off, Rollo whispered, "Butt fuck me, Bello. I need someone strong inside me."

"Rollo, Rollo," Valerio said. "Calm down." Valerio made him sit back, thought for a moment, and asked, "Know about Bacchus, the god?"

"No," Rollo sniffed, wiping his nose on the back of his hand.

"He's a very old god," Valerio began. "God of wine. In fact, I'll pour him a drink." He uncorked the bottle, poured a drop onto a step, and corked the bottle. "He dies every year, but comes back," he said, setting the bottle down, "just as the vine is cut back every fall, but sprouts again in spring, just as you'll spring back. I know it may seem like everyone's trying to tear you to pieces now, but soon you'll be dancing at the banquet, I swear. Some rich old man'll be peeling a grape for you. Just take good care of yourself till he comes along. OK?"

Rollo glanced at him furtively, then nodded.

"Take me, for example," Valerio added. "Got a call from this guy who says he saw me on the news. Claims he's an agent, can get me modeling jobs. We'll see."

Rollo pressed his fingertips into his eyes and wiped the tears away, but when he opened his eyes, they widened, and his lips parted. When Valerio looked in Rollo's line of sight, he saw a black, four-door Maserati pull along the curb, the car's black shell streaked with marble patterns of light. The car's windows were tinted, and when the driver's window lowered, Valerio saw an older, distinguished-looking, paternal figure, a big man like Castelli, Valerio thought.

"There he is," Valerio smiled.

"Who?" Rollo said, facing Valerio.

"Your rich old man." When the man smiled and nodded, Valerio said, "He means you."

"No, he doesn't."

"Yes, he does. Talk to him. Get down there before Gianluca or Otto moves in."

Rollo, elbows on knees, stared at the man and bit his thumb.

When Valerio said, "I'm not going," Rollo glanced at Valerio, heaved himself up, and limped down the steps.

He stood near the car, talking to the man and blocking Valerio's view of him. Then he glanced over his shoulder at Valerio, talked to the man some more, and turned around, shuffling across the sidewalk.

At the bottom of the steps, he said, "He wants you." Then he just stood there, an idle puppet, head down.

Valerio grabbed the bottle and descended the steps. He was irritated with Rollo for not trying harder. Then, like a cat near a rat, Valerio sensed trouble. Some shepherding instinct kicked in, and he was glad Rollo was out of the picture. He wondered why such an obviously wealthy man would bother with their little flock when he could have his choice of any Adonis, yet his curiosity, like a long rope, kept pulling him toward the car. He could have tugged against it, he knew, but didn't, and when he passed Rollo, he handed him the bottle, vaguely aware that Rollo, clutching it to his chest, was hurrying off the best he could past Gianluca, Otto, and the others.

When Valerio stopped near the car, he put his hands in his pockets and made eye contact with the man. The man's face was deeply furrowed like bark with narrow eyes and faint eyebrows, giving him a faded look reinforced by thinning hair on top and a pale, mottled scalp. The hair on the sides was frost white, impeccably combed straight back, revealing his most distinctive trait, Valerio thought, perfectly flat ears.

"Buona sera," Valerio began, extending his hand. "Come sta?"

"Buona sera," the man said, squeezing Valerio's hand firmly.

When the man smiled, he displayed perfect teeth, and Valerio could smell, over the arid cool of the air-conditioning, the man's musky, balsamic cologne.

"May I help you with something?" Valerio asked, casually fondling himself.

The man noticed and glanced up. "Would you like to make me happy?"

"Of course, but how?"

The man's cordial expression mirrored Valerio's.

"By the way," the man said, "I like the way your cock curves up."

"Thanks."

"Ever notice the way the needles curve up on the upper twigs of a fir?" the man asked. "Reminds me of that."

"Really," Valerio replied, giving him one of his big, charming grins.

"Much bigger, of course."

"Of course," Valerio agreed. "And much sweeter."

"Much sweeter," the man repeated, gazing at the green and blue dash lights.

Valerio glanced at the GPS screen to see what the location looked like.

"Yes," Valerio began again. "My come's as sweet as milk and honey."

Valerio could easily see the man in some very dark painting of a Medieval knight in armor and puffy pantaloons. At the moment, however, he was wearing a handsome, sapphire-blue, double-breasted suit with wide lapels, sets of buttons down the front, and a small lapel pin in the shape of crossed American and Italian flags.

"So," the man said, gazing at him. "How much?"

"Why don't I get in the car?" Valerio suggested. "We could drive around and discuss it?" When the man hesitated, Valerio added, "The air-conditioning feels great."

"No," the man sighed. "Let's settle things first. No sense driving for an eternity only to...." Valerio was listening attentively, but the man trailed off.

"I know an abandoned school," Valerio said. "A field in the country."

"Police a problem?" the man asked, glancing up.

"No," Valerio lied.

"No long arm of the Pope?"

"No," he lied again. "The Pope has better things to do than punish us for having fun."

"Free to do what you want, eh?"

Valerio froze, staring at him. He felt as if some sort of emotional sun was setting inside himself.

"What about extortion?" When Valerio failed to answer, the man eyed him. "Would you play the slave?"

"Not tonight," Valerio said. "I'm master tonight."

"Think so?" the man asked civilly.

"Know so."

"What about token submission, abusive talk?"

"No."

"Even if I pay you well."

"No amount of money."

When the man reached into his coat pocket, Valerio thought he was reaching for his wallet, but the man took out a Beretta with a silencer and pointed it at him. Valerio stood up straight and took his hands out of his pockets. When the other hustlers saw the gun, they fled.

"You wouldn't belittle yourself?"

"I hustle," Valerio said, "but I'm somebody."

The man squinted at him as if trying to figure him out.

"Say you're nothing," he insisted, face placid.

"No," Valerio stated. "I'm Valerio Antonio Guglielmi from San Magno in Puglia, son of a gardener and a seamstress."

"Even if it would save your life?"

Valerio spread his hands, palms up, in an ambiguous religious gesture, but when he smiled wistfully, the gun hissed as if spitting, and a little hole burst open in Valerio's shirt. He wobbled slightly as if rocked by the first subtle shock of an earthquake. He closed his eyes, and his smile transformed to one of someone experiencing comfortable, soothing, deeply satisfying sex. He dropped to his knees with a jolt, head bowed, as if making obeisance, and the bud of the bullet hole bloomed into a big, glistening rose, petals dripping dark crimson berries down the sheen of his shirt. Then he fell back, cracking his head on the sidewalk.

When the man put the gun away, he mussed his tie, which he adjusted. Then he glanced at Valerio's body and crossed himself. When he drove off, a profound hush fell on the scene, a temple-like solemnity stirred to a ripple of voices by two couples approaching in the distance.

Chapter 49: Amanita Phalloides

After class on Monday, Tyler showed up at Erin's apartment with three bars of sweet cooking chocolate. He had promised to come for dinner if she promised not to crash his class.

"I have something for you," he said, pulling the chocolate out of a jacket pocket.

"Oh, chocolate," she said, closing the door. "You remembahd."

The only thing different he was wearing was a raspberry-colored polo shirt, which he thought of as preppy, but Erin, barefoot, was wearing a black bustier with pointed breast cones a la Madonna. During his last visit, he had broken the seal on her mystery, as he thought of it, figured out, to some extent, what she was up to. But why? Then an analogy occurred to him. Even when he smiled a happy smile, it was slightly crooked due to a missing tooth in childhood, an adult tooth pulled for coming in wrong. Then affected now, he realized. And he thought of the vast, incomprehensible alluvium of critical details that his life had carried to that room at that moment. Even if she told him, would he ever really understand why?

"Actually," she said, "weah havin' chocolate gelato for desseht. I went all the way to Paolo's."

He followed her to the refrigerator, where she put away the chocolate. On the counter were two white plates with sautéed mushrooms, as well as a bottle and two glasses of Sangiovese.

When she tried to hand him a glass, he asked, "Where can I put my jacket?"

"Doah to the left in the hall," she said, setting the glass down.

When he hung up the jacket, he saw that the purple tie was gone, and when he returned to the kitchen, Erin was checking the steaks in the oven.

"Mind if I open the sheers?" he asked, picking up the other glass.

"No," she said, closing the oven.

"Kind of claustrophobic in here."

"Sahry. The window by the bed. People can see in the othah when they go in the hall."

He set his glass on the nightstand to the right of the bed, pushed the musty sheers apart, and picked up the glass. He sniffed the wine and, satisfied with it, sipped some, staring out the window.

"I like to pretend it's an ocean view," Erin said, opening the refrigerator. "Sailboats, wind-surfahs. You know, New Hampshah."

He wandered to the table, where she had set out two straw mats, utensils on paper napkins, and, on a plate between the settings, a block of Cheddar with a knife stuck upright in it, a stem with green grapes, and soda crackers. A squat bayberry candle was burning in a saucer.

"Where have I seen bayberry candles?" he asked himself, slicing a wedge of cheese. Hard as he tried, he could not remember.

"Reminds me of Christmas," she said moodily, opening a carton.

"Right," he agreed. The woodsy smell had something to do with freshly cut firs and spices.

He popped the cheese into his mouth, set his glass on the table, and sat facing her. When she noticed he was watching her, she announced what they were having for dinner. She was broiling a couple of sirloins, and when they were done, she was going to put them on the plates and the plates, in turn, in the microwave to re-heat the mushrooms. Then she was going to add potato salad. She had bought the potato salad at the Vortex, she said, because she remembered he had ordered it as his side.

When she looked ready to serve the plates, he stood and asked, "Do you have aspirin or ibuprofen, something for a headache?"

"Uh, yeah," she said, glancing at the plates uneasily. "Hold on a minute."

When the bathroom door clicked open, he sneaked to the kitchen, switched the plates carefully, and coughed twice to cover the *clack* they made on the counter. He stepped to the hall and met her as she came out with a bottle of aspirin. He jiggled a couple of tablets onto his palm, saw the word *aspirin* stamped on them, and screwed the cap back on. She glanced at the plates, took a deep breath as if summoning her courage, and, using dish rags, picked them up and carried them to the table.

"I think that's it," she said, studying everything anxiously.

When she lay the rags aside, they took seats, and he set the aspirin bottle down and swallowed the tablets with wine. Then they cut the steaks and ate in silence, but when the hush became awkward, he decided to pursue a certain tentative line of questioning.

"Aspirin comes from willows, right?"

"Bahk and twigs," she said.

"What herbs are good for a headache?"

"Wintahgreen," she said immediately. "Theh's somethin' in it that also goes in aspirin."

"I thought wintergreen was poison."

"Well, yeah, if swallowed," she hesitated, visibly tense.

"I'm confused. How would I use it for a headache?"

"Tea," she said, morose. "A couple of teaspoons of leaves in boilin' watah."

"And it wouldn't kill me?" he chuckled, forking a piece of potato.

She froze, wide-eyed, a fork with mushrooms poised in the air.

"No."

Again, they ate quietly. Car doors slammed across the street. Chatter and laughter crackled like fire.

"So, what prompted this little domestic scene?" he asked.

"Domestic scene?"

"Erin the homemaker."

"Just wanted to show you I can do standahd stuff."

"Standard stuff," he smiled.

"What a girl's supposed to do." He picked up on the hint of irritation.

At that point, he realized he was a detached observer of the scene, like a camera, not an active participant. He guessed he felt this way because, on some level, he was becoming more and more aware of how curiously solemn she was. The appearance of the marital moment, he thought, had less and less to do with the glum reality of it.

"Eating your mushrooms?" he asked.

"I am," she said, sliding her fork under some.

"Not eating mine if you're not eating yours."

"That game," she said, referring to his previous drink-for-drink rule.

"Well, at least you won't pass out on them."

They studied the bits of mushroom on their forks and slipped them into their mouths.

"Um, good," he moaned.

"They ah," she agreed, squinting.

They chewed and swallowed. He looked amused, she worried.

"I have a riddle for you," he announced.

"A riddle?"

"Yeah." He put his fork down, leaned back, and clasped his hands behind his head. "My cap has gills like a fish," he began slowly, "and my feet like roots are deep in the ground." He thought, then continued. "I thrive on shadow the way other plants thrive on sun." He gazed toward the ceiling, then glanced at her. "I'm wild, but meek. What am I?" When she did not respond, he asked, "Well?"

"Well, what?"

"It's a riddle. What's the answer?"

"Youah not makin' sense," she said, drowsy. "I think youah on somethin'."

"What are *you* on?"

"What do ya mean?"

"You take something?" he asked.

"Yeah," she admitted.

"Nervous?"

"Yeah."

"Why?"

"I don't know," she said. "Youah difficult."

"Difficult?"

"All these questions."

"But you took it before I got here."

"Youah not friendly," she said, blinking. She seemed to be trying to focus on him. "What is it? What did I do? I know it's me. It always is."

"I don't know. What *have* you done?"

"Nothing," she snapped, a hand to the bustier. "Fixed you a steak, sautéed mushrooms for you."

"What kind of mushrooms?"

"What?" she asked. She seemed to drift away, then came back. "What did you say?"

"What kind of mushrooms?"

"I don't know," she groused. "Organic, from the supahmarket."

"Actually," he confessed, "I don't know one mushroom from another."

She ate a bite of steak, closed her eyes as if savoring it, but seemed to have trouble swallowing it.

"Look," she said, touching her throat. "I told you. Most men leave me flaht."

"You liked me at first sight."

"Somethin' like that."

"You know," he warned her, "you'd better be careful bringing strangers here. The last time I was here, I could've fucked you blind. You wouldn't even have known it."

"Fucked me blind," she smiled nervously. "Now theah's a threat. He fucked me blind. He fucked me till I came. From what I recall, your abs are stacked. Maybe tonight I'll finally see that horse's cock of yoahs."

"Horse, huh," he scoffed. "But, Erin, dear, I'm a dark horse."

"What?"

"Everybody underestimates me," he explained. "Nobody expects me to win."

"Don't know what youah talkin' about."

"Probably not." He tilted back in the chair, hands on the table. "I have supernatural powers, you know."

"Cahn't wait."

"For all you know," he claimed, "I could be a mental patient. I could've drugged your drink while you were in the bathroom."

"But you didn't," she said, eyes down as if ashamed.

"No, you're right. I didn't." Out of the blue, he asked, "You met Linda at Sea Cliff?"

Erin flinched as if literally shocked, then just sat there, staring at him.

"How is she?" he asked casually. He rocked his chair forward and watched her batting an invisible bug from her face. "You entice me over here," he said, "like some roach in a bait station, for lack of a better metaphor, and I'm supposed to just eat your bait and die. Don't think so." When he stood suddenly, he accidentally knocked the chair over backward with a clatter. "Think I'm oozing sap?"

"What?" she whispered.

"Think I'm stupid?"

"The room's spinnin'," she said, turning in her chair. "I'm fallin' down a funnel, down a funnel to a – " She broke off, a hand on her stomach. "Oh, god!" She tried to stand, but dropped to her knees.

"Why?" he asked.

"I'm bein' sucked down to the floah."

"How could you do this to someone you don't even know? What did Linda tell you about me? I didn't kill her mother and sister. I loved them."

She slumped onto all fours and laboriously, like an alligator, started crawling toward the bed.

"I just wanted to eat a hamburger in peace," he lamented, "teach my class in peace. I didn't want to hurt anyone, and now look at you. You women!" he snarled, heart crushed by the fact that even a stranger, let alone his daughter, could hate him so much. "Where'd you get the mushrooms, the island?"

She stopped, head down, then murmured, "You ah evil, ahn't you?"

"Evil?"

"You switched plates." Then she crumpled against the floor, palms up by her hips like fins. "Jesus!" she sighed.

"Oh, my god!" he gasped. "They *were* poisoned mushrooms." He knelt beside her, rolled her onto her back, and, shaking her, shouted, "Erin! Erin, wake up!"

When he thumbed an eyelid open, her pupil was dilated, a small, clear glimpse into black. Then he noticed that her crotch was wet. He stood and stared at her, dumbfounded, then glanced around the room for a phone. Then he remembered that she did not have one. He threw open the front door and opened a door to the right, rushing into a hall. He banged on a door and, after a moment, dashed to the next and banged on it.

He heard motion inside, but when no one answered, he yelled, "Hello! Anyone in there? I need help. Call 911! Someone's sick in 1-F. 1-F," he stressed. "Call 911. 911. Please!"

When he could not rouse anyone, he ran outside, around the building, and down the front steps, but when he lunged against the big, wrought-iron gate, it was chained and padlocked. He growled, rattled the gate in frustration, and called toward a row of dark cars parked behind the businesses across the street. He could hear traffic at the nearby intersection.

Then he scrambled up the steps, raced around the building, and slipped in dog shit, waving his arms to keep his balance. He swerved through the gate to the parking lot, jumped down a low retaining wall, and sprinted down the street with the parked cars. There was a passage to a little plaza between a tavern and a second-hand clothing store, and there, he kept desperately asking people if they had a cell phone until a young blonde stopped and nodded.

"Call 911, please," he begged, his fists clenched against his stomach. "Someone's sick at the Hemlock." He pointed down the passage. "Apartment 1-F. It's an emergency. She's been poisoned."

The blonde took her phone out and dialed 911 calmly.

"1-F," she said, placing the phone to her ear.

"Right."

"The Hemlock."

He nodded.

"Know the address?" she asked.

He shook his head. "Tell them to send an ambulance to the back of the building. They can't get in the front. Hurry."

When she said, "Yes, I'd like to report an emergency," he said, "Thanks," and dashed down the passage.

When he burst into the apartment, Erin was grayish-blue with a burgundy gravy of vomit spilling from her lips. When he pressed her neck, he could not feel a pulse, so he turned her head to the side and began frantically scooping the food out of her mouth with his fingers, greasy pieces of meat and potato.

When he sat back on his feet, he noticed her blue fingernails. Then, panting, he became aware of the calm spell cast on the place.

Chapter 50: Morning

Tyler was dreaming that he was swimming against the current at night off the coast of Maine. Then he floated on his back, letting himself be carried out by the tide. Straight up, the moon had eclipsed to a dim blood smear set off by a vague, blue corona. The breeze dropped, the sea went flat, and he woke, refreshed, in a dark hotel room.

He pressed the dial on his watch to see what time it was, got up nude, and crept across the tile floor and one of the rough Oriental rugs, bouncing on the balls of his feet. When he hooked the heavy curtains behind the tiebacks, the soft sheers glowed like clouds. He drew them gingerly, and when he cranked the window open, a light breeze washed over the sill, filling them with air briefly like sails.

He propped on his elbows and leaned out the window, taking in the sunny day. To the north, nine small cumulus clouds were suspended over Rome. Some buildings and side streets were still in shadow, some lit with sunshine, all beautiful, he thought, because of the old stonework, the rich earth tones in the stucco (orange, ochre, moss), and the classic architectural details (pediments, keystones, roofs with terra-cotta tiles). The boisterous traffic blood had just started flowing through the streets, a few relaxed pedestrians strolling along the sidewalks, the Italian flag waving leisurely from a balustrade near the corner – the magical life of a city waking around him. But it wasn't just the city spread out before him, he realized. It was his life, and he really had nothing better to do with it than enjoy it.

When he glanced at Josh, he was wrapped in a sheet, curled up in the big, rustic bed, sleeping peacefully. Natural as a colt, Tyler thought, or one of Caravaggio's adolescent angels. He was what he had now. More than enough.

He crossed the room and carefully sat beside him, a leg on the bed, knee bent, a foot on the floor. He watched him breathing contentedly, flushed with a rosy radiance. He smelled his warm, sensual skin smell, along with the fresh, wholesome scent of the sheets. With his finger, he gently followed a blue vein on the back of Josh's hand. When Josh opened his eyes, he looked at Tyler, smiled sleepily, and sat up slowly, sliding back against the carved headboard.

"Morning," he said, rubbing an eye.

"Morning," Tyler purred, taking his other hand. "How's my new incestuous brother?"

"Incestuous brother, huh?" Josh said. He bit his lower lip, eyeing him mischievously.

"Josh."

"Yeah?"

Tyler glanced at him from under his brows: "I've never been so happy."

"Me too."

When Josh leaned forward, they embraced and crushed each other's mouth in a rapturous kiss. Then they broke apart and just sat there, catching their breath and looking at each other as if marveling at some treasure they had found. Tyler kissed the pink scratch on Josh's chest, then traced it with his tongue lightly. The fruit of the jewelweed, when touched, pops audibly, and when Tyler mouthed the scratch hungrily, Josh flinched and gasped euphorically as if a thrill had flashed through his body. When Tyler leaned back, braced on his elbows, Josh went down on him, and when Tyler turned his head, there it was: Josh's prodigious erection directly in front of him, filling his vision, veined and pulsing and deserving of attention. In one impulsive gulp, he swallowed it, a mouthful of satiny skin, and when he took it down his throat as far as he could, it felt good.

About the Author

As a student, Ken Anderson won Louisiana State University's Caffee Medal for prose and the Louisiana College Writers First Place for fiction and First Place and Grand Prize for drama. A Professor Emeritus of English, he has been a consultant for a fine-arts journal and a gay men's literary quarterly. His fiction and poetry have appeared in over a hundred journals and anthologies, such as *Bay Windows*, *The Gay Review*, and *The James White Review*. His first book was *The Intense Lover: A Suite of Poems*. His second, the novel *Someone Bought the House on the Island: A Dream Journal*, sold out and was a finalist in the Independent Publisher Book Awards. His third was *Hasty Hearts*, a reprint of the novel plus a collection of ten short stories. His fourth was *The Statue of Pan: Six Stories, a Novella, and a Novella-Play*. His play, *Mattie Cushman: A Psychodrama*, has been produced twice and aired on cable, and a stage version of *Someone Bought the House on the Island* won the Saints and Sinners Playwriting Contest. Ken also wrote the libretto for an operatic version of *Someone*, which premiered in Atlanta in 2010. He has also written a screenplay version of *Someone*, as well as screenplay versions of *The Statue of Pan* and *The Crystal Ball*, and is looking for an agent or producer.

CPSIA information can be obtained
at www.ICGtesting.com
Printed in the USA
EDOW031002280313
1031ED